Also edited by Mary Helen Washington

Invented Lives
Narratives of Black Women 1860–1960

Black-Eyed Susans/ Midnight Birds

ANCHOR BOOKS
DOUBLEDAY

NEW YORK   LONDON   TORONTO   SYDNEY   AUCKLAND

Black-Eyed Susans/ Midnight Birds

Stories By and About
Black Women
Edited and with an
Introduction by

Mary Helen Washington

AN ANCHOR BOOK
PUBLISHED BY DOUBLEDAY
a division of Bantam Doubleday Dell Publishing Group, Inc.
666 Fifth Avenue, New York, New York 10103

ANCHOR BOOKS, DOUBLEDAY,
and the portrayal of an anchor are trademarks of Doubleday,
a division of Bantam Doubleday Dell Publishing Group, Inc.

Black-Eyed Susans (1975) and Midnight Birds (1980) were both originally
published by Anchor.

Gwendolyn Brooks for "If You're Light and Have Long Hair" and "At the
Burns Coopers," both from *Maud Martha* in *Blacks*, published by the David
Company, 1987 by Gwendolyn Brooks. Originally published by Harper &
Brothers © 1953. Reprinted by permission of the author.

Library of Congress Cataloging-in-Publication Data
Black-eyed Susans. Midnight birds : stories by and about Black women
/ edited and with an introduction by Mary Helen Washington.
    p. cm.
Bibliography: p.
ISBN 0-385-26015-6
1. Short stories, American—Afro-American authors. 2. Short
stories, American—Women authors. 3. Afro-American women—
Fiction. 4 Women—Fiction. I. Washington, Mary Helen. II. Title:
Midnight birds.
PS647.A35B57   1989
813'.0108352042—dc20   89-16799
                                          CIP

Grateful acknowledgment is made to the following contributors for permission to reprint the material contained within this anthology:

Jean Wheeler Smith for "Frankie Mae," which appeared in *Black World*, 1968.

Paulette Childress White for "The Bird Cage," which appeared in *Redbook*, June 1978, copyright © 1978 by Paulette Childress White, and "Alice," which appeared in *Essence*, January 1977, copyright © 1977 by Paulette Childress White. Reprinted by permission of the author.

Toni Morrison for "SEEMOTHERMOTHERISVERYNICE" from *The Bluest Eye* by Toni Morrison. Copyright © 1970 by Toni Morrison. Reprinted by permission of Henry Holt and Compnay, Inc.

Paule Marshall for "Reena," which appeared in *American Negro Short Stories*. Reprinted by permission of the author.

Gwendolyn Brooks for "If You're Light and Have Long Hair" and "At the Burns Coopers'," both from *Maud Martha* in *Blacks*, published by the David Company, 1987 by Gwendolyn Brooks. Originally published by Harper & Brothers, © 1953. Reprinted by permission of the author.

Gayl Jones for "Asylum" and "Jevata," both from *White Rat: Short Stories*, by Gayl Jones. Copyright © 1971, 1973, 1975, 1977 by Gayl Jones. Reprinted by permission of Random House, Inc.

Louise Meriwether for "A Happening in Barbados," which appeared in *The Antioch Review*, 1968. Reprinted by permission of the Ellen Levine Literary Agency.

Alexis DeVeaux for "Remember Him a Outlaw" in *Black Creation*, Fall 1972, copyright © 1972 by Alexis DeVeaux, and "The Riddles of Egypt Brownstone," © 1977 by Alexis DeVeaux. Reprinted by permission of the author.

Frenchy Hodges for "Requiem for Willie Lee" in *Ms.*, October 1979, copyright © 1979 by Frenchy Hodges. Reprinted by permission of the author.

Sherley Anne Williams for "Meditations on History," copyright © 1976 by Sherley Anne Williams. Reprinted by permission of the author.

Alice Walker for "Everyday Use" from *In Love and Trouble: Stories of Black Women*, copyright © 1973 by Alice Walker, reprinted by permission of Harcourt Brace Jovanovich, Inc., and "A Sudden Trip Home in the Spring," copyright © 1971 by Alice Walker, and "Advancing Luna" copyright © 1977 by Alice Walker, reprinted from her volume *You Can't Keep a Good Woman Down* by permission of Harcourt Brace Jovanovich, Inc.

Ntozake Shange for "comin to terms," copyright © 1979 by Ntozake Shange. First published in *Essence Magazine* April 1979 and "aw babee, you so pretty" copyright © 1980 by Ntozake Shange. Both reprinted by permission of Russell & Volkening as agents for the author.

Toni Cade Bambara for "Medley" and "Witchbird" from *The Sea Birds Are Still Alive*, published by Random House, copyright © 1977 by Toni Cade Bambara. Reprinted by permission of the author.

To the fine women who brought me up:

Malissa Dalton
Bessie Riffe
Cora Riley
Elsie Wilkins
Sarah Mitchell
Helen Brinson
and
Mary Catherine Washington

And to my friend who shared the growing up:

Ponchita Argieard

As promised, I wish to thank publicly all the students of English 357: Black Women Writers, Fall 1988, University of Massachusetts at Boston, who participated in the many discussions which helped me to revise this book:

Laurel Back	Delores Goode	Linda Paine
Elizabeth Berolini	Geraldine Griffin	Elizabeth Quinlan
T. K. Bowers	Bob Hamilton	Jennifer Ryan
Peggy Carter	Elaine Henry	Patricia Sablock
Pamela Colbert	Robbyn Issner	Kathleen Shea
Laura Cummings	Susan Lattanzi	Laraine Sheridan
Christine Curran	Mary Mahoney	Karen Smith
Liz DiMeo	Tracy Martin	Patricia Soat
Stacy Economou	Janet McMurry	Ellen Thompson
Diane Fagan	Beverly Mills	June Walsh
Elsie Fisher	Dierdre Monahan	Lauralyn Williams
Kim Frizzell	Cris Newport	Patricia Williamson

Many thanks to Lisa Schwartz, who provided the information for the bibliographic essays and to Cris Newport, who typed the manuscript on her word processor and, at least, kept me conversant with the age of technology.

And to my 1987 Black Women Writers class at Harvard Divinity School, who struggled with these stories as intensely as I did:

Kimberly Cuddy	Elizabeth Lemon	Rachel Silberstein
Elizabeth Deasy	Ming Yeung-Lu	Michelle Simons
Susan Gallardo	Barbara Nesto	April Taylor
Beth Gerstein	John Overton	Hatsy Thompson
Myron Howie	N. May Roe	Amy Welch
Nancy Kressin	Christine Ruggle	Andre Willis
Kimmerer LaMothe	Esther Scanlan	Julie Worthington

Table Of Contents

Black-Eyed Susans/ Midnight Birds

Re (Visions): Black Women Writers— Their Texts, Their Readers, Their Critics

Editing this collection of short stories has been for me an autobiographical act, so I open this revised volume with a story about what black women writers have meant in my own life. When I left Notre Dame College in June 1962, I had in hand a signed, sealed contract which would deliver me to the Cleveland Public Schools as a certified secondary school teacher the following September. If anyone had told me then that it would take me ten years to feel committed to my work, that I would teach for years without passion and without a sense of fulfillment, a kind of marriage of necessity, I would not have believed it. For the first two years of my working life I taught eleventh- and twelfth-grade English at Glenville High School. I finished a master's degree in literature and taught for two more years at a small women's college in Cleveland, all of this done as though I were sleepwalking, going through the motions without ever feeling truly connected to or passionately involved with my work. Then, in 1968, that year of turning points, I enrolled in a doctoral program at Detroit and in 1970 joined the newly formed Black Studies department at the University of Detroit as an assistant professor. Imagine this: in 1966 I had been in school for nearly twenty years and I had never read a book written by a black woman. I had of course *heard* of Phillis Wheatley—the

YWCA in Cleveland was named after her—but I had never actually read her poetry. Suddenly after 1970, the names proliferated—Zora Neale Hurston, Nella Larsen, Paule Marshall, Margaret Walker, Dorothy West. I can even recall the exact text that introduced me to these writers and their traditions: a slender little paperback (bought for seventy-five cents) with a stylized portrait of Janie Crawford and Jody Starks on the cover—she pumping water at a well, her long hair cascading down her back, her head tilted slightly in his direction with a look of longing and expectancy; he in his fancy silk shirt and purple suspenders, his coat over one arm, his head cocked to one side, with the look that speaks to Janie of the far horizon. The novel was *Their Eyes Were Watching God,* and it set me on the task which would engage me, passionately, for the next twenty years. I began to immerse myself in collecting the stories of black women, and I realized that I had not been able to commit myself to my work because in the literature I had been taught and in the world I was expected to negotiate, my face did not exist. I know that I felt an immediate sense of community and continuity and joy in the discovery of these writers as though I had found something of my ancestry, my future, and my own voice. And I do know that my commitment to my work—to teaching and writing—began when I joined this circle of sisters.

Black-Eyed Susans, published in 1975, and *Midnight Birds,* published in 1980, have been in print fifteen and ten years, respectively, an extraordinary record of endurance for short story anthologies and a testament to the persistence of a literary tradition of black women as well as a reading public hungry for their stories. Much has changed in these fifteen years. In 1975 there was only one Pulitzer Prize winner in these collections: Gwendolyn Brooks won it for her book of poetry, *Annie Allen,* in 1950; now there are three: Alice Walker for her novel *The Color Purple* in 1983; Toni Morrison for her novel *Beloved* in 1988.[1] Black women writers are reviewed in major periodicals. They are taught as part of American

---

[1] A fourth black woman writer, Rita Dove, won the Pulitzer Prize for her book of poetry *Thomas and Beulah* in 1987.

literature courses in many colleges and universities, and they are the subjects of countless dissertations. At the University of Massachusetts, Boston, where I have taught since 1980, black women writers, out of all proportion to their representation in American literature texts, are often chosen by students for their honors projects and master's theses. At least once this year two black women writers, Walker and Morrison, were on the top ten *New York Times* bestseller list at the same time, signaling that these writers have mass appeal as well as critical acceptance. In the early 1970s I taught these writers using stacks of Xeroxed copies of their stories; now because of a number of reprint series, nearly all of the writings of black women are available, even nineteenth-century works that were out of print for decades.[2]

But the most important aspect of this literary renaissance is not how these writers have been received but the changes the writers themselves have made in the way black women are represented in literature. First of all, these writers represent black women in a variety of roles—as mothers, as daughters, as artists and writers, as wives, as domestic workers and teachers, as college students and

[2] Deborah McDowell's Beacon Press series, Rutgers University Press, The Feminist Press, and the Oxford-Schomburg series on nineteenth-century black American women writers edited by Henry-Louis Gates are current series reprinting black American women writers. Black women's spiritual autobiographies have been republished by William Andrews in *Sisters of the Spirit: Three Black Women's Autobiographies of the Nineteenth-Century* (Bloomington, Indiana University Press, 1986) and by Jean McMahon Humez in *Gifts of Power: The Writings of Rebecca Jackson, Black Visionary, Shaker Eldress* (Amherst, University of Massachusetts Press, 1981). Several anthologies have made the writings of black women available: Toni Cade Bambara's landmark *The Black Woman* (New York, New American Library, 1970); Pat Crutchfield Exum's *Keeping the Faith: Writings by Contemporary Black American Women* (Greenwich, Conn., Fawcett Publications, 1974); and Beverly Guy-Sheftall, Roseanne P. Bell, and Bettye J. Parker's *Sturdy Black Bridges: Visions of Black Women in Literature* (Garden City, N.Y.: Doubleday-Anchor, 1979). Gloria Hull has edited the diary of Alice Dunbar-Nelson, *Give Us Each Day* (New York, W. W. Norton, 1984). Jean Fagan Yellin has published an excellent edition of Linda Brent's 1860 slave narrative, *Incidents in the Life of a Slave Girl* (Cambridge, Mass., Harvard University Press, 1987).

world travelers, as beauticians, actresses: as subjects acting in history, as agents in their own lives. Their characters are not always courageous, nor are they always successful, nor should they be; but we as readers are invested in these characters' psychic lives, in their travels, and we hear their voices speaking in their own tongue. I have in my imagination an entire panoply of literary figures who did not exist for me before 1970: Sula, Eva and Hannah Peace, Odessa, Lexie, Sweet Pea, Honey, Hazel Peoples, Egypt, Edith and Esther Brownstone, Zami, Selina and Silla Boyce, Avey Johnson, Merle Kinbona, Frankie Mae, Dee and Maggie, Celie and Shug, Reena, Janie Crawford, Maud Martha, Vyry Brown, Mattie Michael.

What is even more important than their creation of complex women characters is that these writers have chosen to tell their stories and to use language in certain ways, and in doing so have produced art, writerly designs, which constitute a unique literary tradition. One of those designs is the use of the black woman blues singer to express a power and vitality and commitment to art in black women's lives. I mention this design first because it is a code for the writers themselves, signifying their own self-consciousness about their craft, a recognition of their relationship to an artistic legacy, and a willingness to name themselves as artists. Michele Wallace says that the woman blues singer is "a paradigm of commercial, cultural, and historical potency," a metaphor for "reconstructing black female experience as positive ground."[3] The blues singer appears in Gayl Jones's *Corregidora;* in Sherley Anne Williams's "Someone Sweet Angel Chile," a poem about Bessie Smith; in Ann Petry's 1953 novel *The Narrows,* and in Toni Cade Bambara's "Witchbird," which is in this collection. In Morrison's *The Bluest Eye,* Claudia's mother sings the blues so sweetly that Claudia actually looks forward to "the delicious time when 'my man' would leave me." The woman blues singer is always a sign for the woman who lives autonomously by standards she sets for

[3] Michele Wallace, *"The Color Purple*—An *Amos 'n' Andy* for the 80s," *The Village Voice,* Vol. XXI, No. 11, March 18, 1986, p. 21.

herself, a woman like Honey in "Witchbird," deeply involved in her art, sometimes paying a price for her independence and defiance.[4]

In creating these writerly designs, writers speak to other writers. They change, challenge, revise, and borrow from other writers so that the literary tradition might well look like a grid in one of those airline magazines that shows the vast and intricate interweaving patterns of coast-to-coast flight schedules. The formal critical term for this pattern is *intertextuality,* the relationship of one text to another that eventually configures into a literary tradition.[5] Reena telling her story to Paulie in Paule Marshall's 1959 story "Reena" certainly calls to mind Janie in Zora Neale Hurston's 1937 novel

---

[4] See " 'Infidelity Becomes Her': The Ambivalent Woman in the Fiction of Ann Petry and Dorothy West," in *Invented Lives* (New York, Doubleday, 1987), pp. 302–3, for a description of Petry's use of the blues woman to suggest female power.

[5] Henry Louis Gates and Robert Stepto were the first critics to make me aware of this aspect of a literary tradition. Stepto's book *From Behind the Veil: A Study of Afro-American Narrative* (Urbana, University of Illinois Press, 1979) describes this pattern of intertextuality in male writers from the slave narrative to Ellison's *Invisible Man.* Gates's explanation of how a literary tradition is created is a good one, and I include it here to further clarify the term "intertextuality."

Literary works configure into a tradition, not because of some mystical collective unconscious determined by the biology of race or gender, but because writers read other writers and *ground* their representations of experience in models of language provided largely by other writers to whom they feel akin. It is through this mode of literary revision, amply evident in the *texts* themselves—in formal echoes, recast metaphors, even in parody—that a "tradition" emerges and defines itself. —Henry Louis Gates, Jr., "In Her Own Write," Foreword to *Contending Forces* by Pauline E. Hopkins, Schomburg Library of Nineteenth-Century Black Women Writers (New York: Oxford University Press, 1988), p. xviii.

Michael Awkward's *Inspiriting Influences: Tradition, Revision, and Afro-American Women's Novels* (New York: Columbia University Press, 1989) is the first full-length critical study of the literary tradition of Afro-American women writers to analyze these intertextual relationships.

Their Eyes Were Watching God telling her story to her friend
Pheoby. In "Reena," as in *Their Eyes,* a woman's quest for self-
realization is filtered through the story of her relationship with
three men, each of whom represents some aspect of her self. Like
Hurston, Marshall displaces the "perfect lover," leaving her character in a solitary stance, in a room alone. But while Janie is alone in
her bedroom contemplating the past, living by her memories,
Reena is alone in her "living" room, planning a future for herself
and her daughter.

Paulette Childress White's housewife-narrator in "The Bird
Cage" calls to mind Gwendolyn Brooks's 1953 novel *Maud Martha.*
Both White's narrator and Maud Martha are young, articulate,
working-class women with longings for the artistic life, and both
feel cramped and restricted by their domestic lives. But while
Maud Martha can only express her desire for art indirectly, White's
narrator is explicit and direct: she is a painter and a writer, and she
understands how the politics of domesticity interfere with a woman's desire for self-fulfillment through art. Maud Martha's story
ends with a whispered and somewhat bewildered question: "What
what, am I to do with all this life?" but White's narrator knows
where her subversive desires will take her: "I would paint. I would
paint myself."

Louise Meriwether's 1968 story of three women on a journey
to the West Indies, "A Happening in Barbados," can be read in
relationship to Paule Marshall's 1984 novel *Praisesong for the
Widow,* both of which feature three women journeying together to
the West Indies. Although Meriwether intends to extricate her
character from a plot in which she is a sexual object, "Barbados" is
still allied to the romantic plot with its emphasis on female sexual
attractiveness, on heterosexual relationships, and on female jealousy. Marshall's Avey Johnson has begun to cast off all the accoutrements of conventional female attractiveness, discarding makeup,
jewelry, girdles, and stockings, leaving her hair uncombed and her
body unwashed.[6] Marshall sends Avey, one of the first middle-aged

[6] Significantly, Meriwether's character remains unnamed while Avey is a shortened
form of *Avatara,* a name that suggests her role as a spiritual guide.

heroes in black women's fiction, on a spiritual journey that will free her from the dehumanizing materialism of her suburban life and enable her to experience, not sexual passion, but a deeper, more passionate way of living.

What are these revisions and rewritings telling us, and how do these new ways of reading and interpreting women's stories affect our relationship with these texts. To answer those questions I have to return to the autobiographical subplot of this introduction and to my own revisions and rewritings. When I first published *Black-Eyed Susans* and *Midnight Birds,* my task as critic was to recover the writings of black women writers—to retrieve lost works, to introduce newer writers, to celebrate these writers, to create an audience for them. As a reader and critic of black women's literature, I have moved from the stage of recovering these writers from neglect to the stage of interpretation, of looking critically at the narrative practices and the narrative politics of the writers themselves. One of the most significant differences between the earlier anthologies and this one is that I am a more critical reader, made so by the influence and intervention of new critical methods as well as by these writers whose extraordinary creativity and productivity over the past twenty years (1970 to 1990) call for a more sophisticated criticism.

I now ask different questions of the texts, more troublesome and disconcerting questions about the ways in which these writers reveal their own contradictions, their ambivalences and disguises. Critic Robert Scholes cautions us that as we develop skills in interpreting texts, we also have to lose the sense of reverence for those texts:

> The reverential attitude . . . is the attitude of the exegete before the sacred text; whereas, what is needed is a judicious attitude: scrupulous to understand, alert to probe for blind spots and hidden agendas, and, finally, critical, questioning, skeptical.[7]

[7] Robert Scholes, *Textual Power: Literary Theory and the Teaching of English* (New Haven, Yale University Press, 1985), p. 16.

Certainly, as Scholes insists, it is inconceivable that writers who are just as human as the rest of us would not reveal in their writings their own contradictions, their own hidden agendas, their own blind spots.

Sometimes these contradictions surface in the metaphors writers choose. The bird cage metaphor in Paulette Childress White's story "The Bird Cage" entraps her narrator-housewife just as the circumstances of her domestic life also entrap her. For while the bird cage image suggests the restrictions of domesticity, it does not provide for the possibility of change: since birds do not break down their own cages as the narrator imagines at the end of her story, her narrative implies that she can only be freed by some external force, not by her own power—or that she is not yet ready to claim her own freedom.

Ambivalence toward female power often surfaces in texts by women. Look at the differences between two short stories by Alice Walker about the female artist. In "A Sudden Trip Home in the Spring," the patriarchal household allows Sarah Davis, a painter and sculptor, a happy and successful ending. Sarah's militant preacher brother and her stoic grandfather give her the permission she needs in order to work. When Sarah wonders if she can become an artist, her brother reassures her:

> "You learn how to draw the face," he said, "then you learn how to paint me and how to make Grandpa up in stone. Then you can come home or live in Paris, France. It'll be the same thing."

The female household in Walker's stories creates no such optimistic ending. "Everyday Use," centered around a mother and her two daughters, ends with one daughter being rejected in order to effect a reconciliation with the other. All three women are artists of a kind, and Walker says this story represents herself split into three parts; so these stories suggest that the woman artist experiences herself as fragmented and conflicted, that permission to be an artist is still very much controlled by the world of the fathers.

Even Toni Cade Bambara's story of a resourceful and independent woman is marked by ambivalence. Sweet Pea, the main character in Bambara's "Medley," is an A-1 manicurist and a first-rate storyteller. Though she (like most of Bambara's characters) never leaves the black community, her life does not seem at all restricted. She is mobile, financially independent, and adventurous, and as a storyteller she demonstrates a dexterity and power with words that complements her own internal strength. But the storytelling tradition Sweet Pea connects to is one dominated by men. Indeed, her community is peopled almost entirely by men; Sweet Pea's growth takes place in relation to men, and the two figures of female community (her women friends Pot Limit and Sylvia) are consigned to the dark margins of the jazz club where male musicians predominate.

As I have studied contradiction and ambivalence in these writers, I have become more aware of the sources of my own ambivalence. When I wrote *Black-Eyed Susans* and *Midnight Birds,* I was the director of a Black Studies program, and I still had close ties to a black working-class community in Cleveland where I grew up. Stacks of my books were sold from the front shelf of Evelyn King's Beauty Circle hair salon on Seven Mile Road on Detroit's northwest side. I preached my first sermon on black women writers from the pulpit of Ebenezer Baptist Church. Now I write as a member of a predominantly white academic community, as a member of a solidly middle-class black community. I write as the aunt of ten nephews who are struggling to get into the middle class, as the daughter and niece of women who did domestic work to send me to school, as a Catholic, as a feminist, as one who was formed intellectually by the powerful black movements of the 1950s and 1960s.

How do I combine these voices, and how do I understand and live with the contradictions that shape my voice?[8] Certainly I recognize that my critical response to these writers creates another text

[8] These questions were suggested to me by Marianne Hirsch, who poses them at the end of the chapter "Feminist Discourse/Maternal Discourse: 'Cruel Enough to

which the reader then has to judge critically and skeptically, looking for my hidden agendas and blind spots. Like me, the writers in
this anthology write with multiple, sometimes contradictory
voices. Alice Walker, for example, expresses far more optimism and
certainty about the female artist in her essays than she does in her
fiction. The artist figure in her essays—whether it is Walker herself
or Zora Neale Hurston or nineteenth-century quilt makers or African women weaving stunning creations—suffer only from external
interference. But in Walker's fiction women experience many layers of resistance to their art, including their own culturally condi-
tioned doubts and anxieties. Two of Morrison's voices in *The Bluest Eye* are in such conflict that I refer to them as "the dueling
voices." The militantly race-conscious first-person voice of Pauline
Breedlove is constantly undercut by an omniscient narrator who
tames Pauline's anger, insisting on her passivity and powerlessness
before whites. As a critical reader I ask different questions about
literature in this revised text than I asked fifteen years ago, questions about texts "speaking" to one another, about writers and their
ambivalences, about narrators in conflict. These questions are not
easily answered; they demand that we read and reread, that we
continue to probe for deeper, hidden meanings, that readers, too,
become revisionists.

As I have changed, revising my questions, I am well aware that
these writers have also changed. In my introductory essays I have
tried to show how the writers in this collection have been involved
in the act of revision. Jean Wheeler's Smith's 1988 talk about the
Civil Rights movement depicts a struggling southern black community that is radically different from the passive and powerless
community in "Frankie Mae." Paulette Childress White's 1984 narrative, *The Watermelon Dress,* in contrast to "The Bird Cage" and
its failed artist-narrator, shows the female artist insisting on her
right to create. Toni Morrison's 1987 novel *Beloved* and Sherley
Anne Williams's 1986 novel *Dessa Rose* are told from the powerfully race-conscious point of view of the female slave. In Ntozake
Shange's 1982 novel *Sassafrass, Cypress & Indigo* all four women are

---

Stop the Blood,' " in her book *Unspeakable Plots: Mothers/Daughters and Narrative*
(Bloomington, Indiana University Press, 1989).

artists, and, unlike *for colored girls* . . . , the novel shows women in the process of creating art, not being thwarted or restricted but learning the mechanics of their craft, struggling to develop as artists. Toni Cade Bambara's *The Salteaters* (1980), Alexis DeVeaux's *Don't Explain: A Song of Billie Holiday* (1982), and Alice Walker's *The Color Purple* (1982) are all significant revisions of their previous work.

When I think of what makes these writers unique, I do not think first of ambivalence and contradiction, I think of the ways these writers have used language as a sign of resistance, I think of the powerful, articulate, and passionate voices I hear in their writings, especially the voices of those characters who speak in the vernacular. I think of Egypt Brownstone's mother, Esther, as she scratches the word "illegitimate" from a note sent home by the teacher:

> Hand me that god damn pencil eraser girl. Wasn't nobody illegitimate when they was on top pumpin womens in the huts of nigga quarters.

Or Honey in Toni Cade Bambara's "Witchbird" fighting against scripts that try to denigrate her artistic talent and force her into playing stereotypical roles:

> Got to be firm about shit like that, cause if you ain't some bronze Barbie doll or the big fro murder-mouth militant sister, you Aunt Jemima.

I hear the slave woman Odessa in Sherley Anne Williams's "Meditations on History" refusing to tell the white historian the whereabouts of the slave rebels:

> Onlest mind I be knowin' is mines.

And I hear Pauline Williams in Toni Morrison's *The Bluest Eye* recapturing the ecstatic feeling of her lovemaking with Cholly:

> When he does I feel a power. I be strong. I be pretty. I be young.

These gendered and racial voices speak not just for the individual but for a community. They reflect the community's feelings and they take strength from these connections. This is the language of resistance because it reasserts a community which the dominant culture seeks to control and silence.

These connections to a community are at least part of the reason for the extraordinary optimism of these stories. The characters in them are shown in the process of changing their lives—going to college, traveling to distant countries, training for professions, participating in political change, throwing off shackles (some literally, as in "Meditations on History"), contemplating art. How do we account for such optimism, such faith in the possibility of change? I think we have to read a subtext in these stories: the collective political struggle of the 1950s and 1960s generally called the Civil Rights Movement. With the exception of the two stories by Gwendolyn Brooks, all of these stories were published between 1960 and 1979. In some of them, like "Frankie Mae," the Civil Rights Movement provides the specific political and historical context. In others, political references are more oblique: the activist minister in "A Sudden Trip Home in the Spring" empowers his sister Sarah to take her art seriously; the narrator of "Advancing Luna and Ida B. Wells" says that political events of 1965 gave her the courage to go into small Southern towns and teach people to vote.

The autobiographical statements made by the writers in this anthology reflect the same sense of being part of a movement for change. Alice Walker says quite directly that before the Civil Rights Movement she walked in the white world "less real to them than a shadow," that the Civil Rights Movement gave her history, heroes, and hope, that it literally called her to life.[9] While other writers are not so specific about the effects of politics on their lives and their writing, nearly all of them speak about deriving power

[9] Alice Walker, "The Civil Rights Movement: What Good Was It?" in *In Search of Our Mothers' Gardens: Womanist Prose by Alice Walker* (New York: Harcourt Brace Jovanovich, 1983), p. 122.

from the changes in their communities. Paulette White, Alexis DeVeaux, and Louise Meriwether credit their growth as writers to the writers' workshops which sprang up during the '60s and '70s. DeVeaux says that the emergence of Lorraine Hansberry as a playwright in 1959 made her know that it was possible for a black woman to be an artist in the world. Paulette White was first published by Dudley Randall's Broadside Press, a small black publishing house which published nearly all of the black poets of the 1970s.

But there is another subtext inscribed in these stories. The feminist movement (or *womanist,* to use Alice Walker's term) of the 1970s has also affected the stories black women tell. The housewife-narrator of Paulette White's "The Bird Cage" dreams of being an artist and throwing off the burdens of domestic drudgery. Women demand that their lovers meet them on terms of equality. There is a strong focus on friendships among women, on relationships between mothers and daughters, on the importance of work in women's lives. These are the subjects and themes generated by the politics of feminism and by feminist movements.

Both of these movements for political change in our society have revised the lives and the art of black women. In return, black women writers have given us the most complex images of black women in all of American literature. They have made black women central to their narratives; with their stories they have critiqued the racist and sexist practices of the dominant culture. They have revised American literature.

JEAN WHEELER SMITH

In the 1975 edition of *Black-Eyed Susans,* I wrote in the Afterword to "Frankie Mae" that Jean Wheeler Smith's experiences as a civil rights activist in the South in the 1960s strongly influenced her fiction, especially her understanding of how the sharecropping system saps energy and motivation from even so vital a person as Frankie Mae. In the original afterword I was essentially uncritical of this story. I described it as a parable that could represent the lives of millions of poor black girls. I saw Smith's purpose as an attempt to document the physical and emotional destruction caused by poverty and racism. The questions I ask about this story in 1989 engage that text in far different ways. I am more interested in grappling with the politics of Smith's narrative designs, with what this story says about the uses of languages, than in what it says (or—more to the point—is unable to say) about poverty. I am also interested in the stunning way Smith—now a practicing child psychiatrist—revises this story of a struggling Southern black community when she writes about it in 1988.

Why does Smith shape her story into a rather obvious allegory in which Old Man Brown and Mr. White, Jr., symbolically represent the struggle between the black underclass and the white landowner? And why does she choose to have the tale told by an omniscient narrator who controls and interprets the story but re-mains outside the tale and distant from the community she is ob-serving? Both of those choices now seem problematic. To a great extent Frankie Mae is simply the innocent lamb whose sacrifice is necessary in order to bring about redemption. Because of her suf-fering and death, her father is empowered to act—her mother, Mattie, remains an obscure and insignificant figure. But the assault on Frankie is especially painful for us because she is given so little voice in the story. We know little of what Frankie Mae thinks and feels, especially after her father's capitulation to the white boss. We are made to watch her losing interest in life, becoming pregnant at fifteen, growing fat; but we are not given any real insight into the particular reasons for that behavior. While the narrator reports a pattern of behavior that could be considered "typical" for a poor teenage girl, she describes Old Man Brown as highly individual-ized, even his physical appearance:

> Even though he was in his fifties, he was still a handsome man.
> Medium-sized, with reddish-brown skin. His beard set him
> apart from the others.

And, of course, Brown's rejection of his role in the sharecropping system as timekeeper and his support for the strike make him all the more singular and remarkable.

The young black girl victim recurs so often in black American fiction—I am thinking of Pecola in Morrison's *The Bluest Eye,* of the Wild Child in Walker's *Meridian,* Francie and Sukie in *Daddy Was a Number Runner,* Egypt in Alexis DeVeaux's "Riddles of Egypt Brownstones," Celie in *The Color Purple,* Josie in Du Bois's *The Souls of Black Folk*—that they seem to represent something more than social and political realities. Some critics have suggested that these victimized girl children represent the writers' own sense of vulnerability or even the vulnerability of all black people in this society. It is certainly a vulnerability that is not often imposed on little boys in black fiction.

"Frankie Mae" was published in 1968, years before a new feminist discourse made us aware of the gender-based ideologies that connect female sexuality with death (the sexually active Frankie dies after the birth of her fifth child) and trap female characters in passivity and silence. As many feminist critics have pointed out, the script of female death is one of the conventions of dominant narrative which must be challenged so that narratives of defiance, mastery, and heroic action can emerge.

It is interesting to see how the changes of the past twenty years have influenced Smith's attitudes toward the possibility of female voice and power. In a talk she gave in 1988 at the University of Massachusetts at Boston, she constructed the story of her experiences in SNCC (Student Nonviolent Coordinating Committee), not around the suffering female victim, but around the theme of female empowerment. What is even more noteworthy about Smith's 1988 talk is that she describes the Southern black community where she worked as a SNCC organizer not as powerless and victimized, but as shrewd, heroic, resourceful, and collective:

> Try to imagine me and several other SNCC workers in their twenties, the guys dressed in overalls, me in a flowered blouse, a wraparound skirt with little brown-and-yellow flowers, walking into the local cafe in a Mississippi delta town. The cafe always seemed to me to be cool, perhaps because it was dimly lit in reds and blue with tables of different sizes, covered with oilcloth. It would be about the size of a classroom and there'd be a whole lot of life going on in there: around five in the evening, it would be crowded because people had been working since sunup. There'd be maybe six or eight men in their forties eating collard greens and cornbread and trying to enjoy the quiet. Maybe four or five teenagers playing the juke box, drinking sodas and shadow-dancing. Maybe four women who were "worldly" and had figured out how *not* to spend all of their youths in front of a wood stove. Then there'd be about six men in their twenties, who were a little tense. They were the healthiest men in the black community—the ones who could pick the most cotton, and chop the most weeds, and they

were just beginning to drive the machines—a mixed blessing, since the tractors dispensed weed-killing chemicals that reduced the need for people to chop grass.[1]

Unlike the superior and distant narrator of "Frankie Mae," Smith situates herself in relation to that community—as though she is another member:

What was essential to my success was that people believed that I was trustworthy, intelligent, consistent, dependable—and concerned about them. So a lot of the process of organizing *involved them studying me*—seeing that I came back everyday and didn't get scared off by ferocious whites; hearing that I said basically the same things each time I came, observing that I had the good sense not to get involved with their husbands or boyfriends; experiencing that I truly wanted to know what *they* wanted. (One teenage leader said that she joined the movement and led her entire school out to jail because she so appreciated that someone was interested in what she thought. She said, "Nobody in my whole life ever asked me what I thought about anything.") Emphasis mine.

Smith's 1987 narrative highlights the heroic action of a Southern teenager rather than her victimization and shows the community observing the narrator, thus making the narrator an equal rather than a superior. What this 1987 narrative implies is that another and different story is narratable in 1987, one which critiques narrative practices that are themselves authoritarian and hierarchical, one which questions the assumptions upon which "Frankie Mae" is based, one which focuses on the collective struggles of a community and involves the narrator herself in those struggles.

[1] Jean Wheeler Smith, "The Liberation of a People Happens One By One," Monroe Trotter Lecture, University of Massachusetts, Black Studies Department, October 15, 1987.

Jean Wheeler Smith

Frankie Mae

The sun had just started coming up when the men gathered at the gate of the White Plantation. They leaned on the fence, waiting. No one was nervous, though. They'd all been waiting a long time. A few more minutes couldn't make much difference. They surveyed the land that they were leaving, the land from which they had brought forth seas of cotton.

Old Man Brown twisted around so that he leaned sideways on the gate. Even though he was in his fifties, he was still a handsome man. Medium-sized, with reddish-brown skin. His beard set him apart from the others; it was the same mixture of black and gray as his hair, but while his hair looked like wool, the strands of his beard were long and nearly straight. He was proud of it, and even when he wasn't able to take a bath, he kept his beard neatly cut and shaped into a V.

He closed his eyes. The sun was getting too bright; it made his headache worse. Damn, he thought, I sure wouldn't be out here this early on no Monday morning if it wasn't for what we got to do today. Whiskey'll sure kill you if you don't get some sleep long with it. I wasn't never just crazy 'bout doing this, anyway. Wonder what made me decide to go along?

Then he smiled to himself. 'Course. It was on account of Frankie Mae. She always getting me into something.

Frankie was his first child, born twenty-two years ago, during the war. When she was little, she had gone everywhere with him. He had a blue bicycle with a rusty wire basket in the front. He used to put Frankie Mae in the basket and ride her to town with him and to the cafe, and sometimes they'd go nowhere special, just riding. She'd sit sideways so that she could see what was on the road ahead and talk with him at the same time. She never bothered to hold onto the basket; she knew her daddy wouldn't let her fall. Frankie fitted so well into the basket that for a few years the Old Man thought that it was growing with her.

She was a black child, with huge green eyes that seemed to glow in the dark. From the age of four on, she had a look of being full-grown. The look was in her muscular, well-defined limbs that seemed like they could do a woman's work and in her way of seeing everything around her. Most times, she was alive and happy. The only thing wrong with her was that she got hurt so easy. The slightest rebuke sent her crying; the least hint of disapproval left her moody and depressed for hours. But on the other side of it was that she had a way of springing back from pain. No matter how hurt she had been, she would be her old self by the next day. The Old Man worried over her. He wanted most to cushion her life.

When Frankie reached six, she became too large to ride in the basket with him. Also, he had four more children by then. So he bought a car for $40. Not long afterward, he became restless. He'd heard about how you could make a lot of money over in the delta. So he decided to go over there. He packed what he could carry in one load—the children, a few chickens, and a mattress—and slipped off one night.

Two days after they left the hills, they drove up to the White Plantation in Leflore County, Mississippi. They were given a two-room house that leaned to one side and five dollars to make some groceries with for the next month.

The Old Man and his wife, Mattie, worked hard that year. Up at four-thirty and out to the field. Frankie Mae stayed behind to nurse the other children and to watch the pot that was cooking for dinner. At sundown they came back home and got ready for the next day. They did a little sweeping, snapped some beans for dinner the next day, and washed for the baby. Then they sat on the porch together for maybe a half hour.

That was the time the Old Man liked best, the half hour before bed. He and Frankie talked about what had happened during the day, and he assured her that she had done a good job keeping up the house. Then he went on about how smart she was going to be when she started school. It would be in two years, when the oldest boy was big enough to take care of the others.

One evening on the porch Frankie said, "A man from town come by today looking for our stove. You know, the short one, the one ain't got no hair. Said we was three week behind and he was gonna take it. Had a truck to take it back in, too."

The Old Man lowered his head. He was ashamed that Frankie had had to face that man by herself. No telling what he said to her. And she took everything so serious. He'd have to start teaching her how to deal with folks like that.

"What did you tell him, baby?" he asked. "He didn't hurt you none, did he?"

"No, he didn't bother me, sides looking mean. I told him I just this morning seen some money come in the mail from Uncle Ed in Chicago. And I heard my daddy say he was gonna use it to pay off the stove man. So he said, 'Well, I give y'all one more week, one more.' And he left."

The Old Man pulled Frankie to him and hugged her. "You did 'zactly right, honey." She understood. She would be able to take care of herself.

The end of their first year in the delta, the Old Man and Mattie went to settle up. It was just before Christmas. When their turn came, they were called by Mr. White Junior, a short fat man, with a big stomach, whose clothes were always too tight.

"Let me see, Johnnie," he said. "Here it is. You owe two hundred dollars."

The Old Man was surprised. Sounded just like he was back in

the hills. He had expected things to be different over here. He had made a good crop. Should have cleared something. Well, no sense in arguing. The bossman counted out fifty dollars.

"Here's you some Christmas money," Mr. White Junior said. "Pay me when you settle up next year."

The Old Man took the money to town the same day and bought himself some barrels and some pipes and a bag of chopped corn. He had made whiskey in the hills, and he could make it over here, too. You could always find somebody to buy it. Wasn't no reason he should spend all his time farming if he couldn't make nothing out of it. He and Mattie put up their barrels in the trees down by the river and set their mash to fermentate.

By spring, Brown had a good business going. He sold to the colored cafes and even to some of the white ones. And folks knew they could always come to his house if they ran out. He didn't keep the whiskey at the house, though. Too dangerous. It was buried down by the water. When folks came unexpected, it was up to Frankie and her brother next to her to go get the bottles. Nobody noticed children. The Old Man bought them a new red wagon for their job.

He was able to pay off his stove and to give Mattie some money every once in a while. And they ate a little better now. But still they didn't have much more than before, because Brown wasn't the kind of man to save. Also, he had to do a lot of drinking himself to keep up his sales. Folks didn't like to drink by themselves. When he'd start to drinking, he usually spent up or gave away whatever he had in his pocket. So they still had to work as hard as ever for Mr. White Junior. Brown enjoyed selling the whiskey, though, and Mattie could always go out and sell a few bottles in case of some emergency like their lights being cut off. So they kept the business going.

That spring, Mr. White Junior decided to take them off shares. He would pay $1.50 a day for chopping cotton, and he'd pay by the hundred pound for picking. The hands had no choice. They could work by the day or leave. Actually, the Old Man liked it better working by the day. Then he would have more time to see to his whiskey.

Also, Mr. White Junior made Brown the timekeeper over the other hands. Everybody had drunk liquor with him, and most folks liked him. He did fight too much. But the hands knew that he always carried his pistol. If anybody fought him, they'd have to be trying to kill him, 'cause he'd be trying to kill them.

Brown was given a large, battered watch. So he'd know what time to stop for dinner. His job was to see that the hands made a full day in the field and that all the weeds got chopped. The job was easier than getting out there chopping, in all that sun. So Brown liked it. The only hard part was in keeping after the women whose time was about to come. He hated to see them dragging to the field, their bellies about to burst. They were supposed to keep up with the others, which was impossible. Oftentimes, Mr. White Junior slipped up on the work crew and found one of the big-bellied women lagging behind the others.

"Goddammit, Johnnie," he'd say, "I done told you to keep the hands together. Queenester is way behind. I don't pay good money for folks to be standing around. If she sick, she need to go home."

Sometimes the Old Man felt like defending the woman. She had done the best she could. But then he'd think, No, better leave things like they is.

"You sure right, Mr. White Junior. I was just 'bout to send her home myself. Some niggers too lazy to live."

He would walk slowly across the field to the woman. "I'm sorry, Queenester. The bossman done seen you. I told you all to be looking out for him! Now you got to go. You come back tomorrow, though. He won't hardly be back in this field so soon. I try and let you make two more days this week. I know you need the little change."

The woman would take up her hoe and start walking home. Mr. White Junior didn't carry no hands except to eat dinner and to go home after the day had been made.

One day when he had carried the hands in from the field, Mr. White Junior stopped the Old Man as he was climbing down from the back of the pickup truck. While the bossman talked, Brown fingered his timekeeper's watch that hung on a chain from his belt.

"Johnnie," Mr. White Junior said, "it don't look right to me for you to leave a girl at home that could be working when I need all the hands I can get. And you the timekeeper, too. This cotton can't wait on you all to get ready to chop it. I want Frankie Mae out there tomorrow."

He had tried to resist. "But we getting along with what me and Mattie makes. Ain't got nothing, but we eating. I wants Frankie Mae to go to school. We can do without the few dollars she would make."

"I want my cotton chopped," White said, swinging his fat, sweating body into the truck. "Get that girl down here tomorrow. Don't nobody stay in my house and don't work."

That night the Old Man dreaded the half hour on the porch. When Frankie had started school that year, she had already been two years late. And she had been so excited about going.

When the wood had been gathered and the children cleaned up, he followed Frankie onto the sloping porch. She fell to telling him about the magnificent yellow bus in which she rode to school. He sat down next to her on the step.

"Frankie Mae, I'm going to tell you something."

"What's that, Daddy? Mama say I been slow 'bout helping 'round the house since I been going to school? I do better. Guess I lost my head."

"No, baby. That ain't it at all. You been helping your mama fine." He stood up to face her but could not bring his eyes to the level of her bright, happy face.

"Mr. White Junior stopped me today when I was getting off the truck. Say he want you to come to field till the chopping get done."

She found his eyes. "What did you say, Daddy?"

"Well, I told him you wanted to go to school, and we could do without your little money. But he say you got to go."

The child's eyes lost their brilliance. Her shoulders slumped, and she began to cry softly. Tired, the Old Man sat back down on the step. He took her hand and sat with her until long after Mattie and the other children had gone to bed.

The next morning, Frankie was up first. She put on two blouses and a dress and some pants to keep off the sun and found herself a rag to tie around her head. Then she woke up her daddy and the others, scolding them for being so slow.

"We got to go get all that cotton chopped! And y'all laying round wasting good daylight. Come on."

Brown got up and threw some water on his face. Here was Frankie bustling around in her layers of clothes, looking like a little old woman, and he smiled. That's how Frankie Mae was. She'd feel real bad, terrible, for a few hours, but she always snapped back. She'd be all right now.

On the way to the field he said, "Baby, I'm gonna make you the water girl. All you got to do is carry water over to them that hollers for it and keep your bucket full. You don't have to chop none lest you see Mr. White Junior coming."

"No, Daddy, that's all right. The other hands'll say you was letting me off easy 'cause I'm yours. Say you taking advantage of being timekeeper. I go on and chop with the rest."

He tried to argue with her, but she wouldn't let him give her the water bucket. Finally, he put her next to Mattie so she could learn from her. As he watched over the field, he set himself not to think about his child inhaling the cotton dust and insecticide. When his eyes happened on her and Mattie, their backs bent way over, he quickly averted them. Once when he jerked his eyes away, he found instead the bright-yellow school bus bouncing along the road.

Frankie learned quickly how to chop the cotton, and sometimes she even seemed to enjoy herself. Often the choppers would go to the store to buy sardines and crackers and beans for their dinner instead of going home. At the store the Old Man would eat his beans from their jagged-edge can and watch with pride as Frankie laughed and talked with everyone and made dates with the ladies to attend church on the different plantations. Every Sunday, Frankie had a service to go to. Sometimes, when his head wasn't bad from drinking, the Old Man went with her, because he liked so much to see her enjoy herself. Those times, he put a few gallons of his whiskey in the back of the car just in case somebody needed them. When he and Frankie went off to church like that, they didn't usually get back till late that night. They would be done sold all the whiskey and the Old Man would be talking loud about the wonderful sermon that the reverend had preached and all the souls that had come to Jesus.

That year, they finished the chopping in June. It was too late to send Frankie back to school, and she couldn't go again until after the cotton had been picked. When she went back, in November, she had missed four months and found it hard to keep up with the children who'd been going all the time. Still, she went every day that she could. She stayed home only when she had to, when her mother was sick, or when, in the cold weather, she didn't have shoes to wear.

Whenever she learned that she couldn't go to school on a particular day, she withdrew into herself for about an hour. She had a chair near the stove where she sat, and the little children knew not to bother her. After the hour, she'd push back her chair and go to stirring the cotton in the bed ticks or washing the greens for dinner.

If this was possible, the Old Man loved her still more now. He saw the children of the other workers and his own children, too, get discouraged and stop going to school. They said it was too confusing; they never knew what the teacher was talking about, because they'd not been there the day before or the month before. And they resented being left behind in classes with children half their size. He saw the other children get so that they wouldn't hold themselves up, wouldn't try to be clean and make folks respect them. Yet, every other day, Frankie managed to put on a clean, starched dress, and she kept at her lessons.

By the time Frankie was thirteen, she could figure as well as the preacher, and she was made secretary of the church.

That same year, she asked her daddy if she could keep a record of what they made and what they spent.

"Sure, baby," he said. "I be proud for you to do it. We might even come out a little better this year when we settle up. I tell you what. If we get money outta Mr. White Junior this year, I'll buy you a dress for Christmas, a red one."

Frankie bought a black-and-white-speckled notebook. She put in it what they made and what they paid out on their bill. After chopping time, she became excited. She figured that they had just about paid the bill out. What they made from picking would be theirs. She and the Old Man would sit on the porch and go over the figures and plan for Christmas. Sometimes they even talked about taking a drive up to Chicago to see Uncle Ed. Every so often, he would try to hold down her excitement by reminding her that their figures had to be checked by the bossman's. Actually, he didn't expect to do much better than he'd done all the other years. But she was so proud to be using what she had learned, her numbers and all. He hated to discourage her.

Just before Christmas, they went to settle up. When it came to the Old Man's turn, he trembled a little. He knew it was almost too much to hope for, that they would have money coming to them. But some of Frankie's excitement had rubbed off on him.

He motioned to her, and they went up to the table, where there were several stacks of ten and twenty dollar bills, a big ledger, and a pistol. Mr. White Junior sat in the brown chair, and his agent stood behind him. Brown took heart from the absolute confidence with which Frankie Mae walked next to him, and he controlled his trembling. Maybe the child was right and they had something coming to them.

"Hey there, Johnnie," Mr. White Junior said, "see you brought Frankie Mae along. Fine, fine. Good to start them early. Here's you a seat."

The Old Man gave Frankie the one chair and stood beside her. The bossman rifled his papers and came out with a long, narrow sheet. Brown recognized his name at the top.

"Here you are, Johnnie, y'all come out pretty good this year. Proud of you. Don't owe but $65. Since you done so good, gonna let you have $100 for Christmas."

Frankie Mae spoke up. "I been keeping a book for my daddy. And I got some different figures. Let me show you."

The room was still. Everyone, while pretending not to notice the girl, was listening intently to what she said.

Mr. White Junior looked surprised, but he recovered quickly. "Why sure. Be glad to look at your figures. You know it's easy to make a mistake. I'll show you what you done wrong."

Brown clutched her shoulder to stop her from handing over the book. But it was too late. Already she was leaning over the table, comparing her figures with those in the ledger.

"See, Mr. White Junior, when we was chopping last year we made $576, and you took $320 of that to put on our bill. There. There it is on your book. And we borrowed $35 in July. There it is . . ."

The man behind the table grew red. One of his fat hands gripped the table while the other moved toward the pistol.

Frankie Mae finished. "So you see, you owe us $180 for the year."

The bossman stood up to gain the advantage of his height. He seemed about to burst. His eyes flashed around the room, and his hand clutched the pistol. He was just raising it from the table when he caught hold of himself. He took a deep breath and let go of the gun.

"Oh, yeah. I remember what happened now, Johnnie. It was the slip I gave you to the doctor for Willie B. You remember, last year, 'fore chopping time. I got the bill last week. Ain't had time to put it in my book. It came to, let me think. Yeah, that was the $350."

The Old Man's tension fell away from him, and he resumed his normal manner. He knew exactly what the bossman was saying. It was as he had expected, as it had always been.

"Let's go, baby," he said.

But Frankie didn't get up from the chair. For a moment, she looked puzzled. Then her face cleared. She said, "Willie didn't have anything wrong with him but a broken arm. The doctor spent twenty minutes with him one time and ten the other. That couldn't a cost no $350!"

The bossman's hand found the pistol again and gripped it until the knuckles were white. Brown pulled Frankie to him and put his arm around her. With his free hand he fingered his own pistol, which he always carried in his pocket. He was not afraid. But he hated the thought of shooting the man; even if he just nicked him, it would be the end for himself. He drew a line: If Mr. White Junior touched him or Frankie, he would shoot. Short of that, he would leave without a fight.

White spat thick, brown tobacco juice onto the floor, spattering it on the Old Man and the girl. "Nigger," he said, "I know you ain't disputing my word. Don't nobody live on my place and call me a liar. That bill was $350. You understand me?!" He stood tense, staring with hatred at the man and the girl. Everyone waited for Brown to answer. The Old Man felt Frankie's arms go 'round his waist.

"Tell him no, Daddy. We right, not him. I kept them figures all year, they got to be right." The gates of the state farm flashed through the Old Man's mind. He thought of Mattie, already sick from high blood, trying to make a living for eleven people. Frankie's arms tightened.

"Yessir," he said. "I understand."

The girl's arms dropped from him, and she started to the door. The other workers turned away to fiddle with a piece of rope to scold a child. Brown accepted the $50 that was thrown across the table to him. As he turned to follow Frankie, he heard Mr. White Junior's voice, low now and with a controlled violence. "Hey you, girl. You, Frankie Mae." She stopped at the door but didn't turn around.

"Long as you live, bitch, I'm gonna be right and you gonna be wrong. Now get your black ass outta here."

Frankie stumbled out to the car and crawled onto the back seat. She cried all the way home. Brown tried to quiet her. She could still have the red dress. They'd go down to the river tomorrow and start on a new batch of whiskey.

The next morning, he lay in bed waiting to hear Frankie Mae moving around and fussing, waiting to know that she had snapped back to her old self. He lay there until everyone in the house had gotten up. Still he did not hear her. Finally, he got up and went over to where she was balled up in the quilts.

He woke her. "Come on, baby. Time to get up. School bus be here soon."

"I ain't goin' today," she said; "got a stomach-ache."

Brown sat on the porch all day long, wishing that she would get up out the bed and struggling to understand what had happened. This time, Frankie had not bounced back to her old bright-eyed self. The line that held her to this self had been stretched too taut. It had lost its tension and couldn't pull her back.

Frankie never again kept a book for her daddy. She lost interest in things such as numbers and reading. She went to school as an escape from chores but got so little of her lessons done that she was never promoted from the fourth grade to the fifth. When she was fifteen, and in the fourth grade, she had her first child. After that, there was no more thought of school. In the following four years she had three more children.

She sat around the house, eating and growing fat. When well enough, she went to the field with her daddy. Her dresses were seldom ironed now. Whatever she could find to wear would do.

▲   ▲   ▲

Still, there were a few times, maybe once every three or four months, when she was lively and fresh. She'd get dressed and clean the children up and have her daddy drive them to church. On such days she'd be the first one up. She would have food on the stove before anybody else had a chance to dress. Brown would load up his truck with his whiskey, and they'd stay all day.

It was for these isolated times that the Old Man waited. They kept him believing that she would get to be all right. Until she died, he woke up every morning listening for her laughter, waiting for her to pull the covers from his feet and scold him for being lazy.

She died giving birth to her fifth child. The midwife, Esther, was good enough, but she didn't know what to do when there were complications. Brown couldn't get up but sixty dollars of the hundred dollars cash that you had to deposit at the county hospital. So they wouldn't let Frankie in. She bled to death on the hundred-mile drive to the charity hospital in Vicksburg.

The Old Man squinted up at the fully risen sun. The bossman was late. Should have been at the gate by now. Well, it didn't matter. Just a few more minutes and they'd be through with the place forever.

His thoughts went back to the time when the civil rights workers had first come around and they had started their meetings up at the store. They'd talked about voting and about how plantation workers should be making enough to live off of. Brown and the other men had listened and talked and agreed. So they decided to ask Mr. White Junior for a raise. They wanted nine dollars for their twelve-hour day.

They had asked. And he had said, Hell no. Before he'd raise them he'd lower them. So they agreed to ask him again. And if he still said no, they would go on strike.

At first, Brown hadn't understood himself why he agreed to the strike. It was only this morning that he realized why: It wasn't the wages or the house that was falling down 'round him and Mattie. It was that time when he went to ask Mr. White Junior about the other forty dollars that he needed to put Frankie in the hospital.

"Sorry, Johnnieboy," he'd said, patting Brown on the back, "but me and Miz White have a garden party today and I'm so busy. You know how women are. She want me there every minute. See me tomorrow. I'll fix you up then."

A cloud of dust rose up in front of Brown. The bossman was barreling down the road in his pickup truck. He was mad. That was what he did when he got mad, drove his truck up and down the road fast. Brown chuckled. When they got through with him this morning, he might run that truck into the river.

Mr. White Junior climbed down from the truck and made his way over to the gate. He began to give the orders for the day, who would drive the tractors, what fields would be chopped. The twelve men moved away from the fence, disdaining any support for what they were about to do.

One of the younger ones, James Lee, spoke up. "Mr. White Junior, we wants to know is you gonna raise us like we asked."

"No, goddammit. Now go on, do what I told you."

"Then," James Lee continued, "we got to go on strike from this place."

James Lee and the others left the gate and went to have a strategy meeting up at the store about what to do next.

The Old Man was a little behind the rest because he had something to give Mr. White Junior. He went over to the sweat-drenched, cursing figure and handed him the scarred timekeeper's watch, the watch that had ticked away Frankie Mae's youth in the hot, endless rows of cotton.

PAULETTE CHILDRESS WHITE

When I am asked to speak about myself, this necessarily comes first; I am married and the mother of five sons. I cannot imagine an occupation more in conflict with writing than homemaking. I am usually asked where I find the time to write and I usually answer, just as logically, that I don't know. I do as I can.

I was born and have lived all my life in Detroit. At thirty, I am still just becoming a writer. Growing up, I had this dream of being an artist. I did attend art school during the year following my graduation from high school but for a variety of reasons (not the least of which was financial), I didn't last long. I was living and helping out at home and my clerk-typist salary simply didn't cover tuition on a dream.

I married an artist. For a while I was content to watch him paint. I dabbled a bit and had babies and meanwhile began to write these stories that were poems and poems that were stories. While it's true that I'd never been serious about writing, it had always come easily to me. In fact, the one incident that might have turned me on to writing was as negative as it was positive.

My junior year in high school, I had English comp with a fiftyish, white, male teacher whose love of literature was legendary in the school. Often, he'd spend the entire class hour reading, interpreting, explaining, defining and confusing us about every dead or distant writer there was.

Even the brilliant student, Karl Kruger, to whom the teacher's zeal was usually directed, listened dully and commented sparsely while I, unnoticed in my brown and female skin, was rapt. We were required to do two-page theme papers twice weekly and even my best efforts never earned me more than a "B." Then came the day teacher returned my paper, clucking disappointedly, as he gave me a paper marked with the largest, reddest "E" I'd ever seen. I flipped to the back page for an explanation and there he scrawled, "Where did you copy this?"

I was innocent, of course, but my protests fell on deaf ears. I took the matter to the principal (who was also fifty, white and male), and accepted his reluctant promise to look into the matter. Next day, the class was assigned an impromptu theme to be completed within the class period. We were given a choice of five topics listed on the blackboard. I chose "No Man Is an Island," gathered paper, pen and my powers about me and wrote. I suppose I really told him why no man is an island; the following day in class he stood before us and read my paper. When he finished I'd have sworn there were tears reddening his eyes.

Coincidentally, a young Black woman who had graduated a few years previously and was then attending college had chosen this day to pay the old school a visit and was sitting at the back of the class. I remembered her vaguely as one of the colored elite. Teacher called on her for a comment and she stood and very neatly observed that my theme might well have been composed by a sophomore such as herself. I remember thinking that perhaps she too had sat in this class, absorbed in the magic words, given her best for "B's"—in a brown and female skin, sat unseen. Perhaps she had come to slay the dragon, and on that day, we did.

I was returned "No Man Is an Island" with the reddest, largest "A" I'd ever seen. As for the paper that created the stir, it was returned a few days later with one or two corrections of punctuation and my usual "B." And no apologies.

From that point on, I felt a sense of freedom through language that was much the same as I'd always had in my art. As I said, after I married I began to write. I bought myself a desk, a typewriter and a thesaurus and soon I had drawers full of would-be poems. These, I recited to my husband and whoever else was close and kind enough to listen. My husband was encouraging and prompted me to do a few public readings as occasions arose, but for the most part I hid them away, waiting for the magic that would someday make me "ready."

I figured to haul a stack of poems over to Dudley Randall at Broadside Press and be discovered. What I did do, finally, was attend a writers' workshop where poet Naomi Long Madgett was conducting a session on poetry. Ms. Madgett went through the pile of submissions, selected two of my poems, read them to the group and asked me to stay after. In 1975, with Naomi's help (she taught me what a poem really is), I published a collection of my poems out of Lotus Press in Detroit.

Soon after, I was invited to join a small group of talented and dedicated Black women writers in an informal monthly workshop. We'd meet, share our writing, exchange criticism, talk about our lives and give positive support to one another. In 1977, I published my first short story in Essence *magazine. In 1978, I sold my second to* Redbook *magazine. My after-hour sessions on the typewriter and the creative support of the workshop members—Mary Helen Washington, in particular—were making fantastic changes in my life. So now, the second thing I say about myself is that I am a writer.*

—Paulette Childress White

Though Paulette White published her first two stories—"Alice" and "The Bird Cage"—in the 1970s, her fiction recalls Gwendolyn Brooks's 1953 novel *Maud Martha*.[1] The subjects of all three of White's narratives are black women of the inner city—young, articulate, working-class housewives whose subversive dreams of being artists run through the underground of their lives, erupting now and then to complicate the structures of their domestic lives. Both Maud Martha and White's unnamed narrator in "The Bird Cage" experience alienation from their husbands and anger over the limitations and constraints of the roles of wife and mother; but their anger, though it clearly motivates their stories, is repressed and denied. The narrator of "The Bird Cage" smiles "through the

[1] "Alice" first appeared in *Essence* (January 1977) and "The Bird Cage" in *Redbook* (June 1978); *Maud Martha* (New York: Harper & Brothers, 1953).

stupor of marriage" and wonders if she can forgive her husband "his stares and his self-portraits," blaming herself for becoming "this discontent, this willful woman." Maud also maintains a mask of gentility and docility while she accumulates "these scraps of baffled hate," becoming more and more unwilling to play the role of housewife.

Both of these women—Maud and White's housewife-narrator —are artists, though Maud's artistic interactions are revealed only indirectly in her longing for a larger life and her intense preoccupation with color, texture, beauty, and words. White's narrator is very explicit: she is a poet and a painter, even though both of these aims seem incompatible with the life she leads. At the end of "The Bird Cage," as with the ending of *Maud Martha,* the work of the artist and the domestic life remain separate and irreconcilable—in the narrator's life, though not in her husband's.

Neither Brooks nor White is ready to completely abandon the romance-marriage plot, so both narratives end with ambivalent, ineffectual gestures that do not allow any real transformation in their artist-mothers' lives: in the final chapter of Brooks's novel, Maud wonders in whispered tones what she is going to do "with all of this life" and then imagines herself down in a dark cool valley with her arms becoming "wings cutting away at the layers of air." White also ends "The Bird Cage" with the image of flight. She imagines the bird cage destroyed either by the birds within it —a highly unlikely possibility—or by some outside force, images that suggest retreat from the powerful inclinations of her artist self. While both Brooks and White give us characters of artistic genius, they also create plots in which that genius cannot express itself.[2]

[2] In Chapter Six, "To 'Bear My Mother's Name': *Künstlerromane* by Women Writers" in *Writing Beyond the Ending: Narrative Strategies of Twentieth-Century Women Writers* (Bloomington: Indiana University Press, 1985), Rachel Blau du Plessis explains how ambivalence toward the female artist is expressed in this split in which women writers offer "a vocabulary of passionate and frustrated striving" to describe genius but undercut that presentation of the artist with a plot which offers "conciliations and closures demanded by the femaleness of the artist," p. 89.

"Alice" wrestles with another story of female quest—the need for reconciliation between women and the need for people of color to resist the claims of the (so-called) dominant culture. The narrator's vertical ascent into her high-rise government office requires her to cut off her friend Alice, and it is not until she has suffered her own defeats and known sorrow that she is willing to acknowledge Alice and to embrace their sisterhood.[3] Although she chants Alice's name over and over in this story, Alice herself does not speak until after the narrator's change of heart.

This scene of reconciliation is a recurrent one in black literature, and it always involves the hero or narrator affirming aspects of blackness that have been perceived as negative. But in black women's literature the emphasis is on solidarity with other women. When Selina Boyce in Paule Marshall's *Brown Girl, Brownstones* (1959) suffers her first direct encounter with racism, she responds by affirming the bond between herself and the other women of her community: "She was one with them: the mother and the Bajan women, who had lived each day what she had come to know."[4] The seven women in Ntozake Shange's "for colored girls who have considered suicide when the rainbow is enuf" lay hands on one another in an act of communal blessing to heal the scars of their lives. The narrator's chanting of Alice's name is reminiscent of Nel's chant in Toni Morrison's *Sula* when she goes to visit Sula's grave. Realizing that the grief she feels is for the loss of her friend, Nel cries not for Jude but for Sula: " 'O Lord, Sula,' she cried, 'girl, girl, girlgirlgirl.' "

---

[3] "Alice" is actually a good example of an immersion narrative, defined by Robert Stepto as one in which the questing figure in order to gain sufficient tribal literacy to assume the mantle of articulate kinsman forsakes the individualized mobility of the ascent narrative and chooses not to leave the site of greatest oppression (as Frederick Douglass and early slave narrators do) but to locate himself (or herself) there in order to attain a different and perhaps greater freedom. *From Behind the Veil: A Study of Afro-American Narrative* (Chicago: University of Illinois Press, 1979, p. 167).

[4] Mary Helen Washington, "Afterword," *Brown Girl Brownstones* (Old Westbury, N.Y.: Feminist Press, 1981, pp. 311–25).

Since the publication of these two short stories in *Midnight Birds,* Paulette Childress White has published a long narrative poem, *The Watermelon Dress* (Detroit: Lotus Press, 1984), which, in some ways, is a critique of her earlier fiction. The confining and stultifying domestic imagery of "The Bird Cage" becomes, in *The Watermelon Dress,* a symbol of resistance. The housewife-artist imagines the seams of her housedress beginning to stretch, holes appear, the dress no longer fits. The artist-self surfaces and the ripe heart, once eager to be devoured by a man with "impossibly strong arms / and broad shoulders" becomes a feast for the artist herself, as she comes, late, to discover "her own / green wonder."

Paulette Childress White

Alice

Alice. Drunk Alice. Alice of the streets. Of the party. Of the house of dark places. From whom without knowing I hid love all my life behind remembrances of her house where I went with Momma in the daytime to borrow things, and we found her lounging in the front yard on a dirty plastic lawn chair drinking warm beer from the can in a little brown bag where the flies buzzed in and out of the always-open door of the house as we followed her into the cool, dim rank-smelling rooms for what it was we'd come. And I fought frowns as my feet caught on the sticky gray wooden floor but looked up to smile back at her smile as she gave the dollar or the sugar or the coffee to Momma who never seemed to notice the floor or the smell or Alice.

Alice, tall like a man, with soft wooly hair spread out in tangles like a feathered hat and her face oily and her legs ashy, whose beauty I never quite believed because she valued it so little but was real. Real like wild flowers and uncut grass, real like the knotty sky-reach of a dead tree. Beauty of warm brown eyes in a round dark face and of teeth somehow always white and clean and of lips moist and open, out of which rolled the voice and the laughter, deep and breathless, rolling out the strong and secret beauty of her soul.

Alice of the streets. Gentle walking on long legs. Close-kneed. Careful. Stopping sometimes at our house on her way to unknown places and other people. She came wearing loose, flowered dresses and she sat in our chairs rubbing the too-big knees that sometimes hurt, and we gathered, Momma, my sisters and I, to hear the beautiful bad-woman talk and feel the rolling laughter, always sure that she left more than she came for. I accepted the tender touch of her hands on my hair or my face or my arms like favors I never returned. I clung to the sounds of her words and the light of her smiles like stolen fruit.

Alice, mother in a house of dark places. Of boys who fought each other and ran cursing through the wild back rooms where I did not go alone but sometimes with Alice when she caught them up and knuckled their heads and made them cry or hugged them close to her saying funny things to tease them into laughter. And of the oldest son, named for his father, who sat twisted into a wheel-chair by sunny windows in the front where she stayed with him for hours giving him her love, filling him with her laughter and he sat there—his words strained, difficult but soft and warm like the sun from the windows.

Alice of the party. When there was not one elsewhere she could make one of the evenings when her husband was not storm-ing the dim rooms in drunken fits or lying somewhere in darkness filling the house with angry grunts and snores before the days he would go to work. He sat near her drinking beer with what com-pany was there—was always sure to come—greedy for Alice and her husband, who leaned into and out of each other, talking hard and laughing loud and telling lies and being real. And there were rare and wondrously wicked times when I was caught there with Daddy who was one of the greedy ones and could not leave until the joy-shouting, table-slapping arguments about God and Ne-groes, the jumping up and down, the bellowing "what about the time" talks, the boasting and reeling of people drunk with beer and laughter and the ache of each other was over and the last ones sat talking sad and low, sick with themselves and too much beer. I watched Alice growing tired and ill and thought about the boys who had eaten dinners of cake and soda pop from the corner store, and I struggled to despise her for it against the memory of how, smiling they'd crept off to their rooms and slept in peace. And later at home I, too, slept strangely safe and happy, hugging the feel of that sweet fury in her house and in Alice of the party.

Alice, who grew older as I grew up but stayed the same while I grew beyond her, away from her. So far away that once, on a clear early morning in the spring, when I was eighteen and smart and clean on my way to work downtown in the high-up office of my government job, with eyes that would not see I cut off her smile and the sound of her voice calling my name. When she surprised me on a clear spring morning, on her way somewhere or from somewhere in the streets and I could not see her beauty, only the limp flowered dress and the tangled hair and the face puffy from too much drinking and no sleep, I cut off her smile. I let my eyes slide away to say without speaking that I had grown beyond her. Alice, who had no place to grow in but was deep in the soil that fed me.

It was eight years before I saw Alice again and in those eight years Alice had buried her husband and one of her boys and lost the oldest son to the county hospital where she traveled for miles to take him the sun and her smiles. And she had become a grand-mother and a member of the church and cleaned out her house and closed the doors. And in those eight years I had married and become the mother of sons and did not always keep my floors clean or my hair combed or my legs oiled and I learned to like the taste of beer and how to talk bad-woman talk. In those eight years life had led me to the secret laughter.

Alice, when I saw her again, was in black, after the funeral of my brother, sitting alone in an upstairs bedroom of my mother's house, her face dusted with brown powder and her gray-streaked hair brushed back into a neat ball and her wrinkled hands rubbing the tight-stockinged, tumor-filled knees and her eyes quiet and sober when she looked at me where I stood at the top of the stairs. I had run upstairs to be away from the smell of food and the crowd of comforters come to help bury our dead when I found Alice sitting alone in black and was afraid to smile remembering how I'd cut off her smile when I thought I had grown beyond her and was afraid to speak because there was too much I wanted to say.

Then Alice smiled her same smile and spoke my name in her same voice and rising slowly from the tumored knees said, "Come on in and sit with me." And for the very first time I did.

Paulette Childress White

The Bird Cage

It's Monday. Midnight. The house is quiet, my family asleep. The row of sober-faced brick homes leading from my house on the corner is silent now, and the people in them are probably asleep. As is most of Detroit by this time on a Monday night.

Except for me. I spend the hours around midnight back here in the sunroom, sipping cool drinks and looking for some light. Inner light. Inspiration, that I might, before my eyes give out, distill a line or two of poetry.

There is also this troubled flock outside on the street, beyond my green-curtained windows—a boisterous gathering of men. They're bickering again and again and I'm wondering why I ever wanted this house. I knew about the Bird Cage.

"Man, I wont my money," one says. "Hey," comes the answer, "would I stick you like that, man? For five?" "Aw, I don't wont to hear all that," one says again, and a little chorus sings, "Yeah, just give the man his money!"

Three, maybe four, voices—mean, melodious voices—rise and fall. A mad quartet.

These are none of the good neighbors that keep the tidy homes and lawns down our shady street. Those sensible, hard-working folk went to bed at a decent hour and would have no truck with

these out here now. But in my corner house, the left side of which
is exposed to Woodlin Avenue—a semicommercial thoroughfare—
and its noisome night life, I have come to know them.

They are men and women. Young and old. Up and sometimes,
like now, down. They talk too loudly and laugh too hard and they
argue too much. They wear tight, deep-colored clothes—purple
and russet and forest green. Clothes that bind their strongly shaped
bodies too close, as does the fabric of their lives, so that all their
songs become cries. They are bright, nocturnal birds out looking
for some light, for what joy or sustenance they do not have by day.
I know them. In fact, I am one of them. We all take our pleasure in
the night.

But what I wanted here tonight was solitude. None of this
drama. That is for Fridays or Saturdays, when I have nothing to do
but do my feet or my hair. It can be entertaining then to referee
their fights, mull over their philosophies, laugh at their humor, be
one of them while I clip my toenails or put my hair up. But
weekday nights I don't usually waste on such things.

I spent this day, as I have nearly every weekday for the last two
months, in the kitchen on my hands and knees. Between changing
diapers and preparing meals, I'm piecing together a floor of slate
tile in mortar I mix myself.

It's nothing high-minded. I'm not doing it for any kind of
creative expression or fulfillment. I'm doing it because I want a
rustic country kitchen in a rustic country house and doing it myself
may be as close as I get to having one. So what if it's inside a house
that sits on a busy corner in the heart of the city? So what if it takes
me years?

The point is, after I labor over that floor all day—not to
mention the kids—I don't want to be disturbed. This sunroom is
my midnight sanctuary.

"Let me make this run." "Hey . . ." "Is that all right, man?"
"Give the man his money." "Man, you been in there sportin' all night."
"Look, you let me make this run. I'll have your five dollars when I get
back. Is that all right?" "Man, all I wont is my money."

Gracious. All I want! All I want right now is some quiet.

Country quiet would be nice. In fact, I'd like to take this entire city to the country. We could have a sensitivity session. Back to nature. A workshop in life. Be about life and people, about growing things. Rolling hills and thick green fields. But, you know, some people would just drag their city ways on out to the country with them and miss the whole point.

Besides, this is home. My home. And they do say there is no place like home . . . until you move. Until you leave it.

"I wont my money."

Here is proof, I think, that you *can* get the country out of people. Because despite the rural accents, these are definitely city people out there. These people have forgotten all about the country.

But see what happens to me? I sit down to do a really moving piece. Something insightful. Heavy. Then I'm invaded by this silly business of the five dollars and it gets me sidetracked. The situation apparently demands some attention. . . .

▲   ▲   ▲

The Bird Cage is a lounge. A bar. A squat, brown, brick-and-glass storefront bar. The only thing that keeps the Bird Cage and its variegated fowl from my side door is a four-lane street, with litter-laced curbs and two sidewalks, called Woodlin Avenue. Does "avenue" imply strolling leisurely? Quaint little neighborhood shops? Trees or flowers, even?

Not any more. All of that was before the riots of '67. Back when the neighborhood first began to change. Woodlin is like Main Street in Dodge City now, and the Bird Cage is your friendly neighborhood saloon.

Nights, like now, the bulbs of a little square marquee blink the Bird Cage's dumb, unceasing promise of "Girls! Girls!" Girls in the Bird Cage. Days like tomorrow, when I go out back to hang clothes, I'll have to turn my eyes away from the big orange bandage with purple words announcing that the Ice Cream and Cake

Revue is now being featured. (Ice Cream and Cake, a duo obviously as good as its name because the bandage has been up there across the front of the Bird Cage for the entire year that we've been in this house.)

I've seen them as I've passed the Bird Cage—one Black and the other a white blonde, making half-nude dashes around the dance floor. It's almost as if I know them.

No doubt I never will, though I have imagined that one day I might step out past my hedges in these spotted overalls, plastic thongs slapping on my feet, and smilingly introduce myself to them: "Hi. I'm the lady in the house across from the Bird Cage and aren't you Ice Cream and Cake?"

No, that wouldn't do. We're separated by a lot more than Woodlin Avenue. It's just that, like them, I know what it is to be a girl in the bird cage.

"Hey, you gon' give me my money?" "Man, I can't give you what I ain't got."

That's true. And it's also true that sometimes you take what you can get. Like the house. Sure, I'd rather have been able to buy out in Palmer Park like my cousin Sherri, whose husband is in the hauling business (he must be hauling those gold bricks out of Fort Knox) and can afford it. However, this was a deal we couldn't refuse. The man practically gave us the house.

He was the son of a Polish immigrant. The first time we looked at the house, he led us from room to room. It was big and old and in need of some repair. But there was the sunroom. I wanted the sunroom.

"This," he said, "is the sunroom. My mother kept her plants here. For the light, you see . . . all the windows."

It was off the dining room, toward the back of the house. A small, airy room with seven long windows, and through the windows a lush of ivy. Green, green ivy foaming up around the back side of the house, spilling over onto the seven windows, and the sun sifting in softly, greenly, as though the sunlit foliage would spill into the room to touch you.

I like the sunroom, I thought, old wet-eyed white man. We'll take the house of your childhood. Your mother's house. We'll fill it with our own dark dreams. And sun. And plants. Dry your eyes. It is all right to leave the piano. Yes, the old piano, though it isn't any good any more and we don't play. And yes, the attic things. Whatever. We'll use them—or burn them, is what I thought then, seeing the son of the Polish immigrant peer out of a sunroom window, understanding his glance over at the Bird Cage, hearing him think to say, "We have stayed on as long as we could . . . things have changed, now, you know. . . ."

Yes, I wanted the house. And he nearly gave the house away; he was moving on to a place in the country.

"My money!"

And the garage. My husband saw the garage. He is an artist and a keeper of things. A saver and user of things. He is a man who needs a garage. One day the garage, facing Woodlin as it does, will make a fine studio-gallery. A place to hang the unsold paintings and the portraits of himself. Until then it is such a fine place to keep things.

I learned about my husband when I was fifteen, before I ever met him. It was through my Aunt Bertha. She would pick me up some Saturdays and take me to her house, where I was to help her with the cleaning. She, a busy brown squirrel of a woman, would lead, digging through the dust and clutter, wheezing and snorting with asthma, while I followed, confused, pleading from time to time, "What to do . . . what to do with *this?*" And though it would be only a faded calendar or a paper fan or an empty, broken box, her eyes would grab at the thing as if they were saying, "Oh, save it! I want to save that. Yes, save it, save it." When we were done there would be only a paper sack filled with dust to throw away and the mountains of her life would have been merely rearranged. Aunt Bertha—even in repose her hands curled clawlike, clutching nothing. She would not understand that things must be let go of. That nothing is ours to keep.

My husband is like Aunt Bertha. He never lets go. He likes the garage and the huge web of an attic and the dank corners of the basement, for he is a man who saves things, squeezes things, drains things. He says, "Everything I have is important to me. I value everything that's mine. Yes, from the tiniest nail . . . to you."

"Man, I wont my money." "Run me ovah there. My man gonna run me ovah there. I'ma leave my car. I'ma leave the gray goose here. Yeah, leave the gray duck here." Laughter. "The gray goose. Well, whatevah. Go on, get the man five dollars." Laughter. Murderous little ripples of laughter. The sounds of a car leaving. The sharp peck of feet and low, stultified voices crossing the street, back to the Bird Cage.

I have my own arguments to carry on in here. Such as, Why am I here? I did not mean to be here. This is not where I meant to be. By the Bird Cage. In the bird cage. I wanted to go out somewhere in the world. I only wanted to dip down in here on occasion.

"You got a talent, girl. Get yourself a education. So you don't have to depend on no man for nothing. So you have something to fall back on." And I, the little girl, would look up from my drawings at them—Momma, Aunt Bertha and the other mothers of my childhood. I would listen without hearing.

As a child I was safe, safe in my imaginings of a future. In my drawings of television ladies, magazine ladies, ladies with red-lipped smiles and glossy pageboys and pretty, gathered skirts. Safe I was in the vision of myself as one of those free ladies who ruled big houses and wealthy husbands and proper children. Whose lives were orderly and comfortable and clean.

What I got from my real-life mothers came on me as I grew. Was deeper and more lasting. Was understanding—accepting the fact that I was one of them and that life was mean, work-laden, painful. That men were a necessary evil and children a chore.

"If I had known *then* what I know *now* . . . I wouldn't be where I am today." They would say this over a big pot of something boiling and the sweat would make rivulets in the dark folds of their skin and run down; or they would be sitting on low sofas, pushing their baby-filled bellies out for more room, and their eyes would glaze and wizen hard; or they would be blowing over hot coffee they were having after the husband-daddies were gone, when they made time together, their faded dresses limp around them like the once-bright curtains flagging at the open windows. They would say, "I wouldn't *be* where I am today," and suck the scalding coffee through the wreaths of their lips while their eyes traveled slowly toward the open windows and then dropped like stones to the floor.

▲   ▲   ▲

I would not be where I am today. I would be in airy rooms in a quiet place. On a green hill, in a clapboard bungalow with ginger-bread trim, painted sun-yellow. I would have one bed, one chair, one table and one, just one, of anything. I would dress in too-tight jeans that hugged the narrow bow of my hips and in loose shirts through which the unsuckled nipples of my breasts would make interesting twin dots and I would wear a few special pieces of jewelry—gifts that would be remembrances of some gentle soul and that would bring a soft, bittersweet smile to my lips.

I would paint. I would paint myself. On huge canvases I would paint my soul's songs, search out my own truths. I would not write these long, racking poems but make paint talk, smile, cry, touch. My year in art school would not have ended in defeat. In preg-nancy.

Babies. In other rooms I have four sleeping babies. I never had a pregnancy I wanted but I wanted all my babies. Sweet-skinned, newborn babies, I wanted them—how I wanted to want them! Now that their growth is upon me, meaningless is the memory that I had not wanted them. Even as they sleep I sense the cling of their eyes, hear their voices circling round me, "Momma, Momma!" I am theirs.

"Girl, what are you trying to prove?" Women, my friends, asking me, for my own good, "How many babies are you going to have? Do you want? You're gonna be just like your momma. And *you* don't have to be having all these babies. Any more. *Do* some-thing. The Pill . . . oh, you're gonna be just like your momma."

Meaning, they would be meaning, You have become heavier

with each child, heavier and less happy. We see it. Your body will be wasted. Do something. Who will want your baby-scarred body when he has left you, or you him? What will you do when the children grow up to love someone else and then he looks at you and discovers that he, after all, is still young? Oh, what will you do? Meaning, You do not have our support. Meaning, Fool.

Until the last, I smiled. *He* wanted the babies. He *wanted* the babies. That makes a difference. And I was safe enough in the marriage. Who wanted to swallow a pill each day, every day, for forty years? Not I. I smiled through the stupor of marriage until the last birth. Then I cried to the doctor, the good man of a doctor peering down at jelly me, bloody red jelly me, "Fix it," I said. "Fix it that I don't have any more." And his eyes were flat and shocked as a rag doll's when he asked, "Are you sure?"

"Yes." It did not matter that I never gave birth to a girl. What have I to offer a girl? I have yet to give birth to myself.

▲   ▲   ▲

It is late. Outside, feet pattern a senseless music. It is time now to make that climb. To the bedroom. I wonder, if he touches me tonight, will I like it? Perhaps it is enough that I accept it. If I'm not too tired when he touches me, I may forgive him his stares and his self-portraits and whatever it was that made me so angry today.

Disorganization. That I am so disorganized. "Find a place for things and keep them there. Why don't you *think* about what you're doing sometimes?" he asked me. I held back an urge to say, "But if I did, I wouldn't be here," and thereby held off the inevitable fight. I may forgive him, if I'm not too tired.

He probably dreams of soft, supple virgins—innocently, in his sleep, for he is not a bad man. He is steady, moral, true. Still . . . willing, mindful girls eager to be the wife must haunt him.

I have tried. How could we, either of us, have known that I would become this discontent, this willful woman? Who is not mindful; who talks of independence and personhood and freedom;

this closet feminist? Who often, of late, must be brought down? I was easy enough in the beginning, eager prey. Gave myself over to him thoroughly. Now, he says, and it's true, I've got these big ideas and all we do is fight. He must get at least as weary as I. Innocently, in his sleep, he must dream.

"I'ma show that nigga"—glass breaking—*"who he really messin' with." The sounds of bludgeoning against metal and the metal denting, perhaps, but not breaking like the glass. Laughter. "See how he like the gray goose now. Yeah." Feet scratching in the glass. Footsteps dying down the street, heading away, and one voice, raw, epitaphic, shouting back, "I'm tired. I'm tired of people tryin' to mess ovah me!"*

I can understand that. I'm tired too. But I cannot concern myself with these things now. Tomorrow there's the wash, the floor, the kids and more disorganization.

The Bird Cage will take care of itself. Fire may sweep through it in the middle of the night. The birds it cages may find the reason to tear it down. The landlord may grow negligent and the city condemn it. But someday the Bird Cage will come down.

Then we hungry midnight birds will have our chance to swoop at a morning sky.

TONI MORRISON

The Bluest Eye (1970) is the first of Toni Morrison's five novels.[1] As a narrative which includes incest, the disintegration of a family, black self-hatred, and brutality against black people by their neighbors and kin, it has been widely criticized for being mired in pathology and pessimism.[2] The story of the rape of an innocent child and her subsequent madness are certainly painful to read, especially because we are never quite sure whether Morrison is attempting to establish blame or evading the question of blame altogether. This evasiveness becomes apparent at the very beginning of *The Bluest Eye* when Claudia, the main narrator, begins her narration with a deep sense of sadness and resignation that she can account neither for Pecola's madness, nor the death of her baby, nor the disintegration of her family: "There is really nothing more to say—except why. But since *why* is difficult to handle, one must take refuge in *how.*" Now "handle" and "take refuge" are ambigu-

---

[1] Morrison's other novels are *Sula* (1974), *Song of Solomon* (1977), *Tar Baby* (1982) and *Beloved* (1987).

[2] Linda Dittmar, "Will the Circle Be Unbroken?: Toni Morrison's *The Bluest Eye.*" This essay (forthcoming) is the best analysis of Morrison's ambiguous political stance in *The Bluest Eye.* See the bibliography on Morrison for a synopsis of Dittmar's argument.

ous terms, but if Morrison is telling us to direct our attention toward the *how*—that is, to look at the way events occur rather than at reasons or causes—then I maintain that she is urging us to evaluate the construction of her narrative and *how* she has chosen to tell this story.

One of the most important aspects of the construction of *The Bluest Eye* is that the narration of events is shared by many voices in the community, most crucially the mother and father of the raped child. The two central chapters which flashback to the early lives of Pauline and Cholly Breedlove constitute the *how* of this text: Morrison is telling us that to understand the destruction of their daughter, Pecola, we must also understand the histories of the two people who were closest to her and, presumably, able to protect her. Instead, as we know, they become part of the brutalization of Pecola: the victims become the victimizers because, in Morrison's design, their own lives render them incapable of loving parenthood.

We must pay close attention to these flashbacks because ultimately they shape our interpretation of events and mitigate the harshness of our judgment of these parents who brutalize their daughter. Cholly's flashback is told by a third-person narrator who softens our judgment of his actions, insisting that Cholly, having never been parented himself, has no idea how to be a parent. Ironically, Cholly's rape of Pecola, told entirely by this sympathetic narrator makes Cholly seem far less culpable than Pauline.

Pauline's flashback is actually composed of two voices—a duet between Pauline's own first-person narrative and the omniscient third person which "corrects" Pauline's recollection of events and sometimes undermines her credibility. The flashback begins with the omniscient narrator trying "to build a case out of her foot." There is an implied sense of compassion and concern here as this narrator, an attorney for the defense, is, ostensibly, making the best possible "case" for her client. The "concerned" narrator describes Pauline as essentially passive, so passive in fact that a deformed foot and a cavity in her front tooth are the cause of her feelings of separateness and unworthiness. Isolated from her family, Pauline, according to the narrator, is able to exert only a small degree of power over her life and her environment—and then only over inanimate things: she enjoys arranging jars, peach pits, stones, and leaves. The language of the text suggests that she is nearly always acted upon: ". . . she was enchanted by numbers and depressed by words."

While this omniscient narrator presents Pauline as almost totally passive, Pauline's own narration contradicts that judgment. When she fights with Cholly and her white employer, Pauline says defiantly: "I give him good as he got. Had to. Look like working for that woman and fighting with Cholly was all I did." Pauline's first-person voice is, contrary to what Morrison's other narrator implies, assertive, articulate, self-confident, even brash. She is not, as the omniscient narrator tells us, "depressed by words." On the contrary, she loves words, using the imagery of her Southern roots to invent metaphors for her experiences: the purple berries, the yellow lemonade, and the green june bugs symbolize pleasure and sensuality for Pauline. While the omniscient narrator says that Pauline is unable to resist the domination of Hollywood films, her own comparison of the hostility of Northern whites and the snobbishness of Northern blacks shows a keen ability to critique social conditions:

> Northern colored folks was different too. Dicty-like No better than whites for meanness. They could make you feel just as no-count, 'cept I didn't expect it from them (p. 99).

The omniscient narrator's claim that Pauline is given to fantasy and unable to negotiate the "real" world is also contradicted by Pauline's own narration. In the encounters with racist whites, she protests in whatever ways possible. The young white doctor who is told by the older doctors that black women giving birth don't feel the same pain as white women is forced to drop his gaze before her powerful look. Her encounter with her white employer who tries to get her to leave her husband shows that even when Pauline is economically and socially powerless, she maintains both verbal and psychological authority over her experience: "it didn't seem none too bright for a black woman to leave a black man for a white woman . . . But I reckon now she couldn't understand. She married a man with a slash in his face instead of a mouth. So how could she understand." How do we reconcile this militantly race-conscious woman with the Pauline who becomes a household pet for the white Fisher family, identifying with them so totally that she rejects her own daughter and allies herself with the blue-eyed, blond-haired Fisher child?

By the end of this chapter the dueling voices finish with the omniscient narrator finally consuming Pauline's voice and making her equally, if not more culpable as Cholly (whose rape of Pecola is both physically and psychologically damaging) in the destruction of their child. The dreamy, quiet, gentle Pauline of the Kentucky and Alabama country backwoods becomes the brutal, rigid, religious fanatic with an energy for brutalization that makes her seem undeserving of our sympathy, despite what we learned earlier of her own lonely and pathetic childhood.

Why are these two voices so inimical to each other, so diametrically opposed to each other when they are both enlisted in the same service—to tell Pauline's story, to give insight into her life? Pauline's own narration is aggressive, race-conscious, angry with whites, and disdainful of white hypocrisy. Pauline's is a "race" voice, the voice of the poor, uneducated black woman, to be sure, but a powerful indictment of white society. It is the third-person voice that tames that anger, subverts that militant aggressiveness, and offers us a sanitized and disempowered Pauline, obsequious to whites, disloyal to her own black family, and completely dissociated from her earlier defiant self.

I cannot entirely account for the opposition of these two voices. I see it, to some extent, as a complicated response to the dilemma of being a black writer whose audience is primarily white. Will the white audience accept Pauline's undiluted testimony about the circumstances of her life? Will they allow a critique of white racism to be unmediated, unmasked? Is it possible to tell a "black" story without taking the sensitivities of the white audience into account and somehow trying to assuage their fears and anxieties?

On the other hand much of Morrison's fiction has this double-voiced quality. Claudia's autobiographical narration in *The Bluest Eye* is told by both the adult and the child Claudia. It is sometimes difficult to tell them apart, although Morrison allows the child to be angrier. As Linda Dittmar points out, there is another double-edged aspect to *The Bluest Eye*. The fatalistic story of a victimized, powerless family is countered by Morrison's own formidable power with language: "The pessimism is countered by a vibrant, authorial voice."[3] Like the characters Morrison most admires, her voice is experimental, risk-taking, at times contradictory. And, like the issues she chooses to deal with, that voice is complex, disturbing, paradoxical.

[3] Dittmar, p. 10.

Toni Morrison

Seemothermotheris verynice*

The easiest thing to do would be to build a case out of her foot. That is what she herself did. But to find out the truth about how dreams die, one should never take the word of the dreamer. The end of her lovely beginning was probably the cavity in one of her front teeth. She preferred, however, to think always of her foot. Although she was the ninth of eleven children and lived on a ridge of red Alabama clay seven miles from the nearest road, the complete indifference with which a rusty nail was met when it punched clear through her foot during her second year of life saved Pauline Williams from total anonymity. The wound left her with a crooked, archless foot that flopped when she walked—not a limp that would have eventually twisted her spine, but a way of lifting the bad foot as though she were extracting it from little whirlpools that threatened to pull it under. Slight as it was, this deformity explained for her many things that would have been otherwise incomprehensible: why she alone of all the children had no nickname; why there were no funny jokes and anecdotes about funny things she had done; why no one ever remarked on her food preferences—no saving of the wing or neck for her—no cooking of

* From *The Bluest Eye.*

60

the peas in a separate pot without rice because she did not like rice; why nobody teased her; why she never felt at home anywhere, or that she belonged anyplace. Her general feeling of separateness and unworthiness she blamed on her foot. Restricted, as a child, to this cocoon of her family's spinning, she cultivated quiet and private pleasures. She liked, most of all, to arrange things. To line things up in rows—jars on shelves at canning, peach pits on the step, sticks, stones, leaves—and the members of her family let these arrangements be. When by some accident somebody scattered her rows, they always stopped to retrieve them for her, and she was never angry, for it gave her a chance to rearrange them again. Whatever portable plurality she found, she organized into neat lines, according to their size, shape, or gradations of color. Just as she would never align a pine needle with the leaf of a cottonwood tree, she would never put the jars of tomatoes next to the green beans. During all of her four years of going to school, she was enchanted by numbers and depressed by words. She missed—without knowing what she missed—paints and crayons.

Near the beginning of World War I, the Williamses discovered, from returning neighbors and kin, the possibility of living better in another place. In shifts, lots, batches, mixed in with other families, they migrated, in six months and four journeys, to Kentucky, where there were mines and millwork.

"When all us left from down home and was waiting down by the depot for the truck, it was nighttime. June bugs was shooting everywhere. They lighted up a tree leaf, and I seen a streak of green every now and again. That was the last time I seen real june bugs. These things up here ain't june bugs. They's something else. Folks here call them fireflies. Down home they was different. But I recollect that streak of green. I recollect it well."

In Kentucky they lived in a real town, ten to fifteen houses on a single street, with water piped right into the kitchen. Ada and Fowler Williams found a five-room frame house for their family. The yard was bounded by a once-white fence against which Pau-

line's mother planted flowers and within which they kept a few
chickens. Some of her brothers joined the Army, one sister died,
and two got married, increasing the living space and giving the
entire Kentucky venture a feel of luxury. The relocation was especially comfortable to Pauline, who was old enough to leave school.
Mrs. Williams got a job cleaning and cooking for a white minister
on the other side of town, and Pauline, now the oldest girl at
home, took over the care of the house. She kept the fence in repair,
pulling the pointed stakes erect, securing them with bits of wire,
collected eggs, swept, cooked, washed, and minded the two
younger children—a pair of twins called Chicken and Pie, who
were still in school. She was not only good at housekeeping, she
enjoyed it. After her parents left for work and the other children
were at school or in mines, the house was quiet. The stillness and
isolation both calmed and energized her. She could arrange and
clean without interruption until two o'clock, when Chicken and
Pie came home.

When the war ended and the twins were ten years old, they
too left school to work. Pauline was fifteen, still keeping house, but
with less enthusiasm. Fantasies about men and love and touching
were drawing her mind and hands away from her work. Changes
in weather began to affect her, as did certain sights and sounds.
These feelings translated themselves to her in extreme melancholy.
She thought of the death of newborn things, lonely roads, and
strangers who appear out of nowhere simply to hold one's hand,
woods in which the sun was always setting. In church especially
did these dreams grow. The songs caressed her, and while she tried
to hold her mind on the wages of sin, her body trembled for
redemption, salvation, a mysterious rebirth that would simply happen, with no effort on her part. In none of her fantasies was she
ever aggressive; she was usually idling by the riverbank, or gathering berries in a field when a someone appeared, with gentle and
penetrating eyes, who—with no exchange of words—understood;
and before whose glance her foot straightened and her eyes
dropped. The someone had no face, no form, no voice, no odor. He
was a simple Presence, an all-embracing tenderness with strength

and a promise of rest. It did not matter that she had no idea of what to do or say to the Presence—after the wordless knowing and the soundless touching, her dreams disintegrated. But the Presence would know what to do. She had only to lay her head on his chest and he would lead her away to the sea, to the city, to the woods . . . forever.

There was a woman named Ivy who seemed to hold in her mouth all of the sounds of Pauline's soul. Standing a little apart from the choir, Ivy sang the dark sweetness that Pauline could not name; she sang the death-defying death that Pauline yearned for; she sang of the Stranger who *knew* . . .

> *Precious Lord take my hand*
> *Lead me on, let me stand*
> *I am tired, I am weak, I am worn.*
> *Through the storms, through the night*
> *Lead me on to the light*
> *Take my hand, precious Lord, lead me on.*

> *When my way grows drear*
> *Precious Lord linger near,*
> *When my life is almost gone*
> *Hear my cry hear my call*
> *Hold my hand lest I fall*
> *Take my hand, precious Lord, lead me on.*

Thus it was that when the Stranger, the someone, did appear out of nowhere, Pauline was grateful but not surprised.

He came, strutting right out of a Kentucky sun on the hottest day of the year. He came big, he came strong, he came with yellow eyes, flaring nostrils, and he came with his own music.

Pauline was leaning idly on the fence, her arms resting on the crossrail between the pickets. She had just put down some biscuit dough and was cleaning the flour from under her nails. Behind her at some distance she heard whistling. One of these rapid, high-note riffs that black boys make up as they go while sweeping, shoveling, or just walking along. A kind of city-street music where laughter belies anxiety, and joy is as short and straight as the blade of a pocketknife. She listened carefully to the music and let it pull her lips into a smile. The whistling got louder, and still she did not turn around, for she wanted it to last. While smiling to herself and holding fast to the break in somber thoughts, she felt something tickling her foot. She laughed aloud and turned to see. The whistler was bending down tickling her broken foot and kissing her leg. She could not stop her laughter—not until he looked up at her and she saw the Kentucky sun drenching the yellow, heavy-lidded eyes of Cholly Breedlove.

"When I first seed Cholly, I want you to know it was like all the bits of color from that time down home when all us chil'ren went berry picking after a funeral and I put some in the pocket of my Sunday dress, and they mashed up and stained my hips. My whole dress was messed with purple, and it never did wash out. Not the dress nor me. I could feel that purple deep inside me. And that lemonade Mama used to make when Pap came in out the fields. It be cool and yellowish, with seeds floating near the bottom. And that streak of green them june bugs made on the trees the night we left from down home. All of them colors was in me. Just sitting there. So when Cholly come up and tickled my foot, it was like them berries, that lemonade, them streaks of green the june bugs made, all come together. Cholly was thin then, with real light eyes. He used to whistle, and when I heerd him, shivers come on my skin."

Pauline and Cholly loved each other. He seemed to relish her company and even to enjoy her country ways and lack of knowledge about city things. He talked with her about her foot and asked, when they walked through the town or in the fields, if she were tired. Instead of ignoring her infirmity, pretending it was not there, he made it seem like something special and endearing. For the first time Pauline felt that her bad foot was an asset.

And he did touch her, firmly but gently, just as she had dreamed. But minus the gloom of setting suns and lonely riverbanks. She was secure and grateful; he was kind and lively. She had not known there was so much laughter in the world.

They agreed to marry and go 'way up north, where Cholly said steel mills were begging for workers. Young, loving, and full of energy, they came to Lorain, Ohio. Cholly found work in the steel mills right away, and Pauline started keeping house.

And then she lost her front tooth. But there must have been a speck, a brown speck easily mistaken for food but which did not leave, which sat on the enamel for months, and grew, until it cut into the surface and then to the brown putty underneath, finally eating away to the root, but avoiding the nerves, so its presence was not noticeable or uncomfortable. Then the weakened roots, having grown accustomed to the poison, responded one day to severe pressure, and the tooth fell free, leaving a ragged stump behind. But even before the little brown speck, there must have been the conditions, the setting that would allow it to exist in the first place.

In that young and growing Ohio town whose side streets, even, were paved with concrete, which sat on the edge of a calm blue lake, which boasted an affinity with Oberlin, the underground railroad station, just thirteen miles away, this melting pot on the lip of America facing the cold but receptive Canada—What could go wrong?

"Me and Cholly was getting along good then. We come up north; supposed to be more jobs and all. We moved into two rooms up over a furniture store, and I set about housekeeping. Cholly was working at the steel plant, and everything was looking good. I don't know what all happened. Everything changed. It was hard to get to know folks up here, and I missed my people. I weren't used to so much white folks. The ones I seed before was something hateful, but they didn't come around too much. I mean, we didn't have too much truck with them. Just now and then in the fields, or at the commissary. But they wa'nt all over us. Up north they was everywhere—next door, downstairs, all over the streets—and colored folks few and far between. Northern colored folk was different too. Dicty-like. No better than

whites for meanness. They could make you feel just as no-count, 'cept I didn't expect it from them. That was the lonesomest time of my life. I 'member looking out them front windows just waiting for Cholly to come home at three o'clock. I didn't even have a cat to talk to."

In her loneliness, she turned to her husband for reassurance, entertainment, for things to fill the vacant places. Housework was not enough; there were only two rooms, and no yard to keep or move about it. The women in the town wore high-heeled shoes, and when Pauline tried to wear them, they aggravated her shuffle into a pronounced limp. Cholly was kindness still, but began to resist her total dependence on him. They were beginning to have less and less to say to each other. He had no problem finding other people and other things to occupy him—men were always climbing the stairs asking for him, and he was happy to accompany them, leaving her alone.

Pauline felt uncomfortable with the few black women she met. They were amused by her because she did not straighten her hair. When she tried to make up her face as they did, it came off rather badly. Their goading glances and private snickers at her way of talking (saying "chil'ren") and dressing developed in her a desire for new clothes. When Cholly began to quarrel about the money she wanted, she decided to go to work. Taking jobs as a dayworker helped with the clothes, and even a few things for the apartment, but it did not help with Cholly. He was not pleased with her purchases and began to tell her so. Their marriage was shredded with quarrels. She was still no more than a girl, and still waiting for that plateau of happiness, that hand of a precious Lord who, when her way grew drear, would always linger near. Only, now she had a clearer idea of what drear meant. Money became the focus of all their discussions, hers for clothes, his for drink. The sad thing was that Pauline did not really care for clothes and makeup. She merely wanted other women to cast favorable glances her way.

After several months of doing daywork, she took a steady job in the home of a family of slender means and nervous, pretentious ways.

"Cholly commenced to getting meaner and meaner and wanted to fight me all of the time. I give him as good as I got. Had to. Look like working for that woman and fighting Cholly was all I did. Tiresome. But I holt on to my jobs, even though working for that woman was more than a notion. It wasn't so much her meanness as just simpleminded. Her whole family was. Couldn't get along with one another worth nothing. You'd think with a pretty house like that and all the money they could holt on to, they would enjoy one another. She haul off and cry over the leastest thing. If one of her friends cut her short on the telephone, she'd go to crying. She should of been glad she had a telephone. I ain't got one yet. I recollect oncet how her baby brother who she put through dentistry school didn't invite them to some big party he throwed. They was a big to-do about that. Everybody stayed on the telephone for days. Fussing and carrying on. She asked me, 'Pauline, what would you do if your own brother had a party and didn't invite you?' I said ifn I really wanted to go to that party, I reckoned I'd go anyhow. Never mind what he want. She just sucked her teeth a little and made out like what I said was dumb. All the while I was thinking how dumb she was. Whoever told her that her brother was her friend? Folks can't like folks just 'cause they has the same mama. I tried to like that woman myself. She was good about giving me stuff, but I just couldn't like her. Soon as I worked up a good feeling on her account, she'd do something ignorant and start in to telling me how to clean and do. If I left her on her own, she'd drown in dirt. I didn't have to pick up after Chicken and Pie the way I had to pick up after them. None of them knew so much as how to wipe their behinds. I know, 'cause I did the washing. And couldn't pee proper to save their lives. Her husband ain't hit the bowl yet. Nasty white folks is about the nastiest things they is. But I would have stayed on 'cepting for Cholly come over by where I was working and cut up so. He come there drunk wanting some money. When that white woman see him, she turned red. She tried to act strong-like, but she was scared bad. Anyway, she told Cholly to get out or she would call the police. He cussed her and started pulling on me. I would of gone upside his head, but I don't want no dealing with the police. So

*I taken my things and left. I tried to get back, but she didn't want me
no more if I was going to stay with Cholly. She said she would let
me stay if I left him. I thought about that. But later on it didn't seem
none too bright for a black woman to leave a black man for a white
woman. She didn't never give me the eleven dollars she owed me,
neither. That hurt bad. The gas man had cut the gas off, and I
couldn't cook none. I really begged that woman for my money. I went
to see her. She was mad as a wet hen. Kept on telling me I owed her
for uniforms and some old broken-down bed she give me. I didn't
know if I owed her or not, but I needed my money. She wouldn't let
up none, neither, even when I give her my word that Cholly wouldn't
come back there no more. Then I got so desperate I asked her if she
would loan it to me. She was quiet for a spell, and then she told me I
shouldn't let a man take advantage over me. That I should have more
respect, and it was my husband's duty to pay the bills, and if he
couldn't, I should leave and get alimony. All such simple stuff. What
was he gone give me alimony on? I seen she didn't understand that
all I needed from her was my eleven dollars to pay the gas man so I
could cook. She couldn't get that one thing through her thick head.
'Are you going to leave him, Pauline?' she kept on saying. I thought
she'd give me my money if I said I would, so I said 'Yes, ma'am.'
'All right,' she said. 'You leave him, and then come back to work, and
we'll let bygones be bygones.' 'Can I have my money today?' I said.
'No' she said. 'Only when you leave him. I'm only thinking of you
and your future. What good is he, Pauline, what good is he to you?'
How you going to answer a woman like that, who don't know what
good a man is, and say out of one side of her mouth she's thinking of
your future but won't give you your own money so you can buy you
something besides baloney to eat? So I said, 'No good, ma'am. He
ain't no good to me. But just the same, I think I'd best stay on.' She
got up, and I left. When I got outside, I felt pains in my crotch, I
had held my legs together so tight trying to make that woman
understand. But I reckon now she couldn't understand. She married a
man with a slash in his face instead of a mouth. So how could she
understand?"*

One winter, Pauline discovered she was pregnant. When she told Cholly, he surprised her by being pleased. He began to drink less and come home more often. They eased back into a relationship more like the early days of their marriage, when he asked if she was tired or wanted him to bring her something from the store. In this state of ease, Pauline stopped doing daywork and returned to her own housekeeping. But the loneliness in those two rooms had not gone away. When the winter sun hit the peeling green paint of the kitchen chairs, when the smoked hocks were boiling in the pot, when all she could hear was the truck delivering furniture downstairs, she thought about back home, about how she had been all alone most of the time then too, but that this lonesomeness was different. Then she stopped staring at the green chairs, at the delivery truck; she went to the movies instead. There in the dark her memory was refreshed, and she succumbed to her earlier dreams. Along with the idea of romantic love, she was introduced to another—physical beauty. Probably the most destructive ideas in the history of human thought. Both originated in envy, thrived in insecurity, and ended in disillusion. In equating physical beauty with virtue, she stripped her mind, bound it, and collected self-contempt by the heap. She forgot lust and simple caring for. She regarded love as possessive mating, and romance as the goal of the spirit. It would be for her a wellspring from which she would draw the most destructive emotions, deceiving the lover and seeking to imprison the beloved, curtailing freedom in every way.

She was never able, after her education in the movies, to look at a face and not assign it some category in the scale of absolute beauty, and the scale was one she absorbed in full from the silver screen. There at last were the darkened woods, the lonely roads, the riverbanks, the gentle, knowing eyes. There the flawed became whole, the blind sighted, and the lame and halt threw away their crutches. There death was dead, and people made every gesture in a cloud of music. There the black-and-white images came together, making a magnificent whole—all projected through the ray of light from above and behind.

It was really a simple pleasure, but she learned all there was to love and all there was to hate.

"The onliest time I be happy seem like was when I was in the picture show. Every time I got, I went. I'd go early, before the show started. They'd cut off the lights, and everything be black. Then the screen would light up, and I'd move right on in them pictures. White men taking such good care of they women, and they all dressed up in big clean houses with the bathtubs right in the same room with the toilet. Them pictures gave me a lot of pleasure, but it made coming home hard, and looking at Cholly hard. I don't know. I 'member one time I went to see Clark Gable and Jean Harlow. I fixed my hair up like I'd seen hers on a magazine. A part on the side, with one little curl on my forehead. It looked just like her. Well, almost just like. Anyway, I sat in that show with my hair done up that way and had a good time. I thought I'd see it through to the end again, and I got up to get me some candy. I was sitting back in my seat, and I taken a big bite of that candy, and it pulled a tooth right out of my mouth. I could of cried. I had good teeth, not a rotten one in my head. I don't believe I ever did get over that. There I was, five months pregnant, trying to look like Jean Harlow, and a front tooth gone. Everything went then. Look like I just didn't care no more after that. I let my hair go back, plaited it up, and settled down to just being ugly. I still went to the pictures, though, but the meanness got worse. I wanted my tooth back. Cholly poked fun at me, and we started fighting again. I tried to kill him. He didn't hit me too hard, 'cause I were pregnant I guess, but the fights, once they got started up again, kept up. He begin to make me madder than anything I knowed, and I couldn't keep my hands off him. Well, I had that baby—a boy—and after that got pregnant again with another one. But it weren't like I thought it was gone be. I loved them and all, I guess, but maybe it was having no money, or maybe it was Cholly, but they sure worried the life out of me. Sometimes I'd catch myself hollering at them and beating them, and I'd feel sorry for them, but I couldn't seem to stop. When I had the second one, a girl, I 'member I said I'd love it no matter what it looked like. She looked like a black ball of hair. I don't recollect

*trying to get pregnant that first time. But that second time, I actually
tried to get pregnant. Maybe 'cause I'd had one already and wasn't
scairt to do it. Anyway, I felt good, and wasn't thinking on the
carrying, just the baby itself. I used to talk to it whilst it be still in
the womb. Like good friends we was. You know. I be hanging wash
and I knowed lifting weren't good for it. I'd say to it holt on now I
gone hang up these few rags, don't get froggy; it be over soon. It
wouldn't leap or nothing. Or I be mixing something in a bowl for the
other chile and I'd talk to it then too. You know, just friendly talk.
On up til the end I felted good about that baby. I went to the hospital
when my time come. So I could be easeful. I didn't want to have it at
home like I done with the boy. They put me in a big room with a
whole mess of women. The pains was coming, but not too bad. A
little old doctor come to examine me. He had all sorts of stuff. He
gloved his hand and put some kind of jelly on it and rammed it up
between my legs. When he left off, some more doctors come. One old
one and some young ones. The old one was learning the young ones
about babies. Showing them how to do. When he got to me he said
now these here women you don't have any trouble with. They deliver
right away and with no pain. Just like horses. The young ones smiled
a little. They looked at my stomach and between my legs. They never
said nothing to me. Only one looked at me. Looked at my face, I
mean. I looked right back at him. He dropped his eyes and turned red.
He knowed, I reckon, that maybe I weren't no horse foaling. But
them others. They didn't know. They went on. I seed them talking to
them white women: 'How you feel? Gonna have twins?' Just shucking
them, of course, but nice talk. Nice friendly talk. I got edgy, and
when them pains got harder, I was glad. Glad to have something else
to think about. I moaned something awful. The pains wasn't as bad as
I let on, but I had to let them people know having a baby was more
than a bowel movement. I hurt just like them white women. Just
'cause I wasn't hooping and hollering before didn't mean I wasn't
feeling pain. What'd they think? That just 'cause I knowed how to
have a baby with no fuss that my behind wasn't pulling and aching
like theirs? Besides, that doctor don't know what he talking about. He
must never seed no mare foal. Who say they don't have no pain? Just*

'cause she don't cry? 'Cause she can't say it, they think it ain't there?
If they looks in her eyes and see them eyeballs lolling back, see the
sorrowful look, they'd know. Anyways, the baby come. Big old healthy
thing. She looked different from what I thought. Reckon I talked to it
so much before I conjured up a mind's eye view of it. So when I seed
it, it was like looking at a picture of your mama when she was a girl.
You knows who she is, but she don't look the same. They give her to
me for a nursing, and she liked to pull my nipple off right away. She
caught on fast. Not like Sammy, he was the hardest child to feed. But
Pecola look like she knowed right off what to do. A right smart baby
she was. I used to like to watch her. You know they makes them
greedy sounds. Eyes all soft and wet. A cross between a puppy and a
dying man. But I knowed she was ugly. Head full of pretty hair, but
Lord she was ugly."

When Sammy and Pecola were still young, Pauline had to go
back to work. She was older now, with no time for dreams and
movies. It was time to put all of the pieces together, make coher-
ence where before there had been none. The children gave her this
need; she herself was no longer a child. So she became, and her
process of becoming was like most of ours: she developed a hatred
for things that mystified or obstructed her; acquired virtues that
were easy to maintain; assigned herself a role in the scheme of
things; and harked back to simpler times for gratification.

She took on the full responsibility and recognition of bread-
winner and returned to church. First, however, she moved out of
the two rooms into a spacious first floor of a building that had been
built as a store. She came into her own with the women who had
despised her, by being more moral than they; she avenged herself
on Cholly by forcing him to indulge in the weaknesses she despised. She joined a church where shouting was frowned upon,
served on Stewardess Board No. 3, and became a member of Ladies
Circle No. 1. At prayer meeting she moaned and sighed over Cholly's ways, and hoped God would help her keep the children from
the sins of the father. She stopped saying "chil'ren" and said "chil-
dring" instead. She let another tooth fall, and was outraged by

painted ladies who thought only of clothes and men. Holding Cholly as a model of sin and failure, she bore him like a crown of thorns, and her children like a cross.

It was her good fortune to find a permanent job in the home of a well-to-do family whose members were affectionate, appreciative, and generous. She looked at their houses, smelled their linen, touched their silk draperies, and loved all of it. The child's pink nightie, the stacks of white pillow slips edged with embroidery, the sheets with top hems picked out with blue cornflowers. She became what is known as an ideal servant, for such a role filled practically all of her needs. When she bathed the little Fisher girl, it was in a porcelain tub with silvery taps running infinite quantities of hot, clear water. She dried her in fluffy white towels and put her in cuddly night clothes. Then she brushed the yellow hair, enjoying the roll and slip of it between her fingers. No zinc tub, no buckets of stove-heated water, no flaky, stiff, grayish towels washed in a kitchen sink, dried in a dusty backyard, no tangled black puffs of rough wool to comb. Soon she stopped trying to keep her own house. The things she could afford to buy did not last, had no beauty or style, and were absorbed by the dingy storefront. More and more she neglected her house, her children, her man—they were like the afterthoughts one has just before sleep, the early-morning and late-evening edges of her day, the dark edges that made the daily life with the Fishers lighter, more delicate, more lovely. Here she could arrange things, clean things, line things up in neat rows. Here her foot flopped around on deep pile carpets, and there was no uneven sound. Here she found beauty, order, cleanliness, and praise. Mr. Fisher said, "I would rather sell her blueberry cobblers than real estate." She reigned over cupboards stacked high with food that would not be eaten for weeks, even months; she was queen of canned vegetables bought by the case, special fondants and ribbon candy curled up in tiny silver dishes. The creditors and service people who humiliated her when she went to them on her own behalf respected her, were even intimidated by her, when she spoke for the Fishers. She refused beef slightly dark or with edges not properly trimmed. The slightly reeking fish that she accepted for her own family she would all but throw in the fishman's face if he sent it to the Fisher house. Power, praise, and luxury were hers in this household. They even gave her what she had never had—a nickname—Polly. It was her pleasure to stand in her kitchen at the end of a day and survey her handi-work. Knowing there were soap bars by the dozen, bacon by the rasher, and reveling in her shiny pots and pans and polished floors. Hearing, "We'll never let her go. We could never find anybody like Polly. She will *not* leave the kitchen until everything is in order. Really, she is the ideal servant."

Pauline kept this order, this beauty, for herself, a private world, and never introduced it into her storefront, or to her children. Them she bent toward respectability, and in so doing taught them fear: fear of being clumsy, fear of being like their father, fear of not being loved by God, fear of madness like Cholly's mother's. Into her son she beat a loud desire to run away, and into her daughter she beat a fear of growing up, fear of other people, fear of life.

All the meaningfulness of her life was in her work. For her virtues were intact. She was an active church woman, did not drink, smoke, or carouse, defended herself mightily against Cholly, rose above him in every way, and felt she was fulfilling a mother's role conscientiously when she pointed out their father's faults to keep them from having them, or punished them when they showed any slovenliness, no matter how slight, when she worked twelve to sixteen hours a day to support them. And the world itself agreed with her.

It was only sometimes, sometimes, and then rarely, that she thought about the old days, or what her life had turned to. They were musings, idle thoughts, full sometimes of the old dreaminess, but not the kind of thing she cared to dwell on.

"I started to leave him once, but something came up. Once, after he tried to set the house on fire, I was all set in my mind to go. I can't even 'member now what held me. He sure ain't give me much of a life. But it wasn't all bad. Sometimes things wasn't all bad. He used to come easing into bed sometimes, not too drunk. I make out like I'm

asleep, 'cause it's late, and he taken three dollars out of my pocketbook
that morning or something. I hear him breathing, but I don't look
around. I can see in my mind's eye his black arms thrown back
behind his head, the muscles like great big peach stones sanded down,
with veins running like little swollen rivers down his arms. Without
touching him I be feeling those ridges on the tips of my fingers. I sees
the palms of his hands calloused to granite, and the long fingers curled
up and still. I think about the thick, knotty hair on his chest, and the
two big swells his breast muscles make. I want to rub my face hard in
his chest and feel the hair cut my skin. I know just where the hair
growth slacks out—just above his navel—and how it picks up again
and spreads out. Maybe he'll shift a little, and his leg will touch me,
or I feel his flank just graze my behind. I don't move even yet. Then
he lift his head, turn over, and put his hand on my waist. If I don't
move, he'll move his hand over to pull and knead my stomach. Soft
and slow-like. I still don't move, because I don't want him to stop. I
want to pretend sleep and have him keep on rubbing my stomach.
Then he will lean his head down and bite my tit. Then I don't want
him to rub my stomach anymore. I want him to put his hand between
my legs. I pretend to wake up, and turn to him, but not opening my
legs. I want him to open them for me. He does, and I be soft and wet
where his fingers are strong and hard. I be softer than I ever been
before. All my strength in his hand. My brain curls up like wilted
leaves. A funny, empty feeling is in my hands. I want to grab holt of
something, so I hold his head. His mouth is under my chin. Then I
don't want his hand between my legs no more, because I think I am
softening away. I stretch my legs open, and he is on top of me. Too
heavy to hold, and too light not to. He puts his thing in me. In me.
In me. I wrap my feet around his back so he can't get away. His face
is next to mine. The bed springs sounds like them crickets used to
back home. He puts his fingers in mine, and we stretches our arms
outwise like Jesus on the cross. I hold on tight. My fingers and my
feet hold on tight, because everything else is going, going. I know he
wants me to come first. But I can't. Not until he does. Not until I
feel him loving me. Just me. Sinking into me. Not until I know that

*my flesh is all that be on his mind. That he couldn't stop if he had
to. That he would die rather than take his thing out of me. Of me.
Not until he has let go of all he has, and give it to me. To me. To
me. When he does, I feel a power. I be strong, I be pretty, I be
young. And then I wait. He shivers and tosses his head. Now I be
strong enough, pretty enough, and young enough to let him make me
come. I take my fingers out of his and put my hands on his behind.
My legs drop back onto the bed. I don't make no noise, because the
chil'ren might hear. I begin to feel those little bits of color floating up
into me—deep in me. That streak of green from the june-bug light,
the purple from the berries trickling along my thighs, Mama's
lemonade yellow runs sweet in me. Then I feel like I'm laughing
between my legs, and the laughing gets all mixed up with the colors,
and I'm afraid I'll come, and afraid I won't. But I know I will. And
I do. And it be rainbow all inside. And it lasts and lasts and lasts. I
want to thank him, but don't know how, so I pat him like you do a
baby. He asks me if I'm all right. I say yes. He gets off me and lies
down to sleep. I want to say something, but I don't. I don't want to
take my mind offen the rainbow. I should get up and go to the toilet,
but I don't. Besides, Cholly is asleep with his leg throwed over me. I
can't move and don't want to.*

*"But it ain't like that anymore. Most times he's thrashing away
inside me before I'm woke, and through when I am. The rest of the
time I can't even be next to his stinking drunk self. But I don't care
'bout it no more. My Maker will take care of me. I know He will. I
know He will. Besides, it don't make no difference about this old
earth. There is sure to be a glory. Only thing I miss sometimes is that
rainbow. But like I say, I don't recollect it much anymore."*

TONI MORRISON
Bibliography

Toni Morrison's work, like that of Alice Walker, has been at the center of a critical debate over the political function of literature and the social responsibility of black writers. As Morrison's popularity has grown, the disturbing vision of black life offered to an increasingly white audience has troubled many critics. During the late seventies, the critical focus on Morrison shifted from a celebration of her "mythical" worlds to discussions about the nature of Morrison's political perspective. In the eighties, defenses generated in reaction to these criticisms, accompanied by other developments in literary criticism, led many critics to consider the opposition of "negative" and "positive" images too simplistic a strategy for evaluating black literature. Recently, critical response to Morrison has favored a "complicating" of the ways in which literature's effect on culture should be understood.

A paper by Linda Dittmar, "Will the Circle Be Unbroken: Toni Morrison's *The Bluest Eye*" (forthcoming in *Novel*), gives an incisive account of the kinds of indictments leveled at Morrison. Dittmar explores the political implications of Morrison's "pessimistic" world view by analyzing the narrative and verbal structure in *The Bluest Eye*. She argues that the liberating qualities of the novel are strongly undermined by a fatalistic political perspective. Dittmar says that the reader experiences being caught in a trap—a cycle of despair—and that experience suppresses the inspirational possibilities suggested by the text and conveys the sense that social and political change are impossible.

Many critics disagree with the assessment that Morrison's work is overwhelmingly pessimistic, offering various rationale for the prevalence of brutality and alienation in her fictional worlds. In *Fingering the Jagged Grain: Tradition and Form in Recent Black Fiction* (Athens, Ga.: University of Georgia Press, 1985) Keith Byerman compares Morrison to Flannery O'Connor and argues that their troubled worlds serve to point an accusing finger at an immoral and insane social order. Philip M. Royster *("The Bluest Eye"* in *First World,* Winter 1977, pp. 35–43) makes a simpler point, asserting that the harsh depiction of black life is a deliberate effort by Morrison "to root out the symptoms" in order to foreground their causes. In an essay discussing the themes of Morrison's novels, Susan Willis ("Eruptions of Funk: Historicizing Toni Morrison" in *Specifying: Black Women Writing the American Experience* Madison: University of Wisconsin Press, 1987, pp. 83–109) defends Morrison's depiction of fragmentation and alienation as historically correct, arguing that the displacement experienced by black families is an outcome of their relocation from the rural South to the urban North during the Second World War. Willis also points out that folk wisdom's heavy presence in Morrison's work is not—as many maintain—an indication that Morrison is suggesting endurance and not social upheaval as a desired end. Willis says that folk wisdom and social criticism go hand in hand.

Barbara Christian's lengthy chapter on Morrison in *Black American Novelists* and three essays in her recent collection *Black Feminist Criticism* concentrate on elaborations of Morrison's thematic concerns, especially her emphasis on the redemptive power of nature. Christian argues that the most alienated characters are those with the most tenuous ties to the natural world.

Michael Awkward in "Roadblocks and Relatives: Critical Revision in Toni Morrison's *The Bluest Eye*" (*Critical Essays on Toni Morrison,* ed. Nellie F. McKay, Boston: G. K. Hall, 1988, pp. 57–

68) claims that Morrison's novels represent a revision and rework-
ing of earlier male-centered texts, thus creating "canonical space"
for later feminist fiction. Hortense Spillers presents a similar argument in "A Hateful Passion, A Lost Love," *(Feminist Studies,* Summer 1983, pp. 293–323), praising Morrison for a breakthrough to a
"new female being" in *Sula.* Contrasting *Sula* to Hurston's *Their
Eyes Were Watching God* and Margaret Walker's *Jubilee,* Spillers
argues that the novel involves readers in their own "contradictory
motivations concerning issues of individual woman-freedom." By
presenting a sexually active and independent female character,
Morrison dispels the historic need to prove the virtuousness of
black female characters, thus opening up room for other writers to
explore the possibilities of black female experience in more complex ways.

Representative of the contemporary move away from evaluating black literature on the basis of positive or negative literary role
models are two excellent essays by Deborah McDowell and Valerie
Smith in " 'The Self and the Other': Reading Toni Morrison's Sula
and the Black Female Text," in *Critical Essays on Toni Morrison*, ed.
Nellie F. McKay (Boston: G. K. Hall, 1988, pp. 77–90). McDowell
surveys the arguments which come to bear on black feminist literature. She compares the positive/negative oppositions to other bi-
nary oppositions (self/other, male/female, virgin/whore) which
have impeded the social and literary progress of black women
writers. McDowell sees in Morrison's work the fictional rejection
of this dualism: in *Sula,* for example, a character's identity is treated
as a process of becoming rather than as a static role. Valerie Smith's
chapter on Morrison, "Toni Morrison's Narratives on Community" in her book *Self-Discovery and Authority in Afro American
Literature* (Cambridge: Harvard University Press, 1987, pp.
122–53), makes a similar point but approaches it differently. Smith
analyzes Morrison's technique of inserting flashbacks and histories
of minor characters into the protagonist's narrative, thereby "complicating" the act of storytelling and suggesting that the discovery
of self is a cyclic, not a linear, process.

PAULE MARSHALL

As the author of several eloquent essays about her own work, Paule Marshall has directed our attention toward those aspects of her work she considers the most political, specifically the need for black people to affirm their own cultural identity, to claim their history, and to resist the oppressive terms of the dominant culture.[1] It is precisely the eloquence and articulateness of Marshall's statements about her own writing that has made critics less attentive to those aspects of her texts that contradict or problematize her stated political aims.[2] The "political" story of the quest for communal and cultural values is in some ways a mask that deflects our atten-

[1] Paule Marshall, "Shaping the World of My Art," *New Letters,* Vol. 40 No. 1 (Autumn 1973), pp. 106–7. Marshall has also written about her own work in "The Making of a Writer: From the Poets in the Kitchen," which is the Introduction to a collection of her stories, *Reena and Other Stories* (New York: The Feminist Press, 1983), pp. 3–12.

[2] In his essay "Whose Child? The Fiction of Paule Marshall" *(CLA Journal,* Vol. 26 No. 1, September 1980, pp. 1–15), John Cook argues that Marshall's major private subject is sexual conflict and that in some of her early fiction she simply superimposes her political perspective on the story of sexual politics. The correlation of public and private themes, he says finally becomes fully consistent in *The Chosen Place, the Timeless People.*

tion from an even more powerful, perhaps more threatening story. The story of sexual politics, of female resistance to the claims of community, of the emergence of female power, propose an even more radical opposition to dominance than Marshall's more explicitly political story.

The parallels between "Reena" and Zora Neale Hurston's 1937 novel *Their Eyes Were Watching God* suggest how much "Reena," like the Hurston novel, is the story of the conflict between female independence and the claims of a male-dominated community.[3] In both stories the stages of the woman's life are marked by her relationships with three men, each of whom helps the woman (Janie in *Their Eyes* and Reena) to clarify her own identity. In both stories the woman's independence is achieved by leaving those men. In both stories the dominant romantic plot is undercut by the subplot of female community.

Both Janie Crawford and Reena choose for their first romantic relationship a man who belongs to their youthful period when they are innocent and naive and unprepared for the man's ineffectualness and for the hostility that lies beneath his ineptitude. Janie's first husband, Logan, is resentful of her good looks and her independent spirit. Reena's first boyfriend leaves her because his family thinks she is too dark. The second affair, equally disastrous, is undertaken, not out of desire for intimacy and love, but to establish the woman's authority in the larger society. Janie runs off with Jody because she needs to get out of the claustrophobic world of her little village and go beyond being a domestic slave: "he [Jody] did not represent sun-up and pollen and blooming trees, but he spoke for far horizon. He spoke for change and chance" *(Their Eyes,* p. 50). The white man Reena chooses for her second affair is part of her left-wing experimental period, and as she moves away from the provincial world of sororities and college dances, her choice of a white lover, a radical, affirms that growing distance from her former life.

---

[3] Zora Neale Hurston, *Their Eyes Were Watching God* (Urbana: University of Illinois Press, 1978). "Reena" was originally published in *Harper's* (October 1962, pp. 154–63).

Finally both Reena and Janie, having learned crucial lessons about self-division, choose a third relationship which seems to allow them a fidelity to self as well as a commitment to another. But neither Hurston nor Marshall is content to let romantic love be the measure of her character's life. The perfect lover must be made imperfect. Reena fights against being submerged in her husband's problems just as Janie fights being consumed by Tea Cake's madness. These perfect lovers displaced, both women are left at the end of their narratives in a solitary stance—Reena alone in her living room making plans for her and her children's future; Janie alone in her upstairs bedroom (the downstairs "shut and fastened") contemplating the past.[4] But these stories do not end in their characters' isolation. Each woman tells her story to a trusted friend whose hearing of it changes her life and gives the tale new meaning. Janie's friend Pheoby Watson tells her, "Ah done growed ten feet higher from jus' listenin' tuh you, Janie. Ah ain't satisfied wid mah self no mo'." Reena's friend Paulie says that Reena's tale has made vivid for her "what it has meant, what it means, to be a black woman in America." Lee Edwards says of Hurston's novel that it gains its final meanings not from Janie's idyllic relationship with Tea Cake but "from the change this relationship and Janie's survival of its loss make for Pheoby."[5] Thus these two female listeners and female storytellers suggest that the emphasis in both texts is on relationships among women, an emphasis which is also signaled by the presence of a female ancestral figure—Nanny in *Their Eyes* and Aunt Vi in "Reena"—whose life offers an original text of female authority and autonomy. Though this story of female empower-

[4] In my essay " 'I Love the Way Janie Crawford Left Her Husbands': Zora Neale Hurston's Emergent Female Hero," *(Invented Lives: Narratives of Black Women 1860–1960* [New York: Doubleday, 1987], pp. 237–54), I argue that the ending of *Their Eyes* is troublesome because while the language gives the illusion of growth, Janie is alone in the final scene contemplating the past but cutting off any further exploration of the world. The darkened bedroom, the pulling in of the horizon, the dominance of Tea Cake's memory leave Janie in a position of stasis.

[5] Lee R. Edwards, *Psyche As Hero: Female Heroism and Fictional Form* (Middletown, Conn.: Wesleyan University Press, 1984, pp. 219–20.)

ment is relegated to the background of the dominant romantic plot, it continues to assert itself at the same time that it tries to conceal its potentially subversive designs.

"Reena," it must be noted, significantly revises the female quest story of *Their Eyes Were Watching God*. At the end of "Reena" there is no dead lover made even more magnificent by his absence. Reena's ex-husband Dave is attractive but problematic. Reena is not enclosed in her bedroom contemplating the past but in her "living" room planning a future. Unlike Janie, who rejects the wisdom of the ancestral figure, Reena and Paulie pay tribute to Aunt Vi, evoking her memory to celebrate her life and its meanings for them as her descendants. And finally the trusted friend, Paulie, does not, like Pheoby, experience her own life as diminished in comparison to the tale-teller. Paulie, the writer who shapes the tale that Reena tells, is her friend and equal.

Both Hurston and Marshall are making claims for the woman artist, claims that allow her the freedom not to be defined by men, to be immersed in her own story, to be alone, to critique her community. These six love affairs are on one level maneuvers which allow the writers to move their characters beyond the boundaries set up by family and community and into those beginnings which Reena describes as "new and fresh with all kinds of possibilities." Like her luminous literary ancestor, Janie Mae Crawford, Reena has challenged the restrictions the community places on its female artists and has enlarged the spaces women can occupy in the world. It has taken a while for us to recognize that issues of gender *are* political issues; in Marshall's case, the narrative of the woman artist designing her own story and resisting the claims which threaten to stifle that design may very well be the most political of all her tales.

Paule Marshall

Reena

Like most people with unpleasant childhoods, I am on constant guard against the past—the past being for me the people and places associated with the years I served out my girlhood in Brooklyn. The places no longer matter that much since most of them have vanished. The old grammar school, for instance, P.S. 35 ("Dirty 5's" we called it and with justification) has been replaced by a low, coldly functional arrangement of glass and Permastone which bears its name but has none of the feel of a school about it. The small, grudgingly lighted stores along Fulton Street, the soda parlor that was like a church with its stained-glass panels in the door and marble floor have given way to those impersonal emporiums, the supermarkets. Our house even, a brownstone relic whose halls smelled comfortingly of dust and lemon oil, the somnolent street upon which it stood, the tall, muscular trees which shaded it were leveled years ago to make way for a city housing project—a stark, graceless warren for the poor. So that now whenever I revisit that old section of Brooklyn and see these new and ugly forms, I feel nothing. I might as well be in a strange city.

But it is another matter with the people of my past, the faces that in their darkness were myriad reflections of mine. Whenever I encounter them at the funeral or wake, the wedding or christening

—those ceremonies by which the past reaffirms its hold—my guard drops and memories banished to the rear of the mind rush forward to rout the present. I almost become the child again—anxious and angry, disgracefully diffident.

Reena was one of the people from that time, and a main contributor to my sense of ineffectualness then. She had not done this deliberately. It was just that whenever she talked about herself (and this was not as often as most people) she seemed to be talking about me also. She ruthlessly analyzed herself, sparing herself nothing. Her honesty was so absolute it was a kind of cruelty.

She had not changed, I was to discover in meeting her again after a separation of twenty years. Nor had I really. For although the years had altered our positions (she was no longer the lord and I the lackey) and I could even afford to forgive her now, she still had the ability to disturb me profoundly by dredging to the surface those aspects of myself that I kept buried. This time, as I listened to her talk over the stretch of one long night, she made vivid without knowing it what is perhaps the most critical fact of my existence— that definition of me, of her and millions like us, formulated by others to serve out their fantasies, a definition we have to combat at an unconscionable cost to the self and even use, at times, in order to survive; the cause of so much shame and rage as well as, oddly enough, a source of pride: simply, what it has meant, what it means, to be a black woman in America.

We met—Reena and myself—at the funeral of her aunt who had been my godmother and whom I had also called aunt, Aunt Vi, and loved, for she and her house had been, respectively, a source of understanding and a place of calm for me as a child. Reena entered the church where the funeral service was being held as though she, not the minister, were coming to officiate, sat down among the immediate family up front, and turned to inspect those behind her. I saw her face then.

It was a good copy of the original. The familiar mold was there, that is, and the configuration of bone beneath the skin was the same despite the slight fleshiness I had never seen there before;

her features had even retained their distinctive touches: the positive set to her mouth, the assertive lift to her nose, the same insistent, unsettling eyes which when she was angry became as black as her skin—and this was total, unnerving, and very beautiful. Yet something had happened to her face. It was different despite its sameness. Aging even while it remained enviably young. Time had sketched in, very lightly, the evidence of the twenty years.

As soon as the funeral service was over, I left, hurrying out of the church into the early November night. The wind, already at its winter strength, brought with it the smell of dead leaves and the image of Aunt Vi there in the church, as dead as the leaves—as well as the thought of Reena, whom I would see later at the wake.

Her real name had been Doreen, a standard for girls among West Indians (her mother, like my parents, was from Barbados), but she had changed it to Reena on her twelfth birthday—"As a present to myself"—and had enforced the change on her family by refusing to answer to the old name. "Reena. With two e's!" she would say and imprint those e's on your mind with the indelible black of her eyes and a thin threatening finger that was like a quill.

She and I had not been friends through our own choice. Rather, our mothers, who had known each other since childhood, had forced the relationship. And from the beginning, I had been at a disadvantage. For Reena, as early as the age of twelve, had had a quality that was unique, superior, and therefore dangerous. She seemed defined, even then, all of a piece, the raw edges of her adolescence smoothed over; indeed, she seemed to have escaped adolescence altogether and made one dazzling leap from childhood into the very arena of adult life. At thirteen, for instance, she was reading Zola, Hauptmann, Steinbeck, while I was still in the thrall of the Little Minister and Lorna Doone. When I could only barely conceive of the world beyond Brooklyn, she was talking of the Civil War in Spain, lynchings in the South, Hitler in Poland—and talking with the outrage and passion of a revolutionary. I would try, I remember, to console myself with the thought that she was really an adult masquerading as a child, which meant that I could not possibly be her match.

For her part, Reena put up with me and was, by turns, patronizing and impatient. I merely served as the audience before whom she rehearsed her ideas and the yardstick by which she measured her worldliness and knowledge.

"Do you realize that this stupid country supplied Japan with the scrap iron to make the weapons she's now using against it?" she had shouted at me once.

I had not known that.

Just as she overwhelmed me, she overwhelmed her family, with the result that despite a half dozen brothers and sisters who consumed quantities of bread and jam whenever they visited us, she behaved like an only child and got away with it. Her father, a gentle man with skin the color of dried tobacco and with the nose Reena had inherited jutting out like a crag from his nondescript face, had come from Georgia and was always making jokes about having married a foreigner—Reena's mother being from the West Indies. When not joking, he seemed slightly bewildered by his large family and so in awe of Reena that he avoided her. Reena's mother, a small, dry, formidably black woman, was less a person to me than the abstract principle of force, power, energy. She was alternately strict and indulgent with Reena and, despite the inconsistency, surprisingly effective.

They lived when I knew them in a cold-water railroad flat above a kosher butcher on Belmont Avenue in Brownsville, some distance from us—and this in itself added to Reena's exotic quality. For it was a place where Sunday became Saturday, with all the stores open and pushcarts piled with vegetables and yard goods lined up along the curb, a crowded place where people hawked and spat freely in the streaming gutters and the men looked as if they had just stepped from the pages of the Old Testament with their profuse beards and long, black, satin coats.

When Reena was fifteen her family moved to Jamaica in Queens and since, in those days, Jamaica was considered too far away for visiting, our families lost contact and I did not see Reena again until we were both in college and then only once and not to speak to . . .

▲   ▲   ▲

I had walked some distance and by the time I got to the wake, which was being held at Aunt Vi's house, it was well under way. It was a good wake. Aunt Vi would have been pleased. There was plenty to drink, and more than enough to eat, including some Barbadian favorites: coconut bread, pone made with the cassava root, and the little crisp codfish cakes that are so hot with peppers they bring tears to the eyes as you bite into them.

I had missed the beginning, when everyone had probably sat around talking about Aunt Vi and recalling the few events that had distinguished her otherwise undistinguished life. (Someone, I'm sure, had told of the time she had missed the excursion boat to Atlantic City and had held her own private picnic—complete with pigeon peas and rice and fricassee chicken—on the pier at 42nd Street.) By the time I arrived, though, it would have been indiscreet to mention her name, for by then the wake had become—and this would also have pleased her—a celebration of life.

I had had two drinks, one right after the other, and was well into my third when Reena, who must have been upstairs, entered the basement kitchen where I was. She saw me before I had quite seen her, and with a cry that alerted the entire room to her presence and charged the air with her special force, she rushed toward me.

"Hey, I'm the one who was supposed to be the writer, not you! Do you know, I still can't believe it," she said, stepping back, her blackness heightened by a white mocking smile. "I read both your books over and over again and I can't really believe it. My Little Paulie!"

I did not mind. For there was respect and even wonder behind the patronizing words and in her eyes. The old imbalance between us had ended and I was suddenly glad to see her.

I told her so and we both began talking at once, but Reena's voice overpowered mine, so that all I could do after a time was listen while she discussed my books, and dutifully answer her questions about my personal life.

"And what about you?" I said, almost brutally, at the first chance I got. "What've you been up to all this time?"

She got up abruptly. "Good Lord, in here's noisy as hell. Come on, let's go upstairs."

We got fresh drinks and went up to Aunt Vi's bedroom, where in the soft light from the lamps, the huge Victorian bed and the pink satin bedspread with roses of the same material strewn over its surface looked as if they had never been used. And, in a way, this was true. Aunt Vi had seldom slept in her bed or, for that matter, lived in her house, because in order to pay for it, she had had to work at a sleeping-in job which gave her only Thursdays and every other Sunday off.

Reena sat on the bed, crushing the roses, and I sat on one of the numerous trunks which crowded the room. They contained every dress, coat, hat, and shoe that Aunt Vi had worn since coming to the United States. I again asked Reena what she had been doing over the years.

"Do you want a blow-by-blow account?" she said. But despite the flippancy, she was suddenly serious. And when she began it was clear that she had written out the narrative in her mind many times. The words came too easily; the events, the incidents had been ordered in time, and the meaning of her behavior and of the people with whom she had been involved had been painstakingly analyzed. She talked willingly, with desperation almost. And the words by themselves weren't enough. She used her hands to give them form and urgency. I became totally involved with her and all that she said. So much so that as the night wore on I was not certain at times whether it was she or I speaking.

▲   ▲   ▲

From the time her family moved to Jamaica until she was nineteen or so, Reena's life sounded, from what she told me in the beginning, as ordinary as mine and most of the girls we knew. After high school she had gone on to one of the free city colleges, where she had majored in journalism, worked part time in the school library, and, surprisingly enough, joined a houseplan. (Even I hadn't gone that far.) It was an all-Negro club, since there was a tacit understanding that Negro and white girls did not join each other's houseplans. "Integration, northern style," she said, shrugging.

It seems that Reena had had a purpose and a plan in joining the group. "I thought," she said with a wry smile, "I could get those girls up off their complacent rumps and out doing something about social issues. . . . I couldn't get them to budge. I remember after the war when a Negro ex-soldier had his eyes gouged out by a bus driver down South I tried getting them to demonstrate on campus. I talked until I was hoarse, but to no avail. They were too busy planning the annual autumn frolic."

Her laugh was bitter but forgiving and it ended in a long, reflective silence. After which she said quietly, "It wasn't that they didn't give a damn. It was just, I suppose, that like most people they didn't want to get involved to the extent that they might have to stand up and be counted. If it ever came to that. Then another thing. They thought they were safe, special. After all, they had grown up in the North, most of them, and so had escaped the southern-style prejudice; their parents, like mine, were struggling to put them through college; they could look forward to being tidy little schoolteachers, social workers, and lab technicians. Oh, they were safe!" The sarcasm scored her voice and then abruptly gave way to pity. "Poor things, they weren't safe, you see, and would never be as long as millions like themselves in Harlem, on Chicago's South Side, down South, all over the place, were unsafe.

I tried to tell them this—and they accused me of being oversensitive. They tried not to listen. But I would have held out and, I'm sure, even brought some of them around eventually if this other business with a silly boy hadn't happened at the same time. . . ."

Reena told me then about her first, brief, and apparently innocent affair with a boy she had met at one of the houseplan parties. It had ended, she said, when the boy's parents had met her. "That was it," she said and the flat of her hand cut into the air. "He was forbidden to see me. The reason? He couldn't bring himself to tell me, but I knew. I was too black.

"Naturally, it wasn't the first time something like that had happened. In fact, you might say that was the theme of my childhood. Because I was dark I was always being plastered with Vaseline so I wouldn't look ashy. Whenever I had my picture taken they would pile a whitish powder on my face and make the lights so bright I always came out looking ghostly. My mother stopped speaking to any number of people because they said I would have been pretty if I hadn't been so dark. Like nearly every little black girl, I had my share of dreams of waking up to find myself with long, blond curls, blue eyes, and skin like milk. So I should have been prepared. Besides, that boy's parents were really rejecting themselves in rejecting me.

"Take us"—and her hands, opening in front of my face as she suddenly leaned forward, seemed to offer me the whole of black humanity. "We live surrounded by white images, and white in this world is synonymous with the good, light, beauty, success, so that, despite ourselves sometimes, we run after that whiteness and deny our darkness, which has been made into the symbol of all that is evil and inferior. I wasn't a person to that boy's parents, but a symbol of the darkness they were in flight from, so that just as they —that boy, his parents, those silly girls in the houseplan—were running from me, I started running from them . . ."

▲   ▲   ▲

It must have been shortly after this happened when I saw Reena at a debate which was being held at my college. She did not see me, since she was one of the speakers and I was merely part of her audience in the crowded auditorium. The topic had something to do with intellectual freedom in the colleges (McCarthyism was coming into vogue then) and aside from a Jewish boy from City College, Reena was the most effective—sharp, provocative, her position the most radical. The others on the panel seemed intimidated not only by the strength and cogency of her argument but by the sheer impact of her blackness in their white midst.

Her color might have been a weapon she used to dazzle and disarm her opponents. And she had highlighted it with the clothes she was wearing: a white dress patterned with large blocks of primary colors I remember (it looked Mexican) and a pair of intricately wrought silver earrings—long and with many little parts which clashed like muted cymbals over the microphone each time she moved her head. She wore her hair cropped short like a boy's and it was not straightened like mine and the other Negro girls' in the audience, but left in its coarse natural state: a small forest under which her face emerged in its intense and startling handsomeness. I remember she left the auditorium in triumph that day, surrounded by a noisy entourage from her college—all of them white.

"We were very serious," she said now, describing the left-wing group she had belonged to then—and there was a defensiveness in her voice which sought to protect them from all censure. "We believed—because we were young, I suppose, and had nothing as yet to risk—that we could do something about the injustices which everyone around us seemed to take for granted. So we picketed and demonstrated and bombarded Washington with our protests, only to have our names added to the Attorney General's list for all our trouble. We were always standing on street corners handing out leaflets or getting people to sign petitions. We always seemed to pick the coldest days to do that." Her smile held long after the words had died.

"I, we all, had such a sense of purpose then," she said softly, and a sadness lay aslant the smile now, darkening it. "We were forever holding meetings, having endless discussions, arguing, shouting, theorizing. And we had fun. Those parties! There was always somebody with a guitar. We were always singing. . . ." Suddenly, she began singing—and her voice was sure, militant, and faintly self-mocking,

> *"But the banks are made of marble*
> *With a guard at every door*
> *And the vaults are stuffed with silver*
> *That the workers sweated for . . ."*

When she spoke again the words were a sad coda to the song. "Well, as you probably know, things came to an ugly head with McCarthy reigning in Washington, and I was one of the people temporarily suspended from school."

She broke off and we both waited, the ice in our glasses melted and the drinks gone flat.

"At first, I didn't mind," she said finally. "After all, we were right. The fact that they suspended us proved it. Besides, I was in the middle of an affair, a real one this time, and too busy with that to care about anything else." She paused again, frowning.

"He was white," she said quickly and glanced at me as though to surprise either shock or disapproval in my face. "We were very involved. At one point—I think just after we had been suspended and he started working—we even thought of getting married. Living in New York, moving in the crowd we did, we might have been able to manage it. But I couldn't. There were too many complex things going on beneath the surface," she said, her voice strained by the hopelessness she must have felt then, her hands shaping it in the air between us. "Neither one of us could really escape what our color had come to mean in this country. Let me explain. Bob was always, for some odd reason, talking about how much the Negro suffered, and although I would agree with him I would also try to get across that, you know, like all people we also had fun once in a while, loved our children, liked making love— that we were human beings, for God's sake. But he only wanted to hear about the suffering. It was as if this comforted him and eased his own suffering—and he did suffer because of any number of things: his own uncertainty, for one, his difficulties with his family, for another . . .

"Once, I remember, when his father came into New York, Bob insisted that I meet him. I don't know why I agreed to go with him. . . ." She took a deep breath and raised her head very high. "I'll never forget or forgive the look on that old man's face when he opened his hotel-room door and saw me. The horror. I might have been the personification of every evil in the world. His inability to believe that it was his son standing there holding my hand. His shock. I'm sure he never fully recovered. I know I never did. Nor can I forget Bob's laugh in the elevator afterwards, the way he kept repeating: 'Did you see his face when he saw you? Did you . . . ?' He had used me, you see. I had been the means, the instrument of his revenge.

"And I wasn't any better. I used him. I took every opportunity to treat him shabbily, trying, you see, through him, to get at that white world which had not only denied me, but had turned my own against me." Her eyes closed. "I went numb all over when I understood what we were doing to, and with, each other. I stayed numb for a long time."

As Reena described the events which followed—the break with Bob, her gradual withdrawal from the left-wing group ("I had had it with them too. I got tired of being 'their Negro,' their pet. Besides, they were just all talk, really. All theories and abstractions. I doubt that, with all their elaborate plans for the Negro and for the workers of the world, any of them had ever been near a factory or up to Harlem")—as she spoke about her reinstatement in school, her voice suggested the numbness she had felt then. It only stirred into life again when she talked of her graduation.

"You should have seen my parents. It was really their day. My mother was so proud she complained about everything: her seat, the heat, the speaker; and my father just sat there long after everybody had left, too awed to move. God, it meant so much to them. It was as if I had made up for the generations his people had picked cotton in Georgia and my mother's family had cut cane in the West Indies. It frightened me."

I asked her after a long wait what she had done after graduating.

"How do you mean, what I did. Looked for a job. Tell me, have you ever looked for work in this man's city?"

"I know," I said, holding up my hand. "Don't tell me."

We both looked at my raised hand which sought to waive the discussion, then at each other and suddenly we laughed, a laugh so loud and violent with pain and outrage it brought tears.

"Girl," Reena said, the tears silver against her blackness. "You could put me blindfolded right now at the Times Building on 42nd Street and I would be able to find my way to every newspaper office in town. But tell me, how come white folks is so *hard?*"

"Just bo'n hard."

We were laughing again and this time I nearly slid off the trunk and Reena fell back among the satin roses.

"I didn't know there were so many ways of saying 'no' without ever once using the word," she said, the laughter lodged in her throat, but her eyes had gone hard. "Sometimes I'd find myself in the elevator, on my way out, and smiling all over myself because I thought I had gotten the job, before it would hit me that they had really said no, not yes. Some of those people in personnel had so perfected their smiles they looked almost genuine. The ones who used to get me, though, were those who tried to make the interview into an intimate chat between friends. They'd put you in a comfortable chair, offer you a cigarette, and order coffee. How I hated that coffee. They didn't know it—or maybe they did—but it was like offering me hemlock. . . .

"You think Christ had it tough?" Her laughter rushed against the air which resisted it. "I was crucified five days a week and half-day on Saturday. I became almost paranoid. I began to think there might be something other than color wrong with me which everybody but me could see, some rare disease that had turned me into a monster.

"My parents suffered. And that bothered me most, because I

felt I had failed them. My father didn't say anything but I knew because he avoided me more than usual. He was ashamed, I think, that he hadn't been able, as a man and as my father, to prevent this. My mother—well, you know her. In one breath she would try to comfort me by cursing them: 'But Gor blind them,' "—and Reena's voice captured her mother's aggressive accent—" 'if you had come looking for a job mopping down their floors they would o' hire you, the brutes. But mark my words, their time goin' come, 'cause God don't love ugly and he ain't stuck on pretty . . .' And in the next breath she would curse me, 'Journalism! Journalism! Whoever heard of colored people taking up journalism. You must feel you's white or something so. The people is right to chuck you out their office. . . .' Poor thing, to make up for saying all that she would wash my white gloves every night and cook cereal for me in the morning as is I were a little girl again. Once she went out and bought me a suit she couldn't afford from Lord and Taylor's. I looked like a Smith girl in blackface in it. . . . So guess where I ended up?"

"As a social investigator for the Welfare Department. Where else?"

We were helpless with laughter again.

"You too?"

"No," I said, "I taught, but that was just as bad."

"No," she said, sobering abruptly. "Nothing's as bad as working for Welfare. Do you know what they really mean by a social investigator? A spy. Someone whose dirty job it is to snoop into the corners of the lives of the poor and make their poverty more vivid by taking from them the last shred of privacy. 'Mrs. Jones, is that a new dress you're wearing?' 'Mrs. Brown, this kerosene heater is not listed in the household items. Did you get an authorization for it?' 'Mrs. Smith, is that a telephone I hear ringing under the sofa?' I was utterly demoralized within a month.

"And another thing. I thought I knew about poverty. I mean, I remember, as a child, having to eat soup made with those white beans the government used to give out free for days running, sometimes, because there was nothing else. I had lived in Brownsville, among all the poor Jews and Poles and Irish there. But what I saw in Harlem, where I had my case load, was different somehow. Perhaps because it seemed so final. There didn't seem to be any way to escape from those dark hallways and dingy furnished rooms . . . All that defeat." Closing her eyes, she finished the stale whiskey and soda in her glass.

"I remember a client of mine, a girl my age with three children already and no father for them and living in the expensive squalor of a rooming house. Her bewilderment. Her resignation. Her anger. She could have pulled herself out of the mess she was in? People say that, you know, including some Negroes. But this girl didn't have a chance. She had been trapped from the day she was born in some small town down South.

"She became my reference. From then on and even now, whenever I hear people and groups coming up with all kinds of solutions to the quote Negro problem, I ask one question. What are they really doing for that girl, to save her or to save the children? . . . The answer isn't very encouraging."

▲   ▲   ▲

It was some time before she continued, and then she told me that after Welfare she had gone to work for a private social-work agency, in their publicity department, and had started on her master's in journalism at Columbia. She also left home around this time.

"I had to. My mother started putting the pressure on me to get married. The hints, the remarks—and you know my mother was never the subtle type—her anxiety, which made me anxious about getting married after a while. Besides, it was time for me to be on my own."

In contrast to the unmistakably radical character of her late adolescence (her membership in the left-wing group, the affair with Bob, her suspension from college), Reena's life of this period sounded ordinary, standard—and she admitted it with a slightly self-deprecating, apologetic smile. It was similar to that of any number of unmarried professional Negro women in New York or Los Angeles or Washington: the job teaching or doing social work which brought in a fairly decent salary, the small apartment with kitchenette which they sometimes shared with a roommate; a car, some of them; membership in various political and social action organizations for the militant few like Reena; the vacations in Mexico, Europe, the West Indies, and now Africa; the occasional date. "The interesting men were invariably married," Reena said and then mentioned having had one affair during that time. She had found out he was married and had thought of her only as the perfect mistress. "The bastard," she said, but her smile forgave him.

"Women alone!" she cried, laughing sadly, and her raised opened arms, the empty glass she held in one hand made eloquent their aloneness. "Alone and lonely, and indulging themselves while they wait. The girls of the houseplan have reached their majority only to find that all those years they spent accumulating their degrees and finding the well-paying jobs in the hope that this would raise their stock have, instead, put them at a disadvantage. For the few eligible men around—those who are their intellectual and professional peers, whom they can respect (and there are very few of them)—don't necessarily marry them, but younger women without the degrees and the fat jobs, who are no threat, or they don't marry at all because they are either queer or mother-ridden. Or they marry white women. Now, intellectually I accept this. In fact, some of my best friends are white women . . ." And again our laughter—that loud, searing burst which we used to cauterize our hurt mounted into the unaccepting silence of the room. "After all, our goal is a fully integrated society. And perhaps, as some people believe, the only solution to the race problem is miscegenation. Besides, a man should be able to marry whomever he wishes. Emotionally, though, I am less kind and understanding, and I resent like hell the reasons some black men give for rejecting us for them."

"We're too middle-class-oriented," I said. "Conservative."

"Right. Even though, thank God, that doesn't apply to me."

"Too threatening . . . castrating . . ."

"Too independent and impatient with them for not being more ambitious . . . contemptuous . . ."

"Sexually inhibited and unimaginative . . ."

"And the old myth of the excessive sexuality of the black woman goes out the window," Reena cried.

"Not supportive, unwilling to submerge our interests for theirs . . ."

"Lacking in the subtle art of getting and keeping a man . . ."

We had recited the accusations in the form and tone of a litany, and in the silence which followed we shared a thin, hopeless smile.

"They condemn us," Reena said softly but with anger, "without taking history into account. We are still, most of us, the black woman who had to be almost frighteningly strong in order for us all to survive. For, after all, she was the one whom they left (and I don't hold this against them; I understand) with the children to raise, who had to *make* it somehow or the other. And we are still, so many of us, living that history.

"You would think that they would understand this, but few do. So it's up to us. We have got to understand them and save them for ourselves. How? By being, on one hand, persons in our own right and, on the other, fully the woman and the wife. . . . Christ, listen to who's talking! I had my chance. And I tried. Very hard. But it wasn't enough."

▲   ▲   ▲

The festive sounds of the wake had died to a sober murmur beyond the bedroom. The crowd had gone, leaving only Reena and myself upstairs and the last of Aunt Vi's closest friends in the basement below. They were drinking coffee. I smelled it, felt its warmth and intimacy in the empty house, heard the distant tapping of the cups against the saucers and voices muted by grief. The wake had come full circle: they were again mourning Aunt Vi.

And Reena might have been mourning with them, sitting there

amid the satin roses, framed by the massive headboard. Her hands lay as if they had been broken in her lap. Her eyes were like those of someone blind or dead. I got up to go and get some coffee for her.

"You met my husband," she said quickly, stopping me.

"Have I?" I said, sitting down again.

"Yes, before we were married even. At an autograph party for you. He was free-lancing—he's a photographer—and one of the Negro magazines had sent him to cover the party."

As she went on to describe him I remembered him vaguely, not his face, but his rather large body stretching and bending with a dancer's fluidity and grace as he took the pictures. I had heard him talking to a group of people about some issue on race relations very much in the news then and had been struck by his vehemence. For the moment I had found this almost odd, since he was so fair-skinned he could have passed for white.

They had met, Reena told me now, at a benefit show for a Harlem day nursery given by one of the progressive groups she belonged to, and had married a month afterward. From all that she said they had had a full and exciting life for a long time. Her words were so vivid that I could almost see them: she with her startling blackness and extraordinary force and he with his near-white skin and a militancy which matched hers; both of them moving among the disaffected in New York, their stand on political and social issues equally uncompromising, the line of their allegiance reaching directly to all those trapped in Harlem. And they had lived the meaning of this allegiance, so that even when they could have afforded a life among the black bourgeoisie of St. Albans or Teaneck, they had chosen to live if not in Harlem so close that there was no difference.

"I—we—were so happy I was frightened at times. Not that anything would change between us, but that someone or something in the world outside us would invade our private place and destroy us out of envy. Perhaps this is what did happen. . . ." She shrugged and even tried to smile but she could not manage it.

"Something slipped in while we weren't looking and began its deadly work.

"Maybe it started when Dave took a job with a Negro magazine. I'm not sure. Anyway, in no time, he hated it: the routine, unimaginative pictures he had to take and the magazine itself, which dealt only in unrealities: the high-society world of the black bourgeoisie and the spectacular strides Negroes were making in all fields—you know the type. Yet Dave wouldn't leave. It wasn't the money, but a kind of safety which he had never experienced before which kept him there. He would talk about free-lancing again, about storming the gates of the white magazines downtown, of opening his own studio—but he never acted on any one of these things. You see, despite his talent—and he was very talented—he had a diffidence that was fatal.

"When I understood this I literally forced him to open the studio—and perhaps I should have been more subtle and indirect, but that's not my nature. Besides, I was frightened and desperate to help. Nothing happened for a time. Dave's work was too experimental to be commercial. Gradually, though, his photographs started appearing in the prestige camera magazines and money from various awards and exhibits and an occasional assignment started coming in.

"This wasn't enough somehow. Dave also wanted the big, gaudy commercial success that would dazzle and confound that white world downtown and force it to *see* him. And yet, as I said before, he couldn't bring himself to try—and this contradiction began to get to him after awhile.

"It was then, I think, that I began to fail him. I didn't know how to help, you see. I had never felt so inadequate before. And this was very strange and disturbing for someone like me. I was being submerged in his problems—and I began fighting against this.

"I started working again (I had stopped after the second baby). And I was lucky because I got back my old job. And unlucky because Dave saw it as my way of pointing up his deficiencies. I couldn't convince him otherwise: that I had to do it for my own sanity. He would accuse me of wanting to see him fail, of trapping him in all kinds of responsibilities. . . . After a time we both got caught up in this thing, an ugliness came between us, and I began to answer his anger with anger and to trade him insult for insult.

"Things fell apart very quickly after that. I couldn't bear the pain of living with him—the insults, our mutual despair, his mocking, the silence. I couldn't subject the children to it any longer. The divorce didn't take long. And thank God, because of the children, we are pleasant when we have to see each other. He's making out very well, I hear."

▲　　▲　　▲

She said nothing more, but simply bowed her head as though waiting for me to pass judgment on her. I don't know how long we remained like this, but when Reena finally raised her head, the darkness at the window had vanished and dawn was a still, gray smoke against the pane.

"Do you know," she said, and her eyes were clear and a smile had won out over pain, "I enjoy being alone. I don't tell people this because they'll accuse me of either lying or deluding myself. But I do. Perhaps, as my mother tells me, it's only temporary. I don't think so, though. I feel I don't ever want to be involved again. It's not that I've lost interest in men. I go out occasionally, but it's never anything serious. You see, I have all that I want for now."

Her children first of all, she told me, and from her description they sounded intelligent and capable. She was a friend as well as a mother to them, it seemed. They were planning, the four of them, to spend the summer touring Canada. "I will feel that I have done well by them if I give them, if nothing more, a sense of themselves and their worth and importance as black people. Everything I do with them, for them, is to this end. I don't want them ever to be confused about this. They must have their identifications straight from the beginning. No white dolls for them!"

Then her job. She was working now as a researcher for a small progressive news magazine with the promise that once she completed her master's in journalism (she was working on the thesis now) she might get a chance to do some minor reporting. And like most people, she hoped to write someday. "If I can ever stop talking away my substance," she said laughing.

And she was still active in any number of social-action groups. In another week or so she would be heading a delegation of mothers down to City Hall "to give the mayor a little hell about conditions in the schools in Harlem." She had started an organization that was carrying on an almost door-to-door campaign in her neighborhood to expose, as she put it, "the blood suckers: all those slumlords and storekeepers with their fixed scales, the finance companies that never tell you the real price of a thing, the petty salesmen that leech off the poor. . . ." In May she was taking her two older girls on a nationwide pilgrimage to Washington to urge for a more rapid implementation of the school-desegregation law.

"It's uncanny," she said, and the laugh which accompanied the words was warm, soft with wonder at herself, girlish even, and the air in the room which had refused her laughter before rushed to absorb this now. "Really uncanny. Here I am, practically middle-aged, with three children to raise by myself and with little or no money to do it, and yet I feel, strangely enough, as though life is just beginning—that it's new and fresh with all kinds of possibilities. Maybe it's because I've been through my purgatory and I can't ever be overwhelmed again. I don't know. Anyway, you should see me on evenings after I put the children to bed. I sit alone in the living room (I've repainted it and changed all the furniture since Dave's gone, so that it would at least look different)—I sit there making plans and all of them seem possible. The most important plan right now is Africa. I've already started saving the fare."

I asked her whether she was planning to live there permanently and she said simply, "I want to live and work there. For how long, for a lifetime, I can't say. All I know is that I have to. For myself and for my children. It is important that they see black people who have truly a place and history of their own and who are building for a new and, hopefully, more sensible world. And I must see it, get close to it, because I can never lose the sense of being a displaced person here in America because of my color. Oh, I know I should remain and fight not only for integration (even though, frankly, I question whether I want to be integrated into America as it stands now, with its complacency and materialism, its soullessness) but to help change the country into something better, sounder —if that is still possible. But I have to go to Africa. . . .

"Poor Aunt Vi," she said after a long silence and straightened one of the roses she had crushed. "She never really got to enjoy her bed of roses what with only Thursdays and every other Sunday off. All that hard work. All her life . . . Our lives have got to make more sense, if only for her."

We got up to leave shortly afterward. Reena was staying on to attend the burial, later in the morning, but I was taking the subway to Manhattan. We parted with the usual promise to get together and exchanged telephone numbers. And Reena did phone a week or so later. I don't remember what we talked about though.

Some months later I invited her to a party I was giving before leaving the country. But she did not come.

PAULE MARSHALL
Bibliography

Barbara Christian is responsible for much of the early criticism of Paule Marshall's work. A lengthy chapter in her book *Black Women Novelists: The Development of A Tradition, 1892–1976* (Westport, Conn.: Greenwood Press, 1980, pp. 80–136) shows that the great concern of Marshall's fiction is to depict the interdependency of character and culture, a concern that was probably shaped by her own experiences as a first-generation American of West Indian descent. Christian praises Marshall for her ability to portray social and political contexts while keeping her characters unique and complex. Though many critics praise Marshall for these qualities, this chapter in Christian is one of the few to explore all of the major characters of Marshall's first two novels. In *Black Feminist Criticism,* published after Marshall's last novel, *Praisesong for the Widow,* Christian has two chapters on Marshall—"Paule Marshall: A Literary Biography" and "Ritualistic Process and the Structure of Paule Marshall's *Praisesong for the Widow"*—which enlarge the scope of her earlier criticism, explaining the importance of Marshall's place in modern and contemporary black women's fiction. The essay on *Praisesong,* a reprint of Christian's review in *Callaloo,* shows Marshall continuing to examine the relationships between the individual and the culture which shapes her.

Dorothy Denniston's dissertation "Cultural Reclamation: The Development of Pan-African Sensibility in the Fiction of Paule Marshall," argues that Marshall's focus on black cultural history necessitates a criticism which is culturally specific. She says that Marshall moves from an American to an Afro-American/Afro-Caribbean and finally to a Pan-African sensibility, combining the process Western art forms with the style and function of African oral art.

Hortense Spillers is one of the few critics to go beyond discussing character, plot, and theme to explore those narrative devices employed by Marshall to suspend the reader's expectations of traditional literary time and space. Drawing on Kenneth Burke, Roland Barthes, and reader-response theory in her essay *"Chosen Place, Timeless People:* Some Figurations on the New World" in *Conjuring,* Spillers analyzes the "simplistic expectations" of readers and Marshall's persistent frustration of those expectations.

Mary Helen Washington's essay "I Sign My Mother's Name: Alice Walker, Dorothy West, and Paule Marshall" in *Mothering the Mind: Twelve Studies of Writers and Their Silent Partners* (New York: Holmes & Meier, 1984, ed. Ruth Perry and Martine Brownley, pp. 142–63) explores the mother-daughter relationships in the lives and works of Walker, West, and Marshall, showing how the generative power of those relationships, as full of conflict as they may be, has been an important element in the shaping of their narratives.

Marshall's own essay "Shaping the World of My Art" *(New Letters,* Vol. 40 No. 1, Autumn 1973, pp. 97–110) is still one of the best introductions to her work. In it she describes the early influences on her work, specifically the women of the Barbadian community whose vivid and creative use of language taught her the art of storytelling and characterization and whose bitter, angry recollection of Barbadian colonialism made her sensitive to the effects of poverty and exploitation on the lives of oppressed people. She attributes the "essentially political perspective" of her work to their powerful words: "it was those women long ago, perhaps more than any other single factor, who were responsible for laying the foundation of the aesthetic—aesthetic taken to mean here the themes and techniques—which most characterize my work" (p. 105).

Perhaps because of the authority and integrity of Marshall's political and cultural aims, criticism of her work has often been limited to a discussion of theme, plot, and characterization that is often general and descriptive rather than analytic. There is also a tendency on the part of her critics—many of whom are sympathetic to an ideology that so vigorously affirms black culture to accept Marshall's narratives uncritically without examining the contradictions inherent in those or any other narratives. Two exceptions are John Cook's essay "Whose Child? The Fiction of Paule Marshall" in *CLA Journal* (Vol. 26 No. 1, September 1980, pp. 1–15) and Susan Willis's chapter "Describing Arcs of Recovery: Paule Marshall's Relationship to Afro-American Culture" in *Specifying*. Cook questions Marshall's reputation as a political writer, arguing that her work is actually marked by a search for an authentically political statement. Cook uses *Brown Girl Brownstones, Soul Clap Hands and Sing,* and *The Chosen Place, the Timeless People* to demonstrate the ambiguity of Marshall's cultural and political perspectives. Cook concludes by praising *The Chosen Place* as the achievement of a definitive political voice because it claims a Pan-African perspective, unlike earlier works like *Brown Girl Brownstones,* which "affirms no culture" but chooses instead to focus on the clash of cultural perspectives.

Susan Willis sees Marshall's political and cultural critique as a part of her strategy as a utopian writer whose "visionary sense of renewal through the recovery of culture" captures the utopian aspirations of the sixties but may prove ineffective as a political strategy for the eighties. Willis is the only one of Marshall's critics to note the inherent conflict between the oral tradition which Marshall seeks to record and preserve and the tradition of narrative out of which she writes: "The process of writing a novel may well represent the application of a system of meaning and telling originating in dominant culture" (p. 69), and since it is the product of a single individual, it cannot reproduce the multiplicity and diversity of oral storytelling.

GWENDOLYN BROOKS

"If You're Light and Have Long Hair" and "At the Burns-Coopers' " are two chapters from Gwendolyn Brooks's only novel, *Maud Martha,* published in 1953.[1] Set in Chicago's predominantly black south side during the 1930s and 1940s, the novel traces the girlhood and growth to womanhood of a dark-skinned protagonist through whose consciousness the entire story is filtered. In almost every way Maud Martha's life seems to be quite ordinary—she grows up in a working-class black family, dreams of travel and sophistication, but settles for marriage, a family, and domestic life in a little kitchenette apartment. What makes Maud extraordinary is the rich interior life Brooks allows her—a life that in every way runs contrary to the life she has had "to settle" for. On the surface she seems content building a little nest with her husband, Paul, raising her daughter, Paulette, searching for the little ways to enrich that circumscribed life. Inwardly, however, she rebels against this confinement. While she tries to fit herself to the prevailing cultural ideal for women in the 1940s and 1950s of the self-sacrificing housewife and mother, the resentment and anger she expresses inwardly constitute a form of rebellion against that ideal, even

[1] *Maud Martha,* New York: Harper & Brothers, 1953.

though her anger is nearly always expressed in passive or indirect ways.[2]

In a very perceptive and important essay, critic Raymond Hedin says that anger has always been a thorny problem for black writers.[3] Hedin contends that beginning with the slave narrative, black writers have had to repress anger and other emotions that could be interpreted by white audiences as evidence of the brutal nature of black men in order to present a benign humanity that would ease the fears of white readers. Many black writers emphasized rationality and attempted to downplay emotion. Perhaps the best example of this repression is the slave narrative which almost never fully expresses outrage at injustice but tries instead to present the slave narrator as too reasonable to lose control. It seems to me that this argument applies mainly to black male writers and that women have a different though related problem with anger. Women's anger, rather than being replaced by excessive rationality, is often represented as self-destructive, the most extreme forms of which are the suicidal endings of novels like Kate Chopin's *The Awakening* (1899), Edith Wharton's *The House of Mirth* (1905), Nella Larsen's *Quicksand* (1928).[4]

Maud does not commit suicide, but she is, at times, so passive

---

[2] At one point in the early days of their marriage, Maud tries to make herself content with a stove-heated basement apartment which she hates:

> Was her attitude uncooperative? Should she be wanting to sacrifice more, for the sake of her man? A procession of pioneer women strode down her imagination; strong women, bold; praiseworthy, faithful, stout-minded; with a stout light beating in the eyes. Women who could stand low temperatures. Women who would toil eminently, to improve the lot of their men. Women who cooked. She thought of herself, dying for her man. It was a beautiful thought. *(Maud Martha,* pp. 58–59.)

[3] Raymond Hedin, "The Structuring of Emotion in Black American Fiction," *Novel* (Fall 1982): 35–54.

[4] In her forthcoming essay "When Privilege Is No Protection: Class, Race, and Gender in Edith Wharton's *House of Mirth* and Nella Larsen's *Quicksand,*" Linda Dittmar says that rage and rebellion underlie the suicidal endings of these novels.

that she seems to have become an accomplice in her own impotence, suppressing an angry voice and pretending a compliance she does not feel. As she plays the conventional role of self-sacrificing young wife in a marriage that has deeply disappointed her, she evades her own feelings and the narration presents her as worried, not about her own resentments, but about her husband's disillusionment with their marriage and with her:

> She knew that he was tired of his wife, tired of his living quarters, tired of working at Sam's, tired of his two suits . . . He had no money, no car, no clothes, and he had not been put up for membership in the Foxy Cats Club . . . He was not on show . . . Something should happen . . . She knew that he believed he had been born to invade, to occur, to confront, to inspire the flapping of flags, to panic people. *(Maud Martha,* p. 147)

When she and Paul are invited to the Foxy Cats Club Ball, Maud continues to allow these scraps of rage and baffled hate to accumulate while she resists the words that could release her into action. She prepares for the Foxy Cats Ball in language that we know will defeat her:

> "I'll settle," decided Maud Martha, "on a plain white princess-style thing and some blue and black satin ribbon. I'll go to my mother's. I'll work miracles at the sewing machine."
> "On that night, I'll wave my hair. I'll smell faintly of lily of the valley." (p. 82)

The words she uses to refashion herself—*white, princess, wavy, lily* —suggest how complete a transformation she imagines she needs in order to be accepted. Maud knows another language—a street vernacular—fully capable of expressing rage and resistance. When Paul goes off with the beautiful Maella, she imagines how she might use this vernacular speech to confront Maella:

"I could," considered Maud Martha, "go over there and scratch her upsweep down. I could spit on her back. I could scream. 'Listen,' I could scream, 'I'm making a baby for this man and I mean to do it in peace.'" (p. 88)

But Maud says none of this. She continues throughout the first half of the novel to express anger obliquely, especially in the unflattering portraits she paints of those who persecute her.

In the second half of the novel, Brooks does allow Maud to free herself from some of these inhibited responses. When Maud moves away from her claustrophobic world of her little kitchenette apartment and into a larger social world she feels more urgently the need to speak. Beginning with "The Self-Solace" there are several racial incidents which move her closer to expressing her anger. First in a beauty shop, then in a millinery store, then in the home of Mrs. Burns-Cooper, where she is a servant, Maud is exposed to the condescension or veiled hostility of whites. In the beauty shop, she remains evasive, refusing to believe that the white woman has said "nigger" so as to distance herself from her own violent reactions. At Mrs. Burns-Cooper's, she is again indirect but somewhat more defiant. She refers to herself impersonally in the third person: "Why, *one* was a human being," but she also refuses to return to a job she badly needs. And, in recognizing that Paul too has been subjected to the same kind of humiliation, she asserts a racial solidarity that relieves the intense privateness of her own experience.

Gwendolyn Brooks

If You're Light and Have Long Hair*

Came the invitation that Paul recognized as an honor of the first water, and as sufficient indication that he was, at last, a social somebody. The invitation was from the Foxy Cats Club, the club of clubs. He was to be present, in formal dress, at the Annual Foxy Cats Dawn Ball. No chances were taken: "Top hat, white tie and tails" hastily followed the "Formal dress," and that elucidation was in bold type.

Twenty men were in the Foxy Cats Club. All were good-looking. All wore clothes that were rich and suave. All "handled money," for their number consisted of well-located barbers, police-men, "government men," and men with a lucky touch at the tracks. Certainly the Foxy Cats Club was not a representative of that growing group of South Side organizations devoted to moral and civic improvements, or to literary or other cultural pursuits. If that had been so, Paul would have chucked his bid (which was black and silver, decorated with winking cat faces) down the toilet with a yawn. "That kind of stuff" was hardly understood by Paul, and was always dismissed with an airy "dicty," "hincty," or "highfalu-tin." But no. The Foxy Cats devoted themselves solely to the business of being "hep," and each year they spent hundreds of

* From the novel *Maud Martha*.

115

dollars on their wonderful Dawn Ball, which did not begin at dawn, but was scheduled to end at dawn. "Ball," they called the frolic, but it served also the purposes of party, feast, and fashion show. Maud Martha, watching him study his invitation, watching him lift his chin, could see that he considered himself one of the blessed.

Who—what kind soul had recommended him!

"He'll have to take me," thought Maud Martha. "For the envelope is addressed 'Mr. and Mrs.,' and I opened it. I guess he'd like to leave me home. At the Ball, there will be only beautiful girls, or real stylish ones. There won't be more than a handful like me. My type is not a Foxy Cat favorite. But he can't avoid taking me— since he hasn't yet thought of words or ways strong enough, and at the same time soft enough—for he's kind; he doesn't like to injure —to carry across to me the news that he is not to be held permanently by my type, and that he can go on with this marriage only if I put no ropes or questions around him. Also, he'll want to humor me, now that I'm pregnant."

She would need a good dress. That, she knew, could be a problem, on his grocery clerk's pay. He would have his own expenses. He would have to rent his topper and tails, and he would have to buy a fine tie, and really excellent shoes. She knew he was thinking that on the strength of his appearance and sophisticated behavior at this Ball might depend his future admission (for why not dream?) to *membership,* actually, in the Foxy Cats Club!

"I'll settle," decided Maud Martha, "on a plain white princess-style thing and some blue and black satin ribbon. I'll go to my mother's. I'll work miracles at the sewing machine.

"On that night, I'll wave my hair. I'll smell faintly of lily of the valley."

The main room of the Club 99, where the Ball was held, was hung with green and yellow and red balloons, and the thick pillars, painted to give an effect of marble, and stretching from floor to ceiling, were draped with green and red and yellow crepe paper. Huge ferns, rubber plants, and bowls of flowers were at every corner. The floor itself was a decoration, golden, glazed. There was no overhead light; only wall lamps, and the bulbs in these were romantically dim. At the back of the room, standing on a furry white rug, was the long banquet table, dressed in damask, accented by groups of thin silver candlesticks bearing white candles, and laden with lovely food: cold chicken, lobster, candied ham fruit combinations, potato salad in a great gold dish, corn sticks, a cheese fluff in spiked tomato cups, fruit cake, angel cake, sunshine cake. The drinks were at a smaller table nearby, behind which stood a genial mixologist, quick with maraschino cherries, and with lemon, ice, and liquor. Wines were there, and whiskey, and rum, and eggnog made with pure cream.

Paul and Maud Martha arrived rather late, on purpose. Rid of their wraps, they approached the glittering floor. Bunny Bates's orchestra was playing Ellington's "Solitude."

Paul, royal in rented finery, was flushed with excitement. Maud Martha looked at him. Not very tall. Not very handsomely made. But there was that extraordinary quality of maleness. Hiding in the body that was not *too* yellow, waiting to spring out at her, surround her (she liked to think)—that maleness. The Ball stirred her. The Beauties, in their gorgeous gowns, bustling, supercilious; the young men, who at other times most unpleasantly blew their noses, and darted surreptitiously into alleys to relieve themselves, and sweated and swore at their jobs, and scratched their more intimate parts, now smiling, smooth, overgallant; the drowsy lights; the smells of food and flowers, the smell of Murray's pomade, the body perfumes, natural and superimposed; the sensuous heaviness of the wine-colored draperies at the many windows; the music, now steamy and slow, now as clear and fragile as glass, now raging, passionate, now moaning and thickly gray. The Ball made toys of her emotions, stirred her variously. But she was anxious to have it end, she was anxious to be at home again, with the door closed behind herself and her husband. Then, he might be warm.

There might be more than the absent courtesy he had been giving her of late. Then, he might be the tree she had a great need to lean against, in this "emergency." There was no telling what dear thing he might say to her, what little gem let fall.

But, to tell the truth, his behavior now was not very promising of gems to come. After their second dance he escorted her to a bench by the wall, left her. Trying to look nonchalant, she sat. She sat, trying not to show the inferiority she did not feel. When the music struck up again, he began to dance with someone red-haired and curved, and white as a white. Who was she? He had approached her easily, he had taken her confidently, he held her and conversed with her as though he had known her well for a long, long time. The girl smiled up at him. Her gold-spangled bosom was pressed—was pressed against that maleness—

A man asked Maud Martha to dance. He was dark, too. His mustache was small.

"Is this your first Foxy Cats?" he asked.

"What?" Paul's cheek was on that of Gold-Spangles.

"First Cats?"

"Oh. Yes." Paul and Gold-Spangles were weaving through the noisy twisting couples, were trying, apparently, to get to the reception hall.

"Do you know that girl? What's her name?" Maud Martha asked her partner, pointing to Gold-Spangles. Her partner looked, nodded. He pressed her closer.

"That's Maella. That's Maella."

"Pretty, isn't she?" She wanted him to keep talking about Maella. He nodded again.

"Yep. She has 'em howling along the stroll, all right, all right."

Another man, dancing past with an artificial redhead, threw a whispered word at Maud Martha's partner, who caught it eagerly, winked. "Solid, ol' man," he said. "Solid, Jack." He pressed Maud Martha closer. "You're a babe," he said. "You're a real babe." He reeked excitingly of tobacco, liquor, pinesoap, toilet water, and Sen Sen.

Maud Martha thought of her parents' back yard. Fresh. Clean.

Smokeless. In her childhood, a snowball bush had shone there, big above the dandelions. The snowballs had been big, healthy. Once, she and her sister and brother had waited in the back yard for their parents to finish readying themselves for a trip to Milwaukee. The snowballs had been so beautiful, so fat and startlingly white in the sunlight, that she had suddenly loved home a thousand times more than ever before, and had not wanted to go to Milwaukee. But as the children grew, the bush sickened. Each year, the snowballs were smaller and more dispirited. Finally a summer came when there were no blossoms at all. Maud Martha wondered what had become of the bush. For it was not there now. Yet she, at least, had never seen it go.

"Not," thought Maud Martha, "that they love each other. It oughta be that simple. Then I could lick it. It oughta be that easy. But it's my color that makes him mad. I try to shut my eyes to that, but it's no good. What I am inside, what is really me, he likes okay. But he keeps looking at my color, which is like a wall. He has to jump over it in order to meet and touch what I've got for him. He has to jump away up high in order to see it. He gets awful tired of all that jumping."

Paul came back from the reception hall. Maella was clinging to his arm. A final cry of the saxophone finished that particular slice of the blues. Maud Martha's partner bowed, escorted her to a chair by a rubber plant, bowed again, left.

"I could," considered Maud Martha, "go over there and scratch her upsweep down. I could spit on her back. I could scream. 'Listen,' I could scream, 'I'm making a baby for this man and I mean to do it in peace.' "

But if the root was sour what business did she have up there hacking at a leaf?

Gwendolyn Brooks

At the Burns-Coopers'*

It was a little red and white and black woman who appeared in the doorway of the beautiful house in Winnetka.

About, thought Maud Martha, thirty-four.

"I'm Mrs. Burns-Cooper," said the woman, "and after this, well, it's all right this time, because it's your first time, but after this time always use the back entrance."

There is a pear in my icebox, and one end of rye bread. Except for three Irish potatoes and a cup of flour and the empty Christmas boxes, there is absolutely nothing on my shelf. My husband is laid off. There is newspaper on my kitchen table instead of oilcloth. I can't find a filing job in a hurry. I'll smile at Mrs. Burns-Cooper and hate her just some.

"First, you have the beds to make," said Mrs. Burns-Cooper. "You either change the sheets or air the old ones for ten minutes. I'll tell you about the changing when the time comes. It isn't any special day. You are to pull my sheets, and pat and pat and pull till all's tight and smooth. Then shake the pillows into the slips, carefully. Then punch them in the middle.

"Next, there is the washing of the midnight snack dishes. Next,

* From the novel *Maud Martha*.

there is the scrubbing. Now, I know that your other ladies have probably wanted their floors scrubbed after dinner. I'm different. I like to enjoy a bright clean floor all the day. You can just freshen it up a little before you leave in the evening, if it needs a few more touches. Another thing. I disapprove of mops. You can do a better job on your knees.

"Next is dusting. Next is vacuuming—that's for Tuesdays and Fridays. On Wednesdays, ironing and silver cleaning.

"Now about cooking. You're very fortunate in that here you have only the evening meal to prepare. Neither of us has breakfast, and I always step out for lunch. Isn't that lucky?"

"It's quite a kitchen, isn't it?" Maud Martha observed. "I mean, big."

Mrs. Burns-Cooper's brows raced up in amazement.

"Really? I hadn't thought so. I'll bet"—she twinkled indulgently—"you're comparing it to your *own* little kitchen." And why do that, her light eyes laughed. Why talk of beautiful mountains and grains of alley sand in the same breath?

"Once," mused Mrs. Burns-Cooper, "I had a girl who botched up the kitchen. Made a botch out of it. But all I had to do was just sort of cock my head and say, 'Now, now, Albertine!' Her name was Albertine. Then she'd giggle and scrub and scrub and she was *so* sorry about trying to take advantage."

It was while Maud Martha was peeling potatoes for dinner that Mrs. Burns-Cooper laid herself out to prove that she was not a snob. Then it was that Mrs. Burns-Cooper came out to the kitchen and, sitting, talked and talked at Maud Martha. In my college days. At the time of my debut. The imported lace on my lingerie. My brother's rich wife's Stradivarius. When I was in Madrid. The charm of the Nile. Cost fifty dollars. Cost one hundred dollars. Cost one thousand dollars. Shall I mention, considered Maud Martha, my own social triumphs, my own education, my travels to Gary and Milwaukee and Columbus, Ohio? Shall I mention my collection of fancy pink satin bras? She decided against it. She went on listening, in silence, to the confidences until the arrival of the lady's mother-in-law (large-eyed, strong, with hair of a mighty white, and with an eloquent, angry bosom). Then the junior Burns-Cooper was very much the mistress, was stiff, cool, authoritative.

There was no introduction, but the elder Burns-Cooper boomed, "Those potato parings are entirely too thick!"

The two of them, richly dressed, and each with that health in the face that bespeaks, or seems to bespeak, much milk drinking from earliest childhood, looked at Maud Martha. There was no remonstrance; no firing! They just looked. But for the first time, she understood what Paul endured daily. For so—she could gather from a Paul-word here, a Paul-curse there—his Boss! when, squared, upright, terribly upright, superior to the President, commander of the world, he wished to underline Paul's lacks, to indicate soft shock, controlled incredulity. As his boss looked at Paul, so these people looked at her. As though she were a child, a ridiculous one, and one that ought to be given a little shaking, except that shaking was—not quite the thing, would not quite do. One held up one's finger (if one did anything), cocked one's head, was arch. As in the old song, one hinted, "Tut tut! now now! come come!" Metal rose, all built, in one's eye.

I'll never come back, Maud Martha assured herself, when she hung up her apron at eight in the evening. She knew Mrs. Burns-Cooper would be puzzled. The wages were very good. Indeed, what could be said in explanation? Perhaps that the hours were long. I couldn't explain *my* explanation, she thought.

One walked out from that almost perfect wall, spitting at the firing squad. What difference did it make whether the firing squad understood or did not understand the manner of one's retaliation or why one had to retaliate?

Why, one was a human being. One wore clean nightgowns. One loved one's baby. One drank cocoa by the fire—or the gas range—come the evening, in the wintertime.

Black Women Novelists: The Development of a Tradition, 1892–1976 (Westport, Conn.: Greenwood Press, 1980).

Until 1970 there was only one full-length study of Brooks, Henry Shaw's *Gwendolyn Brooks* (Boston: Twayne, 1980), distinguished mainly for a kind of literal-mindedness which focuses on Maud's capitulation to white beauty standards. A much better full-length study is D. H. Melhem's *Gwendolyn Brooks: Poetry of the Heroic Voice* (Lexington, Kent.: University Press of Kentucky, 1987). Again, the novel is relegated to second-class status, given only a few pages; but the information found here is new and important. For the first time we learn of the development of *Maud Martha* from twenty-five poems to the novel it finally became. Using correspondence between Brooks and her editors, Melhem shows the development of the novel as well as the constant interference of editors on the slowly forming work. Melhem also does an excellent job of linking *Maud Martha* to other works by Brooks.

For other notable perspectives on Brooks, see " 'An Order of Constancy': Notes on Brooks and the Feminine" (in *Centennial Review* Vol. 29 No. 2, Spring 1985, pp. 223–48), in which Hortense J. Spillers discusses the possibility and implications of a uniquely feminine perspective in *Maud Martha*. Here Spillers uses, and simultaneously evaluates, feminist criticism. George Kent's chapter on Brooks's "The Poetry of the Unheroic" in *Blackness and the Adventure of Western Civilization* (Chicago: Third World Press, 1972) was one of the first to discuss at length the power, anger, and beauty of Brooks's poetry. Kent contributed an essay to *A Life Distilled* which extends his perceptive analysis through her later work. *College Language Association Journal* devoted several essays to Brooks in its September 1973 issue, among them a brief but telling essay by Gloria J. Hull, who criticizes Brooks's critics for ignoring a "technical, style-oriented" interpretation. For a wonderful autobiographical statement by Brooks herself, see *Black Women Writers, 1950–1980,* ed. Mari Evans (Garden City, N.Y.: Doubleday, 1984), pp. 75–78, and an interview in Claudia Tate's *Black Women Writers at Work* (New York: Continuum Press, 1983, pp. 39–48).

GAYL JONES

Gayl Jones was born in Lexington, Kentucky, November 23, 1949. She attended grade school and high school in Lexington, received a scholarship to Connecticut College in New London, Connecticut, and completed a master's degree in creative writing at Brown University. She taught African-American literature and creative writing at the University of Michigan until the fall of 1983.

She published her first novel, *Corregidora,* when she was only twenty-six and since then has published a second novel, *Eva's Man* (1976); a book of short stories, *White Rat* (1977); and is working on a third novel, *Palmares,* which is about the fugitive slave settlements in Brazil in the seventeenth and eighteenth centuries. The main character in *Palmares* is a slave woman named Almeyda who journeys into the interior of Brazil searching for her husband. According to Jones, Almeyda is a more heroic woman character than the ones she has written about in earlier stories. The black woman as hero—as opposed to the woman who is sexually abused and powerless—represents Jones's attempt to achieve greater balance in her work.

Gayl Jones is the third generation of black women writers in her family. Her grandmother, Amanda Wilson, wrote plays for church programs and schools. Her mother, Lucille Jones, is a published writer. One of Jones's early memories is of her mother sitting at the kitchen table writing at night after working during the day as a domestic. She also wrote stories for Gayl and her brother and read them aloud when they were children. Then, like many women with families to care for, she stopped writing early in the fifties, but recently, with her daughter's encouragement, she has published several stories in *Obsidian* (Spring 1977). In an interview with her mother, Jones admits the similarities of style and subject between her writing and her mother's[1]—in both writers there is the flat conversational tone, a sense of tragedy hidden beneath the ordinariness of everyday life, attention to the psychic and sexual abuse of women. In the *Obsidian* stories, Lucille Jones writes about a young girl kidnapped by white men and forced into prostitution, a wife who slices her husband's jaw with an ax when she finds him with another woman, and a father and son competing in a jealous rivalry for the same woman. These are the kinds of stories that also compel the imagination of her daughter, Gayl.

The influence of the mother on her daughter's writing is significant for many reasons. First because it is a special and rare phenomenon for a black woman to have her mother as a literary model. For Gayl Jones it has unquestionably meant that she has suffered less than most women from "contrary instincts"[2]—those psychological and social hindrances to a woman devoting herself to a writing career. Without question, conflict, or doubt, she is a writer:

> *I used to have an image of myself when I grew up . . . I was this independent woman, I never saw myself as being married or having children or anything like that, and I was always traveling, particularly to Spanish-speaking places, and I was a writer.*[3]

---

[1] "Interview with Lucille Jones," *Obsidian.*

[2] Virginia Woolf coined this phrase in *A Room of One's Own.*

[3] Interview with Michael Harper in *Massachusetts Review,* 18 (Autumn 1977), p. 711.

From her mother, Jones also learned the tradition of oral story-telling, which is so much in evidence in her writing. Jones is insistent upon the importance of words being heard, being said aloud, so that the rhythms and patterns of a language are preserved and the integrity of the oral tradition is maintained. When her characters speak, they are also documenting the experience of black people, utilizing the original language of the people, drawing on the storehouse of folklore which expresses the attitudes and morality contained in that folklore.

> *"If that nigger loved me he wouldn't've throwed me down the steps,"*
>   *I called.*
>
> *"What?" She came to the door.*
>
> *"I said if that nigger loved me he wouldn't've throwed me down the*
>   *steps."*
>
> *"I know niggers love you do worse than that," she said.*[4]

This is Ursa speaking to her friend Catherine in Jones's first novel, *Corregidora*. Spoken aloud, the lines are obviously based on the rhythm and pattern of the three-line blues song. The first line is repeated with slight variation in the second line, the repetition holding us in momentary suspense as we wait for the "resolution" or "answer" in the last line. Catherine's "answer" to Ursa is wise and knowing and calls on a woman's experience with men and love: she is saying that people can love deeply and still hurt each other and one does not necessarily preclude the other.

In all of her writing so far Gayl Jones has performed the ritual of the blues as Ralph Ellison has defined it:

> the impulse to keep the painful details and episodes of a brutal
> experience alive in one's aching consciousness . . . and to tran-

*scend it, not by the consolation of philosophy, but by squeezing from
it a near-tragic, near-comic lyricism.*[5]

In "Jevata," a fifty-year-old woman lives with her eighteen-year-
old lover named Freddy. The story is told through Jevata's middle-
aged friend, Mr. Floyd, a direct descendant of the itinerant blues
singer. Something of a wanderer, homeless and without family, he
is considered a fool by the community because he loves Jevata and
gives her money and friendship without any sexual favors in return; but Mr. Floyd conveys to the reader a true empathy for
Jevata. Because he is attracted to her sixteen-year-old daughter,
Floyd acknowledges his own hidden and unacceptable urges, thus
exposing his own vulnerable humanity and Jevata's pathetic and
unarticulated need. When Floyd tries to get her to explain why she
tried to kill Freddy, she gives the heart-wrenching answer of a
person who is emotionally mute. She cannot explain her feelings
because "It always have took me a long time, Floyd."

Again in "Asylum" the black woman being treated in a hospital for mental patients is unable to defend herself with words.
Against a powerful and baffling and painful reality she retaliates
with hostility and calculated belligerence. The white hospital is a
cold, alien, implacable force—a world in control of her, with
names to define her sickness and thus the power to imprison her.
Her last question to the doctors shows that she too understands the
nature of institutional power and the terms she must submit to if
she wants to be freed. These are the painful details of brutal experiences, endured without consolation.

In preserving the memory of the black past—both the personal
and historical past—Jones uses the language, the symbols, the myths
generated by that tradition. Those specific forms, as Ellison tells us,
represent profoundly a particular group's attempt to humanize the
world.[6] Only a few black writers like Jones have this ability to
recall a past which even now is fleeting. I recall a picture in *Cor-*

[5] "Richard Wright's Blues," in *Shadow and Act* (Random House, 1953, p. 90).
[6] "The Art of Fiction: An Interview," in *Shadow and Act,* p. 172.

regidora of a woman doing hair in the kitchen telling a girl to hold her ear, so she won't burn her when she straightens the edges, and I realized I had almost forgotten that ritualistic scene. Images of torn pages, records destroyed, blacks being cheated out of their land are historical images selected by Jones as she carries out the task of preserving the evidence.

If critics are hard on Jones for what they do not approve of or understand, it is because they understand, it is because they understand so little about black life. Diane Johnson said in *The New York Review of Books* that a white reader, like herself, could not relate to such dehumanized pictures of black life and lamented that all of Jones's women characters were brutalized and dull. As in the blues, Jones's people do not often transcend their lives; they struggle, they cope, they accept the bittersweet irony of their lives and do not expect resolutions. As in the blues, there is little of conventional morality or middle-class American ideals in these lives. Jones's characters drift into or out of marriage or living arrangements without regard for society's standards; they refer to sexual acts in raw street terms; they speak without delicate pretensions. The wild words of the black woman in "Asylum" are an indictment of the white doctor's middle-class hypocrisy: "He writes about my sexual amorality because I wouldn't let that other doctor see my pussy." Perhaps the genteel reader or critic will, like the doctor, want to cringe at this woman's crudeness but only at the risk of avoiding the deeper question Jones is forcing us to face: how do freedom and love survive a brutal history?

One wishes for the heroic voice, for the healing of the past; but it is presumptuous to demand that these things appear before their time. The blues certainly do not encompass the entire black American experience, nor do they admit all of its complexities, but they allow bitterness, infidelity, promiscuity, and pain (as well as humor) to exist. For now Gayl Jones's voice is a blues voice. Some of her people cannot speak standard English and so sound stupid to the outsider; some are emotionally withdrawn; some still have generations of exploitation to extricate themselves from. She is their voice. Their past is in her blood.

Gayl Jones

Asylum

When the doctor coming? When I'm getting examined?

They don't say nothing all these white nurses. They walk around in cardboard shoes and grin in my face. They take me in this little room and sit me up on a table and tell me to take my clothes off. I tell them I won't take them off till the doctor come.

Then one of them says to the other, You want to go get the orderly?

She might hurt herself.

Not me, I won't get hurt.

Then they go out and this big black woman comes in to look after me. They sent her in because they think I will behave around her. I do. I just sit there and don't say nothing. She acts like she's scared. She stands next to the door.

You know, I don't belong here, I start to say, but don't. I just watch her standing up there.

The doctor will come in to see you in a few minutes, she says.

I nod my head. They're going to give me a physical examination first. I'm up on the table but I'm not going to take my clothes off. All I want them to do is examine my head. Ain't nothing wrong with my body.

The woman standing at the door looks like somebody I know.

She thinks I'm crazy, so I don't tell her she looks like somebody I know. I don't say nothing. I know one thing. He ain't examining me down there. He can examine me anywhere else he wants to, but he ain't touching me down there.

The doctor's coming. You can go to the bathroom and empty your bladder and take your clothes off and put this on.

I already emptied my bladder. The reason they got me here is my little nephew's teacher come and I run and got the slop jar and put it in the middle of the floor. That's why my sister's daughter had me put in here.

I take my clothes off but I leave my bloomers on cause he ain't examining me down there.

The doctor sticks his head in the door.

I see we got a panty problem.

I say, Yes, and it's gonna stay.

He comes in and looks down in my mouth and up in my nose and looks in my ears. He feels my breasts and my belly to see if I got any lumps. He starts to take off my bloomers.

I ain't got nothing down there for you.

His nose turns red. I stare at the black woman who's trying not to laugh. He puts a leather thing on my arm and tightens it. He takes blood out of my arm.

I get dressed and the big nurse goes with me down the hall. She doesn't talk. She doesn't smile. Another white man is sitting behind a desk. He is skinny and about my age and he attaches some things to my head and tells me to lay down. I lay down and see all the crooked lines come out. I stare at circles and squares and numbers and move them around and look at little words and put them together anyway I want to, then they tell me to sit down and talk about anything I want to.

How I do?

I can't tell you that, but we can tell you're an intelligent person even though you didn't have a lot of formal education.

How can you tell?

He doesn't say nothing. Then he asks, Do you know why they brought you here?

I peed in front of Tony's teacher.

Did you have a reason?

I just wanted to.

You didn't have a reason?

I wanted to.

What grade is Tony in?

The first.

Did you do it in front of the little boy?

Yeah, he was there.

He doesn't comment. He just writes it all down. He says to-morrow they are going to have me write words down, but now they are going to let me go to bed early because I have had a long day.

It ain't as long as it could've been.

What do you mean?

I look at his blue eyes. I say nothing. He acts nervous. He tells the nurse to take me to my room. She takes me by the arm. I tell her I can walk. She lets my arm go and walks with me to some other room.

▲   ▲   ▲

Why did you do it when the teacher came?

She just sit on her ass and fuck all day and it ain't with herself.

I write that down because I know they ain't going to know what I'm talking about. I write down whatever comes into my mind. I write down some things that after I get up I don't remember.

We think you're sociable and won't hurt anybody and so we're going to put you on this floor. You can walk around and go to the sun room without too much supervision. You'll have your sessions every week. You'll mostly talk to me, and I'll have you write things down everyday. We'll discuss that.

I'll be in school.

He says nothing. I watch him write something down in a book.

He thinks I don't know what he put. He thinks I can't read upside down. He writes about my sexual amorality because I wouldn't let that other doctor see my pussy.

▲   ▲   ▲

My niece comes to visit me. I have been here a week. She acts nervous and asks me how I'm feeling. I say I'm feeling real fine except everytime I go sit down on the toilet this long black rubbery thing comes out a my bowels. It looks like a snake and it scares me. I think it's something they give me in my food.

She screws up her face. She doesn't know what to say. I have scared her and she doesn't come back. It has been over a month and she ain't been back. She wrote me a letter though to tell me that Tony wanted to come and see me but they don't allow children in the building.

I don't bother nobody and they don't bother me. They put me up on the table a few more times but I still don't let him look at me down there. Last night I dreamed I got real slender and turned white like chalk and my hair got real long and the black woman she helped them strap me down because the doctor said he had to look at me down there and he pulled this big black rubbery thing look like a snake out of my pussy and I broke the stirrups and jumped right off the table and I look at the big black nurse and she done turned chalk white too and she tells me to come to her because they are going to examine my head again. I'm scared of her because she looks like the devil, but I come anyway, holding my slop jar.

If the sounds fit put them here.
They don't fit.
How does this word sound?
What?
Dark? Warm? Soft?
Me?
He puts down: libido concentrated on herself.

What does this word make you feel?
Nothing.
You should tell me what you are thinking?
Is that the only way I can be freed?

Gayl Jones

Jevata

I didn't see Jevata when she ran Freddy away from her house, but Miss Johnny Cake said she had a hot poker after him, and would have killed him too, if he hadn't been faster than she was. Nobody didn't know what made her do it. I didn't know either then, and I'm over there more than anybody else is. Now I'm probably the onliest one who know what did happen—me and her boy David. Miss Johnny Cake don't even know, and it seem like she keep busier than anybody else on Green Street. People say what make Miss Johnny so busy is the Urban Renewal come and made her move out of that house she was living in for about forty years, and all she got to do now is sit out there on the porch and be busy. Once she told me she felt dislocated, and I told Jevata what she said, and Jevata said she act dislocated.

Miss Johnny Cake aint the onliest one talking about Jevata neither. All up and down Green Street they talking. They started talking when Jevata went up to Lexington and brought Freddy back with her, and they aint quit. They used to talk when I'd come down from Davis town to visit her. Then I guess they got used to me. I called myself courting her then. We been friends every since we went over to Simmons Street School together, and we stayed friends. I guess all the courting was on my side though, cause she

135

never would have me. I still come to see about her though. I was coming to see about her all during the time that Freddy was living with her.

"I don't see what in the world that good-lookin boy see in her," Miss Johnny Cake would say. "If I was him and eighteen, I wouldn't be courting the mama, I be courting the daughter. He ain't right, is he, Mr. Floyd?"

I wouldn't say anything, just stand with my right foot up on the porch while she sat rocking. She was about seventy, with her gray hair in two plaits.

"I don't see what they got in common," Miss Johnny said.

"Same thing any man and woman got in common," I said.

"Aw, Mr. Floyd, you so nasty."

Before Freddy came, Jevata used to have something to say to people, but after he came she wouldn't say nothing to nobody. She used to say I was the only one that she could trust, because the others always talked about her too much. "Always got something to say about you. Caint even go pee without them having something to say about you." She would go on by and wouldn't say nothing to nobody. People said she got stuck up with that young boy living with her. "Woman sixty-five going with a boy eighteen," some of the women would say. "You seen her going up the street, didn't you? Head all up in the air, that boy trailin behind her. Don't even look right. I be ashamed for anybody to see me trying to go with a boy like that. Look like her tiddies fallen since he came, don't it? But you know she always have been like 'at though, always looking after boys. I stopped Maurice from going down there to play. But you know if he was like anybody else he least be trying to get some from the daughter too."

Now womens can get evil about something like that. Wasn't so much that Jevata was going with Freddy, as she wouldn't say nothing to them while she was doing it. Now if she'd gone over there and said something to them, and let them all in her business and everything, they would felt all right then, and they wouldn't a got evil with her. "Rest of us got man trouble, Miss Jevata must got boy trouble," they'd laugh.

Now the boy's eighteen, but Jevata ain't sixty-five though, she's fifty, cause I ain't but two years older than her myself. I used to try to go with her way back when we was going to Simmons Street School together, but she wouldn't have me then, and she won't have me now. She married some nigger from Paris, Kentucky, one come out to Dixieland dance hall that time Dizzy Gillespie or Cab Calloway come out there. Name was Joe Guy. He stayed with her long enough to give her three children. Then he was gone. I was trying to go with her after he left, but she still wouldn't have me. She mighta eventually had me if he hadn't got to her, but after he got to her, seem like she wouldn't look at no mens. Onliest reason she'd look at me was because we'd been friends for so long. But first time I tried to get next to her right after he left, she said, "Shit, Floyd, me and you friends, always have been and always will be." I asked her to marry me, but she looked at me real evil. I thought she was going to tell me I could just quit coming to see her, but she didn't. After that she just wouldn't let me say nothing else about it, so I just come over there every chance I get. She got three childrens. Cynthy the oldest. She sixteen. Then she got a boy fourteen, name David, and a little boy five, name Pete. Sometime she call him Pete Junebug, sometime Little Pete.

Don't nobody know where in Lexington she went and got Freddy. Some people say she went down to the reform school they got down there and got him. It ain't that he's bad or nothing, it's just that they think something's wrong with him. I didn't know where she got him myself, because it was her business and I figured she tell me when she wanted to, and if she didn't wont to, she wouldn't.

Miss Johnny Cake lives over across the street from Jevata, and everytime I pass by there, she got to call me over. Sometimes I don't even like to pass by there, but I got to. She thinks I'm going to say something about Jevata and Freddy, but I don't. I just listen to what she's got to say. After she's said her piece, sometimes she'll look at me and say, "Clarify things to me, Mr. Floyd." I figure she picked that up from Reverend Jackson, cause he's always saying,

"The Lord clarified this to me, the Lord clarified that to me." I ain't clarified nothing to her yet.

"He's kinda funny, ain't he?" she said one day. That was when Freddy and Jevata was still together. It seemed like Miss Johnny Cake just be sitting out there waiting for me to come up the street, because she would never fail to call me over. Sitting up there, old seventy-year-old woman, couldn't even keep her legs together. One a the men on the street told me she been in a accident, and something happened to that muscle in her thighs, that's supposed to help you keep your legs together. I believed him till he started laughing, and then I didn't know whether to believe him or not.

"That boy just don't act right, do he? He ain't right, is he, Mr. Floyd? Something wrong with him, ain't it?" She waited, but not as if she expected an answer. I guess she'd got used to me not answering. "You reckon he's funny? Naw, cause he wouldn't be with her if he was funny, would he? I guess she do something for him. She must go something he wont. God knows I don't see it. Mr. Floyd, you just stand up there and don't say nothing. Cat got your tongue, and Freddy got hers." She looked at me grinning. I blew smoke between my teeth. "If you wonted to, I bet you could tell me everything that go on in that house."

I said I couldn't.

"Well, I know she sixty-five, cause she used to live down 'ere on Poke Street when I did. She might look like she forty-five, and tell everybody she forty-five, but she ain't. Now, if that boy was *right,* he be trying to go with Cynthy anyway. That's what a *right* boy would do. But he ain't right. He don't even *look* right, do he, Mr. Floyd?"

I told her he didn't look no different from anybody else to me.

Miss Johnny grinned at me. "You just don't wont to say nothin' against her, do you? Ain't no reason for you to take up for him, though, cause he done cut you out, aint he?"

I said I was going across the street. She said she didn't see why I won't to take up for him, cut me out the way he did.

One day when I came down the street, Freddy was standing out in the yard, his shirt sleeves rolled up, standing up against the post, looking across the street at Miss Johnny, looking evil. I didn't think Miss Johnny would bother me this time. I waved to her and kept walking. She said, "Mr. Floyd, ain't you go'n stop and have a few words with me? You got cute too?" I went over to her porch before I got a chance to say anything to Freddy. He was watching us, though. Green Street wasn't a wide street, and if she talked even a little bit as loud as she'd been talking, he would have heard.

"Nigger out there," she said, almost at a whisper. "Keep staring at me. Look at him."

She kept patting her knees. I didn't turn around to look at him. I was thinking, "He see those bloomers you got on."

"Look at him," she said, still low.

"Nice day, ain't it?" I said, loud.

"Fine day," she said, loud, too, then whispered, "I wish he go in the house. I don't even like to look at him."

I said nothing. I lit a cigarette. She started rocking back and forth in her rocker, and closed her eyes, like she was in church. Or like I do when I'm in church.

"You have you a good walk?" she asked, her eyes still closed.

I said, "OK."

We were talking moderate, now.

"You a fool you know that? Walk all the way out here from Davis town, just to see that woman. She got what she need, over there."

I hoped he hadn't heard, but I knew he had. I wondered if I was in his place, if I would have come over and said something to her.

"You know you a fool, don't you?" she asked again, still looking like she was in church.

I didn't answer.

"You know you a fool, Mr. Floyd," she said. She rocked a while more then she opened her eyes.

"But I reckon you say you been a fool a long time, ain't no use quit now."

I turned a little to the side so I could see out of the corner of my eye. He was still standing there. I couldn't tell if he was watch-

ing or not. I felt awkward about crossing the street now. I gave
Miss Johnny a hard look before I crossed. She only smiled at me.

"Mr. Floyd," Freddy said. He always called me "Mr. Floyd."
He was still looking across the street at Miss Johnny. I stood with
my back to her. He asked me to walk back around the yard with
him. I did. I stood with my back against the house, smoking a
cigarette.

"I caint stand that old woman," he said. "You see how she was
setting, didn't you? Legs all open. I never could stand womens sit
up with their legs all open. 'Specially old women."

I said they told me she couldn't help it.

"I had a aunt use to do that," he said. "She can help it. She just
onry. Ain't nothin wrong with that muscle. She just think somebody wont to see her ass. Like my aunt. Used to think I wonted to
see her ass, all the time."

I said nothing. Then I asked "How's Jevata . . . and the children?"

"They awright. Java and Junebug in the house. Other two at
school."

I finished my cigarette and was starting in the house.

"Think somebody wont to see her ass," Freddy said. He stayed
out in the yard.

Jevata was in the kitchen ironing. She took in ironing for some
white woman lived out on Stanley Street.

"How you, Floyd?" she asked.

"Not complaining," I said. I sat down at the kitchen table. She
looked past me out in the back yard where Freddy must have still
been standing.

"What Miss Busy have to say about me today?" she asked,
looking back at me.

"Nothin'."

"You can tell me," she said. "I won't get hurt."

"Miss Johnny wasn't doing nothing but out there talking bout
the weather," I said.

"Weather over here?" she asked.

I smiled.

She looked back out in the yard. I thought Freddy was still standing out there, but when I turned around in my seat to look, he wasn't. He must have gone back around to the front of the house.

"How you been?" she asked me as if she hadn't asked before, or didn't remember asking.

She wasn't looking at me, but I nodded.

"I never did think I be doing this," she said. "You 'member that time I told you Joe and me went down to Yazoo, Mississippi and this ole, white woman come up to me and asked me did I iron, and I said, 'Naw, I don't iron.' I wasn't gonna iron for *her,* anyway."

I said nothing. I had already offered to help Jevata out with money, but she wouldn't let me. I worked with horses, and had enough left over to help. Now, I was thinking, she had *four* kids to take care of.

"He found a job yet?" I asked.

She looked at me, irritated. She was sweating from the heat. "I told him he could take his time. He ain't been here long. He need time to get adjusted."

I was wondering how much adjusting did he need. It was over half a year ago since she went and got him.

"You don't think Freddy's evil, do you?" she asked.

I looked at her. I didn't know why she asked that. I said, "Naw, I don't think he's evil." She went back to ironing. I just sat there in the kitchen, watching her. After a while Freddy came in through the back door. He didn't say anything. He passed by, and I saw him put his hand on her waist. She smiled but didn't turn around to look at him. He went on into the front of the house. I sat there about fifteen or twenty minutes longer, and then I got up and said I was going.

"Glad you stopped by," Jevata said.

I said I'd probably be back by sometime next week, then I went out the back way.

Miss Johnny not only caught me when I was coming to see Jevata, but she caught me when I was leaving.

"I never did think that bastard go in the house," she said.

"Sometime I wish the Urban Renewal come and move me away from here. They dislocate me once, they might as well do it again."

I was thinking she probably heard Reverend Jackson say, "When the devil dislocate you, the Lord relocate you."

"How's Miss Jevata doing?" she asked.

"She's awright," I said.

"Awright as you can be with a nigger like that on your hands. If it was me, I be ashamed for anybody see me in the street with him. If he wont to go with somebody, he ought to go with Cynthy. I didn't tell you what I seen them doing last night?"

"What?" I asked frowning.

"I seen 'em standing in the door. Standing right up in the door kissing. Thought nobody couldn't see 'em with the light off. But you know how you can see in people's houses. Tha's the only time I seen 'em though. But still if they gonna do something like that, they ought to go back in there where caint nobody see 'em, and do it. Cause 'at ain't right. Double sin as old as she is. And they sinned again, cause you spose to go in your closet and do stuff like that."

I said nothing.

"You know I'm right, Mr. Floyd."

I still said nothing.

"Naw, you prob'ly don't know if I'm right or not," she said.

I looked away from her, over across the street at Jevata's house.

"Tiddies all sinking in," she said. "I don't see what he see in her. Look like she ain't got no tiddies no more. I don't see what he see in her. You think I'm crazy, don't you? I just don't like to see no old womens trying to go with young boys like that. I guess y'all ripe at that age, though, ain't you?"

I said I couldn't remember back that far.

"Floyd, you just a nigger. You just mad cause you been trying to go with her yourself. I bet you thought y'all *was* going together, didn't you? Everybody else thought so too, but not me. I didn't."

I turned around to look at her. She kept watching me.

"Ain't no use you saying nothing neither, cause I know you wasn't. I can tell when a man getting it and when he aint."

I started to tell her I could tell when a woman wonts it and can't have it, but I just told her I'd be seeing her.

"You got a long walk back to Davis town, ain't you, Mr. Floyd?"

▲   ▲   ▲

The next time I was down to Jevata's only the girl was at home. I asked her where her mama was. She said she and Freddy took Junebug downtown to get him some shoes. She told me Jevata had been mad all morning.

"Mad about what?" I asked.

"Mad cause Miss Johnny told Freddy to go up to the store for her."

"To get what?"

"A bottle of Pepsi Cola."

"Did he go?"

"Naw, he sent Davey." Then she said, "I don't know what makes that woman so meddlesome, anyway."

We were in the living room. I hadn't set down when I heard Jevata wasn't there. She was still standing, her arms folded like she was cold. She was frowning.

"What is it?" I asked.

"I guess I do know why she so meddlesome, why they all so meddlesome," she said.

I waited for her to go on.

"They talking about them, ain't they, Mr. Floyd? People all up and down the street talking, ain't they?" She didn't ask the question as if she expected an answer. She was still looking at me, frowning. She was a big girl for sixteen. She could've passed for eighteen. And she acted older than she was. She acted about twenty.

"Sometimes I'm ashamed to go to school. Kids on this street been telling everybody up at school. But you know I wouldn't tell mama. I don't wont to hurt her. I wouldn't do anything to hurt her."

I was thinking Jevata probably already knew, or guessed that people who didn't even know her might be talking about her.

I didn't say anything.

"They saying nasty things," she said.

I still didn't say anything. She kept looking at me. I put my hand on her shoulder. She was the reason I understood how Jevata could feel about Freddy, those times I felt attracted to Cynthy, wanting to touch those big breasts. I took my hand away.

"Just keep trying not to hurt her," I said.

She was looking down at the floor. I kept watching her breasts. They were bigger than her mama's. I was thinking of Mose Mason, who they put out of church for messing with that little girl him and his wife adopted. The deacons came to the house and he said, "I ain't doing nothing but feeling around on her tiddies. I ain't doing nothin' y'all wouldn't do." They was mad, too. "They ack like they ain't never wont to feel on nobody," Moses told me when we was sitting over in Tiger's Inn. "Shit, I bet they do more feeling Saturday night than it take me a whole damn week to do. And then they come sit up under the pulpit on Sunday morning and play like they hands ain't never touched nothin' but the Holy Bible. Saying 'amen' louder than anybody. Shit, don't make me no difference, though, whether I'm with 'em or not cause the Baptist is sneaky, anyway. Sneak around and do they dirt."

"I can hear them," Cynthy said quietly. "I can hear her telling him to hold her. 'Hold me, Freddy,' she say. I can hear her telling him he's better to her than my daddy was."

I couldn't think of anything to tell her. I wanted to touch her again, but didn't dare.

When Jevata came in, she said, "Cynthy tell you what that bitch did?"

I nodded.

"I know what she wonts, bitch," she said. "I know just what she wonts with him."

She asked me if I wanted something to eat. I said, Naw, I'd better be going. I'd been just waiting around to see her.

▲   ▲   ▲

"Why did she try to kill 'im, Mr. Floyd?" Miss Johnny asked. It was a couple of weeks after Jevata had gone after Freddy with the poker.

"I don't know," I said. I had my right foot up on the porch and was leaning on my knee, smoking.

"Got after Cynthy, didn't he? I bet that's what he did."

"He didn't bother Cynthy," I said, angry. But I didn't know whether he did or not.

"I bet tha's what he did. I bet she went somewhere and come back and found them in that house." She started laughing.

"I don't know what happened," I said.

"Seem like she tell you, if she tell anybody," Miss Johnny said.

I threw my cigarette down on the ground, and mashed it out.

"I wish she let me come over there and get some dandelions like I used to, so I can make me some wine out of 'em," she said.

"If Freddy was over there, you could tell him to get you some," I said.

"I wouldn't tell 'at nigger to do nothing for me," she said. She was angry. I looked at her for a moment, and then I walked out of the yard.

When I got to Jevata's, she was sitting in the front room with her housecoat on, the same dirty yellow one Cynthy said she was wearing the day she threatened to kill Freddy. Cynthy said she hadn't been out of the house since she chased Freddy out. I asked her if she was all right.

"Ain't complaining, am I?" she said. She said she had some Old Crow back there in the kitchen if I wanted some. I said, "Naw, thank you." She hadn't been drinking any herself, which surprised me. She didn't drink much anyway, but I thought maybe with Freddy gone, she might.

"Shit, Floyd, why you looking at me like that?" she asked.

"I didn't know I was looking at you any way," I said.

"Well, you was."

I said nothing.

"I seen Miss Bitch call you over there. What she wont this time?"

"She wonts to know why," I said.

"I ain't told *you* why."

"And you won't, will you?"

She looked away from me, then she said, "You know it always have took me a long time, Floyd."

She didn't say anything else, and I tried not to look at her the way I had been looking. She sat on the edge of the couch with her hands together, like she was nervous, or praying. Her shoulders were pulled together in a way that made her look like she didn't have any breasts.

Cynthy came in the front room, and asked me how I was.

"Awright."

"Mama, supper's ready," she said.

"Stay for supper, won't you, Floyd?" Jevata asked me.

"Yeah."

"Cynthy, where's Freddy?" Jevata asked suddenly.

Cynthy looked at me quickly, then back at Jevata.

"He's not here, Mama," Cynthy said.

"Floyd, you ain't seen Freddy, have you?" Jevata asked me.

I just looked at her. I couldn't even have replied as calmly as Cynthy had managed to. I just kept looking at her. Jevata laughed suddenly, a quick, nervous laugh, then said, "Naw, y'all, I don't mean Freddy, I mean where's Little Pete, y'all. I don't mean Freddy I feel like a fool now."

I said nothing.

"He's down the road playing with Ralph," Cynthy said.

"Well, tell him to come on up here and get his supper."

"What about David, Mama?"

"You take his plate in there to him. I don't wont to see him."

"Yes, m'am."

I looked at Cynthy, puzzled, then I said I would take it. Jevata looked at me, but said nothing.

David was lying on the bed. I set his plate down on the chair by the bed. He didn't say anything.

"You know something about this, don't you?" I asked.

He still said nothing.

"I b'lieve you know what happened."

"Go way and leave me alone!" David said. "You ain't my daddy."

I stood looking at him for a moment. He still lay on his belly. He had half turned around when he was hollering, but he hadn't looked at me. I finally left the room. When I came back in the kitchen, Little Pete was sitting at the table and Cynthy was putting the food on the table.

"Where's Jevata?" I asked.

Cynthy said nothing.

"I just ask her when Freddy was coming back and then she start acting all funny. I didn't do nothin', Mr. Floyd."

"I know you didn't," I said.

Cynthy looked at me and sat my plate down on the table. I sat down with them. Jevata didn't come back.

"Don't you think you better take your mama a plate," I said to Cynthy.

"She said she didn't wont nothin'," she said.

I stood up.

"She looked like she didn't wont nothin', Mr. Floyd," Cynthy said.

I sat back down.

I knew there was one place I could find out where Freddy was. I took the bus to Lexington, then went over to the barber shop over in Charlotte Court, right off Georgetown Street.

"Any y'all know Freddy Coleman?" I asked.

They didn't answer. Then, one man sitting up in the chair, getting his hair trimmed around the sides, cause he didn't have any in the top, said, "What you go to do with him?"

"Nothin'," I said. "I just wont to know where he is."

"I used to know. He used to keep the yard down here at Kentucky Village."

Some of the other men started laughing. Kentucky Village was a school for delinquent boys. I asked what was funny.

"Close to them KV boys, wasn't he?" one of the men said.

The man in the chair started laughing. "He never did do nothing. Just used to stand up there with the rake. Womens be passing by looking. Didn't do 'em no good." He asked me why I wanted him.

"I'm just looking for him," I said.

They looked at each other, like people who got a secret. They were trying not to laugh again.

"You can try that liquor store up the street. They tell me his baby hang out over there."

The rest of the men started laughing. I left them and went up to the liquor store. Somebody told me Freddy was living in an apartment up over some restaurant off Second Street.

I found the place and went upstairs and knocked on the door. He wasn't glad to see me.

"How you find me?" he asked.

I came in before he asked me to. I stayed standing.

"What do you wont?" he asked. "Finding out where I am for *her?*"

"Naw, for myself," I said.

I looked around. The living room was small. Only a couch and a couple of chairs, and a low coffee table. On the coffee table was a hat with feathers on it. It was a woman's hat. We were both standing. I didn't sit down without him asking me to. He wasn't saying anything and I wasn't. I was thinking he *was* a good-looking man, almost *too* good-looking. The onliest other man I knew was *that* good-looking was Mr. Pindar, a fake preacher that used to go around stealing people's money. He used to get drunks off the street and have them go before the congregation and play like he had changed their life. And people would believe it, too. He was so good-looking the women would believe it, and preached so good the men would believe it.

Freddy kept standing there looking at me. I kept looking at him.

"Where's my ostrich hat?" It was a man's voice, but somehow it didn't sound like a man.

Freddy looked embarrassed, he was frowning. He hollered he didn't know where it was.

"You seen my ostrich hat, honey?" the man asked again. He came in, like he was swaying, saw me and stopped cold. He said, "How do," snatched the hat from the table and went back in the other room.

Freddy wasn't looking at me. I said I'd better be going.

"He's crazy," Freddy said quickly. "He live down at Eastern State, and he's crazy."

Eastern State was the mental hospital.

"He got a room down at Eastern State," Freddy said. "They let him out everyday so he can get hisself drunk. That's all he do is get hisself drunk."

I said nothing. The man had come back in the room, and was standing near the door, pouting, his lower lip stuck out. Freddy hadn't turned to see him.

I started to go. Freddy reached out to put his hand on my arm, but didn't. He looked like he didn't want me to go.

"I was going to ask you to come back to her," I said, my eyes hard now. I ignored the man standing there, pouting. "I was going to tell you she needs you."

Freddy looked like he wanted to cry. "You know she kill me if I go back there," he said.

"Why?" I asked.

He said nothing.

I went toward the door again and he came with me. He still hadn't turned around to see the man. I asked him why again. Then I wanted another why. I asked him why did he go with her in the first place.

He said nothing for a long time, then he reached out to touch my arm again. I don't know if he would have stopped again this time, but I stood away from him.

"She was going to the carnival. You know the one they have

back behind Douglas Park every year, the one back there. She was passing through Douglas Park and seen me sitting up there all by myself. She ask me if I wont to go to the carnival. I don't know why she did. Maybe she thought I was lonesome, but I wasn't. I was sitting up there all by myself. She took me with her, you know. They had this man in this tent who was swallowing swords and knives, you know like they do. She wanted to take me there, so I went. We was standing up there watching this man, up close to him. We was standing close to each other too, and then all a sudden Miss Jevata kind of turned her head to me, you know, and said kind of quiet like, 'You know, Miss Jevata could teach you how to swallow lightning,' she said. That was all she said. She didn't say nothing else and she didn't say that no more. I don't even know if anybody else heard her. But I think that's why I went back with her. That was the reason I went with her."

I said nothing. When I closed the door, I heard something hit the wall.

"Freddy did something to David, didn't he," I asked her.

"Naw, it wasn't David," Jevata said. She was sitting with her hands together.

I frowned, watching her.

"Petie come and told me Freddy tried to throw him down the toilet. I didn't believe him."

"If he tried he would've," I said. "What did him and David do?"

She kept looking at me. I was waiting.

"I seen him go in the toilet," she said finally. "Him and David went back in the toilet together. He didn't even have his pants zipped up when he come back to the house."

I was over by her when she burst out crying. When she stopped, she asked me if I could do something for her. I told her all she had to do was ask. When she told me she still loved Freddy, that she wanted me to get him back for her, I walked out the door.

I thought I wouldn't see her again. When the farm I worked for wanted me to go up to New Hampshire for a year to help train some horses, I went. I told myself when I did come back, I was through going out there, but I didn't keep my promise to myself.

When I got there, Miss Johnny wasn't sitting out on her porch, but Jevata was sitting out on hers—with a baby, sitting between her breasts. She was tickling the baby and laughing. When she looked up at me, she was still laughing.

"Floyd, Freddy back," she said. "Freddy come back."

I didn't know what to say to her. I asked if Cynthy was at home. She said yes. I went in the house. Cynthy was standing in the living room. She must have seen me coming.

"Freddy back?" I asked.

She put her hands to her mouth, and drew me toward the kitchen.

"Naw, she mean the baby," she said. "She named the baby Freddy."

"Is it his?" I asked.

She hesitated, frowning, then she said, "Yes." She got farther into the kitchen and I went with her.

"She didn't wont to have him at first. At first she tried to get rid of him."

I kept looking at her. She was a grown woman now. I remembered when I first started coming there, right after her daddy left. Everytime I'd come, she'd get the broom and start sweeping around my feet, like she was trying to sweep me out of the house. Now she looked at me, still frowning, but I could tell she was glad to see me. She said she knew I'd been sending them the money, but Jevata thought Freddy had.

I said nothing. I stood there for a moment, then I said I'd better be going.

"You will come back to see us?" she asked quickly, apprehensively. "We've missed you."

I looked at her. I started to move toward her, then I realized that she meant I might be able to help Jevata.

"Yes, I'll be back," I said.

She smiled. I went out the door.

"You little duck, you little duck, Freddy, you little duck," Jevata said, tickling the baby, who was laughing. A pretty child.

"You be back to see us, won't you, Floyd?" she asked when I started down the porch.

"Yes," I said, without turning around to look at her.

GAYL JONES
Bibliography

In the past five years, Gayl Jones has received a great deal of critical attention. This is a mixed blessing because critics tend to retreat from any discussion of the human struggle of her characters into discourses on style. The extent to which Jones redefines and reviews stereotypes about black women is usually neglected in favor of an analysis of her modernistic narrative and linguistic strategies. Male critics are intrigued by her apparently disordered and violent fictional world, while none of the many women publishing full-length studies of black and/or women writers have included Jones in their commentaries.

Of the criticism currently available, the fullest examination of Jones's two novels and short fiction is Jerry W. Ward's essay in *Black Women Writers 1950–1980* (Garden City, N.Y.: Doubleday, 1984), pp. 244–57, entitled "Escape from Trublem: The Fiction of Gayl Jones." Ward demonstrates the connections between Jones's use of linguistic strategies which involve the reader in questioning the nature of narrative authority and her black female perspective, a perspective for which neither history nor fiction have been reliable narrators. Ward uses the work of Wolfgang Iser and Frank Kermode to explain Jones's place in the American, modernist, and Afro-American canons.

Melvin Dixon also has an essay in this volume, a later revision of which is found in his book *Ride Out the Wilderness: Geography and Identity in Afro-American Literature* (Urbana: University of Illinois Press, 1987, pp. 108–20). While discussion of Jones is included in a chapter on Hurston and Walker, Dixon finds more connections to James Baldwin than to her "womanist" companions. Like Ward, Dixon is interested in Jones's use of oral speech to explore the nature and limits of language, and his point is that Jones is not merely transcribing everyday speech but rather is using it to discuss language itself.

In *Fingering the Jagged Grain: Tradition and Form in Recent Black Fiction* (Athens, Ga.: University of Georgia Press, 1985) Byerman pairs Jones and Morrison and the "bizarre, oppressive worlds" he finds in both writers. He draws on the analyses of madness developed by French philosopher Michel Foucault in his book *Madness and Civilization: A History of Insanity in the Age of Reason,* to explain Jones's use of madness in *Eva's Man.*

Michael Cooke devotes several pages to Jones's novel *Corregidora* in his examination of recent black fiction in *Afro-American Literature in the Twentieth-Century* (New Haven: Yale University Press, 1984, pp. 217–22). Like Ward and Dixon, Cooke discusses the epistemological issues raised by the novel, giving particular attention to the blues and their meaning in *Corregidora.*

LOUISE MERIWETHER

I was raised in New York, in Harlem, under what could be called "mean" circumstances if we wish to be polite and avoid more descriptive language. My father was a house painter and my mother did domestic work. There were five of us children (I was the only girl).

My parents were born in South Carolina and were part of that vast black migration to the "promised land" in search of a better way of life. I've been "migrating" a good deal of my life—from Harlem to Washington, D.C.; to the Bronx; Omaha, Nebraska; St. Paul, Minnesota; Los Angeles; and back to New York again—carrying a little bit of Harlem with me wherever I went.

After graduating from Central Commercial High School in New York, I went to work as a secretary. Subsequently I returned to school at night, in the mornings, at noon, and finally I bagged a degree in English from New York University and a master's degree in journalism from the University of California.

After eighteen years on the West Coast, I have discovered that you can "come home again," and I now live in New York.

After publication of my first novel, Daddy Was a Number Runner, *I turned my attention to black history for the kindergarten set, recognizing that the deliberate omission of blacks from American history has been damaging to the children of both races. It reinforces in one a feeling of inferiority and in the other a myth of superiority.*

The Freedom Ship of Robert Smalls (Englewood Cliffs, N.J.: Prentice-Hall, 1971) relates to the hijacking of a Confederate gunboat by eight slaves during the Civil War. The Heart Man (Prentice-Hall, 1972) is a capsule of the life of Dr. Daniel Hale Williams, who performed the world's first successful heart surgery in 1893. Don't Take the Bus on Monday (1973) is the abbreviated story of the gallant lady Rosa Parks.

I was active in the civil rights movement, specifically with CORE in Los Angeles, and spent the summer of '65 toting guns for the Deacons in Bogalusa.

Currently, I am writing a Civil War novel.

—Louise Meriwether

The central character in Meriwether's first novel *Daddy Was a Number Runner* (1971)[1] is twelve-year-old Francie Coffin, who narrates the story and allows us to see the complex community of Harlem in the 1930s—the Depression years—through her perceptions. It is first of all a community where people share the little they have and where everyone knows everyone else's story; where teenagers explore the streets and one another; where Adam Clayton Powell is the major political and religious leader, heading boycotts and denouncing racism; where an entire city block celebrates collectively as a racial sign the victory of Joe Louis over Max Baer in Madison Square Garden. But it is also a threatening world, not only for Francie and her best friend Sukie, who are subjected to sexual assault, but for their entire families. Francie watches each one—her father, mother, and two brothers—beaten down by the daily assaults of poverty, joblessness, and racial discrimination.

Paule Marshall points out in her review of Meriwether's novel that the sexual indignities Francie is subjected to as she tries to get

---

[1] Originally published in 1970 (Englewood Cliffs, N.J.: Prentice-Hall), *Daddy Was a Number Runner* was republished in 1986 by the Feminist Press.

an extra soup bone or bun "are symbolic of the collective and historical violation of black women."[2] Indeed, the collective and historical sense is evident in all of Meriwether's characters, particularly the black women. Meriwether shows Francie's mother in the role many black women have historically been forced to play in the family: leaving the family to do domestic work, worrying about sons and daughters learning too much in the streets, and that final indignity, facing the social welfare interviews to apply for relief. Francie's mama sits in front of the social worker, apologetically, burying her pride to listen to a lecture on the importance of being truthful and obeying welfare laws. Francie looks at her mother's face and wonders where she has seen that look before. It is an ancient look, worn for years before and years to come by those who stayed and took care.

"A Happening in Barbados," which is included in this collection, is different from *Number Runner* and Meriwether's earlier fiction in several important ways. First the narrator is an adult woman with the capacity for choice, not a child victimized by the cruelties of her environment. She is educated, mobile, sophisticated, articulate—and able to interpret history. Meriwether does undermine the narrator's power, however, by making her major quest the desire to be sexually possessed by men. A plot in which women are merely desirable objects (note how much of the dialogue is among men or directed toward men, or is about male desire) threatens to turn the narrator into another female victim. But Meriwether's ultimate aim is to give the narrator responsibility for rescuing herself and to surface another, repressed, story—the relationship of the narrator to other women and to herself. The narrator's consciousness at the end of the story that she has misused another woman to gratify her own ego displaces the earlier story of idyllic romance, sexual jealousy, and feminine charm.

The setting of this story in a Caribbean country (Meriwether's earlier fiction is set in Harlem) has some bearing on the narrator's

[2] Paule Marshall, Review of *Daddy Was a Number Runner* in the *New York Times* (June 26, 1970, p. 31).

freedom of choice. The West Indies is as much a symbolic place as it is a geographical location, functioning imaginatively as a place of empowerment.[3] This setting seems to give the writer permission to create characters with a sense of quest and plots which convey the possibility of fulfilling those quests. Part of the reason that the West Indies signifies, at least aesthetically, a more liberating space is rooted in actual experience. As Barbara Christian explains, blacks were the majority culture in the West Indies, so the land seemed to be theirs and their cultural habits seemed to be predominant.[4]

The journey of a woman to the West Indies in search of some form of fulfillment that surfaces in "A Happening in Barbados" is significantly revised by Paule Marshall in her 1984 novel, *Praisesong for the Widow* (New York: G. P. Putnam's Sons, 1983). While the emphasis in "Barbados" is one of female sexual attractiveness—the narrator's "tall, brown frame squeezed into a skin-tight bathing suit"—Marshall's main character, Avey Johnson, is in the process of discarding all the accoutrements of conventional feminine attractiveness: she strips herself of girdle and stockings, empties her purse, discards makeup and jewelry. With her hair half combed, she begins the journey of spiritual and communal, not sexual and individual, quest. As Avey enters the final stages of this journey, she is bathed by two women as a part of the ritual baptism into a new state of consciousness. Finally she dances, not the indi-

---

[3] Although I have not thoroughly tested this thesis, I can think of several examples from Paule Marshall's fiction which depict the West Indies as a place where blacks experience continuity with their culture. Even *Brown Girl Brownstones,* which criticizes the West Indian homeland for its exploitation of the poor, uses those cultural ties with Barbados to suggest the Barbadian community's strength and purpose. In *The Chosen Place, the Timeless People* (1971), which is set in the West Indies, Merle Kinbona, its major female character, is politically, psychologically, and narratively more powerful than any women characters in black American literature. We find that same kind of power in Avey Johnson of Marshall's third novel, which is also set in a Caribbean country.

[4] Barbara Christian, *Black Women Novelists: The Development of a Tradition 1892–1976* (Westport, Conn.: Greenwood Press, 1980, p. 81).

vidualized act of sexual possession the narrator of "Barbados" experiences, but the collective dance by which she re-establishes her bonds with the past, with history, with the collective struggles of a people for life and dignity.

Louise Meriwether

A Happening in Barbados

The best way to pick up a Barbadian man, I hoped, was to walk alone down the beach with my tall, brown frame squeezed into a skintight bathing suit. Since my hotel was near the beach, and Dorothy and Alison, my two traveling companions, had gone shopping, I managed this quite well. I had not taken more than a few steps on the glittering, white sand before two black men were on either side of me vying for attention.

I chose the tall, slim-hipped one over the squat, muscle-bound man who was also grinning at me. But apparently they were friends, because Edwin had no sooner settled me under his umbrella than the squat one showed up with a beach chair and two other boys in tow.

Edwin made the introductions. His temporary rival was Gregory, and the other two were Alphonse and Dimitri.

Gregory was ugly. He had thick, rubbery lips, a scarcity of teeth, and a broad nose splattered like a pyramid across his face. He was all massive shoulders and bulging biceps. No doubt he had a certain animal magnetism, but personally I preferred a lean man like Edwin, who was well built but slender, his whole body fitting together like a symphony. Alphonse and Dimitri were clean-cut and pleasant looking.

They were all too young—twenty to twenty-five at the most —and Gregory seemed the oldest. I inwardly mourned their youth and settled down to make the most of my catch.

The crystal-blue sky rivaled the royal blue of the Caribbean for beauty, and our black bodies on the white sand added to the munificence of colors. We ran into the sea like squealing children when the sudden raindrops came, then shivered on the sand under a makeshift tent of umbrellas and damp towels waiting for the sun to reappear while nourishing ourselves with straight Barbados rum.

As with most of the West Indians I had already met on my whirlwind tour of Trinidad and Jamaica, who welcomed American Negroes with open arms, my new friends loved their island home, but work was scarce and they yearned to go to America. They were hungry for news of how Negroes were faring in the States.

Edwin's arm rested casually on my knee in a proprietary manner, and I smiled at him. His thin, serious face was smooth, too young for a razor, and when he smiled back, he looked even younger. He told me he was a waiter at the Hilton, saving his money to make it to the States. I had already learned not to be snobbish with the island's help. Yesterday's waiter may be tomorrow's prime minister.

Dimitri, very black with an infectious grin, was also a waiter, and lanky Alphonse was a tile setter.

Gregory's occupation was apparently women, for that's all he talked about. He was able to launch this subject when a bony white woman—more peeling red than white, really looking like a gaunt cadaver in a loose-fitting bathing suit—came out of the sea and walked up to us. She smiled archly at Gregory.

"Are you going to take me to the Pigeon Club tonight, sugar?"

"No, mon," he said pleasantly, with a toothless grin. "I'm taking a younger pigeon."

The woman turned a deeper red, if that was possible, and, mumbling something incoherent, walked away.

"That one is always after me to take her some place," Gregory said. "She's rich, and she pays the bills but, mon, I don't want an old hag nobody else wants. I like to take my women away from white men and watch them squirm."

"Come down, mon," Dimitri said, grinning. "She look like she's starving for what you got to spare."

We all laughed. The boys exchanged stories about their experiences with predatory white women who came to the islands looking for some black action. But, one and all, they declared they liked dark-skinned meat the best, and I felt like a black queen of the Nile when Gregory winked at me and said, "The blacker the berry, mon, the sweeter the juice."

They had all been pursued and had chased some white tail, too, no doubt, but while the others took it all in good humor, it soon became apparent that Gregory's exploits were exercises in vengeance.

Gregory was saying: "I told that bastard, 'You in my country now, mon, and I'll kick your ass all the way back to Texas. The girl agreed to dance with me, and she don't need your permission.' That white man's face turned purple, but he sat back down, and I dance with his girl. Mon, they hate to see me rubbing bellies with their women because they know once she rub bellies with me she wanna rub something else, too." He laughed, and we all joined in. Serves the white men right, I thought. Let's see how they liked licking *that* end of the stick for a change.

"Mon, you gonna get killed yet," Edwin said, moving closer to me on the towel we shared. "You're crazy. You don't care whose woman you mess with. But it's not gonna be a white man who kill you but some bad Bajan."

Gregory led in the laughter, then held us spellbound for the next hour with intimate details of his affair with Glenda, a young white girl spending the summer with her father on their yacht. Whatever he had, Glenda wanted it desperately, or so Gregory told it.

Yeah, I thought to myself, like LSD, a black lover is the thing this year. I had seen the white girls in the Village and at off-Broadway theaters clutching their black men tightly while I, manless, looked on with bitterness. I often vowed I would find me an ofay in self-defense, but I could never bring myself to condone the wholesale rape of my slave ancestors by letting a white man touch me.

We finished the rum, and the three boys stood up to leave, making arrangements to get together later with us and my two girl friends and go clubbing.

Edwin and I were left alone. He stretched out his muscled leg and touched my toes with his. I smiled at him and let our thighs come together. Why did he have to be so damned young? Then our lips met, his warm and demanding, and I thought, what the hell, maybe I will. I was thirty-nine—good-bye, sweet bird of youth—an ungay divorcee, uptight and drinking too much, trying to disown the years which had brought only loneliness and pain. I had clawed my way up from the slums of Harlem via night school and was now a law clerk on Wall Street. But the fight upward had taken its toll. My husband, who couldn't claw as well as I, got lost somewhere in that concrete jungle. The last I saw of him, he was peering under every skirt around, searching for his lost manhood.

I had always felt contempt for women who found their kicks by robbing the cradle. Now here I was on a Barbados beach with an amorous child young enough to be my son. Two sayings flitted unbidden across my mind. "Judge not, that ye be not judged" and "The thing which I feared is come upon me." I thought, ain't it the god-damned truth?

Edwin kissed me again, pressing the length of his body against mine.

"I've got to go," I gasped. "My friends have probably returned and are looking for me. About ten tonight?"

He nodded; I smiled at him and ran all the way to my hotel.

At exactly ten o'clock, the telephone in our room announced we had company downstairs.

"Hot damn," Alison said, putting on her eyebrows in front of the mirror. "We're not going to be stood up."

"Island men," I said loftily, "are dependable, not like the bums you're used to in America."

Alison, freckled and willowy, had been married three times and was looking for her fourth. Her motto was, if at first you don't succeed, find another mother. She was a real-estate broker in Los Angeles, and we had been childhood friends in Harlem.

"What I can't stand," Dorothy said from the bathroom, "are those creeps who come to your apartment, drink up your liquor, then dirty up your sheets. You don't even get a dinner out of the deal."

She came out of the bathroom in her slip. Petite and delicate with a pixie grin, at thirty-five Dorothy looked more like one of the high school girls she taught than their teacher. She had never been married. Years before, while she was holding onto her virginity with a miser's grip, her fiancé messed up and knocked up one of her friends.

Since then, all of Dorothy's affairs had been with married men, displaying perhaps a subconscious vendetta against all wives.

By ten-twenty we were downstairs and I was introducing the girls to our four escorts, who eyed us with unconcealed admiration. We were looking good in our Saks Fifth Avenue finery. They were looking good, too, in soft shirts and loose slacks, all except Gregory, whose bulging muscles confined in clothing made him seem more gargantuan.

We took a cab and a few minutes later were squeezing behind a table in a small, smoky room called the Pigeon Club. A Trinidad steel band was blasting out the walls, and the tiny dance area was jammed with wiggling bottoms and shuffling feet. The white tourists trying to do the hip-shaking calypso were having a ball and looking awkward.

I got up to dance with Edwin. He had a natural grace and was easy to follow. Our bodies found the rhythm and became one with it while our eyes locked in silent ancient combat, his pleading, mine teasing.

We returned to our seats and to tall glasses of rum and cola tonic. The party had begun.

I danced every dance with Edwin, his clasp becoming gradually tighter until my face was smothered in his shoulder, my arms locked around his neck. He was adorable. Very good for my ego.

The other boys took turns dancing with my friends, but soon preferences were set—Alison with Alphonse and Dorothy with Dimitri. With good humor, Gregory ordered another round and didn't seem to mind being odd man out, but he wasn't alone for long.

During the floor show, featuring the inevitable limbo dancers, a pretty white girl, about twenty-two, with straight, red hair hanging down to her shoulder, appeared at Gregory's elbow. From his wink at me and self-satisfied grin, I knew this was Glenda from the yacht.

"Hello," she said to Gregory. "Can I join you, or do you have a date?"

Well, I thought, that's the direct approach.

"What are you doing here?" Gregory asked.

"Looking for you."

Gregory slid over on the bench, next to the wall, and Glenda sat down as he introduced her to the rest of us. Somehow, her presence spoiled my mood. We had been happy being black, and I resented this intrusion from the white world. But Glenda was happy. She had found the man she'd set out to find and a swinging party to boot. She beamed a dazzling smile around the table.

Alphonse led Alison onto the dance floor, and Edwin and I followed. The steel band was playing a wild calypso, and I could feel my hair rising with the heat as I joined in the wildness.

When we returned to the table, Glenda applauded us, then turned to Gregory. "Why don't you teach me to dance like that?"

He answered with his toothless grin and a leer, implying he had better things to teach her.

White women were always snatching our men, I thought, and now they want to dance like us.

I turned my attention back to Edwin and met his full stare.

I teased him with a smile, refusing to commit myself. He had a lusty, healthy appetite, which was natural, I supposed, for a twenty-one-year-old lad. Lord, but why did he have to be that young? I stood up to go to the ladies' room.

"Wait for me," Glenda cried, trailing behind me.

The single toilet stall was occupied, and Glenda leaned against the wall waiting for it while I flipped open my compact and powdered my grimy face.

"You married?" she asked.

"Divorced."

"When I get married, I want to stay hooked forever."

"That's the way I planned it, too," I said dryly.

"What I mean," she rushed on, "is that I've gotta find a cat who wants to groove only with me."

Oh Lord, I thought, don't try to sound like us, too. Use your own, sterile language.

"I really dug this guy I was engaged to," Glenda continued, "but he couldn't function without a harem. I could have stood that, maybe, but when he didn't mind if I made it with some other guy, too, I knew I didn't want that kind of life."

I looked at her in the mirror as I applied my lipstick. She had been hurt, and badly. She shook right down to her naked soul. So she was dropping down a social notch, according to her scale of values, and trying to repair her damaged ego with a black brother.

"You gonna make it with Edwin?" she asked, as if we were college chums comparing dates.

"I'm not a one-night stand." My tone was frigid. That's another thing I can't stand about white people. Too familiar, because we're colored.

"I dig Gregory," she said, pushing her hair out of her eyes. "He's kind of rough, but who wouldn't be, the kind of life he's led."

"And what kind of life is that?" I asked.

"Didn't you know? His mother was a whore in an exclusive brothel for white men only. That was before, when the British owned the island."

"I take it you like rough men?" I asked.

"There's usually something gentle and lost underneath," she replied.

A white woman came out of the toilet and Glenda went in.

Jesus, I thought, Gregory gentle? The woman walked to the basin, flung some water in the general direction of her hands, and left.

"Poor Daddy is having a fit," Glenda volunteered from the john, "but there's not much he can do about it. He's afraid I'll leave him again, and he gets lonely without me, so he just tags along and tries to keep me out of trouble."

"And he pays the bills?"

She answered with a laugh. "Why not? He's loaded."

Why not, I thought with bitterness. You white women have always managed to have your cake and eat it, too. The toilet flushed with a roar like Niagara Falls. I opened the door and went back to our table. Let Glenda find her way back alone.

Edwin pulled my chair out and brushed his lips across the nape of my neck as I sat down. He still had not danced with anyone else, and his apparent desire was flattering. For a moment, I considered it. That's what I really needed, wasn't it? To walk down the moon-lit beach wrapped in his arms, making it to some pad to be made? It would be a delightful story to tell at bridge sessions. But I shook my head at him, and this time my smile was more sad than teasing.

Glenda came back and crawled over Gregory's legs to the seat beside him. The bastard. He made no pretense of being a gen-tleman. Suddenly, I didn't know which of them I disliked the most. Gregory winked at me. I don't know where he got the impression I was his conspirator, but I got up to dance with him.

"That Glenda," he grinned, "she's the one I was on the boat with last night. I banged her plenty, in the room right next to her father. We could hear him coughing to let us know he was awake, but he didn't come in."

He laughed like a naughty schoolboy, and I joined in. He was a nerveless bastard all right, and it served Glenda right that we were laughing at her. Who asked her to crash our party, anyway? That's when I got the idea to take Gregory away from her.

"You gonna bang her again tonight?" I asked, a new, teasing quality in my voice. "Or are you gonna find something better to do?" To help him get the message I rubbed bellies with him.

He couldn't believe this sudden turn of events. I could almost see him thinking. With one stroke he could slap Glenda down a peg and repay Edwin for beating his time with me on the beach that morning.

"You wanna come with me?" he asked, making sure of his quarry.

"What you got to offer?" I peered at him through half-closed lids.

"Big Bamboo," he sang, the title of a popular calypso. We both laughed.

I felt a heady excitement of impending danger as Gregory pulled me back to the table. The men paid the bill, and suddenly we were standing outside the club in the bright moonlight. Gregory deliberately uncurled Glenda's arm from his and took a step toward me. Looking at Edwin and nodding in my direction, he said, "She's coming with me. Any objections?"

Edwin inhaled a mouthful of smoke. His face was inscrutable. "You want to go with him?" he asked me quietly.

I avoided his eyes and nodded. "Yes."

He flipped the cigarette with contempt at my feet and lit another one. "Help yourself to the garbage," he said, and leaned back against the building, one leg braced behind him. The others suddenly stilled their chatter, sensing trouble.

I was holding Gregory's arm now, and I felt his muscles tense. "No," I said as he moved toward Edwin. "You've got what you want. Forget it."

Glenda was ungracious in defeat. "What about me?" she screamed. She stared from one black face to another, her glance lingering on Edwin. But he wasn't about to come to her aid and take Gregory's leavings.

"You can go home in a cab," Gregory said, pushing her ahead of him and pulling me behind him to a taxi waiting at the curb.

Glenda broke from his grasp. "You bastard. Who in the hell do you think you are, King Solomon? You can't dump me like this." She raised her hands as if to strike Gregory on the chest, but he caught them before they landed.

"Careful, white girl," he said. His voice was low but ominous. She froze.

"But why," she whimpered, all hurt child now. "You liked me last night. I know you did. Why are you treating me like this?"

"I didn't bring you here"—his voice was pleasant again—"so don't be trailing me all over town. When I want you, I'll come to that damn boat and get you. Now get in that cab before I throw you in. I'll see you tomorrow night. Maybe."

"You go to hell." She eluded him and turned on me, asking with incredible innocence, "What did I ever do to you?" Then she was running past toward the beach, her sobs drifting back to haunt me like a forlorn melody.

What had she ever done to me? And what had I just done? In order to degrade her for the crime of being white, I had sunk to the gutter. Suddenly Glenda was just another woman, vulnerable and lonely, like me.

We were sick, sick, sick. All fucked up. I had thought only Gregory was hung up in his love-hate, black-white syndrome, decades of suppressed hatred having sickened his soul. But I was tainted, too. I had forgotten my own misery long enough to inflict it on another woman who was only trying to ease her loneliness by making it with a soul brother. Was I jealous because she was able to function as a woman where I couldn't, because she realized that a man is a man, color be damned, while I was crucified on my own, anti-white-man cross?

What if she were going black trying to repent for some ancient Nordic sin? How else could she atone except with the gift of herself? And if some black brother wanted to help a chick off her lily-white pedestal, he was entitled to that freedom, and it was none of my damned business anyway.

"Let's go, baby," Gregory said, tucking my arm under his.

The black bastard. I didn't even like the ugly ape. I backed away from him. "Leave me alone," I screamed. "Goddamit, just leave me alone!"

For a moment, we were all frozen into an absurd fresco—Alison, Dorothy, and the two boys looking at me in shocked disbelief, Edwin hiding behind a nonchalant smokescreen, Gregory off balance and confused, reaching out toward me.

I moved first, toward Edwin, but I had slammed the door behind me. He laughed, a mirthless sound in the stillness. He knew. I had forsaken him, but at least not for Gregory.

Then I was running down the beach looking for Glenda, hot tears of shame burning my face. How could I have been such a bitch? But the white beach, shimmering in the moonlight, was empty. And once again, I was alone.

LOUISE MERIWETHER
Bibliography

In 1970 every major reviewer and critic recommended Meriwether's first novel, *Daddy Was a Number Runner,* yet her work has not yet received the scholarly appreciation which its placement on these "highly recommended" lists suggests, her book deserves. One of the reasons for the critical neglect of Meriwether is the insistence of many reviewers that her work is significant only as a sociological document—for example, L. E. Sissman's review in *The New Yorker* (July 11, 1970, p. 77). While admiring the novel's "compelling documentation of what slum life is really like," Sissman concludes that "one need not examine the literary merits of a survivor's authentic account of a catastrophe." Since *Daddy Was a Number Runner* is about the *real* threats of the ghetto—hunger, heat, cold, vermin, molestation, violence, despair, the loss of dignity—Sissman argues that we need not consider its literary value. With this damning praise, Sissman insists that the only value of *Number Runner* is as an indictment of a society which permits the poverty and despair of ghetto life and as a warning that America must listen to voices like Meriwether's if any changes are to be made.

This practice of evaluating black literature as sociology is typical of much of the criticism of black writing in the 1960s and early

1970s. Even critics who take black fiction seriously as literature fall into the trap of using these texts to support sociological and psychological arguments. Rita Dandridge in *Negro American Literature Forum* (9:82–85) initially puts Meriwether's novel in a literary context, recognizing it as the first African-American novel to analyze the effects of the Depression on a black family; but she too abandons literary analysis, maintaining that the novel's value lies in its validation of a psychological theory of black adaptation to discrimination.

Because Paule Marshall knows the black literary tradition both as a novelist and critic, she flatly rejects the contention that *Number Runner* is most effective as a sociological or psychological statement. Taking on questions of narrative style and structure in her *New York Times* review (June 26, 1970), Marshall praises Meriwether's use of understatement and her ability to create a wide range of characters while faithfully maintaining the point of view of a twelve-year-old girl.

A study of the commentary on this most popular of Meriwether's works illustrates the difficulty of finding meaningful evaluation of black literature in a context of unexamined assumptions about the relation of culture, political realities, and art.

ALEXIS DeVEAUX

Where Did You Grow Up/Where Born?/How Did You Get to the Place You Are Now?

Grew up in Harlem and the South Bronx in New York City. Born in New York City.

"Wrote no matter what else I had to do, no matter what kinds of nonwriting jobs I had to take to support myself. Have stuck to developing the sacred gift I've been entrusted with. And I have not allowed myself to misuse or abuse that gift. Every step I have made, every word or piece I have written have led me to this particular point in time. It has been both magic and hard, often lonely work. Though I would not say that I have "arrived," I would say that I am successfully alive, in good health, and creative, for it is not my desire to "make it." It is only my desire to live and evolve as a human being.

Is Your Relationship to Your Mother an Important Influence?

Yes. The more I unravel my life, the better I understand hers, and the better I am able to communicate with her and to her about our life. My mother's mother died when my own mother was very young, so my mother never really had the benefit of a mother-daughter relationship or the dynamics of that kind of communication. Because of that, she was unable to communicate to my brothers and sisters and me. Wanting to communicate on an intimate level with her was, I believe, part of the reason I started writing.

Important Experiences That Have Helped Shape Me As a Writer

I have always been attached to books, words. Ever since elementary school. I was an overzealous Book-Report—writer and thoroughly meticulous about compositions, my handwriting, anything that had to do with books. In the street/at home, I eavesdropped on other people's conversations. Being just plain nosy, but not terribly communicative, shy. I would write poems a lot then. And I always had teachers who encouraged me to write. Writing became a way of talking. . . . The Literary Renaissance of the sixties and the whole re-examination of the Harlem Renaissance of the twenties were important influences on me as far as developing a sociopolitical consciousness with respect to writing. Without that movement, and its liberating thrust, my writing would not have had the strength, and the connection to my "root/source," the neo-Africanist point of view it has now. The literary movement and the movement for freedom which engulfs us provides me with the knowledge of a vitally rich, ancient continuum.

Importance of Formal Education in Development of My Writing

It wasn't. I never studied writing or how to write while in school. School kept alive my interest in books, but the actual craft of writing was something I studied and sought out on my own, outside the traditional educational environment. I found workshops and programs where creative writing was stressed. I became active in a couple of community organizations where writers' workshops were offered. That's how I got to meet other writers, known and unknown, to hear what they were doing, saying, feeling, striving for. By the time I got a B.A. through an indepen-

dent study program (and several aborted attempts to finish college in all the wrong, but socially acceptable majors, including psych and sociology), I was fully entrenched in writing, not only as a career, but as a way of life.

OTHER IMPORTANT INFLUENCES THAT HAVE SHAPED ME AS A WRITER

The emergence of Lorraine Hansberry (in 1959) as a gifted, spirited, visionistic woman. And the power behind her work. The fact that she was writing for the theater made no difference since I did not see any boundaries between what was on the stage and what was on the page (and I still don't; often combine techniques of one form with those of another). The image of a Black woman as artist and writer living in the world at the same time I was, was a powerfully mesmerizing image for me. Also, meeting such writers as James Baldwin, Toni Morrison, Paule Marshall, J. E. Franklin (of Black Girl), Adrienne Kennedy, etc. made the possibility of becoming a writer, and surviving at it, a viable one; meeting and seeing them in the flesh made the reality of a lifestyle/career in writing all the more plausible and exciting.

CONNECTIONS BETWEEN MY PERSONAL LIFE AND THE IDEAS/ IMAGES, ETC. I WRITE ABOUT

There is an inseparable connection between who I am and what I realize I must write about. Be it a poem, short story, book, or play. Writing helps me unravel the images and forces at work in my own life, and, therefore, by extension, in the lives of Black women and Black people around me. I hope to communicate something not just about my life, but about our life. It's all one life—isn't it? And I'm very concerned about the images of Black women in literature because whatever is written down becomes the word, and the word is permanent, and stays, long after the writer and the people are gone. I want to say something about the Black woman as three-dimensional human being. So often we've seen her depicted as White man's concubine, mammy, tragic mulatto, maid, prostitute, destitute, one stereotype after another: ugly and useless. I want to change that.

In the most radical and revolutionary ways possible. I want to explore her questions, strengths, concerns, madnesses, love, evils, weaknesses, lack of love, pain, and growth. Her perversities and her moralities. I draw on my own feelings as a source of material, and then I try to flesh out these feelings in characters who may or may not have had my particular experiences but who certainly reflect my own concerns, politics, philosophies, etc. I said earlier that as a young person I was shy. I think that shyness came out of smothered feelings, and a sense of inferiority, an ugliness (anything Black is ugly) vis-à-vis White society. Writing is a way of conquering those feelings of inferior beauty, inferior life, and giving vent to an extremely active imagination. When I am creating characters and the threads of their stories, I am able to free myself, cleanse myself, of old feelings/old scars, psychic imagery, desires, etc. Writing is a healing art/experience; it is a form of meditation.

WHAT TURNING POINTS IN YOUR CAREER/LIFE HAVE BEEN TRANSFORMING?

1. *Winning the Black Creation Literary Contest in the Fall of '72.*
2. *Having my first play produced* (Circles) *in '73.*
3. *Getting my first book published* (Spirits in the Street) *in '73.*
4. *Witnessing the immensity of poverty in Haiti in the summer of '75.*
5. *Going to Milan, Italy, in March of '78.*
6. *Turning thirty.*
7. *Giving up all meats, cigarettes, and drugs in '77.*

CHILDREN AND MARITAL STATUS

At present I have no children and my marital status does not make a difference to my career. I write whether I am single or married.

—Alexis DeVeaux

The two narrators of Alexis DeVeaux's stories, "The Riddles of Egypt Brownstones" and "Remember Him a Outlaw," experience a dual reality in their lives. They are college-bound women who have escaped the ghetto world they are writing about, and they are young women still very much affected by that world. The duality of their lives is present in the formal structure of DeVeaux's narratives. The italicized narration featuring snatches of blues songs, black idioms, children's rhymes, the voices of the men, women, and children from the narrators' childhood is balanced against the controlling voice which explains and interprets. Sometimes a distant third-person narrator is replaced by a personal and self-revealing first-person voice. Short, angry, staccato sentences are followed by long series of unpunctuated sentences. Egypt's royal heritage, her place on the Nile of ancient history is sharply contrasted with the demeaning social statistics of New York authorities: "Girl Negro sex female" . . . "illegitimate." The colors of Egypt's birth—purple, lavender, and blue—give way to the "white metal light" and the "sterilized galaxies of nurses and doctors" of the white world.

The narrators of these two stories—Egypt in "The Riddles of Egypt Brownstones" and Lexie in "Remember Him a Outlaw"—are both insiders and outsiders. At the end of "Riddles," Egypt is in a college classroom in City College of New York studying French and contemplating living with the worldly and sophisticated teacher from Martinique—Madame duFer. Lexie's picture in the white newspaper announces her eight-thousand-dollar scholarship to an Ivy League college in the farm country of upstate New York. But the very fact that these two stories dwell on the past and depict that past quite vividly shows that neither narrator has separated from nor dismissed her history. When Madame duFer asks Egypt about herself, she reminds her that she is connected to her absent father: "I believe in riddles like my father," and the story ends with Egypt at the funeral of her father dressed in his blue suede shoes. Lexie's command that Uncle Willie's story be remembered is the first and last line, as well as the title, of that story.

As insiders, Lexie and Egypt are able to show that though there is little change possible in these ghetto worlds, there are a vibrancy and beauty and energy about these places that often go unrecorded.

In both of these stories color has a vivid emotional significance. Egypt's heritage is symbolized by Egypt's black skin, her mother's red tribal markings and butternut face, her father's "midnight blue" suede shoes. Uncle Willie in "Outlaw" is a "dream in green"; when he comes to visit, "the sun has a new face." Richie's skin is the color of new coal, Willie's liquor medicine is purple-sweet juice, the hallways are "empty-blue." The colors shift, melting into neutrals, as Egypt enters the world of college: "I am sitting in a beige classroom full of right-handed beige desks."

While the colors of their childhood worlds suggest a vibrancy and life, much of the power for movement and change is given to objects, while people, except for the narrators, seem incapable of change or growth. DeVeaux personifies objects, describing cars and buildings as hung over, windows that give voice to lovers' desires; the rap of a ball against the pavement "sings against the Sunday summer morning concrete." The ball, of course, is the most power-ful object in "Riddles," for it is through the ball that Egypt vents the rage she feels toward those who have abused her throughout her life. The "black palm to pink rubber" represents Egypt's anger as she beats against the walls of the confining and hostile world around her. The ball is there at the end, bouncing and pounding fiercely against the hospital wall where her father, who remains a fragile presence throughout the story, is dead. The lives of people, on the other hand, have a static quality. Richie in "Outlaw" rolls from his bed over bottles in a perpetual state of sleep and unaware-ness. The mothers of these two stories are viewed mainly from second-floor windows as they peer down at their children but never venture outside. Uncle Willie is killed by someone who shoots him full of dope.[1]

The unconventional style that DeVeaux uses in all of her work —fragments of African culture, bits of slang, no capital letters, childhood riddles—continues to suggest the duality her narrators experience, a mixture of both pain and triumph over that pain. In

---

[1] I am indebted to one of my students at the University of Massachusetts—Boston, Jan Peterson, for many of the insights on DeVeaux's work.

her biographical poem about Billie Holiday, *Don't Explain: A Song of Billie Holiday,* another unconventional narrative, DeVeaux gives a description of artistry of Billie Holiday that comments on her own narrative art:

> Relaxed and in total control of her own voice . . .
> She wanted her listeners to see and feel
> beauty in the painful story . . .
> She could create/triumph out of crisis.[2]

Biographers, as has been noted, choose their subjects because they represent some aspect of themselves. Holiday's unconventional style is clearly a paradigm for DeVeaux's own artistry. Both of them tell painful stories but with a feeling for the beauty that is embedded in the pain. Both create triumph out of crisis.

---

[2] Alexis DeVeaux, *Don't Explain: A Song of Billie Holiday* (New York: Harper & Row, 1980, p. 33).

The Riddles of Egypt Brownstone

Push sweat violent lavender blue pain sing woman
come sing one hundred ninety nine
sweat girl dance the thigh dance pain
ninety eight ninety seven ninety six
born to push grunt rip life
tear out tear through purple birth murmurings
through sterilized galaxies of nurses and doctors
sing/ninety five ninety four stompin at the savoy

Above her body outstretched on the hospital table a white metal light licked at the starched gown pulled over her stomach heaving.

Bring baby down the Nile

Esther let her knees shut Esther let her eyes buck.

Momma October 13th shoulder pads and zoot suit city
sing woman Lena Horne momma hit the number ninety
three

one two buckle my shoe who? whos the father yes no
maybe so
doctor/lawyer/indian chief

She screamed sweat wet and birth crazy

  Rich man poor man beggar man thief

Harlem Hospital. City of New York. Attending physician Dr. Ed-
mund Greer. October 13 1945. 6:43am. Race Negro sex girl. Name
Girl Brownstone. Mother's name Esther Brownstone. Address 50
West 138. Date of Birth April 9 1928. Occupation usher. Age 17.
Previous births now living none. Place of Employment RKO The-
atre 116th Street was her mother's side of the birth certificate. Her
father's side was blank.

In search of lush black nipple the minuscule mouth beside Esther in
the hospital bed made a sucking sound.

  "I named her Egypt, momma."

Edith Brownstone leaned over. A tiny West Indian silver bracelet
she slipped on the grandchild's wrist.

  "Blackest lil girl I ever saw" Edith said.

She collected riddles growing up. They fascinated her. After school
at the library. Reading books on silver barges through the royal
night. Excursions up the Nile of ancient history. Riddle me this.
Riddle me that. Time and the twentieth century: what has a
mother who is a father name a child Girl Negro sex female born
feet first.

"My teacher say you got to sign this free lunch paper momma."
"Who wrote this word here Egypt?"
"Miss Jackowitz did. Everybody got one."
"Hand me that god damn pencil eraser girl. Wasnt nobody illegiti-
mate when they *was on top pumpin womens in the huts of nigga*
quarters."

▲   ▲   ▲

She had thick red hair dusty black skin at 13. One brown and one
light brown eye. Grew big titties. Was shorter than any of her
friends. A Fanti charm doll she considered herself deformed.

> *"E my name is Egypt. (bounce)*
> *My father's name is Esop. (bounce)*
> *We come from Ethiopia. (bounce bounce)*
> *And we sell elephants." (bounce)*

Her spalding ball sang against the sunday summer morning concrete. Bounce bounce. Black palm to pink rubber ball. Feel air and
space outside. Not like upstairs was. Too hot in the bed too many
people. A taste for watermelon. Black ball to pink rubber palm to
Harlem sidewalk. Smell saturday night in sunday street. Cars and
buildings hung over. Bounce bounce ball over short black leg up
over ball over was-white sneakers. Bounce. Bored. Hit the ball
against the stoop.

> *"Who wanna play stoop ball?*
> *Who wanna be on my team?*
> *So what. I can play if I want to.*
> *Mind your own business Georgie Christmas.*
> *I aint no tomboy shit."*

The third floor window opened abrupt. Her mother's face hung
out. Squinted eyes cruised the street below. A camel cigarette stuck

to her lips. Egypt liked her mother's lips. Egypt liked her mother tough but not mean. Esther spotted Egypt bent over pitching fifteen pennies at the stoop step.

"Take that ball out your sock girl. How many times I got to tell you your name aint Henry?"

A stained white was-once a towel wrapped itself around Egypt's mother's head. Henna mud streaked rivers/red tribal markings down her butternut face.

"Go to the grocery store. Tell Prince I say dont forget my cigarettes this time."

Paper floated from Esther's thick fist crumpled. Egypt positioned her reluctant self to catch the sailing grocery list.

why cant somebody else go get the groceries
sometime momma why it always gotta be me
soon as I get grown Im cuttin out she see

The third floor window closed. Down the block Egypt peeled her left sock away letting free the rubber ball.

shoot she know I dont like him
's why I never say nothin when he come see her
he aint my father shoot I aint eatin none a
his ole nasty food

Bounce bounce pink rubber ball to Black angry palm. Across the street through the Taft Projects. A low income public dream. Stack them up stack them higher. One way in one way out. Project families versus tenement families versus the city is everybody's landlord no matter how you frost the cake.

▲   ▲   ▲

On the edges of El Barrio graffiti poems are rainbows that promise Debbie loves Jose forever baby I need your luvin. Windows half open tell the secret of last night's party. Hot thighs sweating teenage blues under skirts with no panties and zippers open standing up/sitting down/upside second hand refrigerators in dark kitchens. Please baby gimme some. I die if you dont. Please sugar oh lord you soo good. Yeah I love you anything baby anything. Oh jesus oh the Shirelles and do-rags conkoline and red lights. From a record player on the tenth floor Etta James crooned. In the center of the projects a gang of kids raced each other to the metal swings. Egypt walked through the artificial park to the other side of time. King Tut somersaulted beside her. He stroked the false beard of Egyptian royalty. King Tut the boy was King Tut the man was King Tut the dancing Pharaoh. She loved his dip and glide intoxicating two step through the monkey bars.

"Are you ready my dear? Shall we go?"
"Cant."
"Oh but my dear why not? I have prepared everything you know."

He dipped and glided a royal strut his robe shimmered divinity.

"Aint solved the serious riddle" she said.
"Whats a what with a who has a what born on the same day one month apart?" he said.

And split for home through a crack in a breath Egypt inhaled.

how come all of a sudden we gotta take his food
why cant she buy food like everybody else mother
maybe he aint there maybe the stores closed

Lenox Avenue and 116th street. A red and white sign proclaimed PRINCE'S GROCERY STORE AND FRUIT STAND was open. To see how many people were inside she peeked through the pane glass window. She saw only Prince. He saw her staring. He winked her inside. The stingy brim olive green hat pushed back made his forehead jut forward. A well groomed mustache hid the true thickness of his upper lip. Stains and chicken do rusted his white butcher's apron. She thought she saw something in his face/ she thought she saw his blood rise. With false boldness Egypt pushed the glass door open. Against the potato bin she leaned and wrestled Esther's grocery list from her dungaree pocket. She held it out to him.

"Hi. Momma said make sure you send her some cigarettes."
"Hi yourself."

He did not take it. He kept stamping 2 for 31¢ on cans of Campbell's Chicken Noodle soup. Egypt watched. Prince watched Egypt watching Prince through the corners of watching eyes. *Do you see me/I see you?*

"What else your momma say?"
"Nothin."
"She tell you come straight back?"
"Yeah."
hurry up Prince shoot take the list gimme the groceries dont be no riddle please Prince why we gotta play this game every week

"Wanna ice cream sandwich?"
"No thanks."
"Nice tee shirt you got."

Egypt laid the crumpled list on the counter. Prince ripped open a second box of soup cans. He watched her watching. Egypt shoved her hands in her pockets and walked around the store. She felt her face hot. She felt her stomach twist in anxious knots.

▲   ▲   ▲

The aisles of the small Lenox Avenue grocery store were pregnant with boxes of canned vegetables crackers canned juices apple sauce jars and toilet paper. Egypt read the labels. Prince watched her wander up and down through the giant mirror at the back he kept for watching shoplifters. He saw her finger her way into a package of Oreo cookies slip several in her pocket one in her mouth and continue a nonchalant journey. He watched her in the mirror. He watched her watching him.

>*"Hey Tuna man. Come out here and finish these cans for me will ya?"*

A good friend an old sailor he never went to sea. Smelled like fridays fish 2 pounds for a dollar. Didn't eat no tuna said they were sacred. He worked for Prince on the weekends. Visited aquariums every wednesday and monday and told fish tales. From the back of the store Tunafish came out whistling *Mona Lisa Mona Lisa* his white sailor cap and white sailor pants stiff with starch.

>*"Prince man why didnt you tell me your daughter was here? How you doing lil bit? Hows your momma?"*
>*"Fine Mr. Tunafish."*

She talking this way and watching that way watching Prince hand Tunafish the can stamper.

>*he aint my father hes my brothers father*
>*hes her boyfriend he aint nothin to me*
>*I dont even like eatin his food when I get home*
>*Im a tell her that*

Prince lit a Pall Mall cigarette and picked up the grocery list puffing smoke his eyes like bird slits his body like Mr. America's only blacker than blackberry brandy jam. From behind the counter he came out not paying Egypt no mind sneaking Oreo cookies out her pocket with her face turned towards the picked over tomatoes

and grapefruits spoiling in the bin near the store door. He slipped
his arm around her shoulder.

"Come on girl" he said *"lets see what your momma want."*

Pushing a shopping cart in front of them he guided her up and
down the aisles. His large ashy hand weighed a ton on her broad
hand ball shoulders. Prince pretended to read what he knew by
heart: salmon eggs white bread white grits pasteurized cheese ready
made food. He let his hand fondle her bra strap tensed. She moved
out of step. He brought her firmly back in.

"Here" he said *"you might as well finish what you started."*

The open package of Oreo cookies betray her like a laughing
enemy. His hand tasted her breast trembling. Long fingers squeezed
roughly.

*"Why you always so quiet, huh girl? Hand me two cans of that
salmon will ya?"*

He let go long enough for her to reach the green and pink cans.

*"Please Prince please cant you see Mr. Tunafish in the mirror
watchin. Please Prince hes laughin he might tell."*

Egypt felt Prince's hand rub and squeeze. At the back of the store
he pressed closer. In front of the meat case Prince stood behind her.
Prince stuck his hand inside her tee shirt.

"You think your momma want some pork chops?"

When he squeezed her hurting he pulled the blue and yellow tee
shirt up over Egypt's tears palpitating incantations to Ra the All
Seeing Eye of Upper and Lower. Ra the father/Lord of Kemet.
Let there be light. Let there be riddles. Amen.

"You gonna tell your momma our secret?"

He said he wasn't going to bite her. He said they ought to be glad he had a grocery store. He said don't ever tell your momma you hear me?

▲   ▲   ▲

The grocery list never changed. She never told. He always sent something extra. It was the first secret she learned to keep from her momma that summer until the sunday morning the grocery list changed. Esther added: one box Kotex and put it in the bathroom on the floor between the toilet and the bath tub without a word but kept walking behind Egypt smelling her odor and waiting and watching Prince who was "her nigga" watching Egypt do the dishes watching him watch her sideways out of one eye. So that sunday Esther finally smelled it Egypt was standing in the kitchen straightening her hair burning her neck in the back when Esther frowning at the door said "aint gone be no woman-wars in this house" and told her not to go to Prince's store no more she had stopped shopping there.

▲   ▲   ▲

Egypt wondered when was the last time Esther kissed Bull. Was it that night they made her on the roof it was too cold to take their coats off he promised? It was long since then she knew when she heard Esther telling Prince:

> *"This aint got nothin to do with you Prince. Thats his kid. Every Christmas he sends her this money. Dont start somethin you cant finish honey. What you talkin bout? Bull didnt leave me. We was just too young my father said. This aint got nothin to do with you Prince."*

▲   ▲   ▲

She had seen him her birthday every year. He waited on the corner
127th Street and St. Nicholas. Bull David Phillips was her father.
She looked like him in the face a little in the eyes. He loved clothes
and imported hats. Esther said he made his own suits and only wore
blue suede shoes. She wanted a pair on her 18th birthday. They
went to every store 125th Street looking for a pair of midnight
blue suede ladies shoes.

▲   ▲   ▲

*"Maintenant, nous étudierons la conjugasion des verbes. Mademoi-
selle Brownstone. Pouvez-vous traduire pour la classe s'il vous
plaît?"*
"Oui Madame. We will now study the conjugation of verbs."

I am sitting in a beige classroom full of right handed beige desks. I
am one of twenty six students in this City College French 101 class.
The instructor is a Black woman name Madame duFer. She has
lived in Martinique Paris Haiti and Guadeloupe among the folk.
Her shoulders are square Egyptian. Her face is moon black. She
drowns me with her slanted eyes. She sees me looking at her mouth
when she speaks. I doodle in my notebook: I am into thick lips (are
good for sucking). She says her hair is au naturel. The world is
changing. Civil rights and Black Power/it's 1963. I'm smiling at
her with my frown. When she calls on me the others know I am
the favorite.

*"Répétez après moi classe. J'ai un secret. Tu as un secret. Il a un
secret. Elle a un secret."*

I like those European tailored suits she wears with the skirts cut just
above her calves. *E my name is Ellie. My father's name is Eclipse. We*

come from Eatonville. And we sell eggplants. Madame duFer looks like a woman. Madame duFer does not look like a woman. Madame duFer looks like more than a woman or a man.

"Ecoutez classe. Listen carefully. Je suis née à Harlem. Tu es née à Harlem. Il est né à Harlem. Elle est née à Harlem."

I am watching her mouth move thickly in a light French dance to conjugate the present past future tense. April is the month of reincarnated verbs: to spring to jazz to poet. Tonight I am invited to her house for dinner. Suite 3c. Eighteen Hamilton Place. The old Sugar Hill section of Harlem.

"My three sisters and I share a bedroom. I do my homework in the bathroom."
"You could live here if you like. When the semester is over we can be friends. You wont have to call me Madame duFer."
"What about your husband?"
"He has his life. I have mine. Are you frightened?"
"Yes."
"You are the most beautiful student I have ever had. Always coming and going. Much as myself."
"I believe in riddles like my father."
"Do you object to being a kept woman?"
"No."

Esther's mother Edith said Bull had been in a bar flashing his money in the wrong woman's face when he fell out. In the hospital a doctor said Mr. Phillips had been quite sick more than a year with a kidney ailment that had gotten progressively worse. Esther said Bull loved himself some Chivas Regal said he always loved to drink a fifth of it for lunch. The electric kitchen clock he had given her last Christmas fell off the wall that morning while she was having coffee and something said "a bull with one horn cant last too long" and instead of going to work Esther turned on the record player and played her favorite Nat King Cole album for old times sake.

▲   ▲   ▲

After Bull's family called Esther called Egypt and Egypt took a cab all the way to Brooklyn. *What has a mother who is a father and who is he 127th Street once a year?*

"*I needed him to solve the riddle momma*"

She told Esther outside the Intensive Care Unit. Pulled up the leg of her dungarees and took a pink rubber ball out her sock. Bounced it fiercely against the hospital wall. It pounded

> *E my name is Ethiopia*
> *My father's name is Egypt*
> *We come from Esop*
> *And we sell Eclipses*

And then it stopped pound-pounding. The doctor handed them a bag of clothes he had worn. Egypt took out her inheritance. Put them on. Stuffed the hospital report in the toes. And wore his blue suede shoes to the funeral.

Alexis DeVeaux

Remember Him a Outlaw

remember him a outlaw. living in the bowery. didnt hardly work. he couldnt he roars. tobacco smiles. in baggy dove-colored khaki pants and big orange workboots. he is slew-foot. doing his wine walk. hips swaying west down 112 street. he tips his cap to the women. he grins at stoops. talking loud to other bums old friends. the sky or garbage. up the street at the corner of 5th & 112 he stops. to salute cars. to wait. to cross. his sober eye always leary. he crosses to our corner.

> *ma! ma! here come uncle willie! ma!*
> *hey uncle willie!*

mommie from somewhere inside the house runs to the window on instinct. she pops out. relief spreads over her yellow face. we run and climb at uncle willie. a mountain to jump on.

> *take me for a piggy-back uncle willie!*
> *take me first!*
> *look! i got on your hat uncle willie oooooh what you*
> *got in your pocket is that candy??*

a long face melts in his shoulder cage. on his head hair beads. eyes like stars and rot-gut wine. medicine for his thick smooth lips. he sweats. his black skin wet tar. a reflection to look at and never see in. a cherub. an old womans son. uncle willie wasnt 43.

he is drunk. desperate to hold all of us. at the same time. he throws a few jabs to odell. ducks. fat vickie is teased. rosie runs to him. hugging me round the neck. twins we walk together. booboo and nell squint their eyes to look up. the sun has a new face.

up to the stoop uncle willie is a father who visits. knows we love him boisterous. he stops to see mommie in the 2nd floor window. she shakes her head and grins. glad to see him. saying nothing saying

> *willie nigger when you gon change?*

uncle willie rears back in the heat. he sways. wipes sweat in a dingy rag from his neck. he throws back his head to talk

> *hey mae! mae! where you get all those ugly children*
> *from?*
> *oh shut up. what you got in your pockets willie what*
> *you done stole?*

the stoop is crowded with our friends. they stare and giggle. they are kidnapped. cannot play ball or rope. fascinated children at a circus. he is their uncle and pied piper. willie breaks up to laugh. he bends over. slaps his knees. we feel his pockets with silent permission. he winks at mommie

> *now mae you know i dont steal. borrows well what*
> *you borrowed?*

we already know. cherries and penny-candies flow from his pockets. it is a stream. it cannot stop.

lord ha' mercy willie. they gon catch you one day on
that market.
look mae. this my family. my nieces an nefew.
hope yall dont make no faggot outta him. they know
uncle willie always gon bring them something they
know uncle willie dont steal. yall give some to your
lil friends.

we are bombarded from the ringside. fingers poke my face hungry.
odell wants more candy. he is searching. he discovers in a back
pocket. spanish neighbors snicker and point. in the window mommie laughs

willie! odell got your stuff!

odell is an imp running. his thin brown-body flies over the sidewalk. over cracks and cans. he cackles. escaping uncle willies chase

come back here boy! dont you fall and break my jug!
if you do ill break both your legs
come here boy!

odell stops to be caught. his miniature face a pearl shining sweat.
uncle willie blows a sigh of relief. he chuckles. glad to have the
pint of purple-wine back safe.

aint he something? dont know where you found that
one at mae. listen momma- im taking rose an lex on
the avenue. buy the kids some ice cream.
we be right back. rest of yall stay here.

we walk on 5th avenue with uncle willie. he stops every 2 feet.
dudes who ran with his brother in 45 and then. numbers runners.
fathers. enemies. remember when niggers wore clothes made in
italy and talked mafia. up and down lenox avenue. on 5th. num-

bers. getting over the war of. the good cocaine guineas brought up town the year before real dope came. jim-jam is dead. 8th avenue turned dope. tried to cheat georgie out some pay off money. found him in the elevator. no head. remember the lames busted. still in there. old playmates. couldnt get high no more off gin or jonnie walker red.

uncle willie pulls us from behind him. marshmallow fingers squeeze and held our shy hands. we sweat and are introduced celebrities.

> *richie in the joint man. yeah. got a pound jack.*
> *blew a nigger in 2 114 street. he dont play jack.*
> *my brother. these his kids. dont they look like him?*
> *mean an black just like they daddy.*
> *richie kids? didnt know that yeah look just like richie*
> *spit!*
> *nawww man*
> *sure they do*
> *here honey. yall buy yourself something*

coins roll out our hands to the sidewalk. silver dimes and quarters run curving in circles. fall on their faces in the gutter. uncle willie chases a nickel. under his boot its freedom is squashed.

we move from one stoop-crowd to another. down the line uncle willie waves. talks. here is black-father the watermelon man. and miss king. always dressed in black. summer or winter. old miss goldberg in the door of her laundromat. spit creeps from a corner of her mouth. she puffs a corn pipe. in front of her uncle willie stops. uncle willie feels her dead tits. leaves. he makes her hairy face turn pink for him. she dribbles as he walks away. she dreams on one day having him. right in the laundromat. on the ground me and rosie are hiding giggles.

uncle willie steps inside the ice cream place. on the big stools our sandaled feet dangle high off the floor. uncle willie reaches to kiss a big woman behind the counter.

*nigger where you been? dont put your greasy lips on
me. much as you smell.
you know you like it. stop actin so funny.
your nigger must be somewhere in here. listen flossy-
let me have 6 cones. yeah 6. these richie kids. whats
the damage on that? put it on my bill you aint got no
bill here
long as this your store momma- i got me a bill*

flossy looks at him. she smiles. her mouth pauses in a day like this
before. when uncle willie walked thru the door. young and polished. he teases her. he waits for closing time. waits to claim the
chocolate gold his night for love.

the sun melts our ice cream-on-credit. outside uncle willie hurries us to the block. we are 3 hurries. careful to hold the melting
vanilla drips over our fingers. against our clothes. the 2 scoops
disappear in to 1. we lick the sweet cream from our hands. as it
runs we turn the corner. back.

*ok mae   take care momma. im going over to see
grammie. everybody got ice cream. uncle willie dont
have nothing. dont get no kiss?*

odell is always first to him. i am always last. we walk back to the
corner. watch as he fades across the street in colors and noises up
the west side. uncle willie moves. hips like a swan. he stops to bum
a cigarette. he shares his purple magic and continues. the beginning
of our sunset.

and after that when he moved out the bowery grammie took
him back. we moved to the bronx. always saw him on saturdays
114 street. in front of 216. uncle willie sweats. looking for a womans packages to carry up. to collect his jug-money. tip his cap.
downstairs he waits. he spots me. grabs my hand. proud to own me.
his sho-nuff blood. rushed upstairs to see grammie. she pleads with
me not to stay long but to stay a virgin. she gives me my allow-

ance. she kisses me behind the door. i say goodbye and go. downstairs uncle willie is waiting.

> come on baby   ill walk you to the subway.
> momma give you your money? dont say nothing.
> shhh

we tip to 7th avenue. grammie rattles in the window. the veins of
her small throat strain and pop. she yells

> willie willie! dont you take that child money!
> dont worry about nothing momma!
> i aint gon take her money just walking to the train
> station. dont want none a these low niggers putting
> they hands on her thats all!

at the liquor store where grammie cannot see i give uncle willie his
50 cent allowance. and wait briefly outside as he turns my quarters
into purple-sweet juice. he is a magician. war counselor. he is my
main man. coming out grinning. he clutches my shoulder. in his
hand is love. we walk. for a quick taste he steps in a hallway. out of
respect for me. it was easy to peep. him his head bent backwards.
wine drops from his mouth. he jams his magic in a favorite pocket.
uncle willie flows back into the light. every saturday our sacred
routine. every year uncle willie and me.

til the week or summer richie came home. back to the pit. go
down make it rich. to snort more poison. to infest his begging
matter. hustle his mother. anybody. make a flunkie of his brothers
love. for him uncle willie runs the street. collects his old boys
together. spreads news richies out. boasting with pride when richie
got his eldorado. never let uncle willie sit in the front seat. grate-
fully taking the 5s and 10s richie shoved at him saying

> nigger you need to buy yourself some new clothes
> man raggidty as you is

pretty little black man, richie hill is a name. like 8th avenue. the powder he peddles. between niggers he shot and the .38 under his left arm pit. sharp fists that splattered a nigger jaw. richie is power over the dope-sick. a fox is a vulture. slick hair nigger back out the joint. black-berry face in skin the color of new coal around smooth lips like uncle willie.

friday is a carnival afternoon 114 street. a vacuum sucks the souls of its people in the nauseous heat. buildings squat together an infinite line of faces. and bodies chatter hanging from the windows. to feel the breezes that never come. women shout from one side of the narrow street to the other. mating calls. and stray husbands in search of the number or gossip. wasting time. pasted on stoops hordes of people. little ones. 1/2 naked tar-babies run from the spray and coldness of a fire hydrant. they are laughing. people fill every empty space here fleeing from the shit poor.

uncle willie prances up and down in front of 216. he grins and sweats. he is fresh and clean. his head is inflated. his eyes strut. in an unnatural fashion he is clean. in shoes of alligator green. italian knit sweater. silk green pants hang loose against his hips. not use to the rich feel of soft fiber. uncle willie is a dream in green. leather cap and green socks silk. the new pants have no back pocket to carry anything. uncle willie sees me. coconut eyes run to him.

hey uncle willie! hey man you looking too good!
when did you fall into this
yeah momma im moving up. now that richie out—
you working for him or something?
make me a cupla bills   you know.
nothing too tough. no more days niggers out here
gon run over me   who that lil monster
you was talking to on the corner.
who, duck?
baby i know you take care of yourself but if one of
these chumps out here mess around we straighten
him out. know none a them wanna run up on richie.

he wanna see you.
momma showed us your picture in the paper black as
you is. always knew you be the one lex. told mae and
momma. mae always fussing cause you in a book.
uncle willie was the first one to recognize you   so
they give you 8-grand for your college huh? where is it
cornell university. upstate next to the farms
what you gon take up momma
everything. psychology. i dont know
when you leaving?
tuesday night it all begins
uncle willie been waiting a long time to see this
baby. im prouda you. gon cut that picture out an put
it right in my new wallet. show all the niggers my
niece going to one the best colleges.
richard around?
yeah got a place 111 street. him an his man red.
told me to bring you over there soon as you came.
hes prouda you momma.

uncle willies new shoes clop a hollow sound. thru the tribes the
faces of poets and whores tangled together we move. up the block
to 8th avenue the air is a vise no one can escape. bloated junkies in
packs like wolves pace down and up. their nervous eyes glitter. at
6:00 the sun cooks the street. smells of chicken and watermelon mix
with us. 8th avenue spreads gangrehea. it is us. rhythms are gospel
from the dark cool bars. fingers pop. bop. in the heats beat. a
toothless woman stops. in the middle of the street. her hips move
like a snake charmed. she is voodoo. she is happy. while the cars
and buses scream. they are in a hurry. they do not understand. she is
free.

at the corner of 111 street we turn. up the long stairs of a $1/2$
condemned building we stop on the 6th floor. knock and puff at
the 2nd door. hear feet slowly answer the noise we make.

>*red! red! willie. open up. i got lexie.*
>*richie here?*

the doors eye opens and closes.

>*yeah   hes in the front. richie! wake up man!*
>*you got company*

down the empty-blue hallway hear glass knock against glass on the floor. a fan hums low. jazz whispers in the walls. it is hot like the street. smell wolves here. red walks behind us. he is skinny. his red bare chest a map of battle scars.

in the tiny front-room 2 chairs and a love seat are squeezed. a big coffee table you step over to get by is covered with coke bottles and cigarette ash.

>*hey richard. whats happn*

in a coarse voice the black-berry face speaks.

>*hi   stuff. scuse me for not having my clothes on.*
>*so hot in this room*

he has been sleeping.
he is asleep.

>*come here baby. let me see you. watch yourself!*
>*willie! get a broom. sweep this mess out the way!*
>*you want her to think we pigs? hey red aint she*
>*grown up stuff? baby red is my right arm.*

uncle willie is a maid. he sweeps the floor. he wipes the coffee table. he sweats in brown garbage bags. he is glad to help. i open a window. the telephone rings in another tiny room richie answers

yeah i got it sucka. just have your man there
when? right now?? no im waiting for sugar. sent him
crosstown. wont be back til 7. cant send red man.
need him here. what??
just lay cool. youll get it in 20 minutes.
ill send willie. yeah man   yeah.

the telephone is quiet. richie stands in the doorway. he looks at
uncle willie. he lights a cigarette.

red! get that thing together. nigger over there cant
wait. look at that lame! gave him 200 dollars. look
what the nigger do. probably bought a case of pluck
by now. willie. willie! pull yourself together man.
need you for something

red goes to the kitchen. his eyes are sealed in sweatcovers. he sleeps.
from the pink kitchen he returns. he shoves pork chops and frozen
hamburgers in a shopping bag.

here it is richie. maybe i should put it in 2 bags.
yeah, willie got enough sense to carry it—just be his
luck to break it. wake up man!
yeah jack yeah. i hear you. what you want me to do
go over to 108 street central park west. where we
stopped off yesterday? the orange stoop. 1st floor left
in the back-
the bald head chump   richie?
uhhuh. suckas name is randolph. the one-hand dude.
owe him a grand. he get it when im ready.
dont know who the lame think he dealing with.
tell him to meet me in joe-blo about 9.
shouldnt take you more than 15 minutes willie.
take it straight there.

red gives the fat shopping bag to uncle willie.

you kidding me   richie??
bulls out there gon think i took off some supermarket.
this randolph cat a butcher jack?
salready dripping blood on me.
take the thing an get back man!
here baby. put this in your pocket. 50 dollars
enough? make sure you come by an see me. take you
downtown monday night. we hang out together.
momma said you leaving tuesday. let me know if you
need some dust. make sure she get to the subway
willie. take care of yourself baby.

hustled out the door   blood comes after business. outside uncle
willie stoops to wipe pale-red juice from his shoes. down the street
we are conspicuous. on the sidewalk pork chops run away. the
shopping bag is too full. 50 dollars causes a fire in my skirt pocket.
hear the siren scream. red city-wagons surround me. pink faces in
gas masks and plastic coats drown me. laughing because i am a fire.
smoke puffs. sail away over roof tops. wonder where my 50 dollars
is. i pat my pocket for an answer.

uncle willie you dont have to walk me to the subway.
go ahead. to 108 street. that bag might break.
nawwwww momma. uncle willie can handle this.
must be something for your father to give away all
this meat. sure you can make it to the train?
tell mae you saw richie. wheres your money keep
your hands on it. chumps out here.
aww aint no body thinking about getting me uncle
willie. ill see you monday or tuesday
before i go.
alright momma get home safely

down 8th avenue uncle willie goes away. he leans to one side
walking. careful to dodge blood drops from the bag. he is a green
dream. he is gone.

i am out. back from the subways and downtown. saturday is 1/2 spent. the paper money in my pocket just change left over from the boxes and bags i carry up stairs. climb 3 flights to #9. the door kicks open. a trumpet is assaulted. trumped by a strange smell. the air is cold. coming out. hollow sound. dont go in. see gray. see mommie quiet. her eyes at me quiver in their sockets. a whisper drips

>*lexie? close the door an come here*
>*put those things there an sit down*

sit. do not move. the couch wants to speak. what i do now. it wasnt me ma. how come vickie is crying? brought home some change just like you told me. whats wrong with rosie? dont ask. choke. think. ithaca. hallucinate new life. grow up. think. in the ivy league wonderland. a cow grows milk from a tree. tuesday bus ticket #94376. fly brown butterfly. farms are cartoon in storybooks. sunsets are black.

>*mommie your eyes have turned in*
>*mommie where are your lips*
>
>*uncle willie died*

burst firecracker. burst. blop. blop. what? too much too many. blop. blop. what?? cows dont grow on trees. huh? speak slow. huh. leave uncle willie? dead. i am in ithaca. white lake in the pink sun. a sable moonface. you kidding me?? mommie i am going apart.

>*no   it isnt cold.*
>   *no more wine.*
>*this is september.*
>   *it aint cold.*

stand up. sit down. my belly is a fever humming. the world spins around.

play trumpet. say.
play. screech. screech. trumpet.
scream notes.

crack my head. mommie is a spiritual

allah, allah
damn!
allah
this is quicksand
stop
dont tell me
grammie called. not too long ago. say police found
him early this morning. on some roof 108 street. ice
box-cold. just his pants an wallet. laid up there. dont
know what he was doing. willie never bes over there.
didnt use that stuff.
willie was too afraid. somebody drew out his blood
seem like   an shot him full of poison.
gets in your blood
makes you fly
  black dot
  heart drops

thats ridiculous. i see uncle willie right now. saw him yesterday.
talk. shine. walk. in purple magic. long face i love you. head of
hair beads. eye of stars and rot-gut. medicine wine for his thick
smooth lips

lexie—

mommie he sweats—

no—

mommie i see him

they will lock you in a box
will they give me to the worms?
they will make you dust   in green

remember him   a outlaw.

ALEXIS DeVEAUX
Bibliography

In spite of a prolific career as fiction writer, poet, dramatist, and literary critic, Alexis DeVeaux's work has received little critical attention. One of the few critical texts besides *Midnight Birds* to include DeVeaux, Barbara Christian's *Black Feminist Criticism: Perspectives on Black Women Writers* (Elmsford, N.Y.: Pergamon Press, 1985) refers only tangentially to DeVeaux's remarkable achievements as a writer and to her place in the Afro-American women's tradition. Christian uses a quote from DeVeaux to open an essay on contemporary Afro-American women's fiction, and she refers several times to DeVeaux's excellent interview with Paule Marshall in *Essence;*[1] but even as she is recognized for her "budding creativity," DeVeaux is consigned to the margins of Christian's text, which otherwise treats contemporary fiction by black women writers so comprehensively. Christian says in the essay on contemporary fiction that her emphasis is on writers whose "exploration of new forms based on the black woman's culture and her story has . . . revitalized the American novel and opened up new avenues of expression, indelibly altering our sense of the novelistic process"

[1] Alexis DeVeaux, "Paule Marshall—In Celebration of Our Triumph," *Essence* 10:1 (May 1980), 70–71, 96, 98, 123, 124, 126, 131, 133, 135.

(p. 185). One wonders how DeVeaux could be excluded from that thesis when her experiments with language have consistently been so daring and original, and so deeply rooted in a black female vernacular. Even in an essay on lesbian themes in black writing, Christian's "No More Buried Lives,"[2] seemingly an obvious forum for discussion of DeVeaux's often explicitly lesbian fiction, De-Veaux is conspicuously absent, while the focus is on writers like Alice Walker who have achieved almost canonical status in black literary criticism.

---

[2] Barbara Christian, "No More Buried Lives: The Theme of Lesbianism in Audre Lord's *Zami*, Gloria Naylor's *The Women of Brewster Place*, Ntozake Shange's *Sassafras, Cypress, and Indigo*, and Alice Walker's *The Color Purple*," in *Black Feminist Criticism*.

FRENCHY HODGES

Born in Dublin, Georgia, in 1940, Frenchy Hodges lived nearly all her growing-up years in the rural South. She went to school in Georgia, including two years at Clark College, in Atlanta. She graduated from Fort Valley State College, in Fort Valley, Georgia. During her college years she spent summers in the North at domestic jobs that the college summer program provided. After two years of teaching English in Georgia, Hodges migrated North in 1966 to Detroit, where she taught English and creative writing in inner-city junior and senior high schools. In 1977 she returned South and is now teaching in Atlanta.

Knowing the various migrations of Frenchy Hodges is essential to understanding her poetry and fiction, because her unique sensibility is a hybrid: a black, southern, rural sensibility transplanted to the North. One of her most anthologized poems, *Belle Isle* (in *Black Wisdom,* Broadside Press, 1971) reveals that duality. Belle Isle, a park in Detroit that in the 1960s became a summer haven for the city's black and mostly poor population, is used to symbolize their ability to transcend the harsh urban reality. The park is transformed by the warmth, wit, and coping power of the folk who use it, and it becomes a surrogate for the front porch they left in the South.

Remembering what front porches meant to blacks in the South is part of Hodges' search for forgotten folk idioms. In another poem, entitled *Piece de Way Home,* from a book by the same title, Hodges recalls that that particular folk expression meant not only that you were grown up enough to go part of the way home with someone but it also announced your gaining a degree of independence from home. This remembrance of things past is not simply self-indulgent nostalgia. It is essential to her vision to re-establish connections with the values that nourish and strengthen her.

The failure of that vision is what assures the death of the young black man in Hodges' story "Requiem for Willie Lee." Because of the misuse of the earth and "good growing things," people like Willie Lee are not able to transcend their fate. Willie Lee is Bigger Thomas, Black Boy, Bobo, Big Boy—all the young blacks of this country whose very inheritance is to be repressed by physical and psychic violence. In "Requiem," Willie Lee is as threatening to the black middle-class schoolteacher as he once was to whites. The act of reconciliation between the schoolteacher and Willie Lee is a recurrent theme in black literature, from Ellison's *Invisible Man* to Paule Marshall's *Brown Girl, Brownstones.* Since all the Willie Lees of this society have been erased from history, it is the most profound act of recognition to see them. To see these invisible ones means confronting the terror of one's own invisibility. The schoolteacher-narrator knows Willie Lee but does not want to acknowledge him. She wants her vacation. She wants to be unmolested. In the story, she achieves sight when the fate of Willie Lee becomes more important than the luxury resort, rustic cabins, and sunning in leisure, when in fact she realizes that her fate and that of Willie Lee are one.

The schoolteacher's relationship with Willie Lee also signifies the relationship between the black writer, who is more and more often middle-class and poor black folks, who are so often the subject of black literature and so rarely the writers of it. "Requiem" may very well represent the dilemma black writers have experienced since the beginning of the black literary tradition: how to deal with the threatening presence of the folk.

Frenchy Hodges

Requiem for Willie Lee

I teach you know, and it was summer, one of the few times we get to be like children again. Summers we pack up and go somewhere that only rich folk year-round can afford. And if we can only afford a day and a night, we take what we can get and do not count the loss. For twenty-four hours we groove fine on the dollar we have to spend, and in my purse with the credit cards was exactly eighteen dollars: a ten, a five, and three ones.

El Habre is a rustic resort area halfway between Los An and Sanfran. Not a swanky place, but fronting two miles of the most beautiful oceanic view, the junglic-beach is splattered with endless numbers of summer-camp type cabins whitewashed and dingy gray measuring about nine by nine and most of them claiming five sleeping places. Crowded with beds, they can only be used for sleeping. Such is El Habre.

But El Habre has one thing more. El Habre has one of the most popular clubhouses in the world and people who have no intention of ever seeing the cabins—some never even knowing they exist—come to enjoy the fun, the food, and the fine show of stars. So, one lazy summer afternoon near the end of my vacation, Gaile (my hostess) and I and her little girl Donaile set out in my trusty old Mercedes for remote El Habre.

Now we, like many people, didn't know of the need for reservations and we experienced a foreboding of the wait to come when we saw the acres and acres of cars in the Temporary Guests' parking lot. We parked and were ushered by red-coated attendants through a multi-turnstile entrance to a waiting room as we cracked private jokes about the three of us and the only occasional dark faces in evidence among the sea of white. The waiting room was a comfortable no-nonsense place with white straight-backed chairs placed everywhere. There were perhaps a hundred people or more. Only three others were black, an older couple looking for all the world like contented grandparents, which in fact they were, as we learned from the restless little boy of about four who was with them. To my right were two hippie couples making jokes and telling stories about places they'd been and things they'd done. Most of the people were encouraging them to keep up this light show by laughing animatedly at every joke and story punch line. I was sorta enjoying them myself, exchanging "ain't-they-sick" glances with Gaile as we kept a wary eye on Donaile across the room playing with the little grandboy.

Somewhere in the middle of all this, the door burst open and in came Willie Lee, tall, lean, reed-slender, country-sun-and-rain-black, and out of place. In his right hand was a little girl's. With his left he closed the door. He then thrust this hand to some hidden place in the bosom of his black denim jacket and stood for a moment deliberately surveying the room. Though he had a pleasant mischievous schoolboy face, he seemed to be about twenty-two or three. Right away I knew him. Well, not *him,* but from some wellspring of intuition I knew into him and sensed some sinister intent enter that room in the winsome grin and bold arresting gaze that played around the room.

Silence played musical chairs around the group and the hippies were *it,* ending a story that was just begun. All eyes were on the man and the child at the door.

He swaggered Saturday-night-hip-style to a seat across the room from Gaile and me, sat, and the little girl leaned between his knees looking smug and in-the-know about something she knew and we did not. Willie Lee his name was, he said, but somewhere later I heard the child call him Bubba.

Oh, Willie Lee, where did you come from and why are you here where you don't belong with that do-rag on your head, and those well-worn used-to-be-bright-tan riding boots on your feet, and that faded blue sweat shirt and those well-worn familiar-looking faded dungarees? Willie Lee, why did you come here and I know it's a gun or a knife in your jacket where your left hand is and you ain't gonna spoil my last-of-summer holiday!

"What do you think?" *sotto voce,* I said to Gaile.

"Methinks the deprived has arrived," *sotto voce,* her reply.

From the time he entered, he took over.

"Don't let me stop nothing, gray boys," he said to the story-tellers. "We just come to have some fun. Yeah! Spread around the goodwill!" He threw back his head and laughed.

That was when I noticed fully the little girl. She was watching him, laughing to him like she knew what was to come and was deliciously waiting, watching him for the sign. She seemed to be about nine. He stuck out his hand and carefully looked at his watch.

"Yeah!" he said, stretching out his legs from some imaginary lounge chair. "Whatcha say, Miss Schoolteacher?" He laughed, looking boldly amused at me.

Years of teaching and I knew him. Smart, a sharp mind, very intelligent and perceptive but reached by so many forces before me, yet coming sometimes and wanting something others had not given, others who didn't know how, some not knowing he needed, grown in the street and weaned on corners, in alleys, and knowing only a wild creative energy seeking something all humans need. I knew him, looked in his eyes and perceived the soul lost and wandering inside.

"I say forget it, Willie Lee. That's what I say."

A momentary look of recognition crossed his face and when he realized what we both knew, he laughed a laugh of surprise that even here some remnant of his failed past jumped out to remind him of the child he'd been, yet appreciating too, I think, that here it was he in charge, not I.

Gaile had tensed as I spoke. "Come here a minute, Baby," she called to Donaile, but the child was already on her way to her mother, and quickly positioned herself between her legs. She stood facing this newly arrived pair and stared at them. The little girl, Willie's sister he said, made a face at the smaller child who then hid her face in her mother's lap. Still, I looked at Willie Lee. Then I looked away, regretting having acknowledged his person only to have that acknowledgement flung laughingly back in my face, and I resolved to have no more to say to him but to try and figure out what his plan was and how to escape it unharmed.

Again, he must have read my mind.

"Folks," he said, "my sister and I just come to have a little fun. She's had a little dry run of what to expect, and it's coming her birthday and I told her, 'Donna,' I say, 'I'ma let you have a little piece of the action up at El Habre.' She'll be seven next week, you know, and well, it's good to learn things while you young." He laughed again.

Then turned to a flushed-looking man sitting on his left.

"Hey, Pops, how's business on Wall Street?" That laugh again.

The poor man looked for help around the room and finding none in the carefully averted eyes, finally perceived Willie Lee waiting soberly for his answer.

"Nnnnn-not in the ssss-stockmarket," he said, to which Willie Lee guffawed.

I found myself looking intently at that laughing face, trying to figure out what to do and how to do it. I reviewed the entrance from the parking lot. We'd come through a turnstile such as large amusement parks have and we'd been ushered to this side room to wait for reservations. Now where were those uniformed ushers who'd directed us here? One had come and called out a party of five about forty minutes ago. I decided to give up my waiting position and be content to read about this fiasco in tomorrow's paper.

So deciding, I stood up resolutely, took Donaile's hand and

said to Gaile, "Let's go," and started for the door. The whole room stumbled from its trance to begin the same pilgrimage.

Coldly, "Stop where you are, *everybody!*" he said, arresting us, and we turned to look at him standing and calmly holding a gun.

Defeated, I dropped the child's hand and stood there watching the others return to their original seats.

You will not hurt me, Willie Lee. I stood still, looking at him.

"Slim, you and the sister can go if you want to," he said looking levelly at me. Dreamlike I saw a little lost boy sitting in my class, wanting something—love maybe—but too lost, misguided and misbegotten and too far along on a course impossible to change and too late if we but knew how.

"Thank you," I said, and Gaile and I went out the door, each of us holding one of Donaile's hands.

▲   ▲   ▲

Something was wrong at the turnstiles, and the sky had turned cloudy and dark. Instead of the neatly dressed ushers we'd seen coming in, there were two do-rags-under-dingy-brim-hatted fellows wearing old blue denims and black denim jackets calmly smoking in the graying day.

When they saw us, I felt the quick tension as cigarettes were halted in midair.

"Where y'all going, Sistuhs?" the short pudgy one said.

"We got tired of waitin' and *he* said we could go," I answered, standing still and looking at them intently.

They looked at each other a moment.

Then, "I think y'all better wait a while longer," the tall droopy-eyed one said.

Some sixth sense told me we'd be safer inside, and then I saw the bulge of the gun at the pudgy one's side sticking from the waist of his pants.

"You're probably right," I said, and with studied casualness, we turned and went back to the room we'd just left.

Things had started to happen inside. Willie Lee was bran-
dishing the little black and sinister gun as he methodically went to
each person collecting any valuables people were wearing and
money from pockets and bags.

"Get your money out, Slim," he said to me as we came back
inside.

Distinctly, I remember returning to my seat, locating my bill-
fold, extracting eight dollars—the five and three ones, thinking I'd
not give any more than I *had* to and holding the three ones in my
hand and stashing the five in my skirt pocket.

He was snatching watches from wrists and rings from fingers
and making people empty their pockets and purses to him and
putting these things in a dingy little laundry bag with a drawstring.
People seemed dazed in their cooperation while the little girl,
Donna, carted booty from all over the room in wild and joyful
glee. The room was hot and deathly quiet. Then her hand was in
my skirt pocket and she was gone to him and his bag with my
three singles and the five.

Gaile was just sitting there and Donaile was leaning quietly
between her legs. And I was thinking. Where is everybody? What
have they done to them? We'd heard nothing before *he* came. Then
I heard something. I heard the sirens and my mouth dropped open.
Oh, no! Don't come now. I sat wishing they had not come just
then with Willie's job unfinished and the child in the throes of her
wild pre-birthday glee!

Then he was standing in front of me.

"I'm sorry, Slim, but you see how it is!" he said with amused
resolution.

He grabbed the not-on-Wall-Street man, pushed him roughly
toward the door.

"Okay, everybody out," he said.

Things got confusing then. Outside we vaguely heard shouts
and what I guess was gunfire, and not the holiday fireworks it
sounded like. We all went rushing to the door. The door got
jammed, then was not. More shots were heard and screams and
cries. Outside, amid rushing legs, a turnstile smoker lay groaning

and bleeding on the ground. The child Donna ran screaming to where he groaned and lay. Holding tight to Donaile's hand, Gaile and I ran toward the turnstile amid wild and crowded confusion. Then someone was holding me.

"Let me go!"

"Bitch, come with me!" a mean voice said. "You too, Bitch, and bring the kid!" This to Gaile.

We were shoved and pushed into the rear seat of a Scaporelli's Flower Delivery station wagon. Crowded next to us were the two hippie girls clinging to each other and crying. The back doors were slammed, and Willie Lee hustled the pleading Wall Street man in the front seat, jumping in behind him. And Droopy-Eye of the turnstile jumped in the driver's seat, and started the car. Donaile was crying and clinging to Gaile. The course we took was bizarre and rash because people were running everywhere. And still more people were running from the gilded entrance of the El Habre Clubhouse to scatter confusedly along the course we sped. Too many people scattered along this fenced-in service drive where running people and a racing car should never be. He tried to dodge them at first, blowing his horn, but they would not hear and heed, so soon he was knocking them down, murdering his way toward a desperate freedom. The blond hippie girl began to heave and throw up on her friend. I closed my eyes begging the nightmare end. And then I smelled the flowers. Looking back, I saw them silently sitting there.

I looked at the back of Willie Lee's head, where he, hunched forward, gun in hand, tensely peered ahead.

"Willie Lee, it just won't work." I kept my eyes on the back of his head.

"Shut up, Bitch," Droopy-Eye said.

Willie Lee looked back to me.

"Man, that's Miss Schoolteacher. She knows *everything*," he exaggerated. "Slim, it'll work 'cause *you* part of our exit ticket now, since Ol' Sam here brought y'all in."

"Willie Lee, give it up," I said.

"Man, let's dump the dizzy bitch! I was just grabbing anybody," he excused himself. Then as an afterthought, "I never did like schoolteachers no way."

Then up ahead they saw the gate.

"Hey, Sam, crash that gate. No time to stop," Willie said, peering behind.

"Man, ain't no cops gonna run down no people. You got time to open that gate!" This from a man who'd run people down.

Willie Lee peered again through the flowers at the road behind.

"Willie Lee, the road will end when you reach the gate. It's a dirt road then where you have to go slow, unless," I added, "you're ready to die and meet your maker."

"Damn, this bitch think she know everything!" Droopy-Eye said while Willie Lee just looked at me.

Donaile was crying still. Gaile was too. Wall Street was now quietly sitting there, just sitting and staring straight ahead. The hippie girls were crying.

I turned around and looked behind. The running people had receded in the distance, framed in stage-like perspective by the big El Habre Clubhouse where we'd been going to enjoy an afternoon show. And tomorrow my vacation would end, if my life didn't end today.

Droopy-Eye stopped the car and Willie Lee got out and opened the gate. Now began dust and sand as the station wagon plowed too fast down the gravelly, dusty road. Down before us, we could see the ocean's white-capped waves. And between us and the ocean was the circular courtyard flanked by four or five small buildings and one other building larger than the rest.

"The road will end at those buildings," I said. "What you gonna do then, Willie Lee?"

"I'ma chunk yo' ass in the ocean, Bitch, if you don't shut up."

I kept looking levelly at Willie Lee. He kept hunched forward looking down the slowly ending road. We reached the courtyard entrance, a latticed, ivy-covered archway, and Droopy drove the station wagon through.

"Oh, shit, the road *do* end!" Droopy moaned as he stopped the car.

When the motor was cut, we heard the ocean's waves, and back in the distance, the people running and screaming behind. Why are they coming this way, I wondered, remembering the time we kids ran home to our burning house. They must be cabin dwellers, I thought.

"What now, Willie Lee?" I said.

Willie and Droopy jumped out of the car.

"Okay, everybody out!" Willie directed.

When Wall Street, the last, had finally climbed out, Willie shouted, "Okay, Slim, y'all take off. Sam, you take Wall Street, and the two girls come with me." And they began to hustle the three toward the bigger building with the cafeteria sign.

Thank you, Willie Lee, for letting me free. Gaile and Donaile ran toward the woods where the cabins were and where beyond was the busy sea. As I ran behind them, I looked back to see Sam and Willie crashing in the cafeteria door, dragging and pushing the man and the girls inside, just as a Wonder Bread truck began to enter the courtyard from behind it. It was filled with guns-ready police. I screamed to Gaile to wait for me.

▲   ▲   ▲

When we'd reached the bottom of the hill, we heard shouting and gunfire. We ran on cutting right to a service path that led through the green woods lush with undergrowth. About every fifty feet on either side of the path were the cabins, whitewashed, dank and gray. Running and running, stopping some to breathe and rest and to try and soothe the terrified child. *You shouldn't have come here, Willie Lee, bringing your sister to see you fail.* Soon we heard others coming, loud and excited in the tragedy of this day.

Why couldn't you stop, Willie Lee, when it started going wrong and kept on going that way? You're not a fool, because I know you from each year you've been in my classes, and when I've tried to teach you, reach you, touch you, love you, you've snarled "Take your hands off me" and I've kept myself to myself and tried my best to forget every one of you and this afternoon at El Habre was part of my plan to get as far away from you as I can and here you are set on tearing up my turf. Will I never get away from you?

Once while I stopped resting, some people passed.

"They killed the one with the droopy-eyes," they said, "but the other was only wounded and got away."

"He's coming this way, they say."

Then another: "I got my gun in the cabin. When I git it, I'ma help hunt'im and I hope I get to blow'im away."

"They say he's looking for his girlfriend, a teacher or some-body that got away."

Willie Lee, why are you looking for me? Why don't you give yourself up and die? Will I never get away from you?

"Gaile, I've got to go find him," I said. "You take Donaile and try to get away."

I didn't stay for her protest but started walking resolutely back over the path we'd come. The day was dark and the woods were dark and the clouds were dark in the sky. I met and passed people who looked curiously at me. He is looking for me, I thought, and maybe they wondered, thought they knew. I had visions of him knocking people down, shooting anyone trying to stop him, keep him from having his way. Still, why *was* he looking for me? And then I knew. For the same reason I was now looking for him. He was my student who'd failed and I was the teacher who'd failed him. Not for hostage, not for harm, but to die! To die near me who knew him. Well, not *him,* but knew into him just the same. He, who's going to die. Is dying. And now he knows. And I'm the only person who knows him and can love the little boy hurting inside.

His jacket was gone and so was his do-rag and blood was caked in his straightened unkempt hair. His eyes unseeing, he peered ahead and stumbled dying past me.

"Willie Lee," I called his name.

He stopped and in slow motion, semi-crouched, gun half-raised, he turned, peering at me through time. In the green-gray light, I opened wide my arms and silently bade him come. He dropped his gun and came paining into my arms.

It was another world then. People continued to run by bumping us as they did. Glancing about, I saw a cabin nearby.

"Let's go in here," I said.

"Yeah, this what I want," he said. "Someplace to stop."

I looked inside and saw the cabin was bare except for the beds. I climbed through the door and helped him in, leading him to the one double bed. Two singles above and one single below on the side.

"What is this place?" he asked in wonder as our eyes grew accustomed to the darker inside. Drab even in this darkened day.

"This is one of the resort cabins," I said. "Part of El Habre too."

"What do they *do* here?" he asked.

"Sun and swim and sleep," I said. "Hear the ocean on the beach below?"

"And for this, shit, people *pay?*" He gestured around the room in unbelieving wonder.

"Yes," I said, "for this, *Shit,*" I looked to him and was held by his waiting eyes, "people pay. For the sun and the earth and the good growing things and the moon, and the dawn and the dew, people take their hard-earned bread and come here and stay and pay. *They pay!*"

Until then, I had been calm. *Steady, Teach, or you'll lose again.* I softer added, *"We* pay. We all pay."

He was quiet then and dropped his head. He looked at his hands and then at his feet. Then he looked at me.

Soberly, "Well, I spoiled it for them today, didn't I? I spoiled it today real bad," he chuckled, "didn't I?" Then he threw back his head and laughed and laughed.

And I threw back my head and just laughed and laughed hugging him.

"Yes, you did!" I said. "Yes, you really did!"

Perhaps our laughter called the people. And there they were

outside the cabin windows peering and laughing in. I went to the windows then and gently pulled the shades and as best I could, I comforted the dying man, making a requiem for him, for myself, and for all the world's people who only know life through death.

SHERLEY ANNE WILLIAMS

I think that what started me on the road to being a writer was searching for books about black people in the library of Edison Jr./Sr. High School in Fresno, California, in the '50's and being too embarrassed, too shamed to ask for help from the librarian. I don't remember precisely how old I was—I entered Edison as a twelve-year-old seventh-grader and graduated five years later in 1962 and much of that time is a blur—maybe thirteen, fourteen, or fifteen. I do know I was having a lot of trouble—with my mother, the one sister who remained at home, my friends, myself. I felt abandoned by my two older sisters, who had married and seldom returned for visits, out of touch with my teachers, even those who befriended me. What did they know about being black, being on welfare, being solicited for sex by older black men in the neighborhood and the old white ones who cruised our streets on the weekends? And though I know now that need must have been written all over me, I would have died before exposing my family life or my longing to them.

Much as I loved Louisa May Alcott and Frank Yerby, they no longer transported me as they once had done. So, on infrequent class trips to the library (I never went unless forced to by class requirements, for I was set off enough from my classmates by my grades and my middle-class aspirations in my obviously underclass body), I roamed the room, surreptitiously studying the shelves, hoping to spot a title that would identify the books as

Black. I read Black Boy, *an obvious title, but worse than useless for me: it wasn't just that I didn't have to cope with that kind of overt racism in Fresno, California, the heart of the farm-rich San Joaquin Valley. I could identify only in part with Wright's conflicts with his family. I would have given a lot for just such signs of caring as his family's attempts to force him even into the Tom role. Rather than prizing my differences, I despised them and sought during this time to conform, only to discover that even my attempts at conformity set me apart.*

I was led, almost inevitably, I think, to the autobiographies of women entertainers—Eartha Kitt, Katherine Dunham, Ethel Waters. The material circumstances of their childhood were so much worse than mine; they too had had to cope with early and forced sex and sexuality, with mothers who could not express love in the terms that they desperately needed. Yet they had risen above this, turned their difference into something that was respected in the world beyond their homes. I, in the free North, could do no less than endure.

And I did, helped immensely, immeasurably by my sister, Ruby, who returned home after the break-up of her marriage; she was eighteen, her daughter almost three. It is almost twenty years since this happened, yet I have never ceased to admire her and be amazed at the change "Ruise" wrought in my life. She worked as a maid/cook for a white family five days a week (and got twenty-five dollars, an amount that was later doubled when she moved to a new job with a new family), attended night school four nights a week to earn the high school diploma that pregnancy and marriage had forced her to abandon, partied at least two nights a week, took care of her daughter and counseled and guided me through the shoals of adolescence that had almost wrecked her own life. She paid for this schedule with ill-health which eventually forced her to quit work and go on welfare—but not before she had that high school diploma.

After my mother's death—I was then sixteen going on seventeen—I was placed in Ruise's custody and the money she received for my care— plus what we got from occasional field work—picking cotton, cutting grapes, holiday work as a stock clerk in a downtown store, the prize money from a story accepted by Scholastic Magazine—*meant that we survived my last year in high school near the subsistence level. Ruise and her friends, young women much like herself, provided me with a commu-*

nity, with models, both real-life and literary. I was by that last year in high school more sophisticated in searching out black literature. But nowhere did I find stories of these heroic young women who despite all they had to do and endure laughed and loved, hoped and encouraged, supported each other with gifts of food and money and fought the country that was quite literally, we were convinced, trying to kill us. My first published story, "Tell Martha Not to Moan" (Mass. Review, 1967?, anthologized in The Black Woman *and elsewhere), had its genesis in those years. Martha and her life are a composite of the women who made up that circle. Their courage and humor helped each other and me thru some very difficult years.*

The years between then and now are not easily capsulized. Those women pushed me out into a world where I could no longer use their lives as guidelines. And much of that time has been spent in wandering from coast to coast, Nashville, Fresno, San Francisco, D.C., Birmingham, back to Fresno, L.A., back to Fresno, Providence, R.I., Fresno, and finally San Diego. I have moved Ruise to San Diego and plan to go back to collect Learn; my oldest sister is dead. The Peacock Poems *(1975, Wesleyan University Press) contains something of that early, early life when my father and mother were alive and we followed the crops; "Someone Sweet Angel Chile," the unpublished and unfinished second collection of poems, will contain more because I think that our migrations are an archetype of those of the dispossessed and I want somehow to tell the story of how the dispossessed become possessed of their own history without losing sight, without forgetting the meaning or the nature of their journey.*

I am not a very political person in the sense of joining organizations or espousing political philosophies—my disenchantment with the exponents of Black Power began in 1967 while a graduate student at Howard University when a friend and Black Power advocate disparaged my writing because I wasn't writing Richard Wright. I remain, more firmly now than then, a proponent of Black consciousness, of the "The Black Aesthetic," and so I am a political writer. I try to elucidate those elements in our lives on which constructive political changes, those that do more than blackwash or femalize the same old power structure, can be built.

Graduate school was necessary for my current livelihood—college teacher of Afro-American literature—though even there I drew the line finally at certain kinds of disciplines as extraneous to my real pursuit, which I have accepted as writing. I might have survived in the academic world with more ease had I a Ph.D., but my decision not to continue in the doctoral program at Brown was based on the understanding that I didn't want to spend the rest of my life poring over other people's work and trying to explain the world thru their eyes. Rather, what I gain from books and it is often a great deal—no book affected my life so much as reading Langston Hughes' Montage on a Dream Deferred, *for here was my life and my language coming at me—must be melded with, refracted through my experiences and what I know of my contemporaries, my ancestors, my hopes for my descendants (and the "my" is used in the collective sense, implying* we, *implying* our).

I was a "man" in Give Birth to Brightness *(Dial Press, 1972), and a sexual voice in "The Blues Roots of Contemporary Afro-American Poetry" (*Mass. Review, *1977), both critical works—and each of those disguises has helped me to come into my own voice, clarified my own vision. I am the women I speak of in my stories, my poems. The fact that I am a single mother sometimes makes it hard to bring this forth to embody it in the world, but it is precisely because I am the single mother of an only son that I try so hard to do this. Women must leave a record for their men; otherwise how will they know us?*

—Sherley Anne Williams

I have always read "Meditations on History" as a story with deliberate political intent. Indeed, the opening quotation from Angela Davis's essay on slave women and Sherley Anne Williams's own preface point to the strong ideological focus of Williams's work. It is clearly her intention in "Meditations" to tell the story of the black struggle against slavery, though unlike most of the stories written by men, Williams's tale allows constructive roles in that struggle for both women and men. What Williams sets up here is not conflict between black men and women but between the voice of the white writer and the voice of the black female slave Odessa. The white writer begins as the controller of Odessa's story, intending to exact information which will aid slaveholders to maintain their illusions of power and superiority. Modeled after nineteenth-century pro-slavery tracts, the white writer's journal functions to control the image and dominate the voice of the slave. Assuming the inferiority of the slave, the writer refuses to acknowledge Odessa's intelligence or his own limited understanding, though her powerful presence provokes considerable unease in him: "I must constantly remind myself that she is but a darky and a female at that."

That Williams intends to represent the black female voice as more powerful than the white male one is made clear as soon as Odessa's voice erupts in the story. Odessa constructs a narrative totally disconnected from the writer's questions, one that reflects the creativity and strength of the black community. When the writer questions Odessa, she answers by re-creating her life together with Kaine—a love story of two people who would have been merely economic and political statistics in the nineteenth-century racist imagination. While the writer seeks to elicit information to destroy the rebellion of Odessa and her companions, Odessa insists on telling the stories that are life-affirming for the black slave community: Kaine's love for his "banger"; their resistance to oppression; the child they have created together. Ultimately Odessa controls this tale by revising its ending. Instead of being executed, she joins a maroon settlement with other runaway slaves. Instead of providing the white slave owners with further means to assert white power, she creates an ending whose implications so thoroughly undermine his view of the world that he cannot comprehend its meaning: "She is gone . . . Gone and I not even aware, not even suspecting, just, just—gone."

In juxtaposing Odessa's voice against that of the white writer, Williams is doing more than commenting on nineteenth-century narrative practices. She is also representing the relationship of the black female speaker to a white (male) literary world and challenging the racist and sexist practices of white history and white literature. These intentions are made clear from the beginning of "Meditations," when Williams quite deliberately names all of the more than thirty black people in the story. No matter how minor his or her role, no one is simply or anonymously "a slave." This naming is effective on several levels: It creates a sense of the black community as a group of individuals, demanding that we the reader, who are so used to the literary practices which diminish the humanity of black people, also recognize the individuality of each character. The names evoke black traditions, specifically those nineteenth-century naming rituals by which people were given names from the family Bible, from African memory, or as a reflection of personal status in the community.

The black female voice is represented as essentially oral. Odessa speaks her story aloud to the white writer, who intends to write it down and control her by the power of the written word as people whose culture is transmitted orally have always been dominated by the writer's word. Because of her commitment to writing about the dispossessed (and very few writers have Williams's ability to convey the dignity and strength of poor and working-class people), Williams constantly focuses on the power of the oral word. Odessa speaks in a vernacular that is defiant and resisting, one that the white writer only minimally comprehends. When he tries to get her to betray the others in the insurrection, she answers with double-edged meaning in a clear black idiom: "Onlest mind I be knowin' is mines." In all of her work Williams has represented black dialect as having an integrity and power that standard English does not provide. Those characters whose speech is oral, who remain the guardians of "the speech of walk and shout," who have not been "ruined by this white man's schooling," are always the heroic centers of Williams's narratives. Unlike those early black writers who repress the sounds of black dialect in order to create characters they believed would be more acceptable to their readers and who connected dialect to inferiority and ignorance, Williams uses the dialect to signify a character's inner autonomy and ability to remain connected to sustaining black traditions and to resist white control. In this effort she is not too different from Ralph Ellison, whose folk characters have the warmth, wit, and coping power which allow them to survive intact in a hostile white world.

There is, however, one difference between Ellison and Williams—while Ellison's folk characters are minor figures, Williams treats the dispossessed not as "folk" or minor figures but as central actors in the history of their lives.

Sherley Anne Williams

Meditations on History

*The myth [of the black matriarchy and the castrating black female]
must be consciously repudiated as myth and the black woman in her
true historical contours must be resurrected. We, the black women of
today, must accept the full weight of a legacy wrought in blood by our
mothers in chains . . . as heirs to a tradition of supreme persever-
ance and heroic resistance, we must hasten to take our place wherever
our people are forging on towards freedom.*

> from "Reflections on the Black
> Woman's Role in the Community
> of Slaves" by Angela Davis, to
> whom this story is respectfully,
> affectionately dedicated.

"Sho was hot out there today."

"Yeah, look like it fixin to be a hot, hot summer."

"Hope it don't git too hot."

"Naw, dry up the crop, it do."

The desultory conversation eddied around her but she took no
part in it. The day's heat still hung in the air even though the sun
was only a few minutes from setting. The sweaty dust that clung to
her skin was reminder—and omen—enough of how hot it could

get in the fields. It was enough to feel it; she didn't have to talk about it, too. Even the ones talking, Petey and Brady and them, didn't seem very interested in what they were saying. She smiled. Talkin bout "the weather" and "the crop"—knowin they jes puttin on fo Ta'va.

"I see ol crazy Monroe been ova Mas Jeff'son place agin."

She listened more carefully now. Monroe had been trying for the longest time to get Master's permission to be with some girl over at the Jefferson plantation. But Young Mistress had said all the girl was good for was housework and they didn't need another wench up to the House. And that should have been that, but Monroe kept sneaking over to see her every chance he got—which was no more than saying he made chances. As much as Boss Smith worked people in the fields, there was no way any of them were just going to *find* a chance to wander off and go "visiting." All this was common knowledge among them, though none of them ever said anything about when Monroe left or when Monroe returned unless Boss Smith learned on his own that Monroe had gone visiting before the visit was over.

"What *did* they do him?" she asked when it seemed that no one would answer—had it been Brud who asked the first time? No matter; she knew they didn't want to talk about Monroe in front of Tarver. But talk couldn't hurt Monroe now and Harriet—that had been her talking—shouldn't have brought it up if she didn't want to continue with it. It was too hot to start thinking about something and then have to stop just because Harriet didn't know the difference between "talkin" and "talkin smart." "What they do him?" she asked again.

"Mas jes chain him out to one-a the barns; say he gon sell him," Santee, who walked a couple of feet ahead of her, said over his shoulder.

"Lawd, why won't these chi'ren learn."

Sara was always making as if she were so old, so experienced in dealing with the world. She started to reply but someone else spoke.

"Can't learn a nigga nothin."

The laugh Petey's quick answer brought took away most of the evil Sara's statement and Harriet's reluctance to answer had made her feel.

"Well," Brady said, breaking in on their laughter. "I sho wished I knowed what that lil gal—what her name is?"

"Thank it Alberta," someone supplied.

"Yeah, that's it."

"Well, whatever it is, I sho wished I knowed what she got to make a nigga walk fifteen miles a night and jes be *da'in* a beatin when he get back."

"Don't know," Santee said loudly, "but it sho *gots* to be gooood."

"This one nigga won't never find out." Charlie was laughing with the others even as he said it.

"Now you talkin some sense." She hated it when Tarver broke in on their conversations. Since Boss Smith had made him driver, he thought he knew everything and was better than everybody else. She waited, her lips poked out, knowing whatever he said would make her angry. "Much give-away stuff as it is around here, ain't no way in the world I'd chance what Boss Smith put behind them licks jes to get some mo somewhere else."

Only way *you* get any, at all, is cause if a woman don't, you see Boss Smith or Mas hear bout it. But she didn't say it. Tarver wouldn't even have to run to Boss Smith or Master with that. He'd just slap her in the mouth and no one there would go against the skinny driver. That would mean that two—or however many more helped her—would get whipped instead of just one. But she couldn't resist cutting her eyes knowingly at the women who walked on either side of her. Polly looked as though she wasn't listening but Martha's lips were pushed forward in a taut line that flattened their fullness. Martha was the only lone woman Tarver never passed sly remarks with, and that was saying something. Since he had been made driver, Tarver wasn't even above trying to pat on women who already had men. But Tarver hadn't so much as looked at Martha for some time, now, and if he did say something to her it was only an order about what work she should do.

Martha put her hand on her hip, pulling the shapeless over-blouse she wore tight against her heavy breasts, emphasizing the smallness of her waist, and she swung her hips in an exaggerated arc. Even dirty and with that old sweaty head rag on her hand, she looked good. "Yeah, I give it away—to some; othas got to take it."

There was a choked kind of laughter from the men and the other women hid their smiles behind their hands. Go on, girl, she thought and then, looking over at Tarver, she saw the muscle along his neck jump.

"Too bad you ain't gived Monroe none; if it all that good he might woulda stayed home," she laughed as she said it and pushed Martha lightly on the shoulder.

"Naw, Monroe was one that'd had to take it," Martha said with a sigh that caused even more laughter.

And she relaxed. Tarver was laughing, too.

"I jes meant, I don't want to *love* . . ." She liked to watch the older man shake his head like that when he talked; no matter what he said after he did his head like that, it was bound to be funny. "No, I'm a nigga," and again the shake of his head, "what can't *love* where he don't *live*."

"Listen to Charlie talk!"

She didn't join in their laughter this time. Someone was coming down the quarters. It was him. She knew that even before he raised his hand or opened his mouth—who else could still move like that at the end of the day, like he'd just started out fresh not two minutes ago; even without the banjo banging against his back, she would have known him—and she quickened her steps.

"Somebody sho is walkin fas all a sudden."

She heard the voice behind her as she pushed past the people in front of her but she paid no attention; already, and almost of their own will, her lips were stretched wide in a grin. She could see him clearly now though he was still some distance away, see the big head of nappy hair and the pants hiked up around his waist so that his dusty ankles showed. She stayed in front of the others, but now used the hoe like a cane, swinging it high in pretended nonchalance.

Hey, hey, sweet mamma

His voice, high and sweet and clear as running water in a settled stream, always made her feel so good, so like dancing just for the joy of moving and all the moving would be straight to him.

Say, hey now, hey now, sweet mamma
Don't you hear me callin you?

"Seem like they been wid each otha long nough now fo them to stop all that foolishness."

Huh; you jes mad cause you ain't got nobody to be foolish wid. But she didn't say it aloud. That had been Jean Wee's voice and Jean Wee's man, Tucker, had been sold to Charleston not three months ago. She simply quickened her steps.

Hey, hey, sweet mamma, this Kaine Poppa

His arms were outstretched and though she couldn't hear them, she knew his fingers were snapping to the same rhythm that moved his body.

Kaine Poppa calling his woman's name

Behind her, they were laughing. Kaine could always give you something to laugh about. He made jokes on the banjo, came out with a song made up of old sayings and words that had just popped into his head a second before he opened his mouth, traded words with the men or teased her and the other women. But she never more than half heard the laughter he created. By then she'd thrown the hoe aside and was running, running . . .

He caught her and lifted her off the ground and the banjo banged against her hands as she threw her arms around him. "What you doin down here so early?" She was scared. After that first spurt of joy seeing him always brought, she would get frightened. Lawd, if Boss Smith saw him— And that no-good Ta'va was still behind them— Why he want *do* crazy thangs like this.

"They thank I'm still up there at that ol piece-a greenhouse tryin to make strawberries grow all year round." This was said into her neck and as they turned to walk on. Then he laughed aloud. "Why I jes got hungry fo my woman," he said with a glance back over his shoulder.

There was appreciative laughter from behind, but neither the laughter nor his words eased her fear. There must have been something for him to do back at the Big House. Either Childer could have found him a closet to turn out, some piece of furniture to move so the girls could clean behind it, or Aunt Lefonia might have had some spoons or some such to polish in the kitchen. And she knew Emmalina would have wanted him to help serve supper if there was nothing else he had to do. Master was always complaining about how they couldn't afford to have a nigger sitting around eating his head off while he waited for some flowers to grow. But Young Mistress would cry and say how the gardens at the House had always been the showplace of the county. Then, so Aunt Lefonia said—and Aunt Lefonia always knew—Old Mistress would get a pinched look around her mouth and her nose would turn up like she'd just smelled the assfidity bag Merry-Day wore around her neck when she had a cold in her chest, and start talking about how Master was forever trying to drag the Reeves down in the mud where he and the rest of the Vaunghams had come from. And Master would really get mad then and say the Reeves had finally arrived at their true place in life and since it was his money that kept the House a showplace, that nigger, meaning Kaine, better turn his hand to whatever needed doing. That would be the end of it until the next time Master got peeved about something and he would start again. Kaine wouldn't tell her about it, but Aunt Lefonia and Emmalina did and she was afraid that someday Master wouldn't care about Young Mistress' tears or Old Mistress throwing his family up in his face and would sell Kaine to Charleston or the next coffle that passed their way.

"You jes askin fo trouble, comin down here like this."

"Baby, I'm all *ready* in trouble."

The quarters were filling up now, people coming in from other parts of the plantation, the children who were too small to work coming back from Mamma Hattie's cabin where she kept an eye on them during the day. A few fires had already been lighted and she could smell frying fat-back and wood smoke. Her breath caught at his words.

"What you mean?"

"Mean a nigga ain't born to nothin *but* trouble." Lee Tower, who headed the gang that worked the rice fields, stopped as he spoke, "and if a nigga don't *cou't* pleasure, he ain't likely to git none."

He was the best driver on the plantation, getting work out of his people with as much kindness as he could show, not with the whip like Luke, who headed the gang that Master hired out to cut timber, or Tarver who drove the group she worked with. But she couldn't return Lee Tower's smile or laugh when Carrie Mae, who had come up behind him carrying her baby on her hip, said, "Naw, Mas done sent his butt down here to git it *out* o' trouble; takin care that breedin bidness he been let slide."

"Now yo'all know I be tryin." Kaine was laughing too. "But I got somethin here guaran*teed* to ease a troublin mind." And he patted her shoulder and pinched her lightly in her ribs.

Lee Tower and Carrie Mae laughed and passed on.

"Kaine—"

"Lefonia gived me—"

"Afta how much talkin?"

"Didn't take much."

The laugh was choked out of her; she had looked into his eyes. They were alive, gleaming with dancing lights (no matter what mamma-nem said; his eyes did sparkle) that danced only for her. And when they danced, she would love him so much that she had to touch him or smile. She smiled and he grinned down at her. "Don't neva take much—you got the right word, and you know when it come to eatin beef, I *steal* the right word if it ain't hidin somewhere round my own self tongue," he said as he pulled her in their doorway. She laughed despite herself; he could talk and wheedle just about anything he wanted. "And I pulled some new greens from out the patch and seasoned em wid jes a touch o' fatback."

"A touch was all we had. Kaine, what—"

"Hmmmm mmmmm. But that ain't all I wants a touch of," he said holding her closer and pulling the dirty, sweaty rag from her head. "Touch ain't neva jes satisfied me."

She laughed and relaxed against him. They were inside, the rickety door shut against the gathering dusk. "Us greens gon get cold."

"But us ain't." He stood with one leg pressed lightly between her thighs, his lips nibbling the curve of her neck.

"I got to clean up a little." She said it more to tease, to prolong this little moment, than because she really felt the need to wash. Sometimes he got mad—not because she was dirty, but because the dirt reminded him that she worked the fields all day. She couldn't say why his being angry about this pleased her so, but it did. Or, sometimes, he would start a small tussle: she trying to get to the washbasin, he holding her back, saying she wasn't that dirty and even dirty she was better than most men got when their women were clean. And that response pleased her, too. She liked the little popping sound "men" made as it came from his mouth.

He ran the tip of his tongue down the side of her neck. "Ain no wine they got up to the House good as this." His fingers caught in her short kinky hair, his palms rested gently on her high cheekbones. "Ain't no way I'm eva gon let you get away from me, girl. Where else I gon find eyes like this?" He kissed her closed lids, his hands sliding down her neck to her shoulders and back, his fingers kneading the flesh under her tow sack dress, and she wanted him to touch all of her, trembled as she thought of his lips on her breasts, his hands on her stomach, or his legs between her own. "Mmmmmm mmmm." He pulled up her dress and his hands were inside her long drawers. "I sho like this be-hind." His hands cupped her buttocks. "Tell me all this goodness ain't mine," he dared her. "Whoa! and when it git to movin," and he moved, "and I git to movin and we git to movin— Lawd, I knowed it was gon be sweet but not this doggone *good!*"

This was love talk that made her feel almost as beautiful as the way he touched her. She shivered and pulled at the coarse material of his shirt, not needing the anger or the other words, now, because his hands and mouth made her feel so loved. His skin was warm and dry under her hands and even though she could barely wait to feel all of him against all of her, she leaned a little away from him. "Sho you want to be wid this ol dirty woman? Sho you want—"

His lips were on hers, nibbling and pulling, and the sentence ended in a groan. Her thighs spread for him, her hips moved for him. Lawd, this man sho know how to love . . .

It was gone as suddenly as it had come, the memory so strong, so clear it was like being with him all over again. Muscles contracted painfully deep inside her and she could feel the warm moistness oozing between her thighs. There was only the thin cotton coverlet that provided no weight and little warmth, the noise the corn husk pallet made each time she moved. It was moonlight that shined in her eyes, not his eyes that had been the color of lemon-tea and honey. She lay still but she could not conjure the visions again, and finally she turned her back to the tiny window where the moonlight entered, pulled the coverlet up around her breasts and closed her eyes.

Hey, hey, sweet mamma

(She knew the words; it was his voice that had been the music.)

> *Hey, sweet mamma, this Kaine Poppa*
> *Kaine Poppa callin his woman'name.*
> *He can pop his poppa so good*
> *Make his sweet woman take to a cane.*

MEDITATIONS ON HISTORY

The Hughes Farm
Near Linden
Marengo County, Alabama.

June 9, 1829.

I must admit to a slight yearning for the comfort of the Linden House (comfort that is quite remarkable, considering Linden's out-of-the-way location), but Sheriff Hughes' generous offer of hospitality enables me to be close at hand for the questioning of the negress and this circumstance must outweigh the paucity of creature comforts which his gable room provides.

The negress is housed here in a little-used root cellar until such time as sentencing can be carried out. Hughes told me at dinner tonight the amusing story of how the negress came to be housed in his cellar. It seems that the town drunk, a rather harmless fellow who usually spends some portion of each week in housing provided at public expense, protested the idea of having to share quarters with the negress over an extended period of time. The other blacks involved in the uprising had, of course, been given a speedy trial and the sentences were carried out with equal dispatch, so the drunk—I cannot recall his name—had not been too inconvenienced. He drew the line, however, at protracted living with the wench in the close quarters which the smallness of the jail necessitates. In this he was supported by his wife, a papist from New Orleans but otherwise a good woman and normally a very meek one. She was convinced that the girl had the "evil eye" and was also possessed of a knowledge of the black arts—for how else, she asked at one point, could the negress have supplied the members of the coffle with the files which freed them when there were none to be had (a provocative question, but Hughes says that it was never proved that it was the negress who supplied the files). The woman demanded of Hughes, and later, when Hughes could give her no satisfaction, of the judge, the mayor and several of the large landowners in the vicinity, that the girl be moved or her husband be provided with separate quarters. She raised such a rumpus, invoking saints and all manner of idols, and pestered the gentlemen so repeatedly that Hughes in desperation offered his root cellar and, as his farm is also only a short distance from town, the village fathers jumped at his offer. Calmer reflection showed them the wisdom of this hasty decision: Jemina (a singularly inappropriate name for one of her size), the house servant here, is a noted midwife and excellent care is thus close at hand when the negress's time comes.

There is, however, some uncertainty about when that time will be. The Court, at Wilson's request, has postponed the hanging until after the birth of the child, which, according to Wilson's coffle manifest, should be two to three months hence. Hughes, however, says that it will be sooner. Jemina declares that the wench is eight months gone now and the entire district swears by the woman's prognostications. It is all in one to me, for, however far gone she proves to be, there is ample time for me to conclude my investigation of this incident before the law extracts the final punishment for her crimes. And the price will be paid. She will hang from the same gallows where her confederates forfeited their lives for the part they played in that perfidious and, fortunately, unsuccessful uprising.

It is late and the branches of the huge oak which commands the back yard brush softly at the shutters. It is a restful sound and the sense of urgency which had driven me since first I heard of this latest instance of negro savagery has finally eased. The retelling of this misadventure will make a splendid opening for the book and I am properly elated that I managed to reach Linden before the last of the culprits had come by their just deserts. It will be a curious, an interesting process to delve into the mind of one of the instigators of this dreadful plot. Is it merely the untamed, perhaps even *untamable* savagery of their natures which causes them to rise up so treacherously and repudiate the natural order of the universe which has already decreed their place, or is it something more amenable to human manipulation, the lack of some disciplinary measure or restraining word which brought Wilson and countless others to such

tragic consequences? Useless to ponder now, for if I do not discover the answer with this one negress, I have every confidence that
I shall find an answer in the other investigations I shall make.

▲   ▲   ▲

June 10, 1829.

I have seen her: the virago, the she-devil who even now haunts the
nightmares of Wilson. I had not thought it possible that one of his
calling could be so womanish, for surely slave-trading is a more
hazardous profession than that of doctor, lawyer or *writer*. Yet, this
wench, scarcely more than a pickaninny—and the coffle manifest
puts her age somewhere in the neighborhood of fifteen or sixteen
—and one of such diminutive size at that is the self-same wench
whom Wilson called a "raging nigger bitch." In recollecting the
uprising, it is the thought of *this* darky which even now, weeks
after the events, brings a sweat to his brow and a tremble to his
hand. Why, her belly is bigger than she is and birthing the child she
carries—a strong, lusty one if the size of her stomach is any indication—will no doubt kill her long before the hangman has a chance
at her throat. Oh, she may be sullen and stubbornly silent. Although, in this initial visit, she appeared more like a wild and
timorous animal finally brought to bay, for upon perceiving that
Hughes was not alone she moved quickly if clumsily to the farthest
reaches of the root cellar which her leg iron allows. Hughes attempted to coax her in a really remarkable approximation of what
he says is her own speech, saying that I was not there to aggravate
her with further questions as the other white men had done. She,
however, would approach us no closer than just enough to ease the
tension on her chains. Still, I can imagine the dangerously excitable
state which Hughes confirms characterized her actions upon first
being apprehended. According to Hughes, she was like a cat at that
time, spitting, biting, scratching, apparently unconcerned about the
harm her actions might bring to her child. The prosecutor was
naturally relentless in his questioning and it is only since being

removed to this farm that she has achieved a state of relative calm.
Yet, to see in this one common negress the she-devil of Wilson's
delirium is the grossest piece of nonsense. Hughes agrees with me,
saying privately that he always believed that Wilson's loud harshness toward the blacks in his coffles hid a cowardly nature. Hughes,
of course, has had more opportunity to judge of this than I, for
Wilson has been bringing his coffles through Marengo County for
well onto seven years. And this also confirms my own opinion of
him. Even in that one brief visit I had with him in Selma, I
detected the tone, the attitude of the braggart and bully.

▲   ▲   ▲

I shall speak with Hughes about making other provisions for a
meeting place. Even had I been of a mind to talk with the negress,
the stench of the root cellar—composed almost equally I suspect of
stale negro and whatever else has been stored there through the
years—would have driven me away within the minute. And that
would be a pity for there is no doubt that the negress was one of
the leaders in that bloody proceeding. Her own testimony supports
the findings of the Court. Now, she will be brought to re-create
that event and all that led up to it for me. Ah, the work, *The Work*
has at last begun.

▲   ▲   ▲

June 13, 1829.

Each day I become more convinced of the necessity, the righteous-
ness even of the work I have embarked upon. Think, I say to
myself as I sit looking into the negress's face, think how it might
have been had there been a work such as I envision after the Prosser
uprising of 1800. Would the Vesey conspiracy and all the numerous
uprisings which took place in between these two infamous events,
would they have occurred? Would this wretched wench even now

be huddled before me? No, I say. No, for the evil seeds which blossomed forth in her and her companions would never have been planted. I feel more urgency about the completion of *The Roots of Rebellion and the Means of Eradicating Them* (I have settled upon this as a compelling short title) than ever I did about writing *The Complete Guide for Competent Masters in Dealing with Slaves and Other Dependents*. I am honest enough to agree with those of my detractors who claim that *The Guide* is no more than a compendium of sound, commonsense practices gathered together in book form (they forget, however, that it is I who first hit upon the idea of compiling such a book and the credit of being first must always be mine). *The Guide* was, in some sense, a mere business venture. But *Roots*—even though the first word has yet to be written— looms already in my mind as a *magnum opus*.

Yet, being closeted with the negress within the small confines of the root cellar is an unsettling experience. Thus far, I have not been able to prevail upon Hughes to allow us the freedom of the yard for our meetings. Despite his bluff firmness in dealing with her, he is loath to allow the negress beyond the door of the root cellar. It is preposterous to suppose that anything untoward could happen. He vouches for the loyalty of his own darkies and has strictly forbidden them to have any intercourse whatsoever with her unless a white person is also present. The negress would, of course, be chained and perhaps under the open sky, I can free myself from the oppressive sense of her eyes casting a spell, not so much upon me (I know that should it ever come to a contest, God will prove stronger than the black devils she no doubt worships). No, not upon me is the spell cast, but upon the whole of the atmosphere from which I must draw breath. This last I know is fanciful; I laugh even as I write it, and it is not *the* reason for my long silence. She refused on two occasions to speak with me. I forebore carrying this tale to Hughes. He is a crude, vulgar, even brutal man who would doubtless feel that the best solution to the negress's stubbornness is a judicious application of the whip. In another situation I might be inclined to agree with him—the whip is most often the medicine to cure a recalcitrant slave. In this instance, however, I feel that the information I require must, if it is to be creditable, be freely given. I trust that I have not placed too much dependence upon her intelligence and sensitivity. Or, more likely, upon that innate stubbornness and intractableness for which I believe blacks from certain parts of the dark continent are well known. I think not, for upon the first occasion she appeared unmoved when I reminded her that although the child she carries may save her yet a while from a hanging, it was certainly not proof against a whipping. She cannot be said to roll her eyes (a most lamentable characteristic of her race), rather she *flicks* them across one—much in the same manner a horse uses his tail to flick a bothersome fly. It is a most offensive gesture. It was thus that she greeted this statement. I was so angered that I struck her in the face, soiling my hand and bloodying her nose, and called to Hughes to open the door. I was almost immediately sorry for my impetuous action. Hughes thinks of me as an expert negro tamer and although he has not, as he told me, read *The Guide,* he has heard from respectable sources that it has a "right good bit o' learnin and common sense" in it. I, therefore, do not want it ever to appear, for even a moment, that I have been or will ever be defeated by a negress. As I take pains to point out in *The Guide,* it is seldom necessary to strike a darky with one's hand and to do so, except in the most unusual circumstances, is to lower one's self almost to the same level of random violence which characterizes the action of the blacks among themselves. It is always a lowering, even repellent reflection to know that one has forgotten the sense of one's own teachings. It was Willis, I believe, on the plantation of Mr. Charles Haskin's near Valadosta in Lowndes County, Georgia, who carried a riding whip in order to correct just such subtle signs of insolence as the negress has tried my patience with. But the violence of my reaction has perhaps made any such response unnecessary in the future.

My latest attempt to have speech with her was this morning and I find it difficult to interpret her attitude. We heard upon approaching the cellar a humming or moaning. It is impossible to precisely define it as one or the other. I was alarmed, but Hughes merely laughed it off as some sort of "nigger business." He was perhaps right, for upon opening the door and climbing down the steps into the cellar proper, we found her with her arms crossed in front of her chest, her hands grasping her shoulders. She was seated in the stream of light which comes through the one window—an odd instance in itself for always before she had crouched away from the light so that her eyes gleamed forth from the darkness like those of a beast surprised in its lair. She rocked to and fro and at first I thought the sounds which came from her some kind of dirge or lamentation. But when I ventured to suggest this to Hughes, he merely laughed, asking how else could a nigger in her condition keep happy save through singing and loud noise, adding that a loud nigger was a happy one; it is the silent ones who bear watching. I asked tartly if he made no distinction between moaning and singing. Why should I, he replied with a hearty laugh, the niggers don't. I am obliged to rely upon Hughes' judgment in this matter; as slaveholder and sheriff he has had far greater contact with various types of darkies than I should ever wish for myself. And this last piece of information tallies with what I heard again and again while doing the research for *The Guide*.

Hughes left at this point and I was alone with the wench. I admit to being at a loss as to how to begin, but just as I was about to order her to cease her noise, she lurched to her feet and her voice rose to a climactic pitch. She uttered the words, "I bes. I bes." Just those two words on a loud, yes, I would say, even exultant note. Her arms were now at her side and she stood thus a moment in the light. Her face seemed to seek it and her voice was like nothing I had ever heard before. "I bes. I. And he in air on my tongue the sun on my face. The heat in my blood. I bes he; he me. He me. And it can't end in this place, not this time. Not this time. Not this. But if it do, if it do, it was and I bes. I bes."

I did not exist for her. And I knew then that to talk to her while she remained in such a state would be to talk to the air she now seems to claim to be. We will try what a little pressure can accomplish with her reluctant tongue. Perhaps a day spent on nothing but salt water will make her realize how lightly we have thus far held the reins.

I am somewhat surprised that she feels so little inclined toward boasting of her deeds, dark though they are. I do not make the mistake of putting her silence down to modesty or even fear but the above-mentioned stubbornness. She will find, however, that there are as many ways to wear stubbornness thin as there are to wear away patience.

▲   ▲   ▲

June 17, 1829.

I have spent the last few days at the courthouse, going through the trial records of this appalling incident, hoping to get a better understanding of what transpired and some insight into the motivation of the darkies. It is a measure of Judge Hoffer's confidence in me and the work upon which I am engaged that I was allowed access to the records. While I do not envision a narrative such as was made of the trial records of the Denmark Vesey case (which was later destroyed because of the inflammatory material it contained), I shudder to think of the uses to which the information contained in these records might be put should they fall into the wrong hands. The trials were conducted in closed sessions so that, while the records themselves contain little more than what Wilson and Hughes have already told me, none of this information is for public consumption.

The bare outline is this: Wilson picked up a consignment of slaves in Charleston at the end of March. While in the area, he attended a private sale where he heard of a wench, just entered upon childbearing age, and already increasing, that was being offered for sale on the plantation of Mr. Terrell Vaungham. He inquired at the plantation and was told that the wench was being sold because she had assaulted Vaungham. There is always a ready market for females of childbearing age with proven breeding capacity, so, despite the disquieting circumstances, Wilson chose to inspect the wench. There were still signs of punishment, raw welts and burns across the wench's buttocks and the inside of her thighs. Being in places which would only be inspected by the most careful buyer, such marks were not likely to impair her value. Thus satisfied, Wilson paid three hundred eighty-five dollars species for her: she would fetch at least twice that much in New Orleans. The wench gave every appearance of being completely cowed at the time of purchase and throughout the rest of the journey; thus no special guard was placed upon her. Also purchased at this time, through regular channels, were two bucks who were later whipped and branded as runaways because of their parts in the uprising. These purchases brought the number of slaves in the coffle to eighty: fifty males and thirty females ranging in age from about eleven to thirty (but then, no slave dealer will ever admit that any slave he wants to sell is older than thirty or younger than ten). Wilson will not take pickaninnies on these overland trips, feeling that they are more trouble than the price which they are like to fetch on the block warrants. Wilson and his partner, Darkmon, had with them six other men who acted as guards and drivers. It is generally agreed that this one-to-ten ratio is a proper one on a trip of this nature.

On the morning of March 30, 1829, they set out on the journey which would eventually end in New Orleans around the middle of June—had all gone well. There were no untoward events during the first portions of the journey, in fact, the coffle moved so smoothly that the regular security measures may have been somewhat relaxed (and Wilson's adamant denial of this does not convince me in the least. Men of his stripe are always more than willing to lay the blame for their own ineptness and laxity at someone else's door). As usual, Wilson continued to sell off and buy up slaves at each stop along the way. This practice, according to Wilson, serves to prevent trouble during the journey. The number of slaves on the coffle remains constant; there is, however, a continuous turnover of bodies. Thus, there is little chance for the blacks to become too intimate with one another. However, in checking the manifest (a copy of which was admitted as evidence) against the list of those apprehended, killed or convicted, I discovered a fact which had evidently escaped notice: a small group of twelve slaves had been with the coffle since Charleston. Of these, ten were directly involved in the uprising. It is also significant that two of the other blacks who were named as ringleaders had been with the coffle for some time. One must therefore conclude that a rapid and regular turnover of slaves does much to prevent the spread of discontent among them (perhaps this axiom can be modified and extended to include slaves on plantations and small farms).

Wilson had lately taken to chaining the blacks in groups of four and five to trees or other natural projections when no housing was available at night. He found that this method allowed them a more comfortable repose at night which in turn meant they were able to travel faster during the day and were also in better condition when they arrived at the market. He had saved considerable sums because the slaves no longer required expensive conditioning and grooming before being put up for sale. The darkies were strung together in the familiar single file when the coffle was ready to move. It is my firm belief that had Wilson used the tried and true method all along, he could have saved himself subsequent grief. A group of darkies had only to break away from the central chain which bound them to a projection in order to be free. This is precisely what happened.

In the early morning hours of April 29, the wench and the four bucks in her chain group managed to free themselves (whether with a file—which seems most likely—or because the locks were not properly secured—a terrifying oversight in a coffle of that size —was not revealed, even under the most intensive and painful methods of questioning. And the chains were never found). Two of these went to subdue the guards and drivers while the other three attacked Wilson and Darkmon, searching for the keys which would free the rest of the coffle. The negress attacked Darkmon and it was his death screams which awakened Wilson. He was immediately fighting for his own life, of course, and just as he managed to climb atop the darky and had raised his arm to strike him with the very rock with which he himself had been attacked, the negress fell upon him. She wielded a pick made from a stone sharpened to a stiletto point (the same one which she later used in attacking members of the posse). Evidently, her screams and "gleaming eyes" struck terror in Wilson's heart, for he is unable to recount what happened after this. Apparently, though, after Darkmon had been so foully murdered and while the negress went to the aid of the buck who had attacked Wilson, the other black used Darkmon's keys to free the others in the coffle. These quickly dispatched the drivers and guards who had not been subdued in the first onslaught. The darkies then took the horses and pack animals, some provisions and all the firearms and other weapons, and left Wilson and two of the drivers for dead. These lone survivors were found the next day on the trail to Linden, weak from loss of blood and babbling deliriously. A posse was quickly formed and set out in pursuit. They soon came upon the horses and other animals which the darkies had loosed, the better to cover their trail. The posse also found, throughout the course of their pursuit, a number of darkies who either could not keep up with the main body of renegades or who had repented of their impetuous action in following the malcontents and were eager to help in the capture. After three days of tracking the renegades back and forth in a northwesterly direction, the posse surprised them in a camp they had made some thirty-five miles north of Linden. After a fierce gun battle in which seven of the posse were wounded, two of whom did not recover from their wounds, the slaves were finally subdued in hand-to-hand combat at a cost to the posse of three dead and numerous minor injuries. A few renegades tried to slip away during the battle: they, too, were recaptured. However, three, seeing that the battle was lost, fled, and have thus far eluded capture. All told, there were some sixty-three blacks retaken, four having been killed in the initial skirmish with the drivers, eight, either outright or later as a result of their wounds, in the battle with the posse. The posse came up with the renegades on May 4; on the afternoon of the 6th, they arrived in Linden and the trials were held all day on the 8th. The slaves were tried in three groups: those who were thought to be ringleaders, those who were known to have been mostly directly involved in the attacks, either on the drivers or the posse (these groups often overlapped), and those who, perhaps, had been coerced into participation in these infamous proceedings. The sentences were carried out during the week of the 11th. The slaves were subjected to continual questioning from the time of their arrest until the time at which their sentences were carried out. I must commend the sheriff, the prosecutor and the judge on their ability to obtain so much information in such a short period of time.

Thirty-three blacks were tried (all adults above the age of fifteen): six were hanged and quartered as ringleaders, thirteen were hanged and quartered because of the ferocity with which they fought the posse (of these last two totals, six were females); three were whipped only; seven were branded only and three were whipped and branded (these last punishments infuriated Wilson when he learned of them. Branding makes the slave almost worthless, for no one in his right mind would buy a slave with such an extensive history of running away and rebelliousness as branding signifies. Wilson had preferred that they be hanged along with the others and thus save himself the cost of housing and feeding them). The negress still awaits her fate. The three bucks who eluded the posse were Big Nathan, a major plotter who had been chained with the negress the night of the uprising; Harker, who had been purchased in Atlanta; and Proud's Cully, who had been purchased in Jeffersonville just across the line in Georgia. According to the testimony of the slaves, it was this wench, the men in her chain group and five blacks from another group who were the sole plotters. The others had neither a part in the planning nor in the execution of these plans until all had been set free. This seems rather farfetched to me. Wilson, in his written statement to the Court, said that he changed the chain groupings at regular intervals. This would have made it easy for any plot to spread rapidly through the coffle. But as all maintained this posture, the Court accepted the statement of the blacks as true. In fact, one plotter, Elijah (charged by two of the others with being a "root-man," a dealer in black magic; but as there was no further substantiation of this charge, he was not tried on this count), was even rather contemptuous of the idea of telling any of the other slaves about the rebellion plot. They were, he said, white men's niggers who would have betrayed the plans at the first opportunity and who would accept freedom only if it were shoved down their throats. Big Nathan, Mungo and Elijah, who were hanged and quartered, and Black David, who was killed in the battle with the posse, were to lead them all to freedom, but none could specify where this place of freedom was. Elijah said that God would reveal the direction of and route to the free place at the proper time, that the means of escape had likewise been delivered into their hands by God and he would not question the will of God. This was all the "information" which the Court could obtain from any of them—save that the negress, when asked why she, rather than one of the males, had been chosen for so dangerous a task as securing the keys, would say only that it was best that way. (Questioning of her was not as severe as with the others. Wilson has developed an almost fanatical resolve to see in chains the child she carries and the doctor feared that, should she lose the baby before this had been accomplished, it might overset Wilson's reason. The Court took this medical opinion into account when deciding to delay the consummation of the wench's sentence.) It is my own belief that she was chosen because of her very unlikeliness. Who would think a female so far gone in the breeding process capable of such treacherous conduct?

▲   ▲   ▲

That, in bare outline, is what happened; my chore now is to fill in that outline, to discover and analyze the motivating factors which culminated in this outrage against the public safety. I feel that I have been richly rewarded for these past few days of work. In retelling this outline, I am filled again with a sense of my mission. I look forward to dealing with the negress again on Monday.

▲   ▲   ▲

June 19, 1829.

"Was I white, I might woulda fainted when Emmalina told me that Mas had done gon up-side Kaine head, nelly bout kilt him iff'n he wa'n't dead already. Fainted and not come to myself til it was ova, least ways all of it that could eva get ova. I guess when you faints you be out the world, that how Kaine say it be. Say that how Mist's act up at the House when Mas or jes any lil thang don't be goin to suit her. Faint, else cry and have em all, Aunt Lefonia, Feddy and the rest, comin, runnin and fannin and carin on, askin what wrong, who did it. Kaine hear em from the garden and he say he be laughin fit to split his side and diggin, diggin and laughin to hear how one lil sickly white woman turn a house that big upside down. I neva rightly believe it could be that way. But wa'n't no way fo me to know fo sho—I work the fields and neva goes round the House neitha House niggas, cept only Aunt Lefonia. Kaine, when me and him first be close and see us want be closer, he try to get me up to the House, ask Aunt Lefonia if she see what she can do, talk to Mist's maybe. But Aunt Lefonia say I too light for Mist's and not light nough fo Mas. Mist's ascared Mas gon be likin the high colored gals same as he was fo they was married so she don't low nothin but dark uns up to the House else ones too old for Mas to be beddin. So I stays in the fields like I been. Kaine don't like it when Aunt Lefonia tell him that and he even ask Mist's please could I change, but Mist's see me and say no. Kaine mad but he finally jes laugh, say, what kin a nigga do? But I see Mist's that time close-up and I can't rightly believe all what Kaine say. Maybe he jes make it mo'n it bes so when he tell it I laugh. But I neva do know fo sho. Kaine mus know though. He been round the Houses, most a House nigga hisself, though a House nigga neva say a nigga what tend flovas any betta'n one what tend corn. He jes laugh when Childer try to come the big nigga ova him, tell him, say, Childer, jes cause you open do's for the white folks don't make you white. And Childer puff all up cause he not like it, you don't be treatin him some big and he was raised up with the old Mas, too? Humph. So he say to Kaine, say, steadda Kaine talkin back at the

ones what betta'n him, Kaine betta be seein at findin him a mo
likely gal'n me."

She paused, her head lifted, her eyes closed as though listening.
"He chosed me." I could not read the expression on her face; the
cellar was too dark. Something, however, seemed to have crept
into her voice and I waited, hoping she would continue. "He
chosed me. Mas ain't had nothing to do wid that. It Kaine what
pick me out and say I be his woman. Mas say you lay down wid
this'n or that un and that be the one you lay wid. He tell Carrie
Mae she lay wid that studdin nigga and that who she got to be wid.
And we all be knowin that it ain't fo nothin but to breed and time
the chi'ren be up in age, they be sold off to notha 'tation, maybe
deep south. And she jes a lil bitty thang then and how she gon be
holdin a big nigga like that, carryin that big nigga child. And all
what mamma say, what Aunt Lefonia and Mamma Hattie say don't
make Mas no ne'mind. 'Luke known fo makin big babies on lil
gals,' Mas say and laugh. Laugh so hard, he don't be hearin Mamma
Hattie say how Luke studdin days be ova 'fo' he eva touch Carrie.
Mas, he don't neva know it, but Luke, he know it. But he don't tell
cause the roots stop his mouth from talkin to Mas same as they stop
his seed from touchin Carrie. Mas jes wonder and wonder and
finally he say Luke ain't good fo nothin no mo cept fo to drive
otha niggas inna field and fo to beat the ones what try fo to be bad.
Carrie bedded wid David then and Mas gots three mo niggas fo to
be studs, so he ain't too much carin. And Carrie gots a baby comin.
Baby comin . . . baby comin. . . . But Kaine chosed me. He
chosed me and when Emmalina meet me that day, tell me Kaine
don took a hoe at Mas and Mas don laid into him wid a shovel,
bout bus' in his head, I jes run and when the hoe gits in my way, I
let it fall, the dress git in my way and I holds that up. Kaine jes
layin there on usses pallet, head seepin blood, one eye closed, one
bout gone. Mamma Hattie sittin side him wipin at the blood. 'He
be dead o' sold. Dead o' sold.' I guess that what she say then. She
say it so many times afta that I guess she say it then, too. 'Dead o'
sold.' Kaine jes groan when I call his name. I say all the names I
know, eva heard bout, thought bout, Lawd, Legba, Shango, Jesus.

Anybody, jes so's Kaine could speak. 'Nigga,' Kaine say. Nigga and my name. He say em ova and ova and I hold his hand cause I know that can't be all he wanna say. Nigga and my name, my name and nigga. 'Nigga,' he say. 'Nigga can do.' And he don't say no mo."

And that has what to do with you and the other slaves rising up and killing the trader and the drivers, I asked sharply, for it seemed as though she would not continue.

She opened her eyes and looked at me. Wide and black they are. She had had them closed or only half open as she talked, her head moving now and then, from side to side, in and out of the light coming in through the tiny unshuttered window. She opened her eyes and her head was silhouetted in the light. I understood then what Wilson meant when he talked in his delirium about "devil eyes," a "devil's stare." Long, black and the whites are un-stained by red or even the rheumy color which characterizes the eyes of so many darkies whether of pure or mixed blood, and she does not often blink them. "I kill that white man," she said, and in the same voice in which she talked about being allowed to work in the big house, in which she had talked about the young darky's dying. They were all the same to her. "I kill that white man cause the same reason Mas kill Kaine. Cause I can." And she turned her head to the dark and would not speak with me anymore.

▲   ▲   ▲

I have read again this first day's conversation with the negress. It is all here—even that silly folderol about "roots"—as much in her own words as I could make out. It would seem that one must be acquainted with darkies from one's birth in order to fully under-stand what passes for speech amongst them. It is obvious that I must speak with her again, perhaps several times more, for she answers questions in a random manner, a loquacious, roundabout fashion—if, indeed, she can be brought to answer them at all. This, to one of my habits, is exasperating to the point of fury. I must constantly remind myself that she is but a darky and a female at that. Copious

notes seem to be the order of the day and I will cull what information I can from them. And, despite the rambling nature of today's
discourse, the fact that she did talk remains something of a triumph
for *The Guide*. Light punishment followed by swift relaxation of
the punitive measure is a trick I learned of in Maryland, where they
have long since realized that the whippings which the abolitionists
deplore are not the only way to bring a rebellious darky to heel.

▲   ▲   ▲

June 22, 1829.

She has talked again, perhaps the influence of the open air or
perhaps there was one thing in the long string of questions I asked
which touched her thought more than another. I have asked the
same basic questions at each meeting. Today, I grew more than a
little impatient with the response—or lack thereof—which I have
thus far elicited, and would have despaired of completing my project, if completion depends upon this one negress—which, thank
God! it does not. But it is not in my nature to admit defeat so
readily and so, thinking to return to the one thing about which she
had previously talked, I asked, How did it happen that this darky
of whom you spoke attacked Mr. Vaungham? I had phrased this
question in various ways and been met with silence. I had even
nudged her slightly with the tip of my boot to assure myself that
she had not fallen into a doze (they fall asleep, I am told, much as a
cow will in the midst of a satisfying chew, though I, myself, have
not observed this), but aside from that offensive flicking of the eye,
she would not respond. I contained my irritation and my impatience and went on with my questioning. Was he crazed, drunk?
Where did he get the liquor? She was seated on the ground at my
feet, her back against the tree trunk. The chain which attached to
her ankle was wound once around the tree and fastened to a rung
of the chair in which I sat. The chair was placed to one side and a
little behind so that she would have to look up at me. She would
not. Sometimes she closed her eyes or looked out into space. At

these times she would hum, an absurd, monotonous little tune in a
minor key, the melody of which she repeated over and over. Each
morning, we are awakened by the singing of the darkies and they
often startle one by breaking into song at odd times during the day.
Hughes, of course, finds this comforting. But thus far I have heard
nothing but moaning from this wench. How did it happen that this
darky attacked Mr. Vaungham? and I raised my voice so as to be
heard over her humming.

She stopped humming for a second and when she resumed, she
put words to the melody:

> *"Lawd, gimme wings like Noah's dove*
> *Lawd, gimme wings like Noah's dove*
> *I'd fly cross these fields to the one I loves*
> *Say, hello darlin; say, how you be.*

Mamma Hattie say that playin wid God, puttin yo self on the same
level's His peoples is on. But Kaine jes laugh and say she ain't
knowed no mo bout God and the Bible than what the white folk
tell her and that can't be too much cause Mas say he don't be likin
religion in his slaves. So Kaine jes go on singin his songs to me in
the e'nin afta I gets out the fields. I be layin up on usses pallet and
he be leanin ginst the wall. He play sweet-soft cause he say that
what I needs, soft sweetin put me to sleep afta I done work so all
day. He really feel bad bout that, me inna field and him in the
garden. He even ask Boss Smith could I come work at the House o'
he come work the field. I scared when he do that. Nobody ask Boss
Smith fo nothin cause that make him note you and the onliest way
Boss Smith know to note you is wid that whip. But Boss Smith jes
laugh and tell him he a crazy nigga. But Kaine not crazy. He the
sweetest nigga as eva walk this earth. He play that banger, he play
it so sweet til Mist's even have him up to the House to play and she
talk bout havin a gang o' niggas to play real music fo when they be
parties and such like at the House. Ole Mist's used to would talk
like that, so Aunt Lefonia say, cause that was how they done in Ole

Mist's home. But it don't nothin comma it then, not now neitha. Side, Kaine say the music he know to play be real nough fo him. Say that that his banger. He make it his'n so it play jes what he want play. And he play it. Not jes strum strum wid all his fingers, but so you hear each strang when he touch it and each strang gots a diff'ent thang to say. And they neva talks bout bein sad, bein lonesome cause Kaine say I hep him put all that behind him. Even when us be workin and he be up to the House and I be out inna field, it not bad, cause he be knowin, when the bell rang, I be comin fix that lil bit ration and we lay up on usses pallet. 'Niggas,' he tell me, 'niggas jes only belongs to white folks and that bes all. They don't be belongin to they mammas and daddys, they sista, they brotha.' Kaine Mamma be sold when he lil bit and he not even know her face. And sometime he thank maybe his first Mas o' the driva o' maybe jes some white man passin through be his daddy. Then he say mus been some fine, big, black man muscled up like strong tree what got sold cause he go fo bad. And he be wishin he took looks afta his daddy, be big and strong like him, be *bad,* steadda the way he do look, nappy head and light eyes. Have a black man fo a daddy well as a white man, he say, but he can't neva know, not fo sho, no way. He be sold hisself lotta time fo he come to Mas 'tation. So he don't know bout stayin wid Mamma Hattie til you be big nough to work the fields, o' bein woked up by mamma and eatin dry cornbread and 'lasses fo day in the mornin wid evabody and hearin Jeeter tease the slow pokes and havin mamma fetch you a slap so Boss Smith won't fetch his whip at you fo tarryin so. Onlest folks he eva belongs to is the white folks and that not really like belongin to a body. He say first time he hear anybody play a banger, he have to stop, have to listen cause it seem like it talkin right at him. And the man what play it, he a Af'ca black, not a reg'la nigga like what you see eva day. And this Af'ca man say that the music he play be from his home, and his home be his; it don't be belongs to no white folks. Nobody there belongs to white folks, jes onlest theyselves and each otha. He tell Kaine lotta thang what Kaine don't member cause he lil bit then and this the

first time he be sold. That in Charleston and I know that close to
where I'm is and I wonder how it be if Mas had buyed Kaine then,
steadda when Kaine be grown. But, it happen how it happen and
that time in Charleston Kaine not know all what the Af'ca man
say, cept bout the home and bout the banger, how to make it, how
to play it. And he know that cause he know if he have it, home be
his and the banger be his. Cept he ain't got no home, so he jes
onlest have the banger.

"He make that banger hisself. Make it outen good parchment
and seasoned wood he get hisself and when Mas break it seem like
he break Kaine. Might well as had cause it not right wid him afta
tha. And I can't make it right wid him. I tell him he can make
notha one. I pick up wood fo him from Jim Boys at the carp'ter
shed, get horsehair from Emmalina Joe Big down to the stables.
But Kaine jes look at it. 'Mas can make notha one,' he say, 'Nigga
can't do shit. Mas can step on a nigga hand, nigga heart, nigga life,
and what can a nigga do? Nigga can't do shit.

> *What can a nigga do when Mas house on fire?*
> *What can a nigga do when Mas house on fire?*
> *Bet NOT do mo'n yell, Fire, Fire!*
> *Let some'un else brang the wata*
> *Cause a nigga can't do shit!*

He sing that and laugh. And one day Emmalina meet me when I
come in outten the field and tell me Mas don shoved in the side of
Kaine head."

She looked up at the sun and blinked her eyes rapidly several
times. I did not question her anymore.

This is still a far cry from just how five slaves managed to free
themselves and loose the rest of the coffle, how, having achieved

this, they managed to murder the drivers and one trader and dangerously injure another (and I begin to think, too, that she must have some inkling of where the three darkies that the posse couldn't find have gotten to), but I begin to perceive how I may get to this point. We shall see tomorrow. Enough for tonight. I sat late with Hughes over a very smooth Kentucky whiskey (I must admit to having misjudged Hughes. I had not thought from either the appointments of his house or the fare at his table that he was capable of such fine taste. Perhaps it is only from want of proper exercise that his discriminating faculties are not more in evidence. What I had thought dead may only be dormant. As for means—in the case of the whiskey, I would say that being sheriff must not be without its advantages). It is curious, though, how the negress, well, how she looks in the sun. For a moment today as I watched her I could almost imagine how Vaungham allowed her to get close enough to stick a knife between his ribs.

▲   ▲   ▲

June 23, 1829.

She demanded a bath this morning, which Hughes foolishly allowed her, and in the creek. Being without a bathing dress, she must perforce bathe in her clothes and dry in them also. A chill was the natural outcome, whose severity we have yet to determine. And were that not bad enough, she cut her foot, a deep slash across the instep and ball, while climbing up the bank. Hughes thinks it a reasonably clean cut but she bathed near the place where the live-stock come to water so there is no way of knowing. He claims that he was so nonplussed, "flustered" as he phrases it, at such a novel request coming from a nigger and a wench ready to be brought to light, too, that he had granted the request before he had time to think properly of the possible outcome. Since she was shackled during the whole business he thought no harm could be done, as though darkies are not subject to the same chills and sweats which overtake the veriest pack animals. It seems that I am never to be spared the consequences of dealing with stupid people. Pray God the wench doesn't die before I get my book.

▲   ▲   ▲

June 27, 1829.

A curious session we had of it today. I know not what, even now, to make of it. She spoke of her own accord today, spoke to me, rather than the hot windless air, as has been her custom. The air, even now, is oppressive, hot, still, strangely dry, and it was obvious, even as Hughes brought her up from the cellar, that the negress also felt it. Her movements, always slow, were even slower, her walk, not stumbling but heavy as though her feet were weighted. She eased her bulk onto the ground beneath the tree and leaned back against its trunk. Her dark wooly hair—which fits upon her head almost like a nubby cap—seemed to merge into the deeper shadows cast by the thick low hanging branches of the tree. I sat in my habitual place just behind her, stripped to my shirt sleeves and feeling that even this was not enough to lessen the sun's onslaught. The sharp, bright sunlight was too painful to gaze at from the depth of that shadow and I must look down at the pages of my notebook, blank save for the day's date, or at her. We were silent for some moments after she was seated, I thinking how limited my vision had become and she engaged in God knows what cogitations.

"That writin what you put on that paper?" I was somewhat startled by the question and did not immediately answer. "You be writin down what I say?" She was on her knees, turned to me now to see what was in the notebook. Instinctively, I held it away from her eyes and told her that although I had written nothing that day —we had said nothing so far—(I fear that this little pleasantry escaped her) I did indeed write down much of what she said. On a happy impulse, I flipped back through the pages and showed her the notes I had made on some of our previous sessions. "What that there . . . and there . . . and that, too?" I told her and even read a little to her, an innocuous line or two. She was entranced. "I relly say that?" And when I nodded she sat back on her haunches. "What you gon do wid it?" I told her cautiously that I would use it in a book I hoped to write. I was totally unsure of whether she would comprehend the meaning of that. "Cause why?" She was thoroughly aroused by this time and seemed, despite the chain which bound her, about to flee.

Girl, I said to her, for at that moment, I could not for the life of me remember her name, Girl, what I put in this book cannot hurt you now. You've already been tried and judged. She seemed somewhat calmed by this utterance, perhaps as much by the tone of my voice, which I purposely made gentle, as by the statement itself. "Then for what you wanna do it?"

I told her that I wrote what I did in the hope of helping others to be happy in the life that has been sent them to live, a response with which I am rather pleased. Certainly, it succeeded in its purpose of setting her mind at ease about the possible repercussions to herself in talking freely with me, for she seemed much struck by the statement, looking intently into my face for a long moment before she again settled down into her habitual pose. I allowed her to reflect upon this for a moment. She was silent for so long that I began to suspect her of dozing and leaned forward the better to see her. Her eyes were open (she seemed not to have the same problem as I with the harsh sunlight), her hands cupped beneath the roundness of her stomach. Your baby seems to have dropped; according to the old wives' tale, you'll be brought to bed soon. It was merely an attempt at conversation, of course; I know no more about that sort of business than I know about animal husbandry or the cultivation of cotton. She, of course, did not treat my words as the conversational gambit they were; she jumped as though stung. I cursed my stupidity, knowing what this unthinking comment must have brought to her mind, even as I realized that this was the first time I had seen her hands anywhere near her stomach. After the initial start, she straightened her back and scooted nearer to the tree, but said nothing. I waited, somewhat anxiously, for the blank sullen look to return. It did not, however, and, emboldened, I ventured quietly, Girl, where did the others get the file? even as she said:

"Kaine not want this baby. He want and don't want it. Babies ain't easy fo niggas, but still, I knows this Kaine's and I wants it cause that. And . . . and, when he ask me to go to Aunt Lefonia . . . I, I nelly bout died. I know what Aunt Lefonia be doin, though she don't be doin it too much cause Mas know it gotta be some nigga chi'ren comin in this world. And was anybody but, but Kaine, I do it, too. First time, a anyway. But, but this Kaine and it be like killin parta him, parta me. So I talk wid him; beg him. I say, this us baby, usses. We make it. How you can say, kill it. It mine and it yo's. He jes look at me. 'Same way Lefonia sons be hers when Mas decide that bay geldin he want worth mo to him than they is to her. Dessa,' and I know he don't want hurt me when he call my name, but it so sweet til it do hurt. Dessa, jes soft like that. 'Dess, where yo brotha, Jeeter, at now?' I'm cryin already, can't cry no mo, not fo Jeeter. He be gon, sold, south, somewhere; we neva do know. And finally I say 'run' and he laugh. He laugh and say, 'Run, Dessa (Lawd. Ain't no body neva say my name so sweet. Even when he mad like that, Dessa. Dessa I always know the way he call my name). Dessa, run where?' 'No'th,' I whisper. I whisper cause I don't rightly thank I eva heard no nigga say that out loud like when anybody, even yo own self's shadow could hear you, less'n it right up on you. 'No'th? And how we gon get there?' 'You know, Kaine.' And he know. I know he know. He know if he wanna know. 'And what we gon do when we gets there?' I jes look at him. Cause he know. 'Dessa.' Say my name agin. 'You know what is no'th? Huh? What is no'th? Mo whites. Jes like here. You don't see Aunt Lefonia, I see her fo you.' But I don't go, not then. I waits and one night Kaine talk to me. I don't *know,* not then, bout all what he says, but I try to learn most o' it by heart so I can thank bout it and thank bout it til I does know. He tell me then how he been sold way from some massas, runned way from othas. He run, he say, tryin to find no'th and he lil then and not even know no'th a di-rection and mo places than he eva be able to count. He jes thank he be free o' whippins, free to belongs to somebody what belongs to him jes so long as he be no'th. Last time he runned way, he most get there and he thank, now he know which way free land is, what is a free town, next time he get there. But neva is no next time cause same time's patterrollers takes him back, they takes back a man what been no'th, lived there and what know what free no'th is. 'Now,' Kaine say, 'now this man free, bo'n free, but still, any white man what say he a slave be believed cause a nigga can't talk fo the laws, not ginst no white man, not even fo his own self. So this man gots to get a notha white man fo to say he is free and he couldn't find one quick nough so then the Georgia Man, that be what the no'th man call the patterrollers, they takes him back fo to be slave. That's right. But even fo the patterrollers catched him, white man hit, he not lowed to hit back. He carpt'na but if the white mens on the job say they don't want work wid him, he don't work and sucha thangs as that. He say it hard bein a free man o' color, he don't say nigga, say free man o' color, but it betta'n bein a slave and if he get the chance he gon runned way.' But, Kaine say, he ask hisself, 'That free? How that gon be free? It still be two lists, one say "White Man Can," otha say "Nigga Can't" and white man still be the onliest one what can write on em.' So he don't run no mo. 'Run fo what,' he say. 'Get caught be jes that much worser off. Maybe is a place wid out no white, nigga can be free.' But he don't know where that is. He find it, he say we have us chi'ren then. That why he say go see Aunt Lefonia, but I don't go. I jes can't. I know Kaine be knowin mo'n me. I know that. He— He told me lotta thang I not eva thank bout fo I wid him. But I does know us. I does. Me'n him. I knows that. And I knows this usses baby. And I thank bout what he say and I thank bout what I knows and I know they all bes the same thang. How they gon be diff'ent? I tell Kaine find it, least *try* fo you say see Aunt Lefonia. I don't be cryin now and he don't be mad. Jes, jes touch my face and say me name, Lawd, say my name. Say my name and his body be so hard, so hard and stiff ginst mine and I feel how he want me. 'I try, Dessa. I try what I can do.' No matter though," she said looking up at me. "Mas kill him fo it get time fo us to go."

We were both quiet for some time. I searched around in my

mind for some way to bring her train of thought back to the immediate concern.

"You thank," she asked looking up at me, "you thank what I say now gon hep peoples be happy in the life they sent? If that be true," she said as I opened my mouth to answer, "Why I not be happy when I live it? I don't wanna talk no mo." And she did not.

▲   ▲   ▲

It is only now that I become aware of my failure to employ the strategy I have devised. Yet, she now suffers from no more than a small case of the sniffles and the gash, while painful, perhaps, causes her no more than a slight limp. Monday will thus do as well as today, for I feel that we have achieved a significant level in our relationship. Today was a turning point and I am most optimistic for the future.

▲   ▲   ▲

June 28, 1829.

As has been my custom in the past, I held no formal session with the negress this Sunday. But, in order to further cultivate the tentative rapport achieved in yesterday's session, I read and interpreted for her selected Bible verses. We were in our habitual place under the oak tree and I must admit that the laziness of the hot Sunday afternoon threatened at times to overcome me (as Hughes had warned me it would). As a consequence, he was reluctant to give me the keys to the cellar. He felt my vigilance would be impaired by the heat. I replied that in as much as the negress would remain chained as usual, there was no danger involved in such a venture— unless, of course, he feared that his own darkies would rise up and free her. He was somewhat stung by my retort, but he did surrender the keys. I shall make it my business to obtain another key to

the cellar and to the chains with which she is bound to the tree—
these are the only ones which in her quieted state she now wears. It
is not to my liking to be required to *request* permission each time I
wish to talk with the woman.

My drowsiness was compounded, I finally realized, by the monotonous melody which she hummed. I have grown, it appears, so
accustomed to them that they seem like a natural part of the setting
like the clucking of the hens or the lowing of the cattle. Thinking
to trap her into an admission of inattention, I asked her to repeat
the lessons I had just imparted to her. She did so and I was very
pleased to find her so responsive. However, the humming became
so annoying that I was forced to ask her to cease. She looked up at
me briefly and though I had not threatened her, I believe she was
mindful of previous punishments and of the fact that it is only
through my influence that she is able to escape from her dark hole
for these brief periods.

"Oh, this ain't no good-timmin song. It say bout the righteous-
ness and heaven, same as what you say."

I asked her to sing it and I set it down here as I remember and
understand it:

> Gonna march away in the gold band in the army bye'n
> bye.
> Gonna march away in the gold band in the army bye'n
> bye.
> Sinner, what you gon do that day?
> Sinner, what you gon do that day?
> When the fire arollin behind you in the army bye'n bye?

It is, of course, only a quaint piece of doggerel which the darkies
cunningly adapt from the scraps of scripture they are taught. Nev-
ertheless, the tune was quite charming when sung; the words
seemed to put new life into an otherwise annoying melody and I
was quite pleased that she had shared it with me. We were both
quiet for several moments after she had done. The heat was, by this

time, an enervating influence upon me. She, too, seemed to be spent by that brief spurt of animation. After a few more moments of silence, I closed the Bible, prayed briefly for the deliverance of her soul, then returned her to the cellar.

▲   ▲   ▲

June 29, 1829.

I asked how to pronounce the name of the young darky with whom she had lived (I am puzzled in my own mind about how to refer to him. Certainly, they were not married and she never speaks of having gone through even the slave ceremony of jumping over the broom). Did Kaine—is that how you pronounce—how you *say* his name? I asked her.

"You say it the same way you . . . you . . . spell? Spell it!"

Did Kaine talk much about freedom? This is part of my strategy, to frame all the questions in such a way that Kaine can be referred to in some manner. Her attachment to this Kaine appears quite sincere and while it is probably rooted in the basest of physical attractions, I cannot summon up the same sense of contempt with which I first viewed this liaison. I must confess also that I feel some slight twinge— Not of guilt, rather of *compassion* in using her attachment to the young darky as a means of eliciting information from her. But the fact is that my stratagems—while not perhaps of the most noble *type*—are used in the service of a greater good and this consideration must sweep all else before it. And I fear that in concentrating upon obtaining this greater good, I had finished asking the first question before I realized that she had made a slight jest. Looking at her in some surprise, I told her that it was quite a good joke, both in what she had said and in my own rather slow and dull reaction to her pleasantry. She in turn smiled, revealing for the first time in my memory the even white teeth behind the long thick lips of her mouth. Kaine did speak, then, a great deal about freedom?

She sat back. "Don't no niggas be talkin too much bout freedom, cause they be knowing what good fo em."

I did not believe her, but I chose, for the time being at least, to
allow her to think that I did. Then what was your idea in trying to
escape from the coffle?

She picked up a twig and began to mark in the dirt and to hum
—not the same tune as the previous days, but one equally monotonous. She looked up at me, finally, and widened her eyes. "Was
you black, you wanna be sold deep south? I neva been deep south,
but Boss Smith, he always threats lazy niggas wid that and they
don't be too lazy no mo."

And the others, I asked, was this what was in their mind?

She shrugged her shoulders. "Onlest mind I be knowin is
mines. Why fo you didn't ask them first?" I believe this was not
insolence, rather it seems more simple curiosity, and I allowed it to
pass, explaining that I had not heard of the incident until too late
to speak with the others who had been charged as leaders. "You
thank there be a place wid out no whites?" I looked at her in some
surprise and she continued to herself, in a deeper dialect than she
had heretofore used, really almost a mumble, something about Emmalina's Joe Big (I have yet to determine if this is the name of
Emmalina's son or her "husband." Because the father is seldom, if
ever, of any consequence after conception, the children of these
unions take their surnames from their owners and are distinguished
from others of the same given names by prefacing their names with
a possessive form of the mother's. This form of address, however, is
also used in referring to spouses. The question of Joe Big's relationship to Emmalina, while of passing interest, is certainly extraneous
to the present discussion, so I did not interrupt her ramblings)
telling Kaine something and going, but where I could not make
out. "They caught Bi— They caught the others what run?"

I asked quickly, perhaps too quickly, if she knew where they
were and the blank sullen look immediately returned to her face.
The humming started again. She moved as though uncomfortable
and touched, almost as if frightened, the big mound which rises
beneath her dress. When she spoke it was in the voice of the first

day. "This all I gotta Kaine. Right here, in my belly. Mist's slap my face when I tell her that, say, don't lie, say, it must be Terrell, that how she call Mas, Terrell, say it mus be hissen, why else Mas want kill Kaine, best gard'er they eva has, what cost a pretty penny. She say, well, Terrell live, he live knowin his woman and his brat south in worser slavery than they eva thought of and Aunt Lefonia stop me fo I kills her, too."

It was almost like listening to the first day's recital and I knew when she turned her head from me that for this day, anyway, I had gotten all from her that I could. This, together with the oppressive heat (the air has now become laden with moisture—a relief from the furnace-like dryness of the last few days—and the whole atmosphere is pregnant with the storm which must break soon), made me close my notebook for the day. But I now know that the thick-lipped mouth, so savage in its sullen repose, can smile and even utter small jests, that lurking behind her all too often blank gaze is something more than the cunning stubbornness which, alone, I first perceived, even noted that her skin, which appeared an ashen black in the light of the root cellar, is the color of strong tea and that even in the shade it is tinged with gold (surely this is a sign of good health in her. The baby should fetch Wilson a handsome price to repay him in some measure for what he has had to suffer through her agency). So, this lapse does not unduly discourage me. I know that she does not understand the project—it would be a wretched piece of business if she did—but she begins to have less distrust of me. She was not overly free in her speech but I begin to believe that she inclines towards this more than in the past. I fancy that I am not overly optimistic in predicting that one, perhaps two more sessions and I will have learned all I need from her. I shall have to think of a provocative title for the section in which I deal with the general principles apparent in her participation in this bloody business. "The Female of the Species," something along those lines, perhaps.

▲   ▲   ▲

Later

Hughes says there is talk of a "maroon" settlement, an encampment of runaway slaves, somewhere nearby. There have been signs of marauding about some of the farms and plantations farther out from town. In the latest incident, several blacks (the wife of the farmer could not give an accurate count) stole into a small farm about twenty miles east of here and took provisions and the farm animals and murdered the farmer when he tried to protect his property. Fortunately, the wife was hidden during the raid and thus escaped injury. Hughes was inclined to treat this as an isolated incident—claiming that the other cases had happened so long ago that they had become greatly exaggerated in the telling—and thus dismiss the maroon theory as merely a fearful figment in the imagination of the larger slaveholders. He put down the missing provisions and the occasional loss of livestock to the thieving of the planters' own darkies. I am aware, as I told him, that an unsupervised darky will steal anything which is not nailed down, yet, in light of Odessa's talk of a place without whites and her concern about the three renegades who escaped capture by the posse—talk which I repeated—I cannot dismiss the theory of an encampment of some sort so easily. It is, of course, pure conjecture, but not, I believe, groundless to say, as I did to Hughes, that perhaps these three had joined the maroons—which would certainly be one place without whites. And, despite the babbling of the fanatic Elijah, it is obvious that the darkies from the coffle had been making for *someplace* when they were apprehended. Hughes was much impressed with my theorizing and invited me to join the posse which leaves at dawn tomorrow in search of the renegades. I readily accepted, for, even knowing the imaginative flights to which the darky's mind is prone, I put much faith in this information precisely because it was given inadvertently. What information Hughes and the prosecutor were able to obtain from the others and from Odessa herself regarding the uprising is as nothing compared to this plum.

▲   ▲   ▲

On the Trail
North and West of Linden

June 30, 1829.

We set out early this morning, picking up the trail of the renegades
at the farm where they were last seen. It led us in a northerly
direction for most of the day and then, just before we stopped for
the night, it turned to the west. Most of the posse feel this is a good
sign, for had the trail continued north we should have soon found
ourselves in Indian territory and, with two enemies to contend
with, the chances of being surprised in ambush would have greatly
increased. The trackers expect to raise some fresher sign of them
tomorrow, for they are laden with supplies and we are not (a fact
to which my stomach can well attest. Dried beef and half-cooked,
half-warmed beans are *not* my idea of appetizing fare). And, I am
told, if the weather holds humid as it has been and does not rain,
their scent will hold fresh for quite a while and the dogs will be
able to follow wherever it leads.

▲   ▲   ▲

I did see Odessa this morning before we departed. I heard singing
and, at first, taking it to be the usual morning serenade of Hughes'
darkies, I took no notice of it. My attention was caught, however,
by the plaintive note of this song, a peculiar circumstance, for
Hughes frowns upon the singing of any but the most lively airs. I
listened and finally managed to catch the words:

> *Tell me, sista   tell me, brotha   how long will it be?*
> *Tell me, brotha   tell me, sista   how long will it be*
> *That a poor sinner got to suffer, suffer here?*
> *Tell me, sista   tell me, brotha   when my soul be free?*

but what can such news avail her in that cellar? And she merely responded with a dumb stare. I am not even sure that she had understood what I said, for she asked, "You a *real* white man, fo true? You don't be talkin like one. Sometime I don't even be knowin what you be sayin. You don't be talkin like Mas and he a real uppity up white man, but not like trash neitha. Kaine says it bes white man what don't talk white man talk. You one like that, huh?" I had been angered, and, yes, I admit, a trifle offended by her question, and her emendations to the question only slightly mollified my emotions. I answered, somewhat haughtily, that I and others like me taught her master and his kind how to speak. My hauteur was, of course, lost on her, for she exclaimed happily that I was a "teacher man." It seemed unnecessarily heartless to destroy her felicitous mood by further probing so I held my peace, which proved to be a fortuitous choice. She continued, "Was a teacher man on the coffle. He teached hisself to read from the Bible, then he preach. But course, that only be to the niggas and he be all right til he want teach otha niggas fo to read the Good Word. That be what he call it, 'The Good Word,' and when his Mas find out what he be doin he be sold south same's if he be teachin a bad word or be a bad nigga or a prime field hand." I seized upon this, feeling that perhaps I had discovered the key to the insurrection, for no one of this description—except perhaps Elijah—had been implicated in the plot. Is he the one who obtained the file, I asked, and she laughed. She laughed. "Onlest freedom he be knowin is what he say the 'righteous freedom,' that what the Lawd be givin him or what the Mas be givin him and he was the firstest one the patter-rollers kills." She moved back into the darkness of the cellar still laughing softly and when I called to her she would not respond. Finally she moved back so that I could see the outline of her form. "Whatcho want?" she called. "Whatcho want?" I could feel my anger rising at the insolence of her tone, but just then Hughes called that we were ready to start. I rose and brushed the dirt from the knees of my trousers. I did not want to leave then, for I felt that some barrier had risen between us which must be breached. I realize now, however, that it was a fortuitous circumstance that

Hughes called at just that moment. Otherwise I might have been betrayed into some impetuous action that might have permanently harmed this project. You will learn what I require when I return, I flung at her, and went to join Hughes. I could hear her voice raised, joining with the others in the new song which the other darkies had commenced during my conversation with her:

> *Good news, Lawd, Lawd, good news.*
> *My brotha got a seat and I so glad.*
> *I hearda from heav'n today.*
> *Good news, Lawdy, Lawd, Lawd. Good news.*
> *I don't mind what Satan say*
> *Cause I heard, yes I heard, well I heard from heav'n*
> *today.*

Pray God that nothing happens to upset the mood evinced by her singing. We have much to talk about, Odessa and I, when we resume our conversations.

▲   ▲   ▲

Somewhere West of Linden

July 3, 1829.

A wild-goose chase and a sorry time we have had of it. There is doubt in my mind that such an encampment, as I first conceived of, exists, at least in this vicinity, for we have searched a large area and come up with nothing conclusive. Several times, we sighted what might have been members of such a band, but the dogs could not tree them and it was more than we ourselves could do to catch more than what we *hope* were fleeting glimpses of black bodies. Whether they took, indeed, to the trees, as some in the posse maintain, or vanished into the air, I have no way of knowing. If they exist, they are as elusive as Indians, nay, as elusive as *smoke* and I feel it beyond the ability of so large a posse as ours to move

warily enough to take them unawares. To compound matters, the
storm which has been threatening for days finally broke this morning, putting an end to our search and drenching us in the process.
We have stopped to rest the horses, for Hughes estimates that if we
push hard, we should reach Linden by nightfall. A bed will be most
welcome after having spent so many days upon the back of this
wretched horse, and I look forward to resuming my conversations
with Odessa. She has a subtle presence, almost an influence which I
have only become aware of in its absence. Perhaps—but that is
useless speculation and must wait upon the certainty of Wilson's
return. Hughes has given the call to mount and so we are off.

▲   ▲   ▲

July 4, 1829.
Early Morning.

I put the date in wearied surprise. We have been out most of the
night scouring the countryside for signs of Odessa, but there were
none that we found and the rain has by now washed away what we
must have missed. It is as though the niggers who crept in and stole
away with her were not human blood, human flesh, but sorcerers
who whisked her away by magic to the accursed den they inhabit.
Hughes maintained that the devil merely claimed his own and gave
up the search around midnight. But reason tells me that the niggers
were not supernatural, not spirits or "haints." They are flesh and
bone and so must leave some trace of their coming and going. The
smallest clue would have sufficed me, for I should have followed it
to its ultimate end. Now the rain has come up and even that small
chance is gone, vanished like Odessa.

And we did not even know that she was gone, had, in fact, sat
down to eat the supper left warming at the back of the stove
against the chance that we would return, to talk of the futile
venture of the last few days, to conjecture on God knows what.
Unsuspecting we were, until the darky that sleeps with Jemina
came asking for her. Hughes went to inquire of his wife—who had

not arisen upon our return, merely called down to us that she was unwell and that food had been left for us. I was immediately alarmed, prescience I now know, upon learning that the woman had not seen Jemina since the wench had taken supper to Odessa earlier in the evening. And Hughes' assurances that Jemina was a good girl, having been with the wife since childhood, did nothing to calm my fears. Such a slight indisposition as his wife evidently had was no reason to entrust the keeping of so valuable a prisoner to another negress who is no doubt only slightly less sly than Odessa herself. I protested thus to Hughes, too strongly I now see, for he replied heatedly that if I did not keep my tongue from his wife—I marvel, even now in my exhaustion, at the quaintness of his phrasing—my slight stature would not keep me from a beating. I am firm in my belief that these impetuous words of mine were a strong factor in his early abandonment of the search and I regret them accordingly. There are stronger words in my mind now, but I forbore, at that time, carrying the discussion farther. I knew, even then, without really knowing why, that time was of the essence. But he shall find on the morrow that even one of my *slight stature* has the means of prosecuting him for criminal neglect. To think of leaving Odessa in the care of another nigger!

The root cellar when we reached it was locked, but the relief I felt was short-lived. It was Jemina inside and the wench set up such a racket, then, when it could not possibly serve any useful purpose, that one would have thought the hounds of hell pursued her. Even had I not recognized that such a cacophony could never issue from Odessa's throat, Hughes' startled exclamation was enough to alert me. The wench was, of course, incoherent—when was a nigger in excitement ever anything else?—but we finally pieced together, between the wench's throwing her apron over her head and howl-ing, "oh, Mas, it terr'ble; they was terr'ble fierce," and pointing to her muddied gown to prove it, what must have happened. Three niggers (she said three the first time and the number has increased with each successive telling; perhaps there were only one or two, but I settle upon three as the most likely number, for they were obviously the niggers with whom Odessa was in league in the uprising on the coffle. I could scream to think that even as we were out chasing shadows, the cunning devils were even then lying in wait to spirit her away. And to think that she—*she* was so deep as to give never an indication that they were then lurking about. Both Jemina and that woman of Hughes swear that except for a natural melancholy—which in itself was not unusual—*I* have been the only one to succeed in coaxing her into animated spirits—there was nothing out of the ordinary in Odessa's demeanor these last days. And knowing now the cupidity of which she is capable, I must believe them). The three bucks overpowered the wench just as she opened the door to the cellar to hand down the evening meal to Odessa. At this point, Hughes ejaculated something to the effect that it was a good thing "my Betty" was not present, at which the negress began what must have been, had I not intervened, a long digression on the "Mist's" symptoms and how she might, at long last, be increasing. But I could *feel* those niggers getting farther away with Odessa and so could not bear the interruption. The niggers forced Jemina into the cellar, bound her, took up Odessa and escaped into the night. The wench swears she heard no names called, that except for one exclamation from Odessa, of surprise or dismay, she could not tell which, they fled in silence, swears also that she could not see well enough to describe either of the niggers, save to state that they were big and black and terrible as though that would help to distinguish them from any of the hundreds, *thousands* of niggers in this world who are equally as big and as black and as terrible. The wench could not even tell whether they went on horseback or afoot, nor explain how a woman almost nine months gone could move so quickly and so quietly as to give no clue to the direction they took, nor less explain how it came about that she herself did not cry out, for surely if she had someone must have heard. This last question was again the occasion for that banshee-like wail about how "terr'ble fierce" the niggers were.

Hughes numbers among his four slaves one he termed an expert tracker, skilled in the ways of the Indians in hunting and trapping, but we did not need his help in finding the place where they had lain in wait for someone to open the cellar door. The earlier rain had made their sign quite plain. We found, also, with heartening ease the place where they had tied their animals. It was muddied and much trampled so we could not tell what kind of animals they were—whether horses or mules—nor even how many. Hughes' jocular, and inappropriately so, prediction that we should find Odessa and her newborn brat—for what female as far gone as she could stand the strain of a quick flight without giving birth to something—lying beside the trail within a mile or so proved incorrect, for the tracks disappeared into the deep underbrush a short distance from the place where the animals had been tied. Both the nigger and the one bloodhound Hughes keeps were alike worthless in the quest. And then the rain came up, driven by a furious wind, lashing the needle-like drops into our faces; washing away all trace of Odessa. Hughes, in giving up the hunt, charged that I acted like one possessed. He could not say by what and I know that this was merely his own excuse for failing in his lawful duty. For myself, I have searched, hunted, called and am now exhausted. She is gone. Even the smallest clue—but there was nothing, no broken twig to point a direction, no scent which the hound could hold for more than a short distance. Gone. And I not even aware, not even suspecting, just—just gone.

SHERLEY ANNE WILLIAMS
Bibliography

Until the publication of *Dessa Rose,* Sherley Anne Williams was known more for her critical contributions than for her creative works. Despite her award-winning poetry *(Someone Sweet Angel Chile,* published in 1982, and *The Peacock Poems,* which was nominated for a National Book Award in 1976) and the considerable notice given to *Dessa Rose* by reviewers, there are only two scholarly articles devoted to that novel. In "(W)riting the Work and Working the Rites" by Mae G. Henderson (in *Gender and Theory: A Dialogue Between the Sexes,* ed. Linda Kauffman, London: Basil Blackwell, in press), Henderson argues that *Dessa Rose,* by involving the reader in challenging the authority of the verbal, narrative, and thematic structures in William Styron's *Confessions of Nat Turner* constitutes a "powerful questioning" and "revision" of the Styron text, and by extension, questions the integrity and accuracy of white male scholarly interpretations of black female experience.

Deborah McDowell's "Negotiating Between Tenses: Witnessing Slavery After Freedom—*Dessa Rose,*" in *Slavery and the Literary Imagination: Selected Papers from the English Institute,* ed. Deborah McDowell and Arnold Rampersad, (Johns Hopkins University Press, 1989, pp. 144–63), demonstrates the ways in which Williams stages multiple and often contradictory versions of Dessa Rose's

278

experience. For McDowell, Williams is distinctive, for while she involves us in the problematic nature of finding and representing "truth," she never succumbs to contemporary "empty nations of radical indeterminacy." Instead, McDowell writes, "while there might not be one 'truth' about Dessa (or about slavery more generally) there are 'certainties' that the text stubbornly claims and validates and those it tries to subvert." McDowell also argues that the post-sixties outpouring of fiction about slavery written by women suggests a trend which "dramatizes not what was *done* to slave women but what they did to what was done to them."

Of the many reviews devoted to *Dessa Rose,* Michelle Wallace's essay in *Women's Review of Books* (Vol. 4 No. 1, October 1986) is the most helpful. Supplying literary and historical contexts for the novel, Wallace shows how its female point of view decenters patriarchal authority, allowing finally a definition of friendship as collective struggle that ultimately transcends both race and class. Other reviews include those by Marcia Gillespie in *Ms.* (September 1986, p. 20); by Doris Davenport in *Black American Literature Forum* (Fall 1986, p. 335); and by David Bradley in *The New York Times Book Review* (August 2, 1986, p. 7).

ALICE WALKER

Although Alice Walker is known primarily as a novelist and short story writer, she has written three landmark essays about the woman artist which, taken together, reveal a strikingly different portrait of the black woman as artist from the one found in her fiction. The three essays, published within five years of one another, from 1974 to 1979, follow a similar pattern. Each essay begins with a very moving story of an artist struggling amidst desperate circumstances to keep the creative spark alive. These portraits of desperate and despairing artists lead Walker to consider the many ways the creativity of black women artists was kept alive in spite of the most demeaning kinds of physical and intellectual subjugation. Having considered the implications of this history of suppressed creativity and the ways in which many black women artists subvert it, Walker ends each essay with a female figure whose powerful presence has helped to nurture and sustain her own art: in the first essay, her mother; in the second, Zora Neale Hurston; and in the third, her daughter, Rebecca. The three essays end with a sense that satisfactory and even triumphant solutions have been found for difficult and complex problems, harmony constructed by a narrative of individual and personal triumph. While Walker's essays on black women's creativity are forceful and compelling and self-assured, her fiction suggests that the problems of artistic creation for women, rooted in women's own ambivalence to female power and patriarchal politics are far more intractable and resistant to resolution than her essays would lead us to believe.

In the most famous of these essays, "In Search of Our Mothers' Gardens," Walker gives us a collective portrait of nineteenth-century black women, whose rich creative genius, undiscovered and unused in lives dominated by back-breaking work, child-bearing, and sexual abuse, must have, she believes, driven them insane. In this essay, Walker imagines these heart-breaking possibilities for a nineteenth-century black woman artist:

> [Perhaps she] died under some ignorant and depraved white overseer's lash? Or was she required to bake biscuits for a lazy backwater tramp, when she cried out in her soul to paint watercolors of sunsets, or the rain falling on the green and peaceful pasturelands? Or was her body broken and forced to bear children . . . when her one joy was the thought of modelling heroic figures of Rebellion in stone or clay?[1]

But, of course, Walker knows that the story of black women's creativity does not end with insanity or despair. Black women, as she shows us in this essay, have found countless ways to inscribe themselves in art—from quiltmaking and blues singing and oral storytelling to the famous gardens created by Walker's own mother, Minnie Lou Walker, who inspired this essay. Walker acknowledges that the art of the present generation of black women —from the sweet sounds of Roberta Flack to Walker's own fiction —bears the signature of these singers, weavers, quilters, garden makers, and storytellers of the past who preserved and passed on a rich artistic legacy.

In the second essay, "Saving the Life That Is Your Own: The

---

[1] Alice Walker, "In Search of Our Mothers' Gardens," in *In Search of Our Mothers' Gardens: Womanist Prose by Alice Walker* (New York: Harcourt Brace Jovanovich, 1983, p. 233).

Importance of Models in the Artist's Life," the struggling artist is Vincent Van Gogh as he sits in a mental institution in France writing to a friend in desperation and anguish over the difficulties of the artist's life: "Society makes our existence wretchedly difficult at times; hence our impotence and the imperfection of our work . . . I myself am suffering under an absolute lack of models."[2] Six months later, Walker reminds us, Van Gogh committed suicide. If the lack of models was a hardship for Van Gogh, it is, according to Walker, an even greater hazard for black women writers. In Walker's own career as artist, despite four years at prestigious colleges (one black, one white), she tells us that she had to search long and hard for a tradition of black women writing to sustain and guide her own writing. In this essay the saving female figure again appears to offer that guidance; it is Zora Neale Hurston, whose folklore studies, as well as her fiction and autobiography, provide for Walker a basis for artistic continuity between Hurston's generation and her own. Not only does Hurston provide the historical underpinnings for Walker's fiction, she also provides a mine of authentic black folklore which empowers Walker to understand and use folklore in her own work.

In the third essay, "One Child of One's Own: A Meaningful Digression Within the Work(s)," the struggling and desperate artist is Walker herself, trying to survive the harshness of a New England winter with a baby under two years of age, both mother and child suffering from illnesses brought on by the transition from Mississippi to Massachusetts. In this essay, the woman artist who, of course, survives, proceeds to examine the assumption of many feminists that bearing children can be a hindrance to a woman trying to be an artist. Walker considers this possibility and, though she doubts that a woman committed to her art can have more than one child, she concludes that her experiences teach her that racism and sexism (the latter coming often from white feminists) are far more threatening obstacles to her work than her own child. Walker

[2] "Saving the Life That Is Your Own: The Importance of Models in the Artist's Life" in *In Search of Our Mothers' Gardens,* p. 4.

ends this essay, as she does the other two, with a female figure who nurtures and sustains the writer. This time it is her own daughter, Rebecca, who becomes her friend and sister, standing with the writer as a firm ally "against whatever denies us all that we are."[3]

The three stories by Walker in this anthology, also about the female artist, suggest that the female artist's relationship to her art is a far more problematic one than her essays allow. Walker's fiction does not express the optimism and the certainties of her essays, and often the artist's empowerment is achieved through an accommodation to male authority, not through female bonding. While Walker as essayist is able to ward off the disturbing threat of male dominance and female anxiety over that threat, her fiction, particularly her early short stories, reveal quite openly that the black woman artist, while she must deal with the ways a white racist culture suppresses and denies her creativity, still finds herself up against "all those patriarchal definitions that intervene between herself and herself."[4]

In "A Sudden Trip Home in the Spring" (1971), the black woman artist, Sarah Davis, is a painter and sculptor, studying at an Ivy League Women's College (much like Walker's own alma ma-

[3] Alice Walker, "One Child of One's Own: A Meaningful Digression Within the Work(s)" in *In Search of Our Mothers' Gardens,* p. 382. In her essay "Maternal Anger/Maternal Love: Silent Themes and Meaningful Digressions," in *Unspeakable Plots: Mothers, Daughters, and Narratives* (Bloomington: Indiana University Press, 1989), Marianne Hirsch maintains that in "One Child of One's Own," Walker idealizes both motherhood and the bond she has with her child, running a risk, therefore, of turning the child into an adoring "maternal" figure and thereby erasing her.

[4] In *The Madwoman in the Attic: The Woman Writer and the Nineteenth-Century Literary Imagination* (New Haven: Yale University Press, 1979), Sandra M. Gilbert and Susan Gubar explore very perceptively the relationship between the female writer and the male literary tradition, and, while they are dealing specifically with a white tradition, their analysis of the *female* struggles of the female author against male literary authority are clearly applicable in many ways, to black women writers. In her essays on the necessity of precursors for the woman writer, Walker is actually the precursor to *Madwoman.*

ter, Sarah Lawrence). In the original edition of *Black-Eyed Susans,*
published in 1975, this was the closing story, selected precisely
because of what seemed to me then its clear-eyed optimism. The
resolution of that story, in which the young black woman is given
"permission" for her art through her relationship with a wise and
loving older brother and a patriarchal grandfather, did not strike
me then as contradictory but as recuperative. A black woman,
unable to paint the faces of black men because of the defeat she sees
there, re-establishes connections with her militant preacher brother
and her solemnly heroic grandfather at the funeral of her father.
Unlike her literary ancestor, Richard Wright, the only black writer
named in the story, Sarah Davis is released into art by this reunion
with her male relatives.[5] Many questions about the black woman
artist are raised in this story but not answered. We don't know, for
example, how Sarah's reconciliation with her father and her changing attitude toward black men will affect the way she depicts black
women, whom she describes stereotypically as "matronly, massive
or arm, with a weary victory showing in their eyes." Nor do we
get any sense of Sarah's relationship with women other than a
rather condescending one with her grandmother and the almost
hostile, reserved one she maintains with her schoolmates.

In "Everyday Use," published two years later in 1973, all three
women characters are artists of some kind: Mama, as the narrator,
tells her own story; Maggie is the quiltmaker, and Dee, the photographer and collector of the arts, has designed her jewelry, dress, and
hair so deliberately and self-consciously that she appears in the
story as a kind of self-creation. Walker herself has said that she
thinks of these characters as herself split into three parts, each
woman representing a different aspect of herself as artist: ·

---

[5] Richard Wright's reunion with his father is, of course, very different from Sarah
Davis's reconciliation with her father. Wright tells us in his autobiography, *Black
Boy* (1945) that when he visited his father after twenty-five years had elapsed, he
saw only a peasant whose experiences were so limited and limiting that father and
son would be strangers forever.

In other words I really see that story as almost about one person, the old woman and two daughters being one person. The one who stays and sustains—this is the older woman—who has on the one hand a daughter who is the same way, who stays and abides and loves, plus the part of them—this autonomous person, the part of them that also wants to go out into the world to see change and be changed . . . I do in fact have an African name that was given to me, and I love it and use it when I want to, and I love my Kenyan gowns and my Ugandan gowns—the whole bit—it's a part of me. But, on the other hand, my parents and grandparents were part of it, and they take precedence.[6]

The male triumvirate of "A Sudden Trip Home in the Spring" has been replaced by three women characters, but this female community does not generate a sense of reconciliation. The narrator-mother remains hostile to Dee throughout the story, setting up an opposition between the two daughters which seems to mirror Walker's own internal struggle as an artist. Maggie, the daughter who stays and abides, is homely and fearful and shy, (somewhat the way Walker describes herself as a child), but it is she who knows the tradition and has the skill to make the quilts. Mama chooses Maggie and rejects the daughter who would turn these family traditions into art. Dee, the photographer and outsider, returning to claim the artifacts whose meaning is located in the family relationships, in some ways represents the black writer (Walker herself at another stage) appropriating the oral tradition in order to turn it into a written artifact which will no longer be available for "everyday use" by its originators.

Susan Willis points out in *Specifying: Black Women Writing the American Experience* that when the black writer takes the materials of folk culture and subjects them to fiction, a system of meaning and telling that originates in the dominant culture, she is engaged

[6] Interview with Mary Helen Washington, June 1972, Jackson, Mississippi.

in "an enterprise fraught with contradiction."[7]The oppositions in "Everyday Use," between mother and daughters and sisters, between art for everyday use and art for art's sake, between insider and outsider, certainly capture that sense of contradiction and conflict. The story ends with Mama choosing Maggie and rejecting Dee, but Dee, who represents Walker herself as the artist who returns home, at least imaginatively, in order to collect the material for her art, certainly cannot be repressed. In this story, as in her essays, Walker shows that the quiltmaker, who has female precursors and female guidance, has an easier relationship with her art than the "deviant" female who finds herself outside of acceptable boundaries.

Walker's central character and narrator in the third story, "Advancing Luna . . . and Ida B. Wells," finding herself outside of those boundaries, experiences such a crisis that she is unable to write an ending to her own story. Trying to confront the reality of her friend's rape, she breaks off her narrative several times, once to interview Ida B. Wells, who tells her to say nothing in order to protect black men.[8] Then the narrator appends a section called "Second Thoughts," in which she and a male lover somewhat condescendingly agree that the rape should be classified as "morally wrong" and "shameful." Over the years the narrator adds other endings, one which offers further characteristics of Luna and one ("Imaginary Knowledge") which tries to explain why Luna later consents to sleep with her rapist. The narrator then "requires" Luna and her rapist to struggle together over his power to rape her and her power "to intimidate an entire people"—until the two of them

[7] Susan Willis, *Specifying: Black Women Writing the American Experience* (Madison: University of Wisconsin Press, 1987, pp. 69–70).

[8] Ida B. Wells (1862–1929), intellectual and activist, formed a one-woman crusade against lynching in the nineteenth and early twentieth centuries. As a journalist and one of the editors of the *Memphis Free Speech,* a black newspaper, she began publishing the facts about lynching, showing that the crime of "rape" which precipitated many lynchings was often an interracial affair between two consenting parties, white women and black men. For publishing these incendiary facts, Wells was driven out of Memphis. She continued her work in New York and Chicago.

have removed "the stumbling block of the rape." Aside from the callousness of forcing the rape victim to discuss her rape with her rapist, the narrator continues to distance herself and the reader from Luna, first by sexualizing the story of the rape by having Luna later sleep with the rapist and finally by replacing the original story of friendship between two women with a friendship between herself and a man. The man is Luna's total opposite. Luna is just barely attractive, slightly asthmatic, pimply-faced, and naive, and she goes off to Goa, a Portuguese colony, to live on the beach. The mural-ist-photographer is "a handsome, brown, erect individual, politi-cally committed and sophisticated enough to understand that the government may have engineered Luna's rape in order to discredit a political movement. Luna is now merely a "character," whereas the narrator and the muralist are presumably "real people, "capable of acting outside of the fiction(s) which dominate Luna. The narra-tor, however, has also been subsumed under the muralist's fiction as the ending of her tale is supplied by the voice of the male author-ity, dominating both the narrator and her art. I think Walker re-veals a great deal (perhaps inadvertently) in this story about the male dominance of the black political movements of the sixties and early seventies. There are fifteen references to important political men in the story; only one woman, Ida B. Wells, is mentioned, and her name is invoked on behalf of men. Those references capture the spirit of the black political events of the sixties, the dominance of the male voice and the male presence and the sense of women as marginalized (not in actual political work but certainly in the reporting of it).

What then does this story say about the black woman as writer and artist? Why does this narrator legitimize male experience and repress the female voice? Is the narrator's inability to finish her narrative until a male supplies the authoritative ending an indica-tion of women's ambivalent relation to the act of writing? The masculine values that prevail here fracture the female text as they have fractured the female friendship.[9] The break with Luna paral-

---

[9] Elizabeth Abel, "Narrative Structure(s) and Female Development: The Case of *Mrs. Dalloway*" in *The Voyage In: Fictions of Female Development* ed. Elizabeth

lels the break in the narrative, and both separations are caused by the insertion of male power.

Much of Walker's fiction from the 1970s poses male dominance as the primary threat to the woman artist.[10] But in "A Sudden Trip Home in the Spring" Walker poses male authority and male acceptance as the keys which unlock the doors to the house of art. In "Advancing Luna . . ." the male voice represses female art. Both positions suggest how problematic fiction writing is for women. Unlike quiltmaking and garden making and even blues singing, which are part of a woman's tradition, the writing of fiction is still done under the shadow of men, without female authority. The self-assurance and sense of vocation bequeathed to women artists in fields where women are predominant create the fire behind Walker's essays. Her fiction tells us, however, that when the woman's art is writing she will have to struggle against many layers of resistance to her art—including her own internal conflicts.

Abel, Marianne Hirsch, and Elizabeth Langland (Hanover, N.H.: University Press of New England, 1983), I am indebted to Elizabeth Abel for this remarkable essay on Virginia Woolf and to Woolf herself for her analysis of how masculine values invade the culture and therefore the literature, "inserting a duality into the female narrative" which separates women from themselves and their values. Abel writes, "This schizoid perspective can fracture the female text" (p. 163). The relationship between black women's texts and male power has rarely been discussed, but as my readings of Walker show, the "discomfort" black women experience in that relationship is embedded in the plots of their stories.

[10] Perhaps the paradigmatic story of male dominance of black women's writing is Walker's chilling story "The Child Who Favored Daughter" in her short story collection *In Love and Trouble* (New York: Harcourt Brace Jovanovich, 1973, pp. 35–46). In this story the young daughter is a letter writer whose love letter to a white man is intercepted by her jealous and domineering father. The letter is so powerful that even when it is rainsoaked the father can still make out " 'I love you' written in a firm hand." For her defiance and rebelliousness, as she refuses to deny the letter, the daughter is brutally assaulted by her father. It does not take too much stretching of the imagination to see the letter as a representation of black women's writing (especially in light of the letter-writing structure of *The Color Purple)* and to see the father's need to destroy the writer as the patriarchal control which intervenes between the writer and her art.

Alice Walker

A Sudden Trip Home in the Spring

FOR THE WELLESLEY CLASS

I

Sarah walked slowly off the tennis court, fingering the back of her head, feeling the sturdy dark hair that grew there. She was popular. As she walked along the path toward Talfinger Hall, her friends fell into place around her. They formed a warm, jostling group of six. Sarah, because she was taller than the rest, saw the messenger first.

"Miss Davis," he said, standing still until the group came abreast of him, "I've got a telegram for ye." Brian was Irish and always quite respectful. He stood with his cap in his hand until Sarah took the telegram. Then he gave a nod that included all the young ladies before he turned away. He was young and good-looking, though annoyingly servile, and Sarah's friends twittered.

"Well, open it!" someone cried, for Sarah stood staring at the yellow envelope, turning it over and over in her hand.

"Look at her," said one of the girls, "isn't she beautiful! Such eyes, and hair, and *skin!*"

Sarah's tall, caplike hair framed a face of soft brown angles, high cheekbones, and large, dark eyes. Her eyes enchanted her

290

friends because they always seemed to know more, and to find more of life amusing, or sad, than Sarah cared to tell.

Her friends often teased Sarah about her beauty; they loved dragging her out of her room so that their boy friends, naïve and worldly young men from Princeton and Yale, could see her. They never guessed she found this distasteful. She was gentle with her friends, and her outrage at their tactlessness did not show. She was most often inclined to pity them, though embarrassment sometimes drove her to fraudulent expressions. Now she smiled and raised eyes and arms to heaven. She acknowledged their unearned curiosity as a mother endures the prying impatience of a child. Her friends beamed love and envy upon her as she tore open the telegram.

"He's dead," she said.

Her friends reached out for the telegram, their eyes on Sarah.

"It's her father," one of them said softly. "He died yesterday. Oh, Sarah," the girl whimpered, "I'm so sorry!"

"Me too." "So am I." "Is there anything we can do?"

But Sarah had walked away, head high and neck stiff.

"So graceful!" one of her friends said.

"Like a proud gazelle," said another. Then they all trooped to their dormitories to change for supper.

Talfinger Hall was a pleasant dorm. The common room just off the entrance had been made into a small modern-art gallery with some very good original paintings, lithographs, and collages. Pieces were constantly being stolen. Some of the girls could not resist an honest-to-God Chagall, signed (in the plate) by his own hand, though they could have afforded to purchase one from the gallery in town. Sarah Davis' room was next door to the gallery, but her walls were covered with inexpensive Gauguin reproductions, a Reubens ("The Head of a Negro"), a Modigliani, and a Picasso. There was a full wall of her own drawings, all of black women. She found black men impossible to draw or to paint; she could not bear to trace defeat onto blank pages. Her women figures were matronly, massive of arm, with a weary victory showing in their eyes. Surrounded by Sarah's drawings was a red SNCC poster of an

old man holding a small girl whose face nestled in his shoulder.
Sarah often felt she was the little girl whose face no one could see.

To leave Talfinger even for a few days filled Sarah with fear.
Talfinger was her home now; it suited her better than any home
she'd ever known. Perhaps she loved it because in winter there was
a fragrant fireplace and snow outside her window. When hadn't
she dreamed of fireplaces that really warmed, snow that almost
pleasantly froze? Georgia seemed far away as she packed; she did
not want to leave New York, where, her grandfather had liked to
say, "the devil hangs out and catches young gals by the front of
their dresses." He had always believed the South the best place to
live on earth (never mind that certain people invariably marred the
landscape), and swore he expected to die no more than a few miles
from where he had been born. There was tenacity even in the gray
frame house he lived in, and in scrawny animals on his farm who
regularly reproduced. He was the first person Sarah wanted to see
when she got home.

There was a knock on the door of the adjoining bathroom, and
Sarah's suite mate entered, a loud Bach Concerto just finishing
behind her. At first she stuck just her head into the room, but seeing
Sarah fully dressed she trudged in and plopped down on the bed.
She was a heavy blond girl with large, milk-white legs. Her eyes
were small and her neck usually gray with grime.

"My, don't you look gorgeous," she said.

"Ah, Pam," said Sarah, waving her hand in disgust. In Georgia
she knew that even to Pam she would be just another ordinarily
attractive *colored* girl. In Georgia there were a million girls better
looking. Pam wouldn't know that, of course, she'd never been to
Georgia; she'd never even seen a black person to speak to—that is,
before she met Sarah. One of her first poetic observations about
Sarah was that she was "a poppy in a field of winter roses." She had
found it weird that Sarah did not own more than one coat.

"Say, listen, Sarah," said Pam, "I heard about your father. I'm
sorry. I really am."

"Thanks," said Sarah.

"Is there anything we can do? I thought, well, maybe you'd

want my father to get somebody to fly you down. He'd go himself but he's taking mother to Madeira this week. You wouldn't have to worry about trains and things."

Pamela's father was one of the richest men in the world, though no one ever mentioned it. Pam only alluded to it at times of crisis, when a friend might benefit from the use of a private plane, train, or ship; or, if someone wanted to study the characteristics of a totally secluded village, island, or mountain, she might offer one of theirs. Sarah could not comprehend such wealth, and was always annoyed because Pam didn't look more like a billionaire's daughter. A billionaire's daughter, Sarah thought, should really be less horsy and brush her teeth more often.

"Gonna tell me what you're brooding about?" asked Pam.

Sarah stood in front of the radiator, her fingers resting on the window seat. Down below, girls were coming up the hill from supper.

"I'm thinking," she said, "of the child's duty to his parents after they are dead."

"Is that all?"

"Do you know," asked Sarah, "about Richard Wright and his father?"

Pamela frowned. Sarah looked down at her.

"Oh, I forgot," she said with a sigh, "they don't teach Wright here. The poshest school in the U.S. and the girls come out ignorant." She looked at her watch, saw she had twenty minutes before her train. "Really," she said almost inaudibly, "why Tears Eliot, Ezratic Pound, and even Sara Teacake, and no Wright?" She and Pamela thought e. e. cummings very clever with his perceptive spelling of great literary names.

"Is he a poet, then?" asked Pam. She adored poetry, all poetry. Half of America's poetry she had, of course, not read, for the simple reason that she had never heard of it.

"No," said Sarah, "he wasn't a poet." She felt weary. "He was a man who wrote, a man who had trouble with his father." She began to walk about the room, and came to stand below the picture of the old man and the little girl.

"When he was a child," she continued, "his father ran off with another woman, and one day when Richard and his mother went to ask him for money to buy food, he laughingly rejected them. Richard, being very young, thought his father Godlike—big, omnipotent, unpredictable, undependable, and cruel; entirely in control of his universe; just like God. But, many years later, after Wright had become a famous writer, he went down to Mississippi to visit his father. He found, instead of God, just an old, watery-eyed field hand, bent from plowing, his teeth gone, smelling of manure. Richard realized that the most daring thing his 'God' had done was run off with that other woman."

"So?" asked Pam. "What 'duty' did he feel he owed the old man?"

"So," said Sarah, "that's what Wright wondered as he peered into that old, shifty-eyed Mississippi Negro face. What was the duty of the son of a destroyed man? The son of a man whose vision had stopped at the edge of fields that weren't even his. Who was Wright without his father? Was he Wright the great writer? Wright the Communist? Wright the French farmer? Wright whose wife could never accompany him to Mississippi? Was he, in fact, still his father's son? Or was he freed by his father's desertion to be nobody's son, to be his own father? Could he disavow his father and live? And if so, live as what? As whom? And for what purpose?"

"Well," said Pam, swinging her hair over her shoulders and squinting her small eyes, "if his father rejected him I don't see why Wright even bothered to go see him again. From what you've said, Wright earned the freedom to be whoever he wanted to be. To a strong man a father is not essential."

"Maybe not," said Sarah, "but Wright's father was one faulty door in a house of many ancient rooms. Was that one faulty door to shut him off forever from the rest of the house? That was the question. And though he answered this question eloquently in his work, where it really counted, one can only wonder if he was able to answer it satisfactorily—or at all—in his life."

"You're thinking of his father more as a symbol of something, aren't you?" asked Pam.

"I suppose," said Sarah, taking a last look around her room. "I see him as a door that refused to open, a hand that was always closed. A fist."

Pamela walked with her to one of the college limousines, and in a few minutes she was at the station. The train to the city was just arriving.

"Have a nice trip," said the middle-aged driver courteously as she took her suitcase from him. But, for about the thousandth time since she'd seen him, he winked at her.

Once away from her friends, she did not miss them. The school was all they had in common. How could they ever know her if they were not allowed to know Wright? she wondered. She was interesting, "beautiful," only because they had no idea what made her, charming only because they had no idea from where she came. And where they came from, though she glimpsed it—in themselves and in F. Scott Fitzgerald—she was never to enter. She hadn't the inclination or the proper ticket.

II

Her father's body was in Sarah's old room. The bed had been taken down to make room for the flowers and chairs and casket. Sarah looked for a long time into the face, as if to find some answer to her questions written there. It was the same face, a dark, Shake-spearean head framed by gray, woolly hair and split almost in half by a short, gray mustache. It was a completely silent face, a shut face. But her father's face also looked fat, stuffed, and ready to burst. He wore a navy-blue suit, white shirt, and black tie. Sarah bent and loosened the tie. Tears started behind her shoulder blades but did not reach her eyes.

"There's a rat here under the casket," she called to her brother, who apparently did not hear her, for he did not come in. She was alone with her father, as she had rarely been when he was alive. When he was alive she had avoided him.

"Where's that girl at?" her father would ask. "Done closed herself up in her room again," he would answer himself.

For Sarah's mother had died in her sleep one night. Just gone to bed tired and never got up. And Sarah had blamed her father.

Stare the rat down, thought Sarah; surely that will help. *Perhaps it doesn't matter whether I misunderstood or never understood.*

"We moved so much, looking for crops, a place to *live,*" her father had moaned, accompanied by Sarah's stony silence. "The moving killed her. And now we have a real house, with *four* rooms, and a mailbox on the *porch,* and it's too late. She gone. *She* ain't here to see it." On very bad days her father would not eat at all. At night he did not sleep.

Whatever had made her think she knew what love was or was not?

Here she was, Sarah Davis, immersed in Camusian philosophy, versed in many languages, a poppy, of all things, among winter roses. But before she became a poppy she was a native Georgian sunflower, but still had not spoken the language they both knew. Not to him.

Stare the rat down, she thought, and did. The rascal dropped his bold eyes and slunk away. Sarah felt she had, at least, accomplished something.

Why did she have to see the picture of her mother, the one on the mantel among all the religious doodads, come to life? Her mother had stood stout against the years, clean gray braids shining across the top of her head, her eyes snapping, protective. Talking to her father.

"He called you out your name, we'll leave this place today. Not tomorrow. That be too late. Today!" Her mother was magnificent in her quick decisions.

"But what about your garden, the children, the change of schools?" Her father would be holding, most likely, the wide brim of his hat in nervously twisting fingers.

"He called you out your name, we go!"

And go they would. Who knew exactly where, before they moved? Another soundless place, walls falling down, roofing gone; another face to please without leaving too much of her father's pride at his feet. But to Sarah then, no matter with what alacrity her father moved, foot-dragging alone was visible.

The moving killed her, her father had said, but the moving was also love.

Did it matter now that often he had threatened their lives with the rage of his despair? That once he had spanked the crying baby violently, who later died of something else altogether . . . and that the next day they moved?

"No," said Sarah aloud, "I don't think it does."

"Huh?" It was her brother, tall, wiry, black, deceptively calm. As a child he'd had an irrepressible temper. As a grown man he was tensely smooth, like a river that any day will overflow its bed.

He had chosen a dull gray casket. Sarah wished for red. Was it Dylan Thomas who had said something grand about the dead offering "deep, dark defiance"? It didn't matter; there were more ways to offer defiance than with a red casket.

"I was just thinking," said Sarah, "that with us Mama and Daddy were saying NO with capital letters."

"I don't follow you," said her brother. He had always been the activist in the family. He simply directed his calm rage against any obstacle that might exist, and awaited the consequences with the same serenity he awaited his sister's answer. Not for him the philosophical confusions and poetic observations that hung his sister up.

"That's because you're a radical preacher," said Sarah, smiling up at him. "You deliver your messages in person with your own body." It excited her that her brother had at last imbued their childhood Sunday sermons with the reality of fighting for change. And saddened her that no matter how she looked at it this seemed more important than Medieval Art, Course 201.

III

"Yes, Grandma," Sarah replied. "Cresselton is for girls only, and *No,* Grandma, I am not pregnant."

Her grandmother stood clutching the broad, wooden handle of her black bag, which she held, with elbows bent, in front of her stomach. Her eyes glinted through round, wire-framed glasses. She spat into the grass outside the privy. She had insisted that Sarah accompany her to the toilet while the body was being taken into the church. She had leaned heavily on Sarah's arm, her own arm thin and the flesh like crepe.

"I guess they teach you how to really handle the world," she said. "And who knows, the Lord is everywhere. I would like a whole lot to see a great-grand. You don't specially have to be married, you know. That's why I felt free to ask." She reached into her bag and took out a Three Sixes bottle, which she proceeded to drink from, taking deep, swift swallows with her head thrown back.

"There are very few black boys near Cresselton," Sarah explained, watching the corn liquor leave the bottle in spurts and bubbles. "Besides, I'm really caught up now in my painting and sculpturing . . ." Should she mention how much she admired Giacometti's work? No, she decided. Even if her grandmother had heard of him, and Sarah was positive she had not, she would surely think his statues much too thin. This made Sarah smile and remember how difficult it had been to convince her grandmother that even if Cresselton had not given her a scholarship she would have managed to go there anyway. Why? Because she wanted somebody to teach her to paint and to sculpture, and Cresselton had the best teachers. Her grandmother's notion of a successful granddaughter was a married one, pregnant the first year.

"Well," said her grandmother, placing the bottle with dignity back into her purse and gazing pleadingly into Sarah's face, "I sure would 'preshate a great-grand." Seeing her granddaughter's smile, she heaved a great sigh, and, walking rather haughtily over the stones and grass, made her way to the church steps.

As they walked down the aisle, Sarah's eyes rested on the back of her grandfather's head. He was sitting on the front middle bench in front of the casket, his hair extravagantly long and white and softly kinked. When she sat down beside him, her grandmother sitting next to him on the other side, he turned toward her and gently took her hand in his. Sarah briefly leaned her cheek against his shoulder and felt like a child again.

IV

They had come twenty miles from town, on a dirt road, and the hot spring sun had drawn a steady rich scent from the honeysuckle vines along the way. The church was a bare, weatherbeaten ghost of a building with hollow windows and a sagging door. Arsonists had once burned it to the ground, lighting the dry wood of the walls with the flames from the crosses they carried. The tall, spreading red-oak tree under which Sarah had played as a child still dominated the churchyard, stretching its branches widely from the roof of the church to the other side of the road.

After a short and eminently dignified service, during which Sarah and her grandfather alone did not cry, her father's casket was slid into the waiting hearse and taken the short distance to the cemetery, an overgrown wilderness whose stark white stones appeared to be the small ruins of an ancient civilization. There Sarah watched her grandfather from the corner of her eye. He did not seem to bend under the grief of burying a son. His back was straight, his eyes dry and clear. He was simply and solemnly heroic, a man who kept with pride his family's trust and his own grief. *It is strange,* Sarah thought, *that I never thought to paint him like this, simply as he stands; without anonymous, meaningless people hovering beyond his profile; his face turned proud and brownly against the light.* The defeat that had frightened her in the faces of black men was the defeat of black forever defined by white. But that defeat was nowhere on her grandfather's face. He stood like a rock, outwardly calm, the grand patriarch of the Davis family. The family alone defined him, and he was not about to let them down.

"One day I will paint you, Grandpa," she said as they turned to go. "Just as you stand here now, with just," she moved closer and touched his face with her hand, "just the right stubborn tenseness of your cheek. Just that look of Yes and No in your eyes."

"You wouldn't want to paint an old man like me," he said,

looking deep into her eyes from wherever his mind had been. "If you want to make me, make me up in stone."

The completed grave was plump and red. The wreaths of flowers were arranged all on one side, so that from the road there appeared to be only a large mass of flowers. But already the wind was tugging at the rose petals and the rain was making dabs of faded color all over the greenfoam frames. In a week, the displaced honeysuckle vines, the wild roses, the grapevines, the grass, would be back. Nothing would seem to have changed.

V

"What do you mean, come *home?*" Her brother seemed genuinely amused. "We're all proud of you. How many black girls are at that school? Just *you?* Well, just one more besides you, and she's from the North. That's really something!"

"I'm glad you're pleased," said Sarah.

"Pleased! Why, it's what Mama would have wanted, a good education for little Sarah; and what Dad would have wanted too, if he could have wanted anything after Mama died. You were always smart. When you were two and I was five you showed me how to eat ice cream without getting it all over me. First, you said, nip off the bottom of the cone with your teeth, and suck the ice cream down. I never knew *how* you were supposed to eat the stuff once it began to melt."

"I don't know," she said; "sometimes you can want something a whole lot, only to find out later that it wasn't what you *needed* at all."

Sarah shook her head, a frown coming between her eyes. "I sometimes spend *weeks,*" she said, "trying to sketch or paint a face that is unlike every other face around me, except, vaguely, for one. Can I help but wonder if I'm in the right place?"

Her brother smiled. "You mean to tell me you spend *weeks* trying to draw one face, and you still wonder whether you're in the right place? You must be kidding!" He chucked her under the chin and laughed out loud. "You learn how to draw the face," he said, "then you learn how to paint me and how to make Grandpa up in stone. Then you can come home or go live in Paris, France. It'll be the same thing."

It was the unpreacher-like gaiety of his affection that made her cry. She leaned peacefully into her brother's arms. She wondered if Richard Wright had had a brother.

"You are my door to all the rooms," she said; "don't ever close."

And he said, "I won't," as if he understood what she meant.

VI

"When will we see you again, young woman?" he asked later as he drove her to the bus stop.

"I'll sneak up one day and surprise you," she said.

At the bus stop, in front of a tiny service station, Sarah hugged her brother with all her strength. The white station attendant stopped his work to leer at them, his eyes bold and careless.

"Did you ever think," said Sarah, "that we are a very old people in a very young place?"

She watched her brother from a window on the bus; her eyes did not leave his face until the little station was out of sight and the big Greyhound lurched on its way toward Atlanta. She would fly from there to New York.

VII

She took the train to the campus.

"My," said one of her friends, "you look wonderful! Home sure must agree with you!"

"Sarah was home?" someone who didn't know asked. "Oh, *great,* how was it?"

Well, how was it? went an echo in Sarah's head. The noise of the echo almost made her dizzy.

"How was it?" she asked aloud, searching for, and regaining, her balance.

"How was it?" She watched her reflection in a pair of smiling hazel eyes.

"It was fine," she said slowly, returning the smile, thinking of her grandfather. "Just fine."

The girl's smile deepened. Sarah watched her swinging along toward the back tennis courts, hair blowing in the wind.

Stare the rat down, thought Sarah; *and whether it disappears or not, I am a woman in the world. I have buried my father, and shall soon know how to make my grandpa up in stone.*

Alice Walker

Everyday Use

I will wait for her in the yard that Maggie and I made so clean and wavy yesterday afternoon. A yard like this is more comfortable than most people know. It is not just a yard. It is like an extended living room. When the hard clay is swept clean as a floor and the fine sand around the edges lined with tiny, irregular grooves, anyone can come and sit and look up into the elm tree and wait for the breezes that never come inside the house.

Maggie will be nervous until after her sister goes: she will stand hopelessly in corners, homely and ashamed of the burn scars down her arms and legs, eying her sister with a mixture of envy and awe. She thinks her sister has held life always in the palm of one hand, that "no" is a word the world never learned to say to her.

You've no doubt seen those TV shows where the child who has "made it" is confronted, as a surprise, by his own mother and father, tottering in weakly from backstage. (A pleasant surprise, of course: what would they do if parent and child came on the show only to curse out and insult each other?) On TV mother and child embrace and smile into each other's faces. Sometimes the mother and father weep, the child wraps them in his arms and leans across the table to tell how he would not have made it without their help. I have seen these programs.

Sometimes I dream a dream in which Dee and I are suddenly brought together on a TV program of this sort. Out of a dark and soft-seated limousine I am ushered into a bright room filled with many people. There I meet a smiling, gray, sporty man like Johnny Carson who shakes my hand and tells me what a fine girl I have. Then we are on the stage and Dee is embracing me with tears in her eyes. She pins on my dress a large orchid, even though she has told me once that she thinks orchids are tacky flowers.

In real life I am a large big-boned woman with rough, man-working hands. In the winter I wear flannel nightgowns to bed and overalls during the day. I can kill and clean a hog as mercilessly as a man. My fat keeps me hot in zero weather. I can work outside all day, breaking ice to get water for washing; I can eat pork liver cooked over the open fire minutes after it comes steaming from the hog. One winter I knocked a bull calf straight in the brain between the eyes with a sledgehammer and had the meat hung up to chill before nightfall. But of course all this does not show on television. I am the way my daughter would want me to be; a hundred pounds lighter, my skin like an uncooked barley pancake. My hair glistens in the hot bright lights. Johnny Carson has much to do to keep up with my quick and witty tongue.

But that is a mistake. I know even before I wake up. Who ever knew a Johnson with a quick tongue? Who can even imagine me looking a strange white man in the eye? It seems to me I have talked to them always with one foot raised in flight, with my head turned in whichever way is farthest from them. Dee, though. She would always look anyone in the eye. Hesitation was no part of her nature.

▲　▲　▲

"How do I look, Mama?" Maggie says, showing just enough of her thin body enveloped in pink skirt and red blouse for me to know she's there almost hidden by the door.

"Come out into the yard," I say.

Have you ever seen a lame animal, perhaps a dog run over by some careless person rich enough to own a car, sidle up to someone who is ignorant enough to be kind to him? That is the way my Maggie walks. She has been like this, chin on chest, eyes on ground, feet in shuffle, ever since the fire that burned the other house to the ground.

Dee is lighter than Maggie, with nicer hair and a fuller figure. She's a woman now, though sometimes I forget. How long ago was it that the other house burned? Ten, twelve years? Sometimes I can still hear the flames and feel Maggie's arms sticking to me, her hair smoking and her dress falling off her in little black papery flakes. Her eyes seemed stretched open, blazed open by the flames reflected in them. And Dee. I see her standing off under the sweet-gum tree she used to dig gum out of; a look of concentration on her face as she watched the last dingy gray board of the house fall in toward the red-hot brick chimney. Why don't you do a dance around the ashes? I'd wanted to ask her. She had hated the house that much.

I used to think she hated Maggie too. But that was before we raised the money, the church and me, to send her to Augusta to school. She used to read to us without pity; forcing words, lies, other folks' habits, whole lives upon us two, sitting trapped and ignorant underneath her voice. She washed us in a river of make-believe, burned us with a lot of knowledge we didn't necessarily need to know. Pressed us to her with the serious way she read, to shove us away, like dimwits, at just the moment we seemed about to understand.

Dee wanted nice things. A yellow organdy dress to wear to her graduation from high school; black pumps to match a green suit she'd made from an old suit somebody gave me. She was deter-mined to stare down any disaster in her efforts. Her eyelids would not flicker for minutes at a time. Often I fought off the temptation to shake her. At sixteen she had a style of her own: and knew what style was.

I never had an education myself. After second grade the school was closed down. Don't ask me why: in 1927 colored asked fewer questions than they do now. Sometimes Maggie reads to me. She stumbles along good-naturedly but can't see well. She knows she is not bright. Like good looks and money, quickness passed her by. She will marry John Thomas (who has mossy teeth in an earnest face), and then I'll be free to sit here and I guess just sing church songs to myself. Although I never was a good singer. Never could carry a tune. I was always better at a man's job. I used to love to milk till I was hooked in the side in '49. Cows are soothing and slow and don't bother you, unless you try to milk them the wrong way.

I have deliberately turned my back on the house. It is three rooms, just like the one that burned, except the roof is tin; they don't make shingle roofs anymore. There are no real windows, just some holes cut in the sides, like the portholes in a ship, but not round and not square, with rawhide holding the shutters up on the outside. This house is in a pasture too, like the other one. No doubt when Dee sees it she will want to tear it down. She wrote me once that no matter where we "choose" to live, she will manage to come see us. But she will never bring her friends. Maggie and I thought about this and Maggie asked me, "Mama, when did Dee ever *have* any friends?"

She had a few. Furtive boys in pink shirts hanging about on washday after school. Nervous girls who never laughed. Impressed with her, they worshiped the well-turned phrase, the cute shape, the scalding humor that erupted like bubbles in lye. She read to them.

When she was courting Jimmy T she didn't have much time to pay to us, but turned all her fault-finding power on him. He *flew* to marry a cheap city girl from a family of ignorant, flashy people. She hardly had time to recompose herself.

When she comes I will meet . . . but there they are!

Maggie attempts to make a dash for the house, in her shuffling way, but I stay her with my hand. "Come back here," I say. And she stops and tries to dig a well in the sand with her toe.

It is hard to see them clearly through the strong sun. But even the first glimpse of leg out of the car tells me it is Dee. Her feet were always neat looking, as if God himself had shaped them with a certain style. From the other side of the car comes a short, stocky man. Hair is all over his head a foot long and hanging from his chin like a kinky mule tail. I hear Maggie suck in her breath. "Uhnnnh," is what it sounds like. Like when you see the wriggling end of a snake just in front of your foot on a road. "Uhnnnh."

Dee, next. A dress down to the ground, in this hot weather. A dress so loud it hurts my eyes. There are yellows and oranges enough to throw back the light of the sun. I feel my whole face warming from the heat waves it throws out. Earrings gold too, and hanging down to her shoulders. Bracelets dangling and making noises when she moves her arm up to shake the folds of the dress out of her armpits. The dress is loose and flows, and as she walks closer, I like it. I hear Maggie go "Uhnnnh" again. It is her sister's hair. It stands straight up like the wool on a sheep. It is black as night and around the edges are two long pigtails that rope about like small lizards disappearing behind her ears.

"Wa-su-zo-Tean-o!" she says, coming on in that gliding way the dress makes her move. The short stocky fellow with the hair to his navel is all grinning and he follows up with, "Asalamalakim, my mother and sister!" He moves to hug Maggie but she falls back, right up against the back of my chair. I feel her trembling there, and when I look up I see the perspiration falling off her skin.

"Don't get up," says Dee. Since I am stout it takes something of a push. You can see me trying to move a second or two before I make it. She turns, showing white heels through her sandals, and goes back to the car. Out she peeks next with a Polaroid. She stoops down quickly and snaps off picture after picture of me sitting there in front of the house with Maggie cowering behind me. She never takes a shot without making sure the house is included. When a cow comes nibbling around the edge of the yard she snaps it and me and Maggie *and* the house. Then she puts the Polaroid on the back seat of the car, and comes up and kisses me on the forehead.

Meanwhile Asalamalakim is going through motions with Maggie's hand. Maggie's hand is as limp as a fish, and probably as cold, despite the sweat, and she keeps trying to pull it back. It looks like Asalamalakim wants to shake hands but wants to do it fancy. Or maybe he don't know how people shake hands. Anyhow, he soon gives up on Maggie.

"Well," I say. "Dee."

"No, Mama," she says. "Not 'Dee,' Wangero Leewanika Kemanjo!"

"What happened to 'Dee'?" I wanted to know.

"She's dead," Wangero said. "I couldn't bear it any longer, being named after the people who oppress me."

"You know well as me you was named after your aunt Dicie," I said. Dicie is my sister. She named Dee. We called her "Big Dee" after Dee was born.

"But who was *she* named after?" asked Wangero.

"I guess after Grandma Dee," I said.

"And who was she named after?" asked Wangero.

"Her mother," I said, and saw Wangero was getting tired. "That's about as far back as I can trace it," I said. Though, in fact, I probably could have carried it back beyond the Civil War through the branches.

"Well," said Asalamalakim, "there you are."

"Uhnnnh," I heard Maggie say.

"There I was not," I said, "before 'Dicie' cropped up in our family, so why should I try to trace it that far back?"

He just stood there grinning, looking down on me like somebody inspecting a Model A car. Every once in a while he and Wangero sent eye signals over my head.

"How do you pronounce this name?" I asked.

"You don't have to call me by it if you don't want to," said Wangero.

"Why shouldn't I?" I asked. "If that's what you want us to call you, we'll call you."

"I know it might sound awkward at first," said Wangero.

"I'll get used to it," I said. "Ream it out again."

Well, soon we got the name out of the way. Asalamalakim had

a name twice as long and three times as hard. After I tripped over it two or three times he told me to just call him Hakim-a-barber. I wanted to ask him was he a barber, but I didn't really think he was, so I didn't ask.

"You must belong to those beef-cattle peoples down the road," I said. They said "Asalamalakim" when they met you too, but they didn't shake hands. Always too busy: feeding the cattle, fixing the fences, putting up salt-lick shelters, throwing down hay. When the white folks poisoned some of the herd, the men stayed up all night with rifles in their hands. I walked a mile and a half just to see the sight.

Hakim-a-barber said, "I accept some of their doctrines, but farming and raising cattle is not my style." They didn't tell me, and I didn't ask, whether Wangero (Dee) had really gone and married him.

We sat down to eat and right away he said he didn't eat collards and pork was unclean. Wangero, though, went on through the chitlins and corn bread, the greens and everything else. She talked a blue streak over the sweet potatoes. Everything delighted her. Even the fact that we still used the benches her daddy made for the table when we couldn't afford to buy chairs.

"Oh, Mama!" she cried. Then turned to Hakim-a-barber. "I never knew how lovely these benches are. You can feel the rump prints," she said, running her hands underneath her and along the bench. Then she gave a sigh and her hand closed over Grandma Dee's butter dish. "That's it!" she said. "I knew there was something I wanted to ask you if I could have." She jumped up from the table and went over in the corner where the churn stood, the milk in it clabber by now. She looked at the churn and looked at it.

"This churn top is what I need," she said. "Didn't Uncle Buddy whittle it out of a tree you all used to have?"

"Yes," I said.

"Uh huh," she said happily. "And I want the dasher too."

"Uncle Buddy whittle that too?" asked the barber.

Dee (Wangero) looked up at me.

"Aunt Dee's first husband whittled the dash," said Maggie so low you almost couldn't hear her. "His name was Henry, but they called him Stash."

"Maggie's brain is like an elephant's," Wangero said, laughing. "I can use the churn top as a centerpiece for the alcove table," she said, sliding a plate over the churn, "and I'll think of something artistic to do with the dasher."

When she finished wrapping the dasher the handle stuck out. I took it for a moment in my hands. You didn't even have to look close to see where hands pushing the dasher up and down to make butter had left a kind of sink in the wood. In fact, there were a lot of small sinks; you could see where thumbs and fingers had sunk into the wood. It was beautiful light yellow wood, from a tree that grew in the yard where Big Dee and Stash had lived.

After dinner Dee (Wangero) went to the trunk at the foot of my bed and started rifling through it. Maggie hung back in the kitchen over the dishpan. Out came Wangero with two quilts. They had been pieced by Grandma Dee, and then Big Dee and me had hung them on the quilt frames on the front porch and quilted them. One was in the Lone Star pattern. The other was Walk Around the Mountain. In both of them were scraps of dresses Grandma Dee had worn fifty and more years ago. Bits and pieces of Grandpa Jarrell's paisley shirts. And one teeny faded blue piece, about the size of a penny matchbox, that was from Great Grandpa Ezra's uniform that he wore in the Civil War.

"Mama," Wangero said sweet as a bird. "Can I have these old quilts?"

I heard something fall in the kitchen, and a minute later the kitchen door slammed.

"Why don't you take one or two of the others?" I asked. "These old things was just done by me and Big Dee from some tops your grandma pieced before she died."

"No," said Wangero. "I don't want those. They are stitched around the borders by machine."

"That'll make them last better," I said.

"That's not the point," said Wangero. "These are all pieces of dresses Grandma used to wear. She did all this stitching by hand. Imagine!" She held the quilts securely in her arms, stroking them.

"Some of the pieces, like those lavender ones, come from old clothes her mother handed down to her," I said, moving up to touch the quilts. Dee (Wangero) moved back just enough so that I couldn't reach the quilts. They already belonged to her.

"Imagine!" she breathed again, clutching them closely to her bosom.

"The truth is," I said, "I promised to give them quilts to Maggie, for when she marries John Thomas."

She gasped, like a bee had stung her.

"Maggie can't appreciate these quilts!" she said. "She'd probably be backward enough to put them to everyday use."

"I reckon she would," I said. "God knows I been saving 'em for long enough with nobody using 'em. I hope she will!" I didn't want to bring up how I had offered Dee (Wangero) a quilt when she went away to college. Then she had told me they were old-fashioned, out of style.

"But they're *priceless!*" she was saying now, furiously; for she has a temper. "Maggie would put them on the bed and in five years they'd be in rags. Less than that!"

"She can always make some more," I said. "Maggie knows how to quilt."

Dee (Wangero) looked at me with hatred. "You just will not understand. The point is these quilts, *these* quilts!"

"Well," I said, stumped, "what would *you* do with them?"

"Hang them," she said. As if that was the only thing you *could* do with quilts.

▲   ▲   ▲

Maggie, by now, was standing in the door. I could almost hear the sound her feet made as they scraped over each other.

"She can have them, Mama," she said, like somebody used to

never winning anything, of having anything reserved for her. "I can 'member Grandma Dee without the quilts."

I looked at her hard. She had filled her bottom lip with checkerberry snuff, and it gave her face a kind of dopey, hangdog look. It was Grandma Dee and Big Dee who taught her how to quilt herself. She stood there with her scarred hands hidden in the folds of her skirt. She looked at her sister with something like fear, but she wasn't mad at her. This was Maggie's portion. This was the way she knew God to work.

When I looked at her like that something hit me in the top of my head and ran down to the soles of my feet. Just like when I'm in church and the spirit of God touches me and I get happy and shout. I did something I never had done before: hugged Maggie to me, then dragged her on into the room, snatched the quilts out of Miss Wangero's hands and dumped them into Maggie's lap. Maggie just sat there on my bed with her mouth open.

"Take one or two of the others," I said to Dee.

But she turned without a word and went out to Hakim-a-barber.

▲   ▲   ▲

"You just don't understand," she said, as Maggie and I came out to the car.

"What don't I understand?" I wanted to know.

"Your heritage," she said. And then she turned to Maggie, kissed her, and said, "You ought to try to make something of yourself too, Maggie. It's really a new day for us. But from the way you and Mama still live you'd never know it."

She put on some sunglasses that hid everything above the tip of her nose and her chin.

Maggie smiled; maybe at the sunglasses. But a real smile, not scared. After we watched the car dust settle I asked Maggie to bring me a dip of snuff. And then the two of us sat there just enjoying, until it was time to go in the house and go to bed.

Alice Walker

Advancing Luna and Ida B. Wells*

I met Luna the summer of 1965 in Atlanta where we both attended
a political conference and rally. It was designed to give us the
courage, as temporary civil rights workers, to penetrate the small
hamlets farther South. I had taken a bus from Sarah Lawrence in
New York and gone back to Georgia, my home state, to try my
hand at registering voters. It had become obvious from the high
spirits and sense of almost divine purpose exhibited by black people
that a revolution was going on, and I did not intend to miss it.
Especially not this summery, student-studded version of it. And I
thought it would be fun to spend some time on my own in the
South.

Luna was sitting on the back of a pickup truck, waiting for
someone to take her from Faith Baptist, where the rally was held,
to whatever gracious black Negro home awaited her. I remember
because someone who assumed I would also be traveling by pickup
introduced us. I remember her face when I said, "No, no more back
of pickup trucks for me. I know Atlanta well enough, I'll walk."
She assumed of course (I guess) that I did not wish to ride beside

* Luna and Freddie Pye are composite characters, and their names are made up.
This is a fictionalized account suggested by a number of real events.

her because she was white, and I was not curious enough about what she might have thought to explain it to her. And yet I was struck by her passivity, her *patience* as she sat on the truck alone and ignored, because someone had told her to wait there quietly until it was time to go.

This look of passively waiting for something changed very little over the years I knew her. It was only four or five years in all that I did. It seems longer, perhaps because we met at such an optimistic time in our lives. John Kennedy and Malcolm X had already been assassinated, but King had not been and Bobby Kennedy had not been. Then too, the lethal, bizarre elimination by death of this militant or that, exiles, flights to Cuba, shoot-outs between former Movement friends sundered forever by lies planted by the FBI, the gunning down of Mrs. Martin Luther King, Sr., as she played the Lord's Prayer on the piano in her church (was her name Alberta?), were still in the happily unfathomable future.

We believed we could change America because we were young and bright and held ourselves *responsible* for changing it. We did not believe we would fail. That is what lent fervor (revivalist fervor, in fact; we would *revive* America!) to our songs, and lent sweetness to our friendships (in the beginning almost all interracial), and gave a wonderful fillip to our sex (which, too, in the beginning, was almost always interracial).

What first struck me about Luna when we later lived together was that she did not own a bra. This was curious to me, I suppose, because she also did not need one. Her chest was practically flat, her breasts like those of a child. Her face was round, and she suffered from acne. She carried with her always a tube of that "skin-colored" (if one's skin is pink or eggshell) medication designed to dry up pimples. At the oddest times—waiting for a light to change, listening to voter registration instructions, talking about her father's new girlfriend she would apply the stuff, holding in her other hand a small brass mirror the size of her thumb, which she also carried for just this purpose.

We were assigned to work together in a small, rigidly segregated South Georgia town whose city fathers, incongruously and years ago, had named Freehold, Georgia. Luna was slightly asthmatic and when overheated or nervous she breathed through her mouth. She wore her shoulder-length black hair with bangs to her eyebrows and the rest brushed behind her ears. Her eyes were brown and rather small. She was attractive, but just barely and with effort. Had she been the slightest bit overweight, for instance, she would have gone completely unnoticed, and would have faded into the background where, even in a revolution, fat people seem destined to go. I have a photograph of her sitting on the steps of a house in South Georgia. She is wearing tiny pearl earrings, a dark sleeveless shirt with Peter Pan collar, Bermuda shorts, and a pair of those East Indian sandals that seem to adhere to nothing but a big toe.

The summer of '65 was as hot as any other in that part of the South. There was an abundance of flies and mosquitoes. Everyone complained about the heat and the flies and the hard work, but Luna complained less than the rest of us. She walked ten miles a day with me up and down those straight Georgia highways, stopping at every house that looked black (one could always tell in 1965) and asking whether anyone needed help with learning how to vote. The simple mechanics: writing one's name, or making one's "X" in the proper column. And then, though we were required to walk, everywhere, we were empowered to offer prospective registrants a car in which they might safely ride down to the county courthouse. And later to the polling places. Luna, almost overcome by the heat, breathing through her mouth like a dog, her hair plastered with sweat to her head, kept looking straight ahead, and walking as if the walking itself was her reward.

I don't know if we accomplished much that summer. In retrospect, it seems not only minor, but irrelevant. A bunch of us, black and white, lived together. The black people who took us in were unfailingly hospitable and kind. I took them for granted in a way that now amazes me. I realize that at each and every house we visited I *assumed* hospitality, I *assumed* kindness. Luna was often startled by my "boldness." If we walked up to a secluded farmhouse and half a dozen dogs ran up barking around our heels and a large black man with a shotgun could be seen whistling to himself under a tree, she would become nervous. I, on the other hand, felt free to yell at this stranger's dogs, slap a couple of them on the nose, and call over to him about his hunting.

That month with Luna of approaching new black people every day taught me something about myself I had always suspected: I thought black people superior people. Not simply superior to white people, because even without thinking about it much, I assumed almost everyone was superior to them; but to everyone. Only white people, after all, would blow up a Sunday school class and grin for television over their "victory," *i.e.,* the death of four small black girls. Any atrocity, at any time, was expected from them. On the other hand, it never occurred to me that black people *could* treat Luna and me with anything but warmth and concern. Even their curiosity about the sudden influx into their midst of rather ignorant white and black Northerners was restrained and courteous. I was treated as a relative, Luna as a much welcomed guest.

Luna and I were taken in by a middle-aged couple and their young school-age daughter. The mother worked outside the house in a local canning factory, the father worked in the paper plant in nearby Augusta. Never did they speak of the danger they were in of losing their jobs over keeping us, and never did their small daughter show any fear that her house might be attacked by racists because we were there. Again, I did not expect this family to complain, no matter what happened to them because of us. Having understood the danger, they had assumed the risk. I did not think them particularly brave, merely typical.

I think Luna liked the smallness—only four rooms—of the house. It was in this house that she ridiculed her mother's lack of taste. Her yellow-and-mauve house in Cleveland, the eleven rooms, the heated garage, the new car every year, her father's inability to remain faithful to her mother, their divorce, the fight over the property, even more so than over the children. Her mother kept the house and the children. Her father kept the car and his new girlfriend, whom he wanted Luna to meet and "approve." I could hardly imagine anyone disliking her mother so much. Everything Luna hated in her she summed up in three words: *"yellow-and-mauve."*

I have a second photograph of Luna and a group of us being bullied by a Georgia state trooper. This member of Georgia's finest had followed us out into the deserted countryside to lecture us on how misplaced—in the South—was our energy, when "the Lord knew" the North (where he thought all of us lived, expressing disbelief that most of us were Georgians) was just as bad. (He had a point that I recognized even then, but it did not seem the point where we were.) Luna is looking up at him, her mouth slightly open as always, a somewhat dazed look on her face. I cannot detect fear on any of our faces, though we were all afraid. After all, 1965 was only a year after 1964 when three civil rights workers had been taken deep into a Mississippi forest by local officials and sadistically tortured and murdered. Luna almost always carried a flat black shoulder bag. She is standing with it against her side, her thumb in the strap.

At night we slept in the same bed. We talked about our schools, lovers, girlfriends we didn't understand or missed. She dreamed, she said, of going to Goa. I dreamed of going to Africa. My dream came true earlier than hers: an offer of a grant from an unsuspected source reached me one day as I was writing poems under a tree. I left Freehold, Georgia, in the middle of summer, without regrets, and flew from New York to London, to Cairo, to Kenya, and finally, Uganda, where I settled among black people with the same assumptions of welcome and kindness I had taken for granted in Georgia. I was taken on rides down the Nile as a matter of course, and accepted all invitations to dinner, where the best local dishes were superbly prepared in my honor. I became, in fact, a lost relative of the people, whose ancestors had foolishly strayed, long ago, to America.

I wrote to Luna at once.

▲   ▲   ▲

But I did not see her again for almost a year. I had graduated from college, moved into a borrowed apartment in Brooklyn Heights, and was being evicted after a month. Luna, living then in a tenement on East Ninth Street, invited me to share her two-bedroom apartment. If I had seen the apartment before the day I moved in I might never have agreed to do so. Her building was between Avenues B and C and did not have a front door. Junkies, winos, and others often wandered in during the night (and occasionally during the day) to sleep underneath the stairs or to relieve themselves at the back of the first-floor hall.

Luna's apartment was on the third floor. Everything in it was painted white. The contrast between her three rooms and kitchen (with its red bathtub) and the grungy stairway was stunning. Her furniture consisted of two large brass beds inherited from a previous tenant and stripped of paint by Luna, and a long, high-backed church pew which she had managed somehow to bring up from the South. There was a simplicity about the small apartment that I liked. I also liked the notion of extreme contrast, and I do to this day. Outside our front window was the decaying neighborhood, as ugly and ill-lit as a battleground. (And allegedly as hostile, though somehow we were never threatened with bodily harm by the Hispanics who were our neighbors, and who seemed, more than anything, *bewildered* by the darkness and filth of their surroundings.) Inside was the church pew, as straight and spare as Abe Lincoln lying down, the white walls as spotless as a monastery's, and a small, unutterably pure patch of blue sky through the window of the back bedroom. (Luna did not believe in curtains, or couldn't afford them, and so we always undressed and bathed with the lights off and the rooms lit with candles, causing rather nun-shaped shadows to be cast on the walls by the long-sleeved high-necked nightgowns we both wore to bed.)

Over a period of weeks, our relationship, always marked by mutual respect, evolved into a warm and comfortable friendship which provided a stability and comfort we both needed at that time. I had taken a job at the Welfare Department during the day, and set up my typewriter permanently in the tiny living room for work after I got home. Luna worked in a kindergarten, and in the evenings taught herself Portuguese.

▲   ▲   ▲

It was while we lived on East Ninth Street that she told me she had been raped during her summer in the South. It is hard for me, even now, to relate my feeling of horror and incredulity. This was some time before Eldridge Cleaver wrote of being a rapist/revolutionary; of "practicing" on black women before moving on to white. It was also, unless I'm mistaken, before LeRoi Jones (as he was then known; now of course Imamu Baraka, which has an even more presumptuous meaning than "the King") wrote his advice to young black male insurrectionaries (women were not told what to do with *their* rebelliousness): "Rape the white girls. Rape their fathers." It was clear that he meant this literally and also as: to rape a white girl *is* to rape her father. It was the misogynous cruelty of this latter meaning that was habitually lost on black men (on men in general, actually), but nearly always perceived and rejected by women of whatever color.

"Details?" I asked.

She shrugged. Gave his name. A name recently in the news, though in very small print.

He was not a Movement star or anyone you would know. We had met once, briefly. I had not liked him because he was coarse and spoke of black women as "our" women. (In the early Movement, it was pleasant to think of black men wanting to own us as a group; later it became clear that owning us meant exactly *that* to them.) He was physically unattractive, I had thought, with something of the hoodlum about him: a swaggering, unnecessarily mobile walk, small eyes, rough skin, a mouthful of wandering or absent teeth. He was, ironically, among the first persons to shout the slogan everyone later attributed solely to Stokeley Carmichael —Black Power! Stokeley was chosen as the originator of this idea by the media, because he was physically beautiful and photogenic and articulate. Even the name—Freddie Pye—was diminutive, I thought, in an age of giants.

"What did you do?"

"Nothing that required making a noise."

"Why didn't you scream?" I felt I would have screamed my head off.

"You know why."

I did. I had seen a photograph of Emmett Till's body just after it was pulled from the river. I had seen photographs of white folks standing in a circle roasting something that had talked to them in their own language before they tore out its tongue. I knew why, all right.

"What was he trying to prove?"

"I don't know. Do you?"

"Maybe you filled him with unendurable lust," I said.

"I don't think so," she said.

Suddenly I was embarrassed. Then angry. Very, very angry. *How dare she tell me this!* I thought.

▲   ▲   ▲

Who knows what the black woman thinks of rape? Who has asked her? Who *cares?* Who has even properly acknowledged that *she* and not the white woman in this story is the most likely victim of rape? Whenever interracial rape is mentioned, a black woman's first thought is to protect the lives of her brothers, her father, her sons, her lover. A history of lynching has bred this reflex in her. I feel it as strongly as anyone. While writing a fictional account of such a rape in a novel, I read Ida B. Wells's autobiography three times, as a means of praying to her spirit to forgive me.

My prayer, as I turned the pages, went like this: *"Please forgive me. I am a writer."* (This self-revealing statement alone often seems to me sufficient reason to require perpetual forgiveness; since the writer is guilty not only of always wanting to know—like Eve—but also of trying—again like Eve—to find out.) *"I cannot write contrary to what life reveals to me. I wish to malign no one. But I must struggle to understand at least my own tangled emotions about interracial rape. I know, Ida B. Wells, you spent your whole life protecting, and trying to protect, black men accused of raping white women, who were lynched by white mobs, or threatened with it. You know, better than I ever will, what it means for a whole people to live under the terror of lynching. Under the slander that their men, where white women are concerned, are creatures of uncontrollable sexual lust. You made it so clear that the black men accused of rape in the past were innocent victims of white criminals that I grew up believing black men literally did not rape white women. At all. Ever. Now it would appear that some of them, the very twisted, the terribly ill, do. What would you have me write about them?"*

Her answer was: *"Write nothing. Nothing at all. It will be used against black men and therefore against all of us. Eldridge Cleaver and LeRoi Jones don't know who they're dealing with. But you remember. You are dealing with people who brought their children to witness the murder of black human beings, falsely accused of rape. People who handed out, as trophies, black fingers and toes. Deny! Deny! Deny!"*

And yet, I have pursued it, *"some black men themselves do not seem to know what the meaning of raping someone is. Some have admitted rape in order to denounce it, but others have accepted rape as a part of rebellion, of 'paying whitey back.' They have gloried in it."*

"They know nothing of America," she says. *"And neither, apparently, do you. No matter what you think you know, no matter what you feel about it, say nothing. And to your dying breath!"*

Which, to my mind, is virtually useless advice to give to a writer.

▲   ▲   ▲

Freddie Pye was the kind of man I would not have looked at then, not even once. (Throughout that year I was more or less into exotica: white ethnics who knew languages were a peculiar weakness; a half-white hippie singer; also a large Chinese mathematician who was a marvelous dancer and who taught me to waltz.) There was no question of belief.

But, in retrospect, there was a momentary *suspension* of belief, a kind of *hope* that perhaps it had not really happened; that Luna had made up the rape, "as white women have been wont to do." I soon realized this was unlikely. I was the only person she had told.

She looked at me as if to say: "I'm glad *that* part of my life is over." We continued our usual routine. We saw every interminable, foreign, depressing, and poorly illuminated film ever made. We learned to eat brown rice and yogurt and to tolerate kasha and odd-tasting teas. My half-black hippie singer friend (now a well-known reggae singer who says he is from "de *I*-lands" and not Sheepshead Bay) was "into" tea and kasha and Chinese vegetables.

And yet the rape, the knowledge of the rape, out in the open, admitted, pondered over, was now between us. (And I began to think that perhaps—whether Luna had been raped or not—it had always been so; that her power over my life was exactly the power *her word on rape* had over the lives of black men, over *all* black men, whether they were guilty or not, and therefore over my whole people.)

Before she told me about the rape, I think we had assumed a lifelong friendship. The kind of friendship one dreams of having with a person one has known in adversity; under heat and mosquitoes and immaturity and the threat of death. We would each travel, we would write to each other from the three edges of the world.

We would continue to have an "international list" of lovers whose amorous talents or lack of talents we would continue (giggling into our dotage) to compare. Our friendship would survive everything, be truer than everything, endure even our respective marriages, children, husbands—assuming we *did,* out of desperation and boredom someday, marry, which did not seem a probability, exactly, but more in the area of an amusing idea.

But now there was a cooling off of our affection for each other. Luna was becoming mildly interested in drugs, because everyone we knew was. I was envious of the open-endedness of her life. The financial backing to it. When she left her job at the kindergarten because she was tired of working, her errant father immediately materialized. He took her to dine on scampi at an expensive restaurant, scolded her for living on East Ninth Street, and looked at me as if to say: "Living in a slum of this magnitude must surely have been your idea." As a cullud, of course.

For me there was the welfare department every day, attempting to get the necessary food and shelter to people who would always live amid the dirty streets I knew I must soon leave. I was, after all, a Sarah Lawrence girl "with talent." It would be absurd to rot away in a building that had no front door.

▲   ▲   ▲

I slept late one Sunday morning with a painter I had met at the welfare department. A man who looked for all the world like Gene Autry, the singing cowboy, but who painted wonderful surrealist pictures of birds and ghouls and fruit with *teeth*. The night before, three of us—me, the painter, and "an old Navy buddy" who looked like his twin and who had just arrived in town—had got high on wine and grass.

That morning the Navy buddy snored outside the bedrooms like a puppy waiting for its master. Luna got up early, made an immense racket getting breakfast, scowled at me as I emerged from my room, and left the apartment, slamming the door so hard she damaged the lock. (Luna had made it a rule to date black men almost exclusively. My insistence on dating, as she termed it "any-one," was incomprehensible to her, since in a politically diseased society to "sleep with the enemy" was to become "infected" with the enemy's "political germs." There is more than a grain of truth in this, of course, but I was having too much fun to stare at it for long. Still, coming from Luna it was amusing, since she never took into account the risk her own black lovers ran by sleeping with "the white woman," and she had apparently been convinced that a summer of relatively innocuous political work in the South had cured her of any racial, economic, or sexual political disease.)

Luna never told me what irked her so that Sunday morning, yet I remember it as the end of our relationship. It was not, as I at first feared, that she thought my bringing the two men to the apartment was inconsiderate. The way we lived allowed us to *be* inconsiderate from time to time. Our friends were varied, vital, and often strange. Her friends especially were deeper than they should have been into drugs.

The distance between us continued to grow. She talked more of going to Goa. My guilt over my dissolute if pleasurable existence coupled with my mounting hatred of welfare work, propelled me in two directions. South, or to West Africa. When the time came to choose, I discovered that *my* summer in the South had infected me with the need to return, to try to understand, and write about, the people I'd merely lived with before.

We never discussed the rape again. We never discussed, really, Freddie Pye or Luna's remaining feelings about what had happened. One night, the last month we lived together, I noticed a man's blue denim jacket thrown across the church pew. The next morning, out of Luna's bedroom walked Freddie Pye. He barely spoke to me— possibly because as a black woman I was expected to be hostile toward his presence in a white woman's bedroom. I was too surprised to exhibit hostility, however, which was only a part of what I felt, after all. He left.

Luna and I did not discuss this. It is odd, I think now, that we didn't. It was as if he were never there; as if he and Luna had not shared the bedroom that night. A month later, Luna went alone to Goa, in her solitary way. She lived on an island and slept, she wrote, on the beach. She mentioned she'd found a lover there who protected her from the local beachcombers and pests.

Several years later, she came to visit me in the South and brought a lovely piece of pottery which my daughter much later dropped and broke, but which I glued back together in such a way that the flaw improves the beauty and fragility of the design.

AFTERWARDS, AFTERWORDS

Second Thoughts

That is the "story." It has an "unresolved" ending. That is because
Freddie Pye and Luna are still alive, as am I. However, one evening
while talking to a friend, I heard myself say that I had, in fact,
written *two* endings. One, which follows, I considered appropriate
for such a story published in a country truly committed to justice,
and the one above, which is the best I can afford to offer a society
in which lynching is still reserved, at least subconsciously, as a
means of racial control.

I said that if we in fact lived in a society committed to the
establishment of justice for everyone ("justice" in this case encom-
passing equal housing, education, access to work, adequate dental
care, et cetera), thereby placing Luna and Freddie Pye in their
correct relationship to each other, *i.e.,* that of brother and sister,
compañeros, then the two of them would be required to struggle
together over what his rape of her had meant.

Since my friend is a black man whom I love and who loves me,
we spent a considerable amount of time discussing what this particular rape meant to us. Morally wrong, we said, and not to be
excused. Shameful; politically corrupt. Yet, as we thought of what
might have happened to an indiscriminate number of innocent
young black men in Freehold, Georgia, had Luna screamed, it became clear that more than a little of Ida B. Wells's fear of probing
the rape issue was running through us, too. The implications of this
fear would not let me rest, so that months and years went by with
most of the story written but with me incapable, or at least unwilling, to finish or to publish it.

In thinking about it over a period of years, there occurred a
number of small changes, refinements, puzzles, in angle. Would
these shed a wider light on the continuing subject? I do not know.
In any case, I returned to my notes, hereto appended for the use of
the reader.

Luna: Ida B. Wells—Discarded Notes

Additional characteristics of Luna: At a time when many in and out
of the Movement considered "nigger" and "black" synonymous,
and indulged in a sincere attempt to fake Southern "hip" speech,
Luna resisted. She was the kind of WASP who could not easily
imitate another's ethnic style, nor could she even exaggerate her
own. She was what she was. A very straight, clear-eyed, coolly
observant young woman with no talent for existing outside her
own skin.

Imaginary Knowledge

Luna explained the visit from Freddie Pye in this way:
   *"He called that evening, said he was in town, and did I know the
Movement was coming North? I replied that I did know that."*
   When could he see her? he wanted to know.
   "Never," she replied.
   *He had burst into tears, or something that sounded like tears, over the
phone. He was stranded at wherever the evening's fund-raising event had
been held. Not in the place itself, but outside, in the street. The "stars"
had left, everyone had left. He was alone. He knew no one else in the
city. Had found her number in the phone book. And had no money, no
place to stay.*
   *Could he, he asked, crash? He was tired, hungry, broke—and even
in the South had had no job, other than the Movement, for months. Et
cetera.*
   *When he arrived, she had placed our only steak knife in the waist-
band of her jeans.*
   *He had asked for a drink of water. She gave him orange juice, some
cheese, and a couple of slices of bread. She had told him he might sleep on
the church pew and he had lain down with his head on his rolled-up
denim jacket. She had retired to her room, locked the door, and tried to
sleep. She was amazed to discover herself worrying that the church pew
was both too narrow and too hard.*
   At first he muttered, groaned, and cursed in his sleep. Then he fell off

the narrow church pew. He kept rolling off. At two in the morning she unlocked her door, showed him her knife, and invited him to share her bed.

Nothing whatever happened except they talked. At first, only he talked. Not about the rape, but about his life.

"He was a small person physically, remember?" Luna asked me. (She was right. Over the years he had grown big and, yes, burly, in my imagination, and I'm sure in hers.) "That night he seemed tiny. A child. He was still fully dressed, except for the jacket and he, literally, hugged his side of the bed. I hugged mine. The whole bed, in fact, was between us. We were merely hanging to its edges."

At the fund-raiser—on Fifth Avenue and Seventy-first Street, as it turned out—his leaders had introduced him as the unskilled, barely literate, former Southern fieldworker that he was. They had pushed him at the rich people gathered there as an example of what "the system" did to "the little people" in the South. They asked him to tell about the 37 times he had been jailed. The 35 times he had been beaten. The one time he had lost consciousness in the "hot" box. They told him not to worry about his grammar. "Which, as you may recall," said Luna, "was horrible." Even so, he had tried to censor his "ain'ts" and his "us'es." He had been painfully aware that he was on exhibit, like Frederick Douglass had been for the Abolitionists. But unlike Douglass he had no oratorical gift, no passionate language, no silver tongue. He knew the rich people and his own leaders perceived he was nothing: a broken man, unschooled, unskilled at anything . . .

Yet he had spoken, trembling before so large a crowd of rich, white Northerners—who clearly thought their section of the country would never have the South's racial problems—begging, with the painful stories of his wretched life, for their money.

At the end, all of them—the black leaders, too—had gone. They left him watching the taillights of their cars, recalling the faces of the friends come to pick them up: the women dressed in African print that shone, with elaborately arranged hair, their jewelry sparkling, their perfume exotic. They were so beautiful, yet so strange. He could not imagine that one of them could comprehend his life. He did not ask for a ride, because of that, but also because he had no place to go. Then he had remembered Luna.

Soon Luna would be required to talk. She would mention her confusion over whether, in a black community surrounded by whites with a history of lynching blacks, she had a right to scream as Freddie Pye was raping her. For her, this was the crux of the matter.

And so they would continue talking through the night.

▲   ▲   ▲

This is another ending, created from whole cloth. If I believed Luna's story about the rape, and I did (had she told anyone else I might have dismissed it), then this reconstruction of what might have happened is as probable an accounting as any is liable to be. Two people have now become "characters."

I have forced them to talk until they reached the stumbling block of the rape, *which they must remove themselves,* before proceeding to a place from which it will be possible to insist on a society in which Luna's word alone on rape can never be used to intimidate an entire people, and in which an innocent black man's protestation of innocence of rape is unprejudicially heard. Until such a society is created, relationships of affection between black men and white women will always be poisoned—from within as from without—by historical fear and the threat of violence, and solidarity among black and white women is only rarely likely to exist.

Postscript: Havana, Cuba, November, 1976

I am in Havana with a group of other black American artists. We have spent the morning apart from our Cuban hosts bringing each other up to date on the kind of work (there are no apolitical artists among us) we are doing in the United States. I have read "Luna."

High above the beautiful city of Havana I sit in the Havana Libre pavilion with the muralist/photographer in our group. He is in his mid-thirties, a handsome, brown, erect individual whom I have known casually for a number of years. During the sixties he designed and painted street murals for both SNCC and the Black Panthers, and in an earlier discussion with Cuban artists he showed impatience with their explanation of why we had seen no murals covering some of the city's rather dingy walls: Cuba, they had said, unlike Mexico, has no mural tradition. "But the point of a revolution," insisted Our Muralist, "is to make new traditions!" And he had pressed his argument with such passion for the *usefulness,* for revolutionary communication, of his craft, that the Cubans were both exasperated and impressed. They drove us around the city for a tour of their huge billboards, all advancing socialist thought and the heroism of men like Lenin, Camilo, and Che Guevara, and said, "These, *these* are our 'murals'!"

While we ate lunch, I asked Our Muralist what he'd thought of "Luna." Especially the appended section.

"Not much," was his reply. "Your view of human weakness is too biblical," he said. "You are unable to conceive of the man without conscience. The man who cares nothing about the state of his soul because he's long since sold it. In short," he said, "you do not understand that some people are simply evil, a disease on the lives of other people, and that to remove the disease altogether is preferable to trying to interpret, contain, or forgive it. Your 'Freddie Pye,'" and he laughed, "was probably raping white women on the instructions of his government."

Oh ho, I thought. Because, of course, for a second, during which I stalled my verbal reply, this comment made both very little and very much sense.

"I *am* sometimes naïve and sentimental," I offered. I am sometimes both, though frequently by design. Admission in this way is tactical, a stimulant to conversation.

"And shocked at what I've said," he said, and laughed again. "Even though," he continued, "you know by now that blacks could be hired to blow up other blacks, and could be hired *by someone* to shoot down Brother Malcolm, and hired *by someone* to provide a diagram of Fred Hampton's bedroom so the pigs could shoot him easily while he slept, you find it hard to believe a black man could be hired *by someone* to rape white women. But think a minute, and you will see why it is the perfect disruptive act. Enough blacks raping or accused of raping enough white women and any political movement that cuts across racial lines is doomed.

"Larger forces are at work than your story would indicate," he continued. "You're still thinking of lust and rage, moving slowly into aggression and purely racial hatred. But you should be considering money—which the rapist would get, probably from your very own tax dollars, in fact—and a maintaining of the status quo; which those hiring the rapist would achieve. I know all this," he said, "because when I was broke and hungry and selling my blood to buy the food and the paint that allowed me to work, I was offered such 'other work.' "

"But you did not take it."

He frowned. "There you go again. How do you know I didn't take it? It paid, and I was starving."

"You didn't take it," I repeated.

"No," he said. "A black and white 'team' made the offer. I had enough energy left to threaten to throw them out of the room."

"But even if Freddie Pye *had been* hired *by someone* to rape Luna, that still would not explain his second visit."

"Probably nothing will explain that," said Our Muralist. "But assuming Freddie Pye *was* paid to disrupt—by raping a white woman—the black struggle in the South, he may have wised up enough later to comprehend the significance of Luna's decision not to scream."

"So you are saying he *did have* a conscience?" I asked.

"Maybe," he said, but his look clearly implied I would never understand anything about evil, power, or corrupted human beings in the modern world.

But of course he is wrong.

ALICE WALKER
Bibliography

The works of Alice Walker have attracted a great deal of critical and popular interest. While sharing an appreciation for her literary abilities, critics are nonetheless divided when discussing the nature of her political perspective.

Several critics, some using the opportunity of the appearance of the film *The Color Purple,* have written about her work as naive or "ahistoric." They point to portrayals which, they argue, unrealistically emphasize the power of individuals to overcome political conditions through the creative or spiritual process of self-discovery. In a chapter comparing Walker and Bambara (in *Fingering the Jagged Grain,* Athens, Ga.: University of Georgia Press, 1985, pp. 104–70), Keith Byerman argues that her perspective is, at the least, ambiguous, and he defines the source of this ambiguity as a difficult "conjunction" of folk wisdom and political activism: ". . . this conjunction does not always work, since the folk worldview implicitly assumes that endurance rather than political power is its objective. It insists not on overcoming the enemy so much as outwitting and outliving him" (p. 105). Byerman briefly traces the development of her political aesthetic, demonstrating the tension between the "fatalism" of folk wisdom and the energetic impulse to transform political structures inherent in a political worldview which is prevalent in her earlier works. In *The Color Purple,* however, Byerman finds that Walker has lost interest in a political solution, shown by her move "to allegorical form in order to transcend history . . . But in doing so she has neutralized the historical condition of the very folk she values" (p. 170). Trudier Harris's criticism offers a similar indictment of Walker's *The Color Purple* ("On *The Color Purple:* Stereotypes and Silence" in *Black American Literature Forum,* 18:4, pp. 155–61). She criticizes Walker's portrayals of women as passive and victimized, a mode of characterization which Harris argues is inconsistent with history and the need for a strong voice in black women's fiction. Other objections to Walker's representation of political and historical issues are found in Loyle Hairston's review of *In Our Mothers' Garden (Freedomways,* 1984, 3rd quarter, pp. 182–90) and Gerald Early's review *"The Color Purple* as Everybody's Protest Art" in *Antioch Review,* 1985, pp. 261–75). Lauren Berlant in "Race, Gender, and Nation in *The Color Purple"* (*Critical Inquiry* Vol. 14 No. 4, Summer 1988, pp. 831–59) says that the novel's embracing of the myth of Western capitalism to undergird its vision of an Afro-American utopia ultimately undermines its oppositional stance.

On the other side of the critical spectrum are those who praise Walker for her creative and spiritual vision, finding in that vision an awareness of those qualities which compel characters to negotiate and transcend the burdens of history and contemporary political obstacles.

Barbara Christian (in *Black Women Novelists,* Westport, Conn.: Greenwood Press, 1980) sees in Walker's work an "emphasis on the possibilities for change" which, Christian asserts, subsumes political transformation. Citing the characters' search for redemption, which is both personal and social, Christian here discusses only Walker's first two novels. In a later piece (in *Black Feminist Criticism,* Elmsford, N.Y.: Pergamon Press, 1985, pp. 85–102), which is expanded to include works published by 1983, Christian explores the development of several themes in Walker: the importance of preserving cultural heritage, the "relationship between struggle and change," and the transcendence of creative powers over limiting circumstances.

Susan Willis *(Specifying,* pp. 81–107) also praises Walker for her depiction of women's struggles. Willis argues that the question of language has been crucial for black women writers and a central issue in Walker's works since most of Walker's women are poor and uneducated. According to Willis, Walker's solution to the woman writer's problem of finding a viable literary language "outside of the male canon defined predominantly by Richard Wright" has been to use the anecdotal narrative, "which because of its relationship to storytelling and the family . . . closely approximates a woman's linguistic practice . . ." (p. 115).

Deborah McDowell's paper "The Changing Same: Generational Connections and Black Women Novelists" *New Literary History*, Vol. 18, 1986–87, pp. 281–302, compares Harper's *Iola Leroy* to *The Color Purple,* showing that the later novels comment on and revise the "uplift" fiction prevalent during the nineteenth century. While sharing similar plots concerning the loss and recovery of personal identity and familial relationships, Walker, in McDowell's words, "transforms" the notion of "uplift" by presenting characters who speak unapologetically in black idiom, female figures who value sexual experience and, through the use of letters and diaries as the dominant narrative vehicle, "elevate folk forms . . . to the status of art."

Michael Awkward's *Inspiriting Influences: Tradition, Revision, and Afro-American Women's Novels* (New York: Columbia University Press, 1989) uses concepts of Julia Kristeva to explore *The Color Purple*'s relationship to Toomer's *Cane* and Hurston's *Their Eyes Were Watching God.* Awkward is noteworthy for his attempts to address Trudier Harris's critiques. Arguing that Walker uses depictions of passivity only in order to show the place of creativity in overcoming "imposed roles and political realities," Awkward defends Walker against her detractors and ends by claiming that *The Color Purple* represents the "fulfillment of Afro-American women novelists' dream of female [comm]unity."

NTOZAKE SHANGE

Any consideration of the work of Ntozake Shange must begin with her choreopoem *for colored girls who have considered suicide / when the rainbow is enuf.*[1] A successful Broadway production in 1976, nationally and internationally acclaimed, *for colored girls . . .* is composed of fourteen narrative poems—recited, sung, dramatized by seven different women dressed in earth colors and the colors of the rainbow. The narratives move from defeat and despair toward an assertion and celebration of female sexuality, creativity, anger, humor, and pain. Ranging from stories about a wild, teen-aged graduation party to the agonies of rape, abortion, and failed love affairs, *for colored girls . . .* is, in Shange's words, about "our struggle to become all that is forbidden, all that is forfeited by our gender, all that we have forgotten."[2]

While the choreopoem begins with the despair of women victimized by the violence of men and by the violence of their physical and psychological environments, it goes beyond victimization toward a repudiation of those cultural ideals that teach women to

[1] Ntozake Shange. *for colored girls who have considered suicide / when the rainbow is enuf* (New York: Macmillan, 1977).
[2] Ibid., p. xv.

feel inadequacy and self-doubt. Deliberately celebrating those aspects of femaleness that have been deemed unattractive, the lady in green reclaims those signs of her identity she has been taught to despise:

> I want my arm wit the hot iron scar/& my leg wit the flea bite/i want my calloused feet & quik language back in my mouth/ . . . i want my own things . . .

When all the women join together at the end of the play for the laying on of hands, singing in gospel style "i found god in myself/& i loved her/i loved her fiercely," the image evoked is not the culturally accepted one of a white male God but of that African tribal woman whose body and skin color could and did represent divinity.[3]

From New York to San Francisco (I saw the play five times in four different cities: New York, Detroit, Los Angeles, and San Francisco), women (and some men) in the audiences laughed, cried, and shouted their recognition and approval of Shange's representation of black women's lives. From the opening moments of the play, when the lady in red announces that she is ending an affair with a man who "has been of no assistance," to the song of solidarity at the end, *for colored girls* . . . is driven not only by female pain and anger but by the need for women to find ways to survive and to demand their space in the world: "this is a women's trip & i need my stuff." In her introduction to a 1978 book of poems, *nappy edges,* Shange says that the time she has spent in close community with other women artists has helped her to break through the conventional notions that women's realities are not suitable for artistic expression. Because women's experiences, their symbols and myths, run counter to (and subvert) the experiences that men have mythologized and canonized (conquering the frontier, conquering women, male bonding, and other "melodramas of beset manhood"), women writers have to face the demeaning of their stories.

---

[3] Carol P. Christ, *Diving Deep and Surfacing* (Boston, Beacon Press, 1980), p. 117.

The diminishment of women's lives, Shange says, results in the diminishment of their art:

> so anyway they were poets/& this guy well he liked this wom-
> en's work/cuz it wazn't 'personal'/i mean a man can get per-
> sonal in his work when he talks politics or bout his dad/but
> women start all this foolishness bout their bodies & blood &
> kids & what's really goin on at home/well & that ain't poetry/
> that's goo-ey gaw/female stuff.[4]

In spite of these oppositions (or perhaps because of them), Shange has set about creating mythologies in which womanhood means something rich, "not tired and stingy." In her 1982 novel, *Sassafrass, Cypress & Indigo,* the four major women characters are all artists: Sassafrass and the mother are weavers, Cypress dances, Indigo is a fiddler: these signs of their continuity with an artistic life derived from African culture and carried on through slavery, so rarely given to women characters in fiction, become in Shange's fiction signs of women's autonomy and freedom.[5]

Perhaps more than any other black woman writer except Audre Lorde, Shange has tried to demystify the sexual mores that make female sexuality a taboo subject. She refuses to exclude any aspect of female sexuality—menstruation, pregnancy, abortion, sexual pleasure, lesbianism—all are, in her terms, suitable subjects for po- etry and fiction. The two stories in this anthology indicate that Shange locates much of women's oppression in the sexual arena. In "comin to terms" Mandy begins to find a man's body, his incessant demands and needs, an intolerable burden. Her refusal to have sex with Ezra is merely the ground level in the construction of a new relationship between them. But what I find most significant in "comin to terms" is the woman's image of herself as a solitary figure in the world, an image that is echoed in Paulette White's

[4] Ntozake Shange, *nappy edges* (New York, St. Martin's Press, 1978), p. 13.
[5] Ntozake Shange, *Sassafrass, Cypress & Indigo* (New York, St. Martin's Press, 1982).

story "The Bird Cage," in which the young wife and mother of four sons dreams of living alone in a house where there will be "one bed, one chair, one table, and one, just one, of anything." Paule Marshall's Reena, sitting alone at night after her divorce, making plans for herself and her children, says that despite her aloneness, everything seems possible. And in spite of all the affirmations of Janie's ecstatic romantic union with Tea Cake, Zora Hurston represents her at the end of *Their Eyes Were Watching God* as a solitary dreamer. The notion of women as solitary figures in their own worlds suggests that women writers are repudiating the standard romantic plot which demands heterosexual union for women to be complete. It seems to me that one of the main projects of contemporary black women writers has been to dismantle that romantic story, to "write beyond the ending" of the conventional domestic love plot.[6]

Perhaps the ultimate sign of the rejection of male-dominated forms is Shange's rejection of standard English, of conventional spelling, punctuation, and grammar. Carol Christ says this repudiation of standard form reflects Virginia Woolf's assertion that women's experience could not be neatly fit into "the rhythms of dominant and subordinate clauses that were patterned after the ordered and hierarchical world of upper class [white] men."[7] Shange breaks up traditional narrative patterns in *Sassafrass, Cypress & Indigo* with recipes, dreams, letters from Mama. In "aw babee you so pretty," the rejection of standard patterns has perhaps another, though related, function. It allows Shange to mediate two cultures: the middle class, highly educated and sophisticated, young educated black woman narrator who is at home in three cultures—European, North American, and Caribbean—but who also wants to remain

[6] Rachel Blau Du Plessis, *Writing Beyond the Ending: Narrative Strategies of Twentieth-Century Women Writers* (Bloomington, Indiana University Press, 1985. Du Plessis uses the term "writing beyond the ending" to mean the ways writers refuse the patterns of conventional narratives, especially those which demand either death or domesticity for their female characters.

[7] Carol P. Christ, *Diving Deep and Surfacing*, p. 101.

rooted through language in black American culture. As a writer and an intellectual, Shange is also affirming her own rootedness in black culture. In mediating these two historically oppositional signs, women writers like Ntozake Shange, Sherley Anne Williams, and Toni Cade Bambara are representing a way of overcoming the sense of cultural division that writers from Frederick Douglass to Ralph Ellison have struggled against.

Ntozake Shange

comin to terms

they hadnt slept together for months/ the nite she pulled the two thinnest blankets from on top of him & gathered one pillow under her arm to march to the extra room/ now 'her' room/ had been jammed with minor but telling incidents/ at dinner she had asked him to make sure the asparagus didnt burn so he kept adding water & they, of course/ water-logged/ a friend of hers stopped over & he got jealous of her having so many friends/ so he sulked cuz no one came to visit him/ then she gotta call that she made the second round of interviews for the venceremos brigade/ he said he didnt see why that waz so important/ & with that she went to bed/ moments later this very masculine leg threw itself over her thighs/ she moved over/ then a long muscled arm wrapped round her chest/ she sat up/ he waz smiling/ the smile that said 'i wanna do it now.'

  mandy's shoulders dropped/ her mouth wanted to pout or frown/ her fist waz lodged between her legs as a barrier or an alternative/ a cooing brown hand settled on her backside/ 'listen, mandy, i just wanna little'/ mandy looked down on the other side of the bed/ maybe the floor cd talk to him/ the hand roamed her back & bosom/ she started to make faces & blink a lot/ ezra waznt talkin anymore/ a wet mouth waz sittin on mandy's neck/ & teeth

beginnin to nibble the curly hairs near her ears/ she started to shake
her head/ & covered her mouth with her hand sayin/ 'i waz
dreamin bout cuba & you wanna fuck'/ 'no, mandy, i dont wanna
fuck/ i wanna make love to . . . love to you'/ & the hand became quite aggressive with mandy's titties/ 'i'm dreamin abt goin
to cuba/ which isnt important/ i'm hungry cuz you ruined dinner/
i'm lonely cuz you embarrassed my friend: & you wanna fuck'/ 'i
dont wanna fuck/ i told you that i wanna make love'/ 'well you
got it/ you hear/ you got it to yr self/ cuz i'm goin to dream abt
goin to cuba'/ & with that she climbed offa the hand pummelin her
ass/ & pulled the two thinnest blankets & one pillow to the extra
room.

▲   ▲   ▲

the extra room waz really mandy's anyway/ that's where she
read & crocheted & thot/ she cd watch the neighbors' children &
hear miz nancy singin gospel/ & hear miz nancy give her some-
timey lover who owned the steepin tavern/ a piece of her mind/ so
the extra room/ felt full/ not as she had feared/ empty & knowin
absence. in a corner under the window/ mandy settled every nite
after the cuba dreams/ & watched the streetlights play thru the lace
curtains to the wall/ she slept soundly the first few nites/ ezra didnt
mention that she didnt sleep with him/ & they ate the breakfast she
fixed & he went off to the studio/ while she went off to school he
came home to find his dinner on the table & mandy in her room/
doing something that pleased her. mandy was very polite & gra-
cious/ asked how his day waz/ did anything exciting happen/ but
she never asked him to do anything for her/ like lift things or
watch the stove/ or listen to her dreams/ she also never went in the
room where they usedta sleep together/ tho she cleaned everywhere else as thoroughly as one of her mother's great-aunts cleaned
the old house on rose tree lane in charleston/ but she never did any
of this while ezra waz in the house/ if ezra waz home/ you cd be
sure mandy waz out/ or in her room.

▲   ▲   ▲

one nite just fore it's time to get up & the sky is lightening up
for sunrise/ mandy felt a chill & these wet things on her neck/ she
started slappin the air/ & without openin her eyes/ cuz she cd/ feel
now what waz goin on/ ezra pushed his hard dick up on her thigh/
his breath covered her face/ he waz movin her covers off/ mandy
kept slappin him & he kept bumpin up & down on her legs & her
ass/ 'what are you doin ezra'/ he just kept movin. mandy
screamed/ 'ezra what in hell are you doin.' & pushed him off her.
he fell on the floor/ cuz mandy's little bed waz right on the floor/
& she slept usually near the edge of her mattress/ ezra stood & his
dick waz aimed at mandy's face/ at her right eye/ she looked
away/ & ezra/ jumped up & down/ in the air this time/ 'what are
you talkin abt what am i doin/ i'm doin what we always do/ i'm
gettin ready to fuck/ awright so you were mad/ but this cant go
on forever/ i'm goin crazy/ i cant live in a house with you & not
fu . . . / not make love. i mean.' mandy still lookin at the puls-
ing penis/ jumpin around as ezra jumped around/ mandy sighed
'ezra let's not let this get ugly/ please, just go to sleep/ in yr bed &
we'll talk abt this tomorrow.' 'what do you mean tomorrow i'm
goin crazy' . . . mandy looked into ezra's scrotum/ & spoke
softly 'you'll haveta be crazy then' & turned over to go back to
sleep. ezra waz still for a moment/ then he pulled the covers off
mandy & jerked her around some/ talkin bout 'we live together &
we're gonna fuck now'/ mandy treated him as cruelly as she wd
any stranger/ kicked & bit & slugged & finally ran to the kitchen/
leavin ezra holdin her torn nitegown in his hands.

▲   ▲   ▲

'how cd you want me/ if i dont want you/ i dont want you
niggah/ i dont want you' & she worked herself into a sobbin
frigidaire-beatin frenzy . . . ezra looked thru the doorway

mumblin. 'i didnt wanna upset you, mandy. but you gotta understand. i'm a man & i just cant stay here like this with you . . . not
bein able to touch you or feel you'/ mandy screamed back 'or fuck
me/ go on, say it niggah/ fuck.' ezra threw her gown on the floor
& stamped off to his bed. we dont know what he did in there.

▲   ▲   ▲

mandy put her gown in the sink & scrubbed & scrubbed til she
cd get his hands off her. she changed the sheets & took a long bath
& a douche. she went back to bed & didnt go to school all day she
lay in her bed. thinkin of what ezra had done. i cd tell him to
leave/ she thot/ but that's half the rent/ i cd leave/ but i like it
here/ i cd getta dog to guard me at nite/ but ezra wd make friends
with it/ i cd let him fuck me & not move/ that wd make him mad
& i like to fuck ezra/ he's good/ but that's not the point/ that's not
the point/ & she came up with the idea that if they were really
friends like they always said/ they shd be able to enjoy each other
without fucking without having to sleep in the same room/ mandy
had grown to cherish waking up a solitary figure in her world/ she
liked the quiet of her own noises in the night & the sound of her
own voice soothin herself/ she liked to wake up in the middle of
the nite & turn the lights on & read or write letters/ she even liked
the grain advisory show on tv at 5:30 in the mornin/ she hadda
lotta secret nurturin she had created for herself/ that ezra & his
heavy gait/ ezra & his snorin/ ezra & his goin-crazy hard-on wd/
do violence to . . . so she suggested to ezra that they continue to
live together as friends/ & see other people if they wanted to have
a more sexual relationship than the one she waz offering . . . ezra
laughed. he thot she waz a little off/ til she shouted 'you cant
imagine me without a wet pussy/ you cant imagine me without yr
goddamed dick stickin up in yr pants/ well yr gonna learn/ i dont
start comin to life cuz you feel like fuckin/ yr gonna learn i'm
alive/ ya hear' . . . ezra waz usually a gentle sorta man/ but he
slapped mandy this time & walked off . . . he came home two

days later covered with hickeys & quite satisfied with himself.
mandy fixed his dinner/ nothin special/ & left the door of her
room open so he cd see her givin herself pleasure/ from then on/
ezra always asked if he cd come visit her/ waz she in need of some
company/ did she want a lil lovin/ or wd she like to come visit
him in his room/ there are no more assumptions in the house.

Ntozake Shange

aw, babee, you so pretty

not only waz she without a tan, but she held her purse close to her hip like a new yorker or someone who rode the paris métro. she waz not from here, but from there.

there some coloureds, negroes, blacks, cd make a living big enough to leave there to come here: but no one went there much any more for all sorts of reasons. the big reason being immigration restrictions & unemployment. nowadays, immigration restrictions of every kind apply to any non-european persons who want to go there from here. just like unemployment applies to most non-european persons without titles of nobility or north american university training. some who want to go there from here risk fetching trouble with the customs authority there. or later with the police, who can tell who's not from there cuz the shoes are pointed & laced strange/the pants be for august & yet it's january/the accent is patterned for port-au-prince, but working in crown heights. what makes a person comfortably ordinary here cd make him dangerously conspicuous there.

so some go to london or amsterdam or paris, where they are so many no one tries to tell who is from where. still the far right wing of every there prints lil pamphlets that say everyone from here shd leave there & go back where they came from.

anyway the yng woman i waz discussing waz from there & she was alone. that waz good. cuz if a man had no big brother in groningen. no aunt in rouen. no sponsor in chicago. this brown woman from there might be a good idea. everybody knows that rich white girls are hard to find. some of them joined the weather underground, some the baader-meinhof gang. a whole bunch of them gave up men entirely. so the exotic-lover-in-the-sun routine becomes more difficult to swing/if she wants to talk abt plastic explosives & the resistance of the black masses to socialism insteada giving head as the tide slips in or lending money just for the next few days. is hard to find a rich white girl who is so dumb, too.

anyway, the whole world knows, european & non-european alike, the whole world knows that nobody loves the black woman like they love farrah fawcett-majors. the whole world dont turn out for a dead black woman like they did for marilyn monroe. (actually, the demise of josephine baker waz an international event, but she waz also a war hero) the worldwide un-beloved black woman is a good idea, if she is from there & one is a yng man with gd looks, piercing eyes, knowledge of several romantic languages, the best dancing spots, the hill where one can see the entire bay at twilight, the beach where the seals & pelicans run free, the hidden "local" restaurants; or in paris, a métro map. in mexico city the young man might know where salsa is played, not that the jalisco folklorico is not beautiful. but if she is from there & black she might want to dance a dance more familiar. such a yng man with such information exists in great numbers everywhere. he stops a yng woman with her bag on her hip, demanding she come to his house for dinner that night. (they are very hospitable) when the black woman from there says she must go to antwerp at 6:00/ he says, then, when she comes back. his friends agree. (they are persistent) he asks, as he forces his number into her palm, are you alone. this is important. for the yng man from here with designs on a yng woman from there respects the territorial rights of another man, if he's in the country.

that is how the approach to the black woman works in the street. "aw babee/ you so pretty" begins often in the lobby of hotels where the bright handsome yng men wd be loiterers were they not needed to tend the needs of the black women from there. tourists are usually white people or asians who didnt come all this way to meet a black woman who isnt even foreign. so the hotel managers wink an eye at the yng men in the lobby or by the bar who wd be loitering, but they are going to help her have a gd time. maybe help themselves, too.

everybody in the world, everybody knows the black woman from there is not treated as a princess, as a jewel, a cherished lover. that's not how sapphire got her reputation, nor how mrs. jefferson perceives the world. "you know/ babee/ you dont act like them. aw babee/ you so pretty."

the yng man in the hotel watches the yng black woman sit & sit & sit, while the european tourists dance with one another & the dapper local fellas mambo frenetically with secretaries from arizona. in search of the missing rich white girl. so our girl sits & sits & sits & sits. maybe she is courageous & taps her foot. maybe she is bold & enjoys the music, smiling, shaking shoulders. let her sit & know she is unwanted. she is not white and she is not from here. let her know she is not pretty enough to dance the next merengue. then appear, mysteriously, in the corner of the bar. stare at her. just stare. when stevie wonder's song "isn't she lovely" blares thru the red-tinted light, ask her to dance & hold her as tyrone power wda. hold her & stare. dance yr ass off. she has been discovered by the non-european fred astaire. let her know she is a surprise . . . an event. by the look on yr face you've never seen anyone like this. black woman from there. you say, "aw/ you not from here?" totally astonished. she murmurs that she is from there. as if to apologize for her unfortunate place of birth, you say, "aw babee/ you so pretty." & it's all over.

a night in a pension near the sorbonne. pick her up from the mattress. throw her gainst the wall in a show of exotic temper & passion: *"maintenant, tu es ma femme. nous nous sommes mariés."* unions of this sort are common wherever the yng black women travel alone. a woman travelling alone is an affront to the non-european man, who is known the world over, to european & non-european alike, for his way with women, his sense of romance, how he can say "aw babee/ you so pretty" & even a beautiful woman will believe no one else ever recognized her loveliness, till he came along.

he comes to a café in willemstad in the height of the sunset. an able-bodied, sinewy yng man who wants to buy one beer for the yng woman. after the first round, he discovers he has run out of money. so she must buy the next round, when he discovers what beautiful legs she has, how her mouth is like the breath of tiger lilies. the taxi driver doesnt speak english, but he knows to drop his countryman off before he takes the yng woman to her hotel. the tab is hers.

but hers are, also, the cheeks that grandma pinches, if the yng man has honorable intentions. all the family will meet the yng black woman from there. the family has been worried abt this yng man for a while. non-european families dont encourage bachelors. bachelorhood is a career we associate with the white people: dandies on the order of errol flynn, robert de niro. the non-european men have women. some women they marry & stay with forever. get chicken on sunday (chicken fricassee, arroz con pollo, poulet grillee, smothered chicken, depending on what kinda black woman she is & whether she is from here or there). then some women they just are with for years or a day. but our families do expect a yng man to waltz in with somebody at sometime. & if she's from there, the family's very excited. they tell the yng woman abt where they are from & how she cd almost be from the same place, except she is from there. but more rousing than coincidental genealogical traits is the torrid declaration: "we shall make love in the . . . how you call it/ yes in the earth, in the dirt. i will have you . . . in my . . . how you say . . . where things grow . . . aw/ yes. i will have you in the soil." probably under the stars & smelling of wine an unforgettable international affair can be consummated.

at 11:30 one evening i waz at the port authority, new york, united states, myself. now i was there & i spoke english & i waz holding approximately $7 american currency, when a yng man from there came up to me from the front of the line of people waiting for the princeton new jersey united states local bus. i mean to say, he gave up his chance for a good seat to come say to me: "i never saw a black woman reading nietzsche." i waz demure enough, i said i had to for a philosophy class. but as the night went on i noticed this yng man waz so much like the yng men from here who use their bodies as bait & their smiles as passport alternatives. anyway the night did go on. we were snuggled together in the rear of the bus going down the jersey turnpike. he told me in english/ which he had spoken all his life in st. louis/ where he waz raised/ that he had wanted all his life to meet someone like me/ he wanted me to meet his family, who hadnt seen him in a long time, since he left missouri looking for opportunity/ opportunity to sculpt. he had been everyplace, he said, & i waznt like any black woman he had ever met anywhere. there or here. he had come back to new york cuz of immigration restrictions & high unemployment among black american sculptors abroad.

just as we got to princeton, he picked my face up from his shoulder where i had been fantasizing like mad & said: "aw babee/ you so pretty." i believe that night i must have looked beautiful for a black woman from there. though a black woman from anywhere cd be asked at any moment to tour the universe. to climb a six-story walk-up with a brilliant & starving painter. to share kadushi. to meet mama. to getta kiss each time the swing falls toward the willow branch. to imagine where he say he from. & more/ she cd/ she cd have all of it/ she cd not be taken/ long as she dont let a stranger be the first to say: "aw babee/ you so pretty." after all, immigration restrictions & unemployment cd drive a man to drink or to lie. so if you know yr beautiful & bright & cherishable awready. when he say, in whatever language, "aw babee/ you so pretty," you cd say, "i know, thank you." & then when he asks yr name again cuz yr answer was inaudible. you cd say: "difficult." then he'll smile. & you'll smile. he'll say: "what nice legs you have." you can say: "yes. they run in the family."

"aw babee/ i've never met any one like you."

"that's strange. there are millions of us."

NTOZAKE SHANGE
Bibliography

Since the production of *for colored girls who have considered suicide /
when the rainbow is enuf,* Shange herself has been the focus of many
interviews and articles. The most in-depth and interesting portrait
of Shange as an artist emerges in Claudia Tate's *Black Women Writers at Work* (New York: Continuum, 1983). Serious analysis of
Shange's plays, poetry, and fiction is much more difficult to find.
One of the few essays to consider *for colored girls . . .* as literature
is Carol P. Christ's " 'i found god in myself . . . & i loved her
fiercely': Ntozake Shange" in *Diving Deep and Surfacing* (Boston:
Beacon Press, 1980, pp. 97–117). Christ describes the play as a
search through the experience of nothingness (a term Christ uses to
describe a state of spiritual emptiness) toward a new image of black
womanhood based on an understanding of the personal and collective histories of black women.

Of Shange's fiction, *Betsy Brown* (New York: St. Martin's Press,
1985) is the most widely reviewed, though most reviews avoid any
serious discussion of the book's aims, literary contexts, or effective-
ness. (For an example, see Nancy Willard's review in *The New York
Times Book Review* (May 12, 1985, p. 12), which merely describes
the plot and then praises Shange for having no ax to grind and for
creating a place "where black and white readers will feel at home."

Critics rarely talk about Shange's work (or Louise Meriwether's) as part of the African-American or mainstream American literary canon. An exception to this is Sherley Anne Williams's review essay "Roots of Privilege: New Black Fiction" in *Ms.* magazine (June 1985, pp. 69–72). While critical of Shange's narrative style, Williams evaluates Shange's work in the context of Afro-American literature, specifically the race-uplift novel, which in the nineteenth and early twentieth centuries was intended as a refutation of black inferiority. Williams praises Shange for depicting a middle-class black family as deeply connected to black culture and a black community, thus solving, at least to some extent, the problem in early black fiction of assuming that black middle-class life must be defined by white cultural standards.

TONI CADE BAMBARA

Toni Cade Bambara's female characters are, typically, independent, resourceful, unconventional, defined by self, not by males or by stereotypic roles. Her girls play competitive sports: her women are uninterested in marriage and conventional motherhood; her old women are interested in sex; her women characters respect themselves for the work they do. They are also articulate speakers, tellers of tall tales, given to exaggeration but fully conscious of their place in the tradition of oral storytellers. At times there is almost too much bravado in these first-person narratives—a blurring of the problems and the grief. In retelling the story of her failed love affair, Sweet Pea's controlled voice does not admit to confusion or vulnerability or anger. In other stories Bambara does allow the suffering to surface but never without a cushion of support.

One of the reasons for the power of Bambara's characters is that her attitude toward her women is deeply partisan—she is fully invested in them, likes them, wants them to succeed, refuses to diminish them. In this passionate advocacy she reminds me of Grace Paley whose women characters also have the vitality and buoyancy of Bambara's because, like Bambara, Paley deliberately "plots" successful endings for her characters:

That woman lives across the street. She's my knowledge and invention. I'm sorry for her. I'm not going to leave her there in that house crying.[1]

In contrast to many other female characters in black women's literature, who are defined in terms of male desire or whose passivity and lack of self-esteem cause stagnation and inactivity, Bambara's women define themselves in their own terms as worthy of respect. They are workers and proud of the work they do. In "Medley," Sweet Pea is, in her own words, "an A-1 manicurist," and she plans to end her relationship with her boyfriend, Larry, because "I got one item on my agenda, making a home for me and my kid." And in "Witchbird" Honey protests the stereotypical black matriarch role that friends, lovers, and coworkers try and force on her, asserting her own definition of self: "Shit, I ain't nobody's mother. I'm a singer. I'm an actress. I'm a landlady look like. Hear me. Applaud me. Pay me."

For Honey, as for most of Bambara's women, the energy for independence and self-definition is fueled by the character's relationship to work and community.

A supportive, nurturing woman's community functions in most of Bambara's fiction. In "Witchbird," Gayle and Laney get dumped at Honey's house by an ex-boyfriend, but Honey takes them in because "it's hard to say no to a sister with no place to go" and their intimacy invokes a plot in which collective survival and communal growth are central.[2] Small details in Bambara's stories reinforce this sense of a community: In "Witchbird," the three women carry a meal to Miz Mary; girls play jump rope in the

---

[1] Grace Paley, "A Conversation with My Father," in *Enormous Changes at the Last Minute* (New York: Dell Publishing Co., 1975, p. 173).

[2] Rachael Blau Du Plessis, *Writing Beyond the Ending: Narrative Strategies of Twentieth-Century Women Writers* (Bloomington: Indiana University Press, 1985, p. 179). Du Plessis argues in the final chapter of *Writing Beyond the Ending* that collectivity and communality signal a critique of the old plots in which women characters were repressed or destroyed.

yard; mothers in the neighborhood look for their children, worrying over the safety of their sons who bear "the outlaw hue"; and Honey collapses finally in the shampoo chair, knowing that in this world of "beauty" there is also balm for the soul.

Sometimes the woman's community in Bambara's fiction is a historical one. Bambara enlists the names of women singers in "Medley" as Sweet Pea soars into her own melodic range; and in "Witchbird" women blues singers are summoned by Honey to empower her own search for artistic self-expression. Honey also hears the voices of historical figures like Harriet Tubman and Mammy Pleasant and voodoo queens helping her to resist the stereotypical scripts and the people who will "trap you in a fiction." Bambara uses women blues singers—Ma Rainey, Trixie Smith, Bessie Smith, Lena Horne—to symbolize both the creativity and the captivity of black women artists, for it was these women who captured in song, and in their own lives, the pain, the humor, the vitality of black life; and for many years they were the only black women allowed to express themselves as creative artists. These blues women represent a historical sisterhood, an embodiment of possibility for women a new literary myth.[3] Like Toni Cade Bambara's blues women, they lived with their pain concealed behind a smile and a flip, sardonic attitude. Beneath the sequins and the ostrich plumes, their lives, like Bambara's women, were ambiguous and bittersweet but nonetheless their own.

---

[3] Michele Wallace, *"The Color Purple*—An *Amos 'n' Andy* for the 80's," in *The Village Voice,* Vol. 31 No. 11 (March 18, 1986). In this excellent discussion of black women's literary traditions, Michele Wallace argues that the woman blues singer is a metaphor for the reconstruction of black female experience as positive ground. As used by Gayl Jones, Ntozake Shange, Gloria Naylor, and Alice Walker, "the black female blues singer [is] a paradigm of commercial, cultural, and historical potency [in] twentieth-century Afro-American literature by women" (p. 22).

Toni Cade Bambara

Medley

I could tell the minute I got in the door and dropped my bag, I wasn't staying. Dishes piled sky-high in the sink looking like some circus act. Glasses all ghosty on the counter. Busted tea bags, curling cantaloupe rinds, white cartoons from the Chinamen, green sacks from the deli, and that damn dog creeping up on me for me to wrassle his head or kick him in the ribs one. No, I definitely wasn't staying. Couldn't even figure why I'd come. But picked my way to the hallway anyway till the laundry-stuffed pillowcases stopped me. Larry's bass blocking the view to the bedroom.

"That you, Sweet Pea?"

"No, man, ain't me at all," I say, working my way back to the suitcase and shoving that damn dog out the way. "See ya round," I holler, the door slamming behind me, cutting off the words abrupt.

Quite naturally sitting cross-legged at the club, I embroider a little on the homecoming tale, what with an audience of two crazy women and a fresh bottle of Jack Daniels. Got so I could actually see shonuff toadstools growing in the sink. Cantaloupe seeds sprouting in the muck. A goddamn compost heap breeding near the stove, garbage gardens on the grill.

"Sweet Pea, you oughta hush, cause you can't possibly keep on lying so," Pot Limit's screaming, tears popping from her eyes. "Lawd hold my legs, cause this liar bout to kill me off."

"Never mind about Larry's housekeeping, girl," Sylvia's soothing me, sloshing perfectly good bourbon all over the table. "You can come and stay with me till your house comes through. It'll be like old times at Aunt Merriam's."

I ease back into the booth to wait for the next set. The drummer's fooling with the equipment, tapping the mikes, hoping he's watched, so I watch him. But feeling worried in my mind about Larry, cause I've been through days like that myself. Cold cream caked on my face from the day before, hair matted, bathrobe funky, not a clean pair of drawers to my name. Even the emergency ones, the draggy cotton numbers stuffed way in the back of the drawer under the scented paper gone. And no clean silverware in the box and the last of the paper cups gone too. Icebox empty cept for a rock of cheese and the lone water jug that ain't even half full that's how anyhow the thing's gone on. And not a clue as to the next step. But then Pot Limit'll come bamming on the door to say So-and-so's in town and can she have the card table for a game. Or Sylvia'll send a funny card inviting herself to dinner and even giving me the menu. Then I zoom through that house like a manic work brigade till me and the place ready for white-glove inspection. But what if somebody or other don't intervene for Larry, I'm thinking.

The drummer's messin round on the cymbals, head cocked to the side, rings sparkling. The other dudes are stepping out from behind the curtain. The piano man playing with the wah-wah doing splashy, breathy science fiction stuff. Sylvia checking me out to make sure I ain't too blue. Blue got hold to me, but I lean forward out of the shadows and babble something about how off the bourbon tastes these days. Hate worryin Sylvia, who is the kind of friend who bleeds at the eyes with your pain. I drain my glass and hum along with the opening riff of the guitar and I keep my eyes strictly off the bass player, whoever he is.

Larry Landers looked more like a bass player than ole Mingus himself. Got these long arms that drape down over the bass like they were grown special for that purpose. Fine, strong hands with long fingers and muscular knuckles, the dimples deep black at the joints. His calluses so other-colored and hard, looked like Larry had swiped his grandmother's tarnished thimbles to play with. He'd move in on that bass like he was going to hump it or something, slide up behind it as he lifted it from the rug, all slinky. He'd become one with the wood. Head dipped down sideways bobbing out the rhythm, feet tapping, legs jiggling, he'd look good. Thing about it, though, ole Larry couldn't play for shit. Couldn't never find the right placement for the notes. Never plucking with enough strength, despite the perfectly capable hands. Either you didn't hear him at all or what you heard was off. The man couldn't play for nuthin is what I'm saying. But Larry Landers was baad in the shower, though.

He'd soap me up and down with them great, fine hands, doing a deep bass walking in the back of his mouth. And I'd just have to sing, though I can't sing to save my life. But we'd have one hella-fyin musical time in the shower, lemme tell you. "Green Dolphin Street" never sounded like nuthin till Larry bopped out them changes and actually made me sound good. On "My Funny Valen-tine" he'd do a whizzing sounding bow thing that made his throat vibrate real sexy and I'd cutesy up the introduction, which is, come to think of it, my favorite part. But the main number when the hot water started running out was "I Feel Like Making Love." That was usually the wind up of our repertoire cause you can imagine what that song can do to you in the shower and all.

Got so we spent a helluva lotta time in the shower. Just as well, cause didn't nobody call Larry for gigs. He a nice man, considerate, generous, baad in the shower, and good taste in music. But he just wasn't nobody's bass player. Knew all the stances, though, the pos-tures, the facial expressions, had the choreography down. And right in the middle of supper he'd get some Ron Carter thing going in his head and hop up from the table to go get the bass. Haul that sucker right in the kitchen and do a number in dumb show, all the playing in his throat, the acting with his hands. But that ain't nuthin. I mean that can't get it. I can impersonate Betty Carter if it comes to that. The arms crooked just so, the fingers popping, the body working, the cap and all, the teeth, authentic. But I got sense enough to know I ain't nobody's singer. Actually, I am a mother, though I'm only just now getting it together. And too, I'm an A-1 manicurist.

▲   ▲   ▲

Me and my cousin Sinbad come North working our show in cathouses at first. Set up a salon right smack in the middle of Miz Maybry's Saturday traffic. But that wasn't no kind of life to be bringing my daughter into. So I parked her at a boarding school till I could make some other kind of life. Wasn't no kind of life for Sinbad either, so we quit.

Our first shop was a three-chair affair on Austin. Had a student barber who could do anything—blow-outs, do's, corn rows, weird cuts, afros, press and curl, whatever you wanted. Plus he din't gab you to death. And he always brought his sides and didn't blast em neither. He went on to New York and opened his own shop. Was a bootblack too then, an old dude named James Noughton, had a crooked back and worked at the post office at night, and knew everything about everything, read all the time.

"Whatcha want to know about Marcus Garvey, Sweet Pea?"

If it wasn't Garvey, it was the rackets or the trucking industry or the flora and fauna of Greenland or the planets or how the special effects in the disaster movies were done. One Saturday I asked him to tell me about the war, cause my nephew'd been drafted and it all seemed so wrong to me, our men over there in Nam fighting folks who fighting for the same things we are, to get that bloodsucker off our backs.

Well, what I say that for. Old dude gave us a deep knee bend, straight up eight-credit dissertation on World Wars I and II—the archduke getting offed, Africa cut up like so much cake, Churchill and his cigars, Gabriel Heatter on the radio, Hitler at the Olympics igging Owens, Red Cross doing Bloods dirty refusing donuts and bandages, A. Philip Randolph scaring the white folks to death, Mary McLeod Bethune at the White House, Liberty Bond drives, the Russian front, frostbite of the feet, the Jew stiffs, the gypsies no one mourned . . . the whole johnson. Talked straight through the day, Miz Mary's fish dinner growing cold on the radiator, his one and only customer walking off with one dull shoe. Fell out exhausted, his shoe rag limp in his lap, one arm draped over the left foot platform, the other clutching his heart. Took Sinbad and our cousin Pepper to get the old man home. I stayed with him all night with the ice pack and a fifth of Old Crow. He liked to die.

After while trade picked up and with a better class of folk too. Then me and Sinbad moved to North and Gaylord and called the shop Chez Sinbad. No more winos stumbling in or deadbeats wasting my time talking raunchy shit. The paperboy, the numbers man, the dudes with classier hot stuff coming in on Tuesday mornings only. We did up the place nice. Light globes from a New Orleans whorehouse, Sinbad likes to lie. Brown-and-black-and-silver-striped wallpaper. Lots of mirrors and hanging plants. Them old barber chairs spruced up and called antiques and damn if someone didn't buy one off us for eight hundred, cracked me up.

I cut my schedule down to ten hours in the shop so I could do private sessions with the gamblers and other business men and women who don't like sitting around the shop even though it's comfy, specially my part. Got me a cigar showcase with a marble top for serving coffee in clear glass mugs with heatproof handles too. My ten hours in the shop are spent leisurely. And my twenty hours out are making me a mint. Takes dust to be a mother, don't you know.

It was a perfect schedule once Larry Landers came into my life. He part-timed at a record shop and bartended at Topp's on the days and nights I worked at the shops. That gave us most of Monday and Wednesdays to listen to sides and hit the clubs. Gave me Fridays all to myself to study in the library and wade through them college bulletins and get to the museum and generally chart out a routine for when Debbie and me are a team. Sundays I always drive to Delaware to see her, and Larry detours to D.C. to see his sons. My bankbook started telling me I was soon going to be a full-time mama again and a college girl to boot, if I can ever talk myself into doing a school thing again, old as I am.

▲   ▲   ▲

Life with Larry was cool. Not just cause he wouldn't hear about me going halves on the bills. But cause he was an easy man to be easy with. He liked talking softly and listening to music. And he liked having folks over for dinner and cards. Larry a real nice man and I liked him a lot. And I liked his friend Hector, who lived in the back of the apartment. Ole moon-face Hector went to school with Larry years ago and is some kind of kin. And they once failed in the funeral business together and I guess those stories of them times kinda keep them friends.

The time they had to put Larry's brother away is their best story, Hector's story really, since Larry got to play a little grief music round the edges. They decided to pass up a church service, since Bam was such a treacherous desperado wouldn't nobody want to preach over his body and wouldn't nobody want to come to hear no lies about the dearly departed untimely ripped or cut down or whatever. So Hector and Larry set up some kind of pop stand awning right at the gravesite, expecting close blood only. But seems the whole town turned out to make sure ole evil, hell-raising Bam was truly dead. Dudes straight from the barber chair, the striped ponchos blowing like wings, fuzz and foam on they face and all, lumbering up the hill to the hole taking bets and talking shit, relating how Ole Crazy Bam had shot up the town, shot up the jail, shot up the hospital pursuing some bootlegger who'd come up one keg short of the order. Women from all around come to demand the lid be lifted so they could check for themselves and be sure that Bam was stone cold. No matter how I tried I couldn't think of nobody bad enough to think on when they told the story of the man I'd never met.

Larry and Hector so bent over laughing bout the funeral, I couldn't hardly put the events in proper sequence. But I could surely picture some neighbor lady calling on Larry and Bam's mama reporting how the whole town had turned out for the burying. And the mama snatching up the first black thing she could find to wrap around herself and make an appearance. No use passing up a scene like that. And Larry prancing round the kitchen being his mama. And I'm too stunned to laugh, not at somebody's mama, and somebody's brother dead. But him and Hector laughing to beat the band and I can't help myself.

Thing about it, though, the funeral business stories are Hector's stories and he's not what you'd call a good storyteller. He never gives you the names, so you got all these he's and she's floating around. And he don't believe in giving details, so you got to scramble to paint your own pictures. Toward the end of that particular tale of Bam, all I could picture was the townspeople driving a stake through the dead man's heart, then hurling that coffin into the hole right quick. There was also something in that story about the civil rights workers wanting to make a case cause a white cop had cut Bam down. But looked like Hector didn't have a hold to that part of the story, so I just don't know.

Stories are not Hector's long suit. But he is an absolute artist on windows. Ole Moon-Face can wash some windows and make you cry about it too. Makes these smooth little turns out there on that little bitty sill just like he wasn't four stories up without a belt. I'd park myself at the breakfast counter and thread the new curtains on the rods while Hector mixed up the vinegar solution real cheflike. Wring out the rags just so, scrunch up the newspapers into soft wads that make you think of cat's paws. Hector was a cat himself out there on the sill, making these marvelous circles in the glass, rubbing the hardhead spots with a strip of steel wool he had pinned to his overalls.

Hector offered to do my car once. But I put a stop to that after that first time. My windshield so clear and sparkling felt like I was in an accident and heading over the hood, no glass there. But it was a pleasure to have coffee and watch Hector. After while, though, Larry started hinting that the apartment wasn't big enough for four. I agreed, thinking he meant Earl had to go. Come to find Larry meant Hector, which was a real drag. I love to be around people who do whatever it is they do with style and care.

Larry's dog's named Earl P. Jessup Bowers, if you can get ready for that. And I should mention straightaway that I do not like dogs one bit, which is why I was glad when Larry said somebody had to go. Cats are bad enough. Horses are a total drag. By the age of nine I was fed up with all that noble horse this and noble horse that. They got good PR, horses. But I really can't use em. Was a fire once when I was little and some dumb horse almost burnt my daddy up messin around, twisting, snorting, broncing, rearing up, doing everything but comin on out the barn like even the chickens had sense enough to do. I told my daddy to let that horse's ass burn. Horses be as dumb as cows. Cows just don't have good press agents is all.

I used to like cows when I was real little and needed to hug me something bigger than a goldfish. But don't let it rain, the dumbbells'll fall right in a ditch and you break a plow and shout yourself hoarse trying to get them fools to come up out the ditch. Chipmunks I don't mind when I'm at the breakfast counter with my tea and they're on their side of the glass doing Disney things in the yard. Blue jays are law-and-order birds, thoroughly despicable. And there's one prize fool in my Aunt Merriam's yard I will one day surely kill. He tries to "whip whip whippoorwill" like the Indians do in the Fort This or That movies when they're signaling to each other closing in on George Montgomery but don't never get around to wiping that sucker out. But dogs are one of my favorite hatreds. All the time woofing, bolting down their food, slopping water on the newly waxed linoleum, messin with you when you trying to read, chewin on the slippers.

Earl P. Jessup Bowers was an especial drag. But I could put up with Earl when Hector was around. Once Hector was gone and

them windows got cloudy and gritty, I was through. Kicked that
dog every chance I got. And after thinking what it meant, how the
deal went down, place to small for four and it was Hector not Earl
—I started moving up my calendar so I could get out of there. I
ain't the kind of lady to press no ultimatum on no man. Like
"Choose, me or the dog." That's unattractive. Kicking Hector out
was too. An insult to me, once I got to thinking on it. Especially
since I had carefully explained from jump street to Larry that I got
one item on my agenda, making a home for me and my kid. So if
anybody should've been given walking papers, should've been me.

▲   ▲   ▲

Anyway. One day Moody comes waltzing into Chez Sinbad's
and tips his hat. He glances at his nails and glances at me. And I
figure here is my house in a green corduroy suit. Pot Limit had just
read my cards and the jack of diamonds kept coming up on my
resource side. Sylvia and me put our heads together and figure it
got to be some gambler or hustler who wants his nails done. What
other jacks do I know to make my fortune? I'm so positive about
Moody, I whip out a postcard from the drawer where I keep the
emeries and write my daughter to start packing.

"How much you make a day, Miss Lady?"

"Thursdays are always good for fifty," I lie.

He hands me fifty and glances over at Sinbad, who nods that
it's cool. "I'd like my nails done at four-thirty. My place."

"Got a customer at that time, Mr. Moody, and I like to stay
reliable. How bout five-twenty?"

He smiles a slow smile and glances at Sinbad, who nods again,
everything's cool. "Fine," he says. "And do you think you can
manage a shave without cutting a person's throat?"

"Mr. Moody, I don't know you well enough to have just
cause. And none of your friends have gotten to me yet with that
particular proposition. Can't say what I'm prepared to do in the
future, but for now I can surely shave you real careful-like."

Moody smiles again, then turns to Sinbad, who says it's cool and he'll give me the address. This look-nod dialogue burns my ass. That's like when you take a dude to lunch and pay the check and the waiter's standing there with *your* money in his paws asking *the dude* was everything all right and later for *you*. Shit. But I take down Moody's address and let the rest roll off me like so much steaming lava. I start packing up my little alligator case—buffer, batteries, clippers, emeries, massager, sifter, arrowroot and cornstarch, clear sealer, magnifying glass, and my own mixture of green and purple pigments.

"Five-twenty ain't five-twenty-one, is it, Miss Lady?"

"Not in my book," I say, swinging my appointment book around so he can see how full it is and how neatly the times are printed in. Course I always fill in phony names case some creep starts pressing me for a session.

For six Thursdays running and two Monday nights, I'm at Moody's bending over them nails with a miner's light strapped to my forehead, the magnifying glass in its stand, nicking just enough of the nails at the sides, tinting just enough with the color so he can mark them cards as he shuffles. Takes an hour to do it proper. Then I sift my talc concoction and brush his hands till they're smooth. Them cards move around so fast in his hands, he can actually tell me he's about to deal from the bottom in the next three moves and I miss it and I'm not new to this. I been a gambler's manicurist for more years than I care to mention. Ten times he'll cut and each time the same fifteen cards in the top cut and each time in exactly the same order. Incredible.

Now, I've known hands. My first husband, for instance. To see them hands work their show in the grandstands, at a circus, in a parade, the pari-mutuels—artistry in action. We met on the train. As a matter of fact, he was trying to burgle my bag. Some story to tell the grandchildren, hunh? I had to get him straight about robbing from folks. I don't play that. Ya gonna steal, hell, steal back some of them millions we got in escrow is my opinion. We spent three good years on the circuit. Then credit cards moved in. Then choke-and-grab muggers killed the whole tradition. He was reduced to a mere shell of his former self, as they say, and took to putting them hands on me. I try not to think on when things went sour. Try not to think about them big slapping hands, only of them working hands. Moody's working hands were something like that, but even better. So I'm impressed and he's impressed. And he pays me fifty and tips me fifty and shuts up when I shave him and keeps his hands off my lovely person.

I'm so excited counting up my bread, moving up the calendar, making impulsive calls to Delaware and the two of us squealing over the wire like a coupla fools, that what Larry got to say about all these goings-on just rolls off my back like so much molten lead.

"Well, who be up there while he got his head in your lap and you squeezing his goddamn blackheads?"

"I don't squeeze his goddamn blackheads, Larry, on account of he don't have no goddamn blackheads. I give him a shave, a steam, and an egg-white face mask. And when I'm through, his face is as smooth as his hands."

"I'll bet," Larry says. That makes me mad cause I expect some kind of respect for my work, which is better than just good.

"And he doesn't have his head in my lap. He's got a whole barbershop set up on his solarium."

"His what?" Larry squinting at me, raising the wooden spoon he stirring the spaghetti with, and I raise the knife I'm chopping the onions with. Thing about it, though, he don't laugh. It's funny as hell to me, but Larry got no sense of humor sometimes, which is too bad cause he's a lotta fun when he's laughing and joking.

"It's not a bedroom. He's got this screened-in sun porch where he raises African violets and—"

"Please, Sweet Pea. Why don't you quit? You think I'm dumb?"

"I'm serious. I'm serious and I'm mad cause I ain't got no reason to lie to you whatever was going on, Larry." He turns back to the pot and I continue working on the sauce and I'm pissed off cause this is silly. "He sits in the barber chair and I shave him and give him a manicure."

"What else you be giving him? A man don't be paying a good-looking woman to come to his house and all and don't—"

"Larry, if you had the dough and felt like it, wouldn't you pay Pot Limit to come read your cards? And couldn't you keep your hands to yourself and she a good-looking woman? And couldn't you see yourself paying Sylvia to come and cook for you and no funny stuff, and she's one of the best-looking women in town?"

Larry cooled out fast. My next shot was to bring up the fact that he was insulting my work. Do I go around saying the women who pass up Bill the bartender and come to him are after his joint? No, cause I respect the fact that Larry Landers mixes the best piña coladas this side of Barbados. And he's flashy with the blender and the glasses and the whole show. He's good and I respect that. But he cooled out so fast I didn't have to bring it up. I don't believe in overkill, besides I like to keep some things in reserve. He cooled out so fast I realized he wasn't really jealous. He was just going through one of them obligatory male numbers, all symbolic, no depth.

Like the time this dude came into the shop to talk some trash and Sinbad got his ass on his shoulders, talking about the dude showed no respect for him cause for all he knew I could be Sinbad's woman. And me arguing that since that ain't the case, what's the deal? I mean why get hot over what if if what if ain't. Men are crazy. Now there is Sinbad, my blood cousin who grew up right in the same house like a brother damn near, putting me through simple-ass changes like that. Who's got time for grand opera and comic strips, I'm trying to make a life for me and my kid. But men are like that. Gorillas, if you know what I mean.

Like at Topp's sometimes. I'll drop in to have a drink with Larry when he's on the bar and then I leave. And maybe some dude'll take it in his head to walk me to the car. That's cool. I lay it out right quick that me and Larry are a we and then we take it from there, just two people gassing in the summer breeze and that's just fine. But don't let some other dude holler over something like "Hey, man, can you handle all that? Why don't you step aside, junior, and let a man . . ." and blah-de-da-de-dah. They can be the best of friends or total strangers just kidding around, but right away they two gorillas pounding on their chest, pounding on their chest and talking over my head, yelling over the tops of cars just like I'm not a person with some say-so in the matter. It's a man-to-man ritual that ain't got nothing to do with me. So I just get in my car and take off and leave them to get it on if they've a mind to. They got it.

But if one of the gorillas is a relative, or a friend of mine, or a nice kinda man I got in mind for one of my friends, I will stick around long enough to shout em down and point out that they are some ugly gorillas and are showing no respect for me and therefore owe me an apology. But if they don't fit into one of them categories, I figure it ain't my place to try to develop them so they can make the leap from gorilla to human. If their own mamas and daddies didn't care whether they turned out to be amoebas or catfish or whatever, it ain't my weight. I got my own weight. I'm a mother. So they got it.

Like I use to tell my daughter's daddy, the key to getting along and living with other folks is to keep clear whose weight is whose. His drinking, for instance, was not my weight. And him waking me up in the night for them long, rambling, ninety-proof monologues bout how the whole world's made up of victims, rescuers, and executioners and I'm the dirty bitch cause I ain't rescuing him fast enough to suit him. Then got so I was the executioner, to hear him tell it. I don't say nuthin cause my philosophy of life and death is this—I'll go when the wagon comes, but I ain't going out behind somebody else's shit. I arranged my priorities long ago when I jumped into my woman stride. Some things I'll go off on. Some things I'll hold my silence and wait it out. Some things I just bump off, cause the best solution to some problems is to just abandon them.

But I struggled with Mac, Debbie's daddy. Talked to his family, his church, AA, hid the bottles, threatened the liquor man, left a good job to play nurse, mistress, kitten, buddy. But then he stopped calling me Dahlin and started calling me Mama. I don't play that. I'm my daughter's mama. So I split. Did my best to sweeten them last few months, but I'd been leaving for a long time.

The silliest thing about all of Larry's grumblings back then was Moody had no eyes for me and vice versa. I just like the money. And I like watching him mess around with the cards. He's exquisite, dazzling, stunning shuffling, cutting, marking, dealing from the bottom, the middle, the near top. I ain't never seen nothing like it, and I seen a whole lot. The thing that made me mad, though, and made me know Larry Landers wasn't ready to deal with no woman full grown was the way he kept bringing it up, always talking about what he figured was on Moody's mind, like what's on my mind don't count. So I finally did have to use up my reserves and point out to Larry that he was insulting my work and that I would never dream of accusing him of not being a good bartender, of just being another pretty face, like they say.

"You can't tell me he don't have eyes," he kept saying.

"What about my eyes? Don't my eyes count?" I gave it up after a coupla tries. All I know is, Moody wasn't even thinking about me. I was impressed with his work and needed the trade and vice versa.

One time, for instance, I was doing his hands on the solarium and thought I saw a glint of metal up under his jacket. I rearranged myself in the chair so I could work my elbow in there to see if he was carrying heat. I thought I was being cool about it.

"How bout keeping your tits on your side of the table, Miss Lady."

I would rather he think anything but that. I would rather he think I was clumsy in my work even. "Wasn't about tits, Moody. I was just trying to see if you had a holster on and was too lazy to ask."

"Would have expected you too. You a straight-up, direct kind of person." He opened his jacket away with the heel of his hand, being careful with his nails. I liked that.

"It's not about you," he said quietly, jerking his chin in the direction of the revolver. "Had to transport some money today and forgot to take it off. Sorry."

I gave myself two demerits. One for the tits, the other for setting up a situation where he wound up telling me something about his comings and goings. I'm too old to be making mistakes like that. So I apologized. Then gave myself two stars. He had a good opinion of me and my work. I did an extra-fine job on his hands that day.

Then the house happened. I had been reading the rental ads and For Sale columns for months and looking at some awful, tacky places. Then one Monday me and Sylvia lucked up on this cute little white-brick job up on a hill away from the street. Lots of light and enough room and not too much yard to kill me off. I paid my money down and rushed them papers through. Got back to Larry's place all excited and found him with his mouth all poked out.

Half grumbling, half proposing, he hinted around that we all should live at his place like a family. Only he didn't quite lay it out plain in case of rejection. And I'll tell you something, I wouldn't want to be no man. Must be hard on the heart always having to get out there, setting yourself up to be possibly shot down, approaching the lady, calling, the invitation, the rap. I don't think I could handle it myself unless everybody was just straight up at all times from day one till the end. I didn't answer Larry's nonproposed proposal cause it didn't come clear to me till after dinner. So I just let my silence carry whatever meaning it will. Ain't nuthin too much changed from the first day he came to get me from my Aunt Merriam's place. My agenda is still to make a home for my girl. Marriage just ain't one of the things on my mind no more, not after two. Got no regrets or bad feelings about them husbands neither. Like the poem says, when you're handed a lemon, make lemonade, honey, make lemonade. That's Gwen Brook's motto, that's mine too. You get a lemon, well, just make lemonade.

▲   ▲   ▲

"Going on the road next week," Moody announces one day through the steam towel. "Like you to travel with me, keep my hands in shape. Keep the women off my neck. Check the dudes at my back. Ain't asking you to carry heat or money or put yourself in no danger. But I could use your help." He pauses and I ease my buns into the chair, staring at the steam curling from the towel.

"Wicked schedule though—Mobile, Birmingham, Sarasota Springs, Jacksonville, then Puerto Rico and back. Can pay you two thousand and expenses. You're good, Miss Lady. You're good and you got good sense. And while I don't believe in nothing but my skill and chance, I gotta say you've brought me luck. You a lucky lady, Miss Lady."

He raises his hands and cracks his knuckles and it's like the talking towel has eyes as well cause damn if he ain't checking his cuticles.

"I'll call you later, Moody," I manage to say, mind reeling. With two thousand I can get my stuff out of storage, and buy Debbie a real nice bedroom set, pay tuition at the college too and start my three-credit-at-a-time grind.

Course I never dreamed the week would be so unnerving, exhausting, constantly on my feet, serving drinks, woofing sisters, trying to distract dudes, keeping track of fifty-leven umpteen goings on. Did have to carry the heat on three occasions and had to do a helluva lotta driving. Plus was most of the time holed up in the hotel room close to the phone. I had pictured myself lazying on the beach in Florida dreaming up cruises around the world with two matching steamer trunks with the drawers and hangers and stuff. I'd pictured traipsing through the casinos in Puerto Rico ordering chicken salad and coffee liqueur and tipping the croupiers with blue chips. Shit no. Was work. And I sure as hell learned how Moody got his name. Got so we didn't even speak, but I kept those hands in shape and his face smooth and placid. And whether he won, lost, broke even, or got wiped out, I don't even know. He gave me my money and took off for New Orleans. That trip liked to kill me.

▲   ▲   ▲

"You never did say nothing interesting about Moody," Pot Limit says insinuatingly, swinging her legs in from the aisle cause ain't nobody there to snatch so she might as well sit comfortable.

"Yeah, she thought she'd put us off the trail with a riproaring tale about Larry's housekeeping."

They slapping five and hunching each other and making a whole lotta noise, spilling Jack Daniels on my turquoise T-straps from Puerto Rico.

"Come on, fess up, Sweet Pea," they crooning. "Did you give him some?"

"Ahhh, yawl bitches are tiresome, you know that?"

"Naaw, naaw," say Sylvia, grabbing my arm. "You can tell us. We wantta know all about the trip, specially the nights." She winks at Pot Limit.

"Tell us about this Moody man and his wonderful hands one more time, cept we want to hear how the hands feeel on the flesh, honey." Pot Limit doing a bump and grind in the chair that almost makes me join in the fun, except I'm worried in my mind about Larry Landers.

Just then the piano player comes by and leans over Sylvia, blowing in her ear. And me and Pot Limit mimic the confectionary goings-on. And just as well, cause there's nothin to tell about Moody. It wasn't a movie after all. And in real life the good-looking gambler's got cards on his mind. Just like I got my child on my mind. Onliest thing to say about the trip is I'm five pounds lighter, not a shade darker, but two thousand closer toward my goal.

"Ease up," Sylvia says, interrupting the piano player to fuss over me. Then the drummer comes by and eases in on Pot Limit. And I ease back into the shadows of the booth to think Larry over.

I'm staring at the entrance half expecting Larry to come into Topp's, but it's not his night. Then too, the thing is ended if I'd only know it. Larry the kind of man you're either living with him or you're out. I for one would've liked us to continue, me and Debbie in our place, him and Earl at his. But he got so grumpy the time I said that, I sure wasn't gonna bring it up again. Got grumpy in the shower too, got so he didn't want to wash my back.

But that last night fore I left for Birmingham, we had us one crazy musical time in the shower. I kept trying to lure him into "Maiden Voyage," which I really can't do without back-up, cause I can't sing all them changes. After while he come out from behind his sulk and did a Jon Lucien combination on vocal and bass, alternating the sections, eight bars of singing words, eight bars of singing bass. It was baad. Then he insisted on doing "I Love You More Today Than Yesterday." And we like to break our arches, stomping out the beat against the shower mat.

The bathroom was all steamy and we had the curtains open so we could see the plants and watch the candles burning. I had bought us a big fat cake of sandalwood soap and it was matching them candles scent for scent. Must've been two o'clock in the morning and looked like the hot water would last forever and ever and ever. Larry finally let go of the love songs, which were making me feel kinda funny cause I thought it was understood that I was splitting, just like he'd always made it clear either I was there or nowhere.

Then we hit on a tune I don't even know the name of cept I like to scat and do my thing Larry calls Swahili wailing. He laid down the most intricate weaving, walking, bopping, strutting bottom to my singing I ever heard. It inspired me. Took that melody and went right on out that shower, them candles bout used up, the fatty soap long since abandoned in the dish, our bodies barely visible in the steamed-up mirrors walling his bathroom. Took that melody right on out the room and out of doors and somewhere out this world Larry changing instruments fast as I'm changing moods, colors. Took an alto solo and gave me a rest, worked an intro up on the piano playing the chords across my back, drove me all up into the high register while he weaved in and out around my head on a flute sounding like them chilly pipes of the Andes. And I was

Yma Sumac for one minute there, up there breathing some rare air
and losing my mind, I was so high on just sheer music. Music and
water, the healthiest things in the world. And that hot water
pounding like it was part of the group with a union card and all.
And I could tell that if that bass could've fit in the tub, Larry
would've dragged that bad boy in there and played the hell out of
them soggy strings once and for all.

I dipped way down and reached way back for snatches of Jelly
Roll Morton's "Deep Creek Blues" and Larry so painful, so sting-
ing on the bass, could make you cry. Then I'm racing fast through
Bessie and all the other Smith singers, Mildred Bailey, Billie and
imitators, Betty Roche, Nat King Cole vintage 46, a little Joe
Carroll, King Pleasure, some Babs. Found myself pulling lines out
of songs I don't even like, but ransacked songs just for the meaningful lines or two cause I realized we were doing more than just
making music together, and it had to be said just how things stood.

Then I was off again and lost Larry somewhere down there
doing scales, sound like. And he went back to that first supporting
line that had drove me up into the Andes. And he stayed there
waiting for me to return and do some more Swahili wailing. But I
was elsewhere and liked it out there and ignored the fact that he
was aiming for a windup of "I Love You More Today Than Yesterday." I sang myself out till all I could ever have left in life was
"Brown Baby" to sing to my little girl. Larry stayed on the ground
with the same supporting line, and the hot water started getting
funny and I knew my time was up. So I came crashing down,
jarring the song out of shape, diving back into the melody line and
somehow, not even knowing what song each other was doing, we
finished up together just as the water turned cold.

Toni Cade Bambara

Witchbird

I

Curtains blew in and wrecked my whole dressing-table arrangement. Then in he came, eight kinds of darkness round his shoulders, this nutty bird screechin on his arm, on a nine-speed model, hand brakes and all. Said, "Come on, we goin ride right out of here just like you been wantin to for long time now." Patting the blanket lassoed to the carrier, leaning way back to do it, straddling the bike and thrusting his johnson out in front, patting, thrusting, insinuating. Bird doing a two-step on the handle bars.

Damn if I'm riding nowhere on some bike. I like trains. Am partial to fresh-smelling club cars with clear windows and cushy seats with white linen at the top for my cheek to snooze against. Not like the hulking, oil-leaking, smoke-belching monstrosity I came home on when the play closed. Leaning my cheek against the rattling windowpane, like to shook my teeth loose. Cigar stench, orange peels curling on the window sills, balls of wax paper greasy underfoot, the linen rank from umpteen different hair pomades. Want the trains like before, when I was little and the porter hauled me up by my wrists and joked with me about my new hat, earning the five my mama slipped him, leisurely. Watching out for my person, saving a sunny seat in the dining car, clearing the aisle of perverts from round my berth, making sure I was in the no-drama section of the train once we crossed the Potomac.

"Well, we can cross over to the other side," he saying, "you in a rut, girl, let's go." Leaning over the edge of the boat, trailing a hand in the blue-green Caribbean. No way. I like trains. Then uncorking the champagne, the bottle lodged between his thighs. Then the pop of the cork, froth cascading all over his lap. I tell you I'm partial to trains. "Well, all right," he sayin, stepping out his pants. "We go the way you want, any way you want. Cause you need a change," he saying, chuggin over my carpet in this bubble-top train he suddenly got. Bird shouting at me from the perch of eye-stinging white linen. And I know something gotta be wrong. Cause whenever I've asked for what I want in life, I never get it. So he got to be the devil or some kind of other ugly no-good thing.

"Get on out my room," I'm trying to say, jaws stuck. Whole right side and left paralyzed like I'm jammed in a cage. "You tromping on my house shoes and I don't play that. Them's the house shoes Heywood gave me for Mother's Day." Some joke. Heywood come up empty-handed every rent day, but that don't stop him from boarding all his ex ole ladies with me freebee. But yellow satin Hollywood slippers with pompoms on Mother's Day, figuring that's what I'm here for. Shit, I ain't nobody's mother. I'm a singer. I'm an actress. I'm a landlady look like. Hear me. Applaud me. Pay me.

"But look here," he saying, holding up a pair of house shoes even finer than mine. Holding em up around his ears like whatshis-name, not the Sambo kid, the other little fellah. "Come on and take this ride with me."

All this talk about crossing over somewhere in dem golden slippers doing something to my arms. They jiggling loose from me like they through the bars of the cage, cept I know I'm under the covers in a bed, not a box. Just a jiggling. You'd think I was holding a hazel switch or a willow rod out in the woods witching for water. Peach twig better actually for locating subterranean springs. And I try to keep my mind on water, cause water is always a good thing. Creeks, falls, foundations, artesian wells. Baptism, candelight ablutions, skinny-dipping in the lake, C&C with water on the side. The root of all worthy civilizations, water. Can heal you. Scrunched up under the quilts, the sick tray pushed to the side, the heal of rain washing against the window can heal you or make you pee the bed one, which'll wake you from fever, from sleep, will save you. Save me. Cause damn if this character ain't trying to climb into my berth. And if there's one thing I can do without, it's phantom fucking.

▲   ▲   ▲

"Honey? You told me to wake you at dark. It's dark." Gayle, the brown-skin college girl my sometime piano player-sometime manager-mosttime friend Heywood dumped on me last time through here, jiggling my arms. Looking sorrowful about waking me up, she knows how sacred sleep can be, though not how scary.

"Here," she says, sliding my house shoes closer to the bed. "You know Heywood was all set to get you some tired old navy-blue numbers. I kept telling him you ain't nobody's grandma," she says, backing up to give me room to stretch, looking me over like she always does, comparing us I guess to flatter her own vanity, or wondering maybe if it's possible Heywood sees beyond friend, colleague, to maybe woman. All the time trying to pry me open and check out is there some long ago Heywood-me history. The truth is there's nothing to tell. Heywood spot him a large, singing, easygoing type woman, so he dumps his girl friends on me is all. I slide into the cold slippers. They're too soft now and give no support. Cheap-ass shoes. Here it is only Halloween, and they falling apart already. I'm sucking my teeth but can't even hear myself good for the caterwauling that damn bird's already set up in the woods, tearing up the bushes, splitting twigs with the high notes. Bird make me think some singer locked up inside, hostage. Cept that bird ain't enchanting, just annoying.

"Laney's fixing a plate of supper for Miz Mary," Gayle is saying, sliding a hand across my dressing-table scarf like she dying to set her buns down and mess in my stuff. My make-up kit ain't even unpacked, I'm noticing, and the play been closed for over a month. I ain't even taken the time to review what that role's done to my sense of balance, my sense of self. But who's got time, what with all of Heywood's women cluttering up my house, my life? Prancing around in shorty nightgowns so I don't dare have company in. A prisoner in my own house.

"Laney say come on, she'll walk to the shop with you, Honey. Me too. I think my number hit today. Maybe I can help out with the bills."

Right. I'd settle for some privacy. Had such other plans for my time right in through here. Bunch of books my nephew sent untouched. Stacks of *Variety* unread under the kitchen table. The new sheet music gathering dust on the piano. Been wanting to go over the old songs, the ole Bessie numbers, Ma Rainey, Trixie Smith, early Lena. So many women in them songs waiting to be released into the air again, freed to roam. Good time to be getting my new repertoire together too instead of rushing into my clothes and slapping my face together just because Laney can't bear walking the streets alone after dark, and Gayle too scared to stay in the place by herself. Not that Heywood puts a gun to my head, but it's hard to say no to a sister with no place to go. So they wind up here, expecting me to absorb their blues and transform them maybe into songs. Been over a year since I've written any new songs. Absorbing, absorbing, bout to turn to mush rather than crystallize, sparkling.

II

Magazine lady on the phone this morning asked if I was boarding any new up-and-coming stars. Very funny. Vera, an early Heywood ex, had left here once her demo record was cut, went to New York and made the big time. Got me a part in the play, according to the phone voice contracted to do a four-page spread on Vera Willis, Star. But that ain't how the deal went down at all.

"I understand you used to room together" was how the phone interview started off. Me arranging the bottles and jars on my table, untangling the junk in my jewelry boxes. Remembering how Vera considered herself more guest than roommate, no problem whatsoever about leaving all the work to me, was saving herself for Broadway or Hollywood one. Like nothing I could be about was all that important so hey, Honey, pick up the mop. Me sitting on the piano bench waiting for Heywood to bring in a batch of cheat sheets, watching Vera in the yard with my nieces turning double dudge. Then Vera gets it in her mind to snatch away the rope and sing into the wooden handle, strolling, sassy, slinky between the dogwoods, taking poses, kicking at the tail of the rope and making teethy faces like Heywood taught her. The little girls stunned by this performance so like their own, only this one done brazenly, dead serious, and by a grown-up lady slithering about the yard.

Staring out the window, I felt bad. I thought it was because Vera was just not pretty. Not pretty and not nice. Obnoxious in fact, selfish, vain, lazy. But yeah she could put a song over, though she didn't have what you'd call musicianship. Like she'd glide into a song, it all sounding quite dull normal at first. Then a leg would shoot out as though from a split in some juicy material kicking the mike cord out the way, then the song would move somewhere. As though the spirit of music had hovered cautious around her chin thinking it over, looking her over, then liking that leg, swept into her mouth and took hold of her throat and the song possessed her, electrified the leg, sparked her into pretty. Later realizing I was staring at her, feeling bad because of course she'd make it, have what she wanted, go everywhere, meet everybody, be everything but self-deserving.

First-class bitch was my two cents with the producers, just to make it crystal clear I didn't intend riding in on her dress tails but wanted to be judged by my own work, my reputation, my audition. Don't nobody do me no favors, please, cause I'm the baddest singer out here and one of the best character actresses around. And just keeping warmed up till a Black script comes my way.

Wasn't much of a part, but a good bit at the end. My daddy used to instruct, if you can't be the star of the show, aim for a good bit at the end. People remember that one good line or that one striking piece of business by the bit player in the third act. Well, just before the end, I come on for my longest bit in the play. I'm carrying this veil, Vera's mama's veil. The woman's so grief-stricken and whatnot, she ain't even buttoned up right and forgot to put on her veil. So here I come with the veil, and the mourners part the waves to give me a path right to the grave site. But once I see the coffin, my brown-sugar honey chile darlin dead and boxed, I forget all about the blood mama waiting for her veil. Forget all about maintaining my servant place in the bourgy household. I snatch off my apron and slowly lift that veil, for I am her true mother who cared for her and carried her through. I raise the hell outta that veil, transforming myself into Mother with a capital M. I let it drape slowly, slowly round my corn rolls, slowly lower it around my brow, my nose, mouth opening and the song bursting my jaws asunder as the curtain—well, not curtain, but the lights, cause we played it in the round, dim. Tore the play up with the song.

Course we did have a set-to about the costume. The designer saw my point—her talents were being squandered copying the pancake box. Playwright saw my point too, why distort a perfectly fine character just cause the director has mammy fantasies. An African patchwork apron was the only concession I'd make. Got to be firm about shit like that, cause if you ain't some bronze Barbie doll type or the big fro murder-mouth militant sister, you Aunt Jemima. Not this lady. No way. Got to fight hard and all the time with the scripts and the people. Cause they'll trap you in a fiction. Breath drained, heart stopped, vibrancy fixed, under arrest. Whole being entrapped, all possibility impaled, locked in some stereotype. And how you look trying to call from the box and be heard much less be understood long enough to get out and mean something useful and for real?

Sometimes I think I do a better job of it with the bogus scripts than with the life script. Fight harder with directors than with friends who trap me in their scenarios, put a drama on my ass. That's the problem with friends sometimes, they invest in who you were or seem to have been, capture you and you're through. Forget what you had in mind about changing, growing, developing. Got you typecasted. That's why I want some time off to think, to work up a new repertoire of songs, of life. So many women in them songs, in them streets, in me, waiting to be freed up.

Dozing, drifting into sleep sometime, the script sliding off the quilts into a heap, I hear folks calling to me. Calling from the box. Mammy Pleasant, was it? Tubman, slave women bundlers, voodoo queens, maroon guerrillas, combatant ladies in the Seminole nation, calls from the swamps, the tunnels, the classrooms, the studios, the factories, the roofs, from the doorway hushed or brassy in a dress way too short but it don't mean nuthin heavy enough to have to explain, just like Bad Bitch in the Sanchez play was saying. But then the wagon comes and they all rounded up and caged in the Bitch-Whore-Mouth mannequin with the dead eyes and the mothball breath, never to be heard from again. But want to sing a Harriet song and play a Pleasant role and bring them all center stage.

Wives weeping from the pillow not waking him cause he got his own weight to tote, wife in the empty road with one slipper on and the train not stopping, mother anxious with the needle and thread or clothespin as the children grow either much too fast to escape the attention of the posse or not fast enough to take hold. Women calling from the lock-up of the Matriarch cage. I want to put some of these new mother poems in those books the nephew sends to music. They got to be sung, hummed, shouted, chanted, swung.

Too many damn ransom notes fluttering in the window, or pitched in through the glass. Too much bail to post. Too many tunnels to dig and too much dynamite to set. I read the crazy scripts just to keep my hand in, cause I knew these newbreed Bloods going to do it, do it, do it. But meanwhile, I gotta work

. . . and hell. Then read one of them books my nephew always sending and hearing the voices speaking free not calling from these new Black poems. Speaking free. So I know I ain't crazy. But fast as we bust one, two loose, here come some crazy cracker throwing a croaker sack over Nat Turner's head, or white folks taking Malcolm hostage. And one time in Florida, dreaming in the hotel room about the Mary McLeod Bethune exhibit, I heard the woman calling from some diary entry they had under glass, a voice calling, muffled under the gas mask they clamped on hard and turned her on till she didn't know what was what. But calling for Black pages.

Then waking and trying to resume the reading, cept I can't remember just whom I'm supposed to try to animate in those dead, white pages I got to deal with till a Blood writes me my own. And catch myself calling to the white pages as I ripple them fast, listening to the pages for the entrapped voices calling, calling as the pages flutter.

Shit. It's enough to make you crazy. Where is my play, I wanna ask these new Bloods at the very next conference I hear about. Where the hell is my script? When I get to work my show?

▲   ▲   ▲

"A number of scandalous rumors followed the run of the play, taking up an inordinate amount of space in the reviews," the lady on the phone was saying, me caught up in my own dialogue. "I understand most of the men connected with the play and Vera Willis had occasion to . . ."

There was Heywood, of course. Hadn't realized they'd gotten back together till that weekend we were packing the play off to New York. Me packing ahead of schedule and anxious to get out of D.C. fast, cause Bradwell, who used to manage the club where I been working for years, had invited me to his home for the weekend. For old times' sake, he'd said. Right. He'd married somebody else, a singer we used to crack on as I recall, not a true note in her, her tits getting her over. And now she'd left him rolling around lonely in the brownstone on Edgecombe Avenue she'd once thought she just had to have. I went out and bought two hussy nightgowns. I was gonna break out in a whole new number. But never did work up the nerve. Never did have the occasion, ole Bradwell crying the blues about his wife. So what am I there for—to absorb, absorb, and transform if you can, ole girl. Absorb, absorb and try to convert it all to something other than fat.

Heywood calling to ask me to trade my suite near the theater for his room clear cross town.

"You can have both," I said, chuckling. "I'm off for the weekend."

"How come? Where you going?"

"Rendezvous. Remember the guy that used to own—"

"Cut the comedy. Where you going?"

"I'm telling you. I got a rendezvous with this gorgeous man I—"

"Look here," he cut in, "I'd invited Laney up to spend the weekend. That was before me and Vera got together again. I was wondering if you'd bail me out, maybe hang out with Laney till I can—"

"Heywood, you deaf? I just now told you I'm off to spend the—"

"Seriously?"

Made me so mad, I just hung up. Hung up and called me a fast cab.

III

Laney, Gayle, and me turn into Austin and run smack into a bunch of ghosts. Skeletons, pirates, and little devils with great flapping shopping bags set up a whirlwind around us. Laney spins around like in a speeded-up movie, holding Mary's dinner plate away from her dress and moaning, comically. Comically at first. But then our bird friend in the woods starts shrieking and Laney moaning for real. Gayle empties her bag into one of the opened sacks, then leans in to retrieve her wallet, though I can't see why. All I got for the kids is a short roll of crumbly Lifesavers, hair with tobacco and lint from my trench coat lining. Screaming and wooo-wooooing, they jack-rabbit on down Austin. Then we heading past the fish truck, my mind on some gumbo, when suddenly Gayle stops. She heard it soon's I did. Laney still walking on till I guess some remark didn't get a uh-hunh and she turns around to see us way behind, Gayle's head cocked to the side.

"What it is?" Laney looking up and down the street for a clue. Other than the brother dumping the last of the ice from the fish truck and a few cats hysterical at the curb, too self-absorbed to launch a concerted attack on the truck, there ain't much to keep the eyes alive. "What?" Laney whispers.

From back of the houses we hear some mother calling her son, the voice edgy on the last syllable, getting frantic. Probably Miz Baker, whose six-foot twelve-year-old got a way of scooting up and down that resembles too much the actions of a runaway bandit to the pigs around here. Mainly, he got the outlaw hue, and running too? Shit, Miz Baker stay frantic. The boy answers from the woods, which starts the bird up again, screeching, ripping through the trees, like she trying to find a way out of them woods and heaven help us if she do, cause she dangerous with rage.

"That him?" Gayle asks, knowing I'm on silence this time of night.

"Who?" Laney don't even bother looking at me, cause she knows I got a whole night of singing and running off at the mouth to get through once Mary lets me out from under the dryer and I get to the club. "Witchbird?" Laney takes a couple steps closer to us. "Yawl better tell me what's up," she says, "cause this here gettin spooookeeee!"

It's mostly getting dark and Laney don't wanna have to take the shortcut through the woods. Witchbird gotta way of screaming on you sudden, scare the shit outta you. Laney trying to balance that plate of dinner and not lose the juice. She is worried you can tell, and not just about Mary's mouth over cold supper. Laney's face easy to read, everything surfaces to the skin. Dug that the day

Heywood brought her by. She knew she was being cut loose, steered safely to cove, the boat shoving off and bye, baby, bye. Sad crinkling round the eyes, purples under the chin, throat pulsating. Gayle harder to read, a Scorpio, she plays it close to the chest unless she can play it for drama.

"Tell me, Gayle. What it is?"

"Heywood back in town."

"Ohhh, girl, don't tell me that." Laney takes a coupla sideways steps, juggling the plate onto one hand so she can tug down the jersey she barmaids in. "You better come on."

"You know one thing," Gayle crooning it, composing a mono-logue, sound like. "There was a time when that laugh could turn me clear around in the street and make me forget just where I thought I was going." On cue, Heywood laughs one of his laughs and Gayle's head tips, locating his whereabouts. She hands me her suede bag heavy with the pic comb and the schoolbooks. It's clear she fixin to take off. "I really loved that dude," she saying, theatrics gone. Laney moves on, cause she don't want to hear nuthin about Heywood and especially from Gayle. "He gets his thing off," La-ney had said to Gayle the night she was dumped, "behind the idea of his harem sprawled all over Honey's house gassing about him. I refuse," she had said and stuck to it.

"I really, really did," Gayle saying, something leaking in her voice.

Laney hears it and steps back. It's spilling on her shoes, her dress, soaking into her skin. She moves back again cause Gayle's zone is spreading. Gayle so filling up and brimming over, she gotta take over more and more room to accommodate the swell. Her leaking splashes up against me too—Heywood taking a solo, teeth biting out a rhythm on the back of his lower lip, Heywood at the wheel leaning over for a kiss fore he cranks up, Heywood wound up in rumpled sheets with his cap pulled down, sweat beading on his nose, waiting on breakfast, Heywood doing the dance of the hot hands and Gayle scrambling for a potholder to catch the coffee-pot he'd reached for with his fool self, Heywood falling off the porch and Gayle's daddy right on him. Gayle's waves wash right up on me and I don't want no parts of it. Let it all wash right through me, can't use it, am to the brim with my own stuff waiting to be transformed. Washes through me so fast the pictures blur and all I feel is heat and sparks. And then I hear the laugh again.

"Oh, shit," Laney says, watching the hem of Gayle's dress turning into the alley. "That girl is craaaaa-zeee, ya heah?" Her legs jiggling to put her in the alley in more ways than one, but that plate leaking pot likker and demanding its due.

Bright's strung up lights in the alley and you can make him out clear, hunched over the bathtub swishing barbeque sauce with a sheet-wrapped broom. Cora visible too, doing a shonuff flower arrangement on the crushed ice with the watermelon slices. And there's Heywood, ole lanky Heywood in his cap he says Babs Gonzales stole from Kenny Clarke and he in turn swiped from Babs. One arm lazy draped around Gayle's shoulders, the other crooked in the fence he lounges against, sipping some of Bright's bad brandy brew, speakeasy style. Other folks around the card table sipping from jelly jars or tin cups. But Heywood would have one of Cora's fine china numbers. He's looking good.

"What's goin on?" Laney asks in spite of herself, but refuses to move where she can see into the yard. All she got to do is listen, cause Heywood is the baritone lead of the eight-part card game opus.

"Ho!"

"Nigger, just play the card."

"Gonna. Gonna do that direckly. Right on yawl's ass."

"Do it to em, Porter."

"Don't tell him nuthin. He don't wanna know nuthin. He ain't never been nuthin but a fool."

Porter spits on the card and slaps it on his forehead.

"Got the bitch right here"—he's pointing—"the bitch that's gonna set ya."

"Nigger, you nasty, you know that? You a nasty-ass nigger and that's why don't nobody never wanna play with yo nasty-ass self."

"Just play the card, Porter."

"Ho!" He bangs the card down with a pop and the table too. "Iz you crazy?"

"If Porter had any sense, he'd be dangerous."

"Sense enough to send these blowhards right out the back door. Ho!"

"You broke the table and the ashtray, fool."

"And that was my last cigarette too. Gimme a dollar."

"Dollar! I look like a fool? If you paying Bright a dollar for cigarettes, you the fool."

"I want the dollar for some barbeque."

"What! What!" Porter sputtering and dancing round the yard. "How come I gotta replace one cigarette with a meal?"

"Okay then, buy some watermelon and some of the fire juice."

"You don't logic, man. You sheer don't logic. All I owe you is a cigarette."

"What about the table?"

"It ain't your table, nigger."

Laney is click-clicking up the street, giving wide berth to the path that leads through the woods. "Why Gayle want to put herself through them changes all over again," she is mumbling, grinding her heels in the broken pavement, squashing the dandelions. "I wouldn't put myself through none of that mess again for all the money." She picking up speed and I gotta trot to catch up. "I don't know how you can stay friends with a man like that, Honey."

"He don't do me no harm," I say, then mad to break my silence.

"Oh, no?" She trying to provoke me into debating it, so she says it again, "Oh, no?"

I don't want to get into this, all I want is to get into Mary's shampoo chair, to laze under Mary's hands and have her massage all the hurt up out of my body, tension emulsified in the coconut-oil suds, all fight sprayed away. My body been so long on chronic red alert messin with them theater folks, messing with stock types, real types, messing with me, I need release, not hassles.

"You think it's no harm the way he uses you, Honey? What are you, his mother, his dumping grounds? Why you put up with it? Why you put up with us, with me? Oh, Honey, I—"

I walk right along, just like she ain't talking to me. I can't take in another thing.

IV

"Well, all right! Here she come, Broadway star," someone bellows at me as the bell over the door jangles.

"Come on out from under that death, Honey," Mary says soon's we get halfway in the door. "Look like you sportin a whole new look in cosmetics. Clown white, ain't it? Or is it Griffin All White applied with a putty knife?" Mary leaves her customer in the chair to come rip the wig off my head. "And got some dead white woman on your head too. Why you wanna do this to yourself, Honey? You auditioning for some zombie movie?"

"Protective covering," Bertha says, slinging the magazine she'd been reading onto the pile. "You know how Honey likes to put herself out of circulation, Mary. Honey, you look like one of them creatures Nanna Mae raised from the dead. What they do to you in New York, girl? We thought you'd come back tired, but not embalmed."

"Heard tell a duppy busted up some posh do on the hill last Saturday," Mary's customer saying. "Lotta zombies round here."

"Some say it was the ghost of Willie Best come back to kill him somebody."

"Long's it's some white somebody, okay by me."

"Well, you know colored folks weren't exactly kind to the man when he was alive. Could be—"

"Heard Heywood's back on the scene," Bertha comes over to say to me. She lifts my hand off the armrest and checks my manicure and pats my hand to make up for, I guess, her not-so-warm greeting. "Be interesting to see just what kinda bundle he gonna deposit on your doorstep this time." Laney cuts her eye at Bertha, surrenders up the juiceless meal and splits. "Like you ain't got nuthin better to do with ya tits but wet-nurse his girls."

I shove Bertha's hand off mine and stretch out in my favorite chair. Mary's got a young sister now to do the scratchin and hot oil. She parts hair with her fingers, real gentle-like. Feels good. I'm whipped. I think on all I want to do with the new music and I'm feelin crowded, full up, rushed.

"No use you trying to ig me, Honey," Bertha says real loud. "Cause I'm Mary's last customer. We got all night."

"Saw Frieda coming out the drugstore," somebody is saying. "Package looked mighty interesting."

Everybody cracking up, Bertha too. I ease my head back and close my eyes under the comb scratching up dandruff.

"Obviously Ted is going on the road again and Frieda gonna pack one of her famous box snacks."

"Got the recipe for the oatmeal cookies richeah," someone saying. "One part rolled oats, one long drip of sorghum, fistful of raisins, and a laaaarge dose of salt-peter."

"Salt pete—er salt pete—er," somebody singing through the nose, outdoing Dizzy.

"Whatchu say!"

"Betcha there'll be plenty straaange mashed potatoes on the table tonight."

The young girl's rubbin is too hard in the part and the oil too hot. But she so busy cracking up, she don't notice my ouchin.

"Saltpetertaters, what better dish to serve a man going on the road for three days. Beats calling him every hour on the half-hour telling him to take a cold shower."

"Best serve him with a summons for being so downright ugly. Can't no woman be really serious about messin with Ted, he too ugly."

"Some that looks ugly . . ." Couldn't catch the rest of it, but followed the giggling well enough after what sounded like a second of silence.

"Mary"—someone was breathless with laughter—"when you and the sisters gonna give another one of them balls?"

"Giiirl," howls Bertha. "Wasn't that ball a natural ball?"

V

Bertha and Mary and me organized this Aquarian Ball. We so busy making out the lists, hooking people up, calling in some new dudes from the Islands just to jazz it up, hiring musicians and all, we clean forgot to get me an escort. I'd just made Marshall the trumpet player give me back my key cause all he ever wanted to do was bring by a passel of fish that needed cleaning and frying, and I was sick of being cook and confidante. I bet if I lost weight, people'd view me different. Other than Marshall, wasn't no man on the horizon, much less the scene. Mary, me and Bertha playing bid whist and I feel a Boston in my bones, so ain't paying too much attention to the fact that this no escort status of mine is serious business as far as Bertha's concerned.

"What about Heywood?" she says, scooping up the kitty.

Right on cue as always, in comes ole lanky Heywood with his cap yanked down around his brow and umpteen scarves around his mouth looking like Jesse James. He's got a folio of arrangements to deliver to me, but likes to make a big production first of saying hello to sisters. So while he's doing his rhyming couplets and waxing lyric and whatnot, I'm looking him over, trying to unravel my feelings about this man I've known, worked with, befriended for so long. Good manager, never booked me in no dumps. Always sees to it that the money ain't funny. A good looker and all, but always makes me feel more mother or older sister, though he four months to the day older than me. Naaw, I conclude, Heywood just my buddy. But I'm thinking too that I need a new buddy, cause he's got me bagged somehow. Put me in a bag when I wasn't looking. Folks be sneaky with their scenarios and secret casting.

"Say, handsome," Bertha say, jumping right on it, "ain't you taking Honey here to the ball?"

"Why somebody got to take her? I thought yawl was giving it."

"That ain't no answer. Can't have Honey waltzin in with-out—"

"Hold on," he saying, unwrapping the scarves cause we got the oven up high doing the meat patties.

"Never mind all that," says Mary. "Who you know can do it? Someone nice now."

"Well, I'll tell you," he says, stretching his arm around me. "I don't know no men good enough for the queen here."

"You a drag and a half," says Bertha.

"And I don't want to block traffic either," he says. "I mean if Honey comes in with my fine self on her arm, no man there is—"

"Never mind that," says Mary, slapping down an ace. "What about your friends, I'm askin you?"

"Like I said, I don't know anybody suitable."

"What you mean is, you only knows the ladies," says Bertha, disgusted. "You the type dude that would probably come up with a basket case for escort anyway. Club foot, hunchback, palsied moron or something. Just to make sure Honey is still available for you to mammify."

"Now wait a minute," he says, rising from the chair and pushing palms against the air like he fending us off. "How I get involved in yawl's arrangements?"

"You a friend, ain't ya? You a drag, that's for sure." Bertha lays down her hand, we thought to hit Heywood, come to find she trump tight.

Heywood puts the folio in my lap and rewraps the scarves for take-off, and we spend the afternoon being sullen, and damn near burnt up the meat patties.

"I'm getting tired of men like that," grumbles Bertha after while. "Either it's 'Hey, Mama, hold my head,' or 'Hey, Sister,' at three in the morning. When it get to be 'Sugar Darling'? I'm tired of it. And you, Honey, should be the tiredest of all."

▲   ▲   ▲

"So I just took my buns right to her house, cause she my friend and what else a friend for?" one of the women is saying. Mary's easing my head back on the shampoo tray, so I can't see who's talking.

"So did you tell her?"

"I surely did. I held her by the shoulders and said, 'Helen, you do know that Amos is on the dope now, don't you?' And she kinda went limp in my arms like she was gonna just crumble and not deal with it."

"A myth all that stuff about our strength and strength and then some," Bertha saying.

" 'If Amos blow his mind now, who gonna take care of you in old age, Helen?' I try to tell her."

"So what she say?"

"She don't say nuthin. She just cry."

"It's a hellafyin thing. No jobs, nary a fit house in sight, famine on the way, but the dope just keep comin and comin."

I don't know Helen or Amos. Can't tell whether Amos is the son or the husband. Ain't that a bitch. But I feel bad inside. I crumple up too hearing it. Picturing a Helen seeing her Amos in a heap by the bathtub, gagging, shivering, defeated, not like he should be. Getting the blankets to wrap him up, holding him round, hugging him tight, rocking, rocking, rocking.

"You need a towel?" Mary whispers, bending under the dryer. No amount of towel's gonna stop the flood, I'm thinking. I don't even try to stop. Let it pour, let it get on out so I can travel light. I'm thinking maybe I'll do Billie's number tonight. Biting my lip and trying to think on the order of songs I'm going to get through this evening and where I can slip Billie in.

"What's with you, Honey?"

"Mary got this damn dryer on KILL," I say, and know I am about to talk myself hoarse and won't be fit for singing.

TONI CADE BAMBARA
Bibliography

While Toni Cade Bambara has written several pieces of criticism herself and granted many interviews, there is little critical commentary on her fiction. Keith Byerman's essay in his book, *Fingering the Jagged Grain: Tradition and Form in Recent Black Fiction* (Athens, Ga.: University of Georgia Press, 1985, pp. 104–28) contains a chapter comparing Bambara and Alice Walker. The pairing is questionable: Byerman's rationale is that Bambara and Walker "tend toward feminist ideology" (p. 105), and that both writers have an uneasy blend of "folk wisdom" and political ideology which renders their worldview ambiguous. Byerman focuses almost exclusively on Bambara's short fiction, examing the impact of gender, family, and community on those characters whose sexual and political conflicts are intertwined. This essay is a survey of plot, theme, and character and, as such, is rather general.

Susan Willis's chapter "Problematizing the Individual" in *Specifying: Black Women Writing the American Experience* (Madison, Wis.: University of Wisconsin Press, 1987, pp. 129–58) is also broad in scope but includes commentary on all of Bambara's fiction. Willis is primarily concerned with Bambara's political development and its reflection in her work as it has evolved from the politically active sixties to the more highly individualized (and therefore, according to Willis, problematic) and less community-centered eighties. The individualism in the earlier stories, which prompted self-affirmation and courage, returns in the later stories as the cause for frustration and anger. "What has changed," Willis contends, "is not so much the individual . . . as the society's ability to offer a place where strength and action may find resonance" (p. 154).

Gloria T. Hull has a very good article on Bambara, " 'What It Is I Think She's Doing Anyhow': A Reading of Toni Cade Bambara's *The Salt Eaters*," in *Conjuring: Black Women, Fiction, and Literary Tradition*, eds. Marjorie Pryse and Hortense Spillers (Bloomington, Ind.: Indiana University Press, 1985, pp. 216–32). Writing from a teacher's perspective, Hull discusses the difficulties readers face when attempting *The Salt Eaters* and offers good arguments for overcoming these difficulties. She argues that Bambara is attempting to raise the problem of the subjective nature of reality while at the same time acknowledging the concrete realities of contemporary life. While sympathetic to the reader's struggle, Hull says that these difficulties in reading reflect the very issues Bambara seeks to raise.

There are two essays on Bambara in *Black Women Writers: (1950–1980): A Critical Evaluation*, ed. Mari Evans (Garden City, N.Y.: Doubleday, 1984). Ruth Burks's essay "From Baptism to Resurrection: Toni Cade Bambara and the Incongruity of Language" (pp. 48–57) discusses Bambara's suspicion of language as an agent of change. Eleanor Traylor's essay "Music as Theme: The Jazz Mode in the Works of Toni Cade Bambara" (pp. 58–70), compares Bambara's work to jazz (concentrating mainly on *The Salt Eaters*) because of their common use of call-and-response patterns. Traylor argues that Bambara's fiction, like jazz, stresses continuity with the past at the same time that it provides a reassessment and revision of that past.

SELECTED WORKS OF FICTION BY AFRO-AMERICAN WOMEN[1]

WILSON, HARRIET E. *Our Nig; or, Sketches from the Life of a Free Black* (1859)

HARPER, FRANCES E. W. *Iola Leroy; Or, Shadows Uplifted* (1892)

NELSON, ALICE DUNBAR. *Violet and Other Tales* (1985)
   The Goodness of St. Rocque and Other Stories (1899)

HOPKINS, PAULINE E. *Contending Forces* (1900)

FAUSET, JESSIE R. *There is Confusion* (1924)
   Plum Bun (1929)
   The Chinaberry Tree (1931)
   Comedy American Style (1933)

LARSEN, NELLA. *Quicksand* (1928)
   Passing (1929)

HURSTON, ZORA NEALE. *Jonah's Gourd Vine* (1934)
   Their Eyes Were Watching God (1937)
   Moses, Man of the Mountain (1939)
   Spunk: The Selected Short Stories of Zora Neale Hurston (1985)

LORDE, AUDRE. *Zami: A New Spelling of My Name* (1982)

PETRY, ANN. *The Street* (1946)
   Country Place (1947)
   The Narrows (1953)
   Miss Muriel and Other Stories (1971)

WEST, DOROTHY. *The Living Is Easy* (1948)

BROOKS, GWENDOLYN. *Maud Martha* (1953)

CHILDRESS, ALICE. *Like One of the Family: Conversations from a Domestic's Life* (1956)

---

[1] List compiled by Professor Richard A. Yarborough, University of California, Los Angeles.

A Hero Ain't Nothin' but a Sandwich (1973)
A Short Walk (1979)

MARSHALL, PAULE. *Brown Girl, Brownstones* (1959)
Soul Clap Hands and Sing (1961)
The Chosen Place, the Timeless People (1969)
Praisesong for the Widow (1983)
Reena and Other Stories (1983)

VROMAN, MARY E. *Esther* (1963)

HUNTER, KRISTIN. *God Bless the Child* (1964)
The Landlord (1966)

WALKER, MARGARET. *Jubilee* (1966)

PHILLIPS, JANE. *Mojo Hand* (1966)

GUY, ROSA. *Bird at My Window* (1966)
The Friends (1973)
Ruby (1976)
A Measure of Time (1983)

POLITE, CARLENE H. *The Flagellants* (1967)
Sister X and the Victims of Foul Play (1975)

WRIGHT, SARAH. *This Child's Gonna Live* (1969)

MERIWETHER, LOUISE. *Daddy Was a Number Runner* (1970)

MORRISON, TONI. *The Bluest Eye* (1970)
Sula (1973)
Song of Solomon (1977)
Tar Baby (1981)
Beloved (1987)

WALKER, ALICE. *The Third Life of Grange Copeland* (1970)
In Love and Trouble (1973)
Meridian (1976)
You Can't Keep a Good Woman Down (1981)
The Color Purple (1982)

The Temple of My Familiar (1989)

HAMILTON, VIRGINIA. *The Planet of Junior Brown* (1971)

BAMBARA, TONI CADE. *Gorilla, My Love* (1972)
The Seabirds Are Still Alive (1977)
The Salteaters (1980)

SHOCKLEY, ANN. *Loving Her* (1974)
Say Jesus and Come to Me (1982)

JONES, GAYL. *Corregidora* (1975)
Eva's Man (1976)
White Rat (1977)

DEVEAUX, ALEXIS. *Don't Explain: A Song of Billie Holiday* (1982)

BUTLER, OCTAVIA. *Patternmaster* (1976)
Survivor (1978)
Kindred (1979)
Wild Seed (1980)
Clay's Ark (1984)
Dawn (1987)
Adulthood Rites (1988)

JOURDAIN, ROSE. *Those The Sun Has Loved* (1978)

SOUTHERLAND, ELLEASE. *Let the Lions Eat Straw* (1979)

CHASE-RIBOUD, BARBARA. *Sally Hemmings* (1979)
Valide (1986)
Echo of Lions (1989)

SHANGE, NTOZAKE. *Sassafras, Cypress & Indigo* (1982)
Betsey Brown (1985)

NAYLOR, GLORIA. *The Women of Brewster Place* (1982)
Linden Hills (1985)
Mama Day (1988)

JONES, NETTIE. *Fish Tales* (1983)

LEE, ANDREA. *Sarah Phillips* (1984)

KINCAID, JAMAICA. *At the Bottom of the River* (1983)
  Annie John (1985)

COOPER, J. CALIFORNIA. *A Piece of Mine* (1984)
  Homemade Love (1986)
  Some Soul to Keep (1987)

DOVE, RITA. *Fifth Sunday* (1985)

MONROE, MARY. *The Upper Room* (1985)

WILLIAMS, SHERLEY ANNE. *Dessa Rose* (1986)

McMILLAN, TERRY. *Mama* (1987)

PAYTON, GEORGIA WILLIAMS. *A Memory to Sweet* (1987)

AUSTIN, DORIS JEAN. *After the Garden* (1987)

CARTIER, XAM WILSON. *Be-Bop, Re-Bop* (1987)

SHAIK, FATIMA. *The Mayor of New Orleans: Just Talking Jazz* (1987)

McELROY, COLLEEN J. *Jesus & Fat Tuesday and Other Stories* (1987)

EDWARDS-YEARWOOD, GRACE. *In the Shadow of the Peacock* (1988)

COLEMAN, WANDA. *A Way of Eyes and Other Stories* (1988)

GOLDEN, MARITA. *A Woman's Place* (1986)
  Long Distance Life (1989)

MARY HELEN WASHINGTON is originally from Cleveland, Ohio. A professor of English at the University of Massachusetts—Boston, she has recently received research fellowships from Harvard University and Wellesley College. She is also the author of *Invented Lives* (Anchor, 1987) and has contributed articles to *Ms.* and *Essence.*

Book Mark

The text of this book was set in the typeface Bembo by
Berryville Graphics, Berryville, Virginia.

The display was set in Kabel and Diskus Bold by Maxwell
Typographers, New York, New York.

It was printed on 45 lb. Mando Prime
and bound by R.R. Donnelley, Crawfordsville, Indiana.

DESIGNED BY ANNE LING